Goddess of the Moon

Polly Iyer

This book is a work of fiction. All names of characters and events are the product of the author's imagination, including some geographical references. I hope no one is offended by the liberties I've taken under artistic license. Any resemblance to persons either living or dead is purely coincidental and beyond the intent of the author.

Cover design by Polly Iyer

Goddess of the Moon
Copyright © 2012 by Polly Iyer
All rights reserved

ISBN-13: 978-1481276504
ISBN-10: 1481276506

To my wonderful, supportive friends.

You know who you are.

Chapter One
The Snatch

Kidnapping *babies used to be easier.* He'd check the charts to be sure he had the right baby and wait for the perfect moment. Then a snip of the plastic bracelet, slide the baby into the satchel in the cleaning cart, and out the employees' door. No one paid attention to a hospital janitor.

Now, impossible-to-remove bar coding and electronic devices on the babies ignited a firestorm of alarms that rivaled warnings of an enemy attack on the homeland. Doors automatically closed, trapping everyone inside. Those hospital precautions demanded an alternative. Breaking into the baby's houses. Tricky, for sure. But he was a master.

One reported kidnapping wasn't even his. The propitious theft kept the police from determining a pattern.

After the mother and child left the hospital, he'd watched the house for days, safely out of sight. This evening, the parents had shown off the infant to their guests, then put her down in the nursery. He saw no activity at the house next door.

Another perfect moment.

Bushes hid the low window. He donned latex gloves, pushed up the screen, and inserted a pry bar into the sliver between the window sash and the outer sill on the right, then on the left. Alternating sides, he pried upward until he'd exerted enough force to break the latch. He raised the window and hoisted himself inside.

The little treasure slept soundly, making those sweet baby noises he loved. He plucked a small plastic bag from the added satchel slung over his shoulder, unzipped it, and extracted a square of gauze soaked with sweet wine. He touched it to the baby's lips, and she drew on her natural instincts to suck. Not too much, he cautioned himself—just enough to act as an anesthesia, a technique rabbis used during a Jewish boy's circumcision. He gingerly placed her inside the satchel and cooed, "Sleep, beautiful one."

So far so good.

As if he were carrying a package of fine porcelain, he carefully let himself out the window, closing it and the screen after he hit the ground.

And he was gone.

Chapter Two
The Call

Diana Racine spent three weeks bronzing in the South Texas sun without one vision of a dead body or potential victim. Today, lying on a chaise with the ocean sounds as background music, she opened one eye, then the other, and settled her gaze on Ernie Lucier. He sat under the patio umbrella reading, his caramel-colored skin safe from the sun's rays. He caught her looking, and his smile crinkled the corners of his gold-flecked hazel eyes.

"This has been the best vacation ever," she said. "Do we have to go home tomorrow?"

"Some people have to work." He rose and was halfway to her when his cell rang. "Damn. I'd forgotten what that nasty thing sounded like." With an apologetic shrug, he returned to his seat and answered.

Diana watched a vee of brown pelicans soar above the palm trees fluttering in the warm breeze off the ocean. She pried herself from her chair and lazily strolled to nestle in Lucier's lap, hoping to distract him from whatever the disruptive call had in store.

"What, Sam? I didn't hear you." Then, sotto voce, Lucier said, "Diana, hold on. Something's happened." He raised his voice, switching the phone to her side of his head so she could listen. "Did you say a baby's been kidnapped?"

Diana pressed her ear next to Lucier's. On the other end, Detective Sam Beecher reported that someone had kidnapped a newborn from a New Orleans home by climbing in the nursery window while the parents were entertaining guests.

"Anything to go on?" Lucier asked.

"Nothing," Beecher said. "No prints other than footprints outside the window, but CSU says nothing unusual in the shoe."

"Where was the baby?" Diana asked, moving into Lucier's phone.

"In a bassinet," Beecher said. "We dusted for prints, but nothing. The kidnapper wore gloves."

"Don't let anyone else near it until I get there," Diana said. "The fewer hands messing up the vibes the better."

Lucier signed off with a promise to return to New Orleans as soon as possible. He rubbed Diana's neck. "Are you sure you want to get back into the psychic business so soon?"

"Darling, I've been doing this since I was a kid. One more time isn't going to send me over the edge. Now, let's pack and get an early plane back. We've no time to lose. You know as well as I that every minute counts in a kidnapping."

"That I do." He pulled her close. "I never wanted this vacation to end, but what do they say about all good things?"

"Settled then." She planted a kiss on his lips and within ten minutes had folded all their belongings into two suitcases while he made plane reservations.

Was it too soon? They'd spent the last three weeks at an oceanfront house on South Padre Island. Sun, salt water, and a man's loving attention did wonders to erase the memory of the serial killer who almost made her his last victim. Tanned and relaxed, she felt almost normal.

But in the eyes of the world, Diana Racine wasn't normal.

Not since, as a six-year old, her telepathic gifts led police to the body of a missing child. Remembering that day and the many that followed sent a familiar icy shiver through her. Entertaining the crowds that filled venues all over the world had saved her sanity. Even so, she'd never be considered normal—except in the eyes of New Orleans police lieutenant Ernie Lucier.

Yeah, she was ready.

Lucier stuck his head in the bedroom door. "Gotta go. It's over twenty miles to the airport, and our plane leaves in an hour and a half."

"Wow, that was fast. I hope we don't hit any traffic."

"No other flights till morning. Beecher and Cash will meet us at the airport. Beecher said he'd drive my car so I can look over the police report on the way." He zipped their suitcases and carried them out to the car.

Diana made a quick run-through of the house. She always forgot something hanging behind the bathroom door or tucked in a drawer, but not this time. Heading for the door, she ran into Lucier.

"One minute." He wrapped his arms around her and pulled her close. "I love you."

"Me too. You, I mean."

"And you're a great lay."

Her laugh echoed through the house and accompanied them to the rental car parked in the driveway.

Chapter Three
The Bassinet

"Welcome back, boss," Beecher said when they exited the secure area of the airport.

"Thanks." Lucier wanted to say it was good to be back, but then he thought of Diana next to him in bed, her lithe, bikini-clad figure on the beach, and he couldn't get the words out.

"Detective Beecher," Diana said formally.

"Ms. Racine," he countered with a sly grin.

"Will you two stop it?" Lucier said.

Diana soft-punched Beecher in the arm. "Hi, Sam."

"Diana. You're looking well." Beecher led them to the baggage claim. "Cash is parked in a marked car outside the entrance. He'll drive your car and we'll follow him to the Seaver house." He said to Diana, "That's the family name of the kidnapped baby. I brought what we have for you to read on the way, Lieutenant."

"Excellent," Lucier said. After picking up their luggage, they headed to the waiting car.

"Glad you're back, Lieutenant," Detective Willy Cash said. "You too, Ms. Racine."

"Nice to be back." Diana shot a glance at Lucier. "Kind of," she mumbled.

The lustful look Diana had on her face bumped up Lucier's heart rate, and he squeezed her knee. When they got to his car, he tossed Cash his keys, and Beecher got in the driver's seat. Lucier turned his attention to the report while the two cars headed to the Seaver house, situated in a quiet Metairie suburb.

"The mother put the baby in the bassinet," Beecher said. "Then when she and her husband went to check on her a couple of hours later, she was gone. The window had been pried open. Mrs. Seaver is under sedation. Mr. Seaver is expecting us. All CSU found were the parents' prints and the footprints outside the window. Agent Stallings is working with us on the case."

"Ralph's a good man," Lucier said. "Does the captain know about Diana?"

"Yup. He thinks it's fine as long as we keep her name quiet. If the public finds out Diana's on the case, all hell will break loose. Jake Griffin will be on her tail, pen in hand, salivating for a story."

"Heaven help us," Diana said. "Besides, you all know I may get absolutely no reading. And don't say a word about looking for an out, okay, Sam?"

"I wasn't gonna say a thing. I'm over that. Saw for myself you're no phony. Took me awhile, but I'm a believer."

"Good. That's what I need. A believer."

"Any idea how this guy zeroed in on the baby?" Lucier asked.

"Dunno," Beecher answered. "The Seavers took the baby home from the hospital's birthing center yesterday morning. They can't think of anyone who'd want to harm them."

"Any of the Seaver neighbors report anything unusual?"

"Nope, and we made a thorough canvass."

"Someone from the hospital?"

"Could be. We have the hospital tapes from the last few days. Halloran's checking them now to see if anyone looks suspicious."

"Good work." Still, with all the visitors and employees in and out of the hospital, finding the right person was like extracting a specific drop of water from the ocean. He studied the report until Beecher stopped the car in the driveway of the Seaver residence.

Mr. Seaver answered the door before anyone chimed their presence. "I didn't want the bell to disturb my wife. She's terribly distraught, as I am. Come in."

"Lieutenant Ernie Lucier, Mr. Seaver." They shook hands and Lucier introduced both Beecher and Cash, saving Diana for last.

"I've seen you perform," Mr. Seaver said. "I'm glad you're here."

"I'm sorry it's under these circumstances. I only hope I can be of help."

"Yes, well…let me show you the nursery."

Lucier squeezed Diana's hand. He figured she was worried about not sensing anything that would help find the Seaver baby. She glanced his way and offered a quick smile. Everyone stepped away as she circled the bassinet. Lifting the crumpled blanket, she studied for a moment, closed her eyes, then stood still. An unearthly silence filled the small room.

Lucier had seen her do this many times before, but whenever she slipped into the trancelike state, she seemed like someone else and not the woman he loved. The invasive effects varied each time—shallow breathing, shaking, REM flutters, even fainting or rest mode, as she euphemistically called it. The enervation that followed each foray into her otherworldly life upset him more than it did her.

Today, Diana's eyes pinched closed. Lucier and Beecher exchanged shrugs but made no move to disrupt her concentration. She stood motionless for almost four minutes.

Opening her eyes, she let out a long, slow breath. "This is strange."

"What?" Lucier asked.

She draped the blanket over the railing, looking confused. "I felt the baby. She's alive, I'm sure, and not being harmed, but I sensed the presence of other babies. I heard them."

Mr. Seaver let out a strangled sigh. Tears filled his eyes. "I'm sorry. This is very emotional for me."

"I understand," Lucier said. "Anything else, Diana?"

Her gaze shifted from Lucier to Beecher to Mr. Seaver and back to Lucier. "She's in a pleasant place. Warm, with sun shining in. Another nursery, I think. The room was painted pink with high ceilings and crown molding, characteristic of an old Victorian house."

She started to say something else but stopped. *Something she didn't want to say in front of the baby's father?* Walking to the window, she touched the sill.

"Are you sure my daughter is okay?" Mr. Seaver asked.

She turned to face him. "Some people don't believe in what I do, Mr. Seaver, and though I don't want to give you false hope, I'd stake my reputation that your daughter is alive and being well taken care of."

He stifled a sob, and this time the tears slid from the corners of his eyes. "Thank you." To Lucier, he said, "Find the man who took our baby, Lieutenant. Find him and lock him away forever."

* * * * *

On their way back to the station, Lucier asked Diana what she *didn't* say at the house.

"What I saw—the room—there was an aura of danger. The baby feels safe, but she's not."

"In what way?" Beecher asked.

"I don't know." Diana wrapped her arms around herself and shivered. "Those babies are in an atmosphere of evil."

Lucier didn't like to show overt affection toward Diana in front of his men, but this time he didn't care. He pulled her close because she shivered in the fear she just described. "Did you see anyone with her?"

"No, I told you everything I saw."

"Get Stallings on the phone, Sam. Ask him if the stats in this case match any other incidents. The feds do it better and faster. I don't recall any baby kidnappings in New Orleans, but there might be a pattern. First, let's verify if we're dealing with a single episode."

They drove into the parking lot of the French Quarter Police Department. "Someone targeted that baby," Lucier said. "I assume you have a list of patients and visitors during the time she was in the hospital?"

"We do. Employees too," Beecher said.

Lucier ruffled Diana's mass of curly black hair and added an affectionate smile. "Maybe Halloran noticed something on the tapes."

* * * * *

"Anything?" Lucier asked when Halloran entered his office.

"I captured some stills of people at the birthing center that week," Halloran said. "Most worked there. One of our guys is there now with the photos to see who hasn't shown up for work."

Lucier ran his fingers through his hair in frustration. "Hope we get lucky."

* * * * *

Diana remembered the first time she walked into the French Quarter police station. Instead of the disdain she'd experienced that first night, today the cops seemed glad to see her. After chatting with a few of them she took the visitor's chair in Lucier's office. The framed degrees and citations still hung on the wall, and the photos of his family sat in the same place on the bookcase, as they should. Only now, her picture faced in his direction on his desk, leaving no doubt they were in a personal relationship.

Beecher entered the office, tucking in his unruly shirt. When they first met, Beecher had called Diana a phony and a charlatan. The epithets weren't new. She'd heard them all before when she gave up helping the police at age fourteen to enter the entertainment world. She usually ignored the comments, but Beecher's attitude had bugged the hell out of her. Her on-target psychic readings had changed his opinion, and their relationship settled into one of mutual respect. In fact, they actually liked one another, but both kept up the adversarial repartee to keep things interesting.

"No one remembers seeing anyone at the hospital who shouldn't have been there," Beecher said. "But the pictures might jog someone's memory."

"What about the Seavers' neighbors?"

"The people on one side weren't home, and the woman on the side of the nursery didn't notice anything. Her young son has a desk by the window, but the boy's autistic. Wouldn't even look at me."

"I saw that window," Diana said. "Was he at home during the time the baby was taken?"

"The mother said yes, but like I said, he's autistic. She said he talks some."

"Hmm, I wonder if she'd let me try to talk to him." Diana said, unable to keep the lilt of hope from her voice. "Sometimes autistics notice things others don't. I know this because I did a reading once for a woman in Boston with an autistic child. She'd read a story about a young man who'd come out of his mental prison and wanted to know if I saw it happening to her son."

"Did you?" Lucier asked.

"No. Not that it couldn't, but I didn't see it. It's very rare. The interesting thing about my client's son was that he could tell the day of any date, either past or future. I asked him what day February 7, 2021, would be, and he told me without hesitation. He was always right."

"That's freaky," Beecher said. "Gives me the willies."

"What makes you think the boy will talk to you?" Lucier asked.

A smile curled her lips. "Maybe he won't talk, but he might speak to me. With or without words."

Chapter Four
Clarity in All the Confusion

Liz Shore, the mother of the autistic boy, agreed to Diana's visit. The Shores' brick ranch boasted a neat lawn, two-car garage, and a generous backyard. Mrs. Shore greeted Diana and Lucier and led them into a large family room. A young boy about eight worked feverishly by the window at a table covered with white drawing paper and an array of crayons neatly organized in color range. Half a dozen vibrant sketches were tacked to a corkboard. An exhibit of his current work, Diana assumed.

Jamie Shore looked like most boys his age, except for the obvious indifference toward his visitors. Sandy-colored hair framed an almost angelic face, and the one time he lifted his head, bright blue eyes showed through a canopy of thick lashes.

"Does Jamie have any special gifts? Anything we can focus on that might help us?" Diana asked Mrs. Shore.

The woman cast an appreciative glance at her son and nodded. From the pride in her expression, she was one of those mothers who devoted time cultivating whatever special talents Jamie possessed.

"He insists everything be neat and organized, and he remembers details. Things you and I wouldn't even notice, Jamie absorbs everything like a sponge."

"Do you think he paid any attention to the house next

door?"

"It's possible, Ms. Racine. When he's not drawing, he watches out the window. Like I told the detective who came over here after the kidnapping, I was busy in the kitchen making dinner. My husband was watching a ballgame. If Jamie had seen something next door, he'll remember everything he saw. He specializes in minutia."

"What will happen if I take his hand?"

"He might pitch a fit, might not. He doesn't like being touched by strangers unless he wants them to or unless he wants to touch them. One never knows what his reaction will be."

"Does he have any special toys? A prized blanket? Something that makes him comfortable."

She offered a weak smile. "He doesn't play with toys, just the crayons."

The strain in Mrs. Shore's voice prompted Diana to reach over and give her a reassuring squeeze. "Will you allow me to touch him?"

"If you think it might help."

Mrs. Shore and Lucier took a seat on the sofa nearby while Diana, armed with the stack of photos Halloran lifted off the hospital tapes, pulled a chair from the other side of Jamie's table to sit by him and meet him at eye level. He continued to draw as if she weren't there. She sat with her eyes closed, sending what she hoped would be positive vibes. She spoke calmly in a soft, steady voice, unlike the exuberance she displayed at her visits to the hospitals' children's wards.

"Hi, Jamie, my name is Diana. Do you mind if I sit here for a minute?" He didn't react to the sound of her voice, but a slight hesitation in his drawing told her he acknowledged her presence.

"Those are beautiful drawings." She reached out for a finished one on the table. "May I have this one?"

He kept coloring as if he didn't hear her, but then he pushed the drawing toward her.

Diana's heart leapt. She glanced at Mrs. Shore, who returned a smile with a hand clasped across her chest. Headway, Diana thought. She talked to him some more about his drawing before she said, "May I touch your hand?" Again, he didn't respond. Slowly, she reached for the hand closest to her.

At first touch, he recoiled, dropped his crayon, and pushed the air in her direction without touching or looking directly at her. His gaze circled the room—up at the ceiling, out the window, and down on the floor, then at his hands, wringing them, concentrating as if they harbored a secret only he knew.

When he quieted, she asked again if she could touch him. He didn't answer. She rested her hand on his forearm. He waved at her again, but she didn't move away nor did he push her away. Other than trying to glean something from his touch, it was important to connect with Jamie physically, to create a bond.

After some minutes without a negative response, Diana placed the dozen black and white photos in Jamie Shore's line of sight. "Jamie, do you remember seeing any of these people at the house next door the other day?"

Jamie's head rotated from side to side as she flipped through the photos slowly. After one pass-through, she started over. This time he slammed his hand on a photo of a man, although his face was mostly hidden by the hood of a sweat jacket. Diana glanced at his mother and patiently waited. Then Jamie spoke in a panicked voice.

"Man, man, man. Man, man, man. Brown coat, brown, brown. Man, man, window. Man, man, brown, brown."

Diana nodded at Lucier sitting quietly with Jamie's mother, both rigid in their seats.

"Bag, bag, bag, bag, Bongo, Bongo, bag, bag, Bongo, man, man, brown, brown, bear, beard, beard, man, man.

"The man had a beard?" Diana said, glancing at Lucier and nodding. "He must have been a very old man with a white beard. Very old, Jamie."

"Red, red, red man, red man, beard, bear, bag, bag, Bongo bag." Jamie stopped, as if a faucet had been turned off. He cast his gaze around the room at everything and at nothing, still wringing his hands, and finally settled his focus outside.

Liz Shore stood up, a clue that the meeting was over. "I think that's enough."

Elated to have culled such important information, Diana removed her hand from Jamie's forearm. She felt sure she could glean more from the boy, but his mother knew best when to stop. "Thank you, Jamie. Thank you very much. You will help us find the baby." But Jamie had gone somewhere Diana couldn't reach, even with a touch. He returned his focus to the papers on his desk, picked up a crayon, and continued his drawing.

The adults moved into the entry hall. "He knew the man carried a baby in the bag," Lucier said. "How?"

Liz nodded. "Hard to tell. He picks up on things others would never see, almost as if he has extrasensory vision, and he remembers everything. Once it's in that complicated brain of his, it's there forever. A year from now, he'll mention the man with the brown coat and the Bongo bag."

"Who's Bongo?" Diana asked.

"Bongo Bear is a TV cartoon show that's been on for

years." Mrs. Shore shook her head. "His world is in another place, and he sees more of what we see and much we don't see at all."

"So there are bags with Bongo Bear's image on them?"

"Bongo's a marketing bonanza. Everything you can think of has Bongo's image on it."

"Where have I been?" Diana said, although she knew. Her life had been restaurants, hotels and theaters, with only newspapers, TV, and magazines to keep her abreast of what was going on in the world.

After a few words of thanks, Diana and Lucier left the Shore house and stepped into the bright sunlight.

"Good job, Diana. He told you what he saw by correcting you. Excellent interrogation tactic. Something to remember."

Diana didn't say anything.

"What's the matter?"

"I can't imagine being locked up inside myself like that, not relating to another human being, not even my mother." She choked back the sadness but couldn't stop the tears filling her eyes. "How hard that must be for Mrs. Shore, wanting to hold him, to share affection, to relate like parents do. Kind of like *Rainman*, huh?"

Lucier put an arm around her shoulder and pulled her to him. "Yeah, I guess so. He possessed a gift too, didn't he?"

"Yes, breaking the bank in Vegas." The thought made her smile and pulled her out of her melancholy. "Now that's a skill."

"Okay, so what do we know? From the picture Jamie targeted, our kidnapper is a short man compared to the others in the background, five-six maybe, with a red beard, probably reddish-brown hair. Age, undetermined."

"Somewhere between seventeen and forty-five, since

Jamie didn't mention any white in his beard. It'd be something he'd notice."

"Good point. Seventeen to forty-five. Not necessarily from New Orleans. That narrows it down considerably." He snorted.

* * * * *

Diana joined Lucier's team in his office, still melancholy over the thought of Jamie's unreachable world.

"Halloran's at the hospital now, showing the picture," Beecher said. "The guy's in too many shots. He has to work there."

"Let's hope. What about the hoodie?" Lucier asked.

"Brown's not a big color for hoodies," Beecher said. "And the padded Bongo Bear bag? There are thousands of those in existence, millions maybe. We'll run a check, but I wouldn't put any hopes on coming up with a hit. Our best bet's the photo."

Lucier looked at the picture. "I agree. Spread it around."

Willy Cash stuck his head in Lucier's office, carrying a rolled-up newspaper. "Big news, Boss. I came up with a similar abduction in Mobile about six months ago. A baby girl taken the same way. The feds hit a dead end with that one. I contacted Stallings. The case is still open. He ran a search for similar baby kidnappings, and found ours is the fourth baby snatch in the last three years. I ordered tapes from the Mobile hospital."

"Good work, Willy," Lucier said. "I remember the one in Mobile. Father was a big wig in some biotech company. The feds thought it was an inside job for ransom. But no one ever called. I'll contact Stallings and get the particulars of the other kidnappings, then call each one to see if anyone's come up with a lead." Lucier poked at his computer. "I hope this isn't what it looks like."

Diana watched him, digging her nails into the palm of her hand. "You're thinking a baby kidnapping ring, aren't you?"

"Has all the earmarks. I'm sure Stallings will agree. If it is, those babies are long gone." He sat on the corner of the desk. "Tell me about the evil you felt, Diana."

"How can anyone explain the unexplainable? Something in the vision of that room creeped me out, something perverse."

"Sorry to interrupt, Lieutenant, but have you seen the morning papers?" Cash threw the *Times Picayune* on the desk.

Diana's picture centered the front page.

Psychic Brought in to Track Kidnapped Baby
By Jake Griffin

Diana's abduction the previous month made headlines all over the world, and Griffin chronicled the story. His account was picked up by every paper in the country and put him on the short list for a Pulitzer.

Oh, yes, Diana thought, Jake Griffin would be all over another story about her, and he wouldn't hesitate to expose the romantic relationship between her and Lucier. Especially since she publicly notified the world that she'd given up show business to settle down and live life out of the spotlight. The two of them made great copy—the cop and the psychic—but as much as she hated the notoriety, she hated it more for Lucier.

"How the hell did he get this story?" Diana asked.

"Shit leaks," Beecher said. "Everyone knows you gave him the story after your ordeal. Hell, he milked it for all it was worth. They probably figured he'd pay for information about anything you're involved in."

"I'm going to put a hex on that little twerp," Diana said.

"Can you do that?" Cash asked with wide-eyed innocence.

Diana chuckled. "No, but I wish I could."

"Well, the story's out in the open now," Beecher said. "Maybe it will ring some bells about other baby abductions."

"I'm sorry, Diana," Lucier said. "I know you didn't want to get involved in this kind of thing anymore. I should have kept you out of it."

"Too late now. Besides, getting involved was my idea. You couldn't have stopped me if you wanted to." She got up and paced the room. "You want to know what will happen after that article hits the street? I'll tell you. Every kook with a baby story will be calling in. Babies who died at birth talking to their mothers from beyond, babies kidnapped by cults and aliens, fathers disappearing with newborns. You'll see. I've been through it all before."

* * * * *

By next day, calls from Maine to California, Florida to Washington State, jammed the switchboards just as Diana predicted. Stories that no police department in the world would take seriously, except those where one or the other parent abducted their children in custody cases.

Brady, the desk sergeant on duty, knocked on the doorjamb. "Sorry to interrupt, Lieutenant, but I found this on my desk. Don't know how it got there. I asked, but no one saw anything."

"Thanks, Sergeant. Let's have a look."

Beecher leaned over the envelope. "Oh-oh, I don't like the look of this."

"Me either," Lucier said. He pulled a pair of gloves from his desk drawer and slit the envelope with a letter opener. He slid a single sheet of paper from the envelope and read what was on it. "Shit. Dust this for prints." He picked up the phone and called Diana at the house she rented near his. "You need to get over here right away. I'm sending Cash to get you."

"Why, what's happened?"

"An envelope just arrived in the mail. It has your name on it. And I don't like what's written inside."

Chapter Five
The Star and the Crescent Moon

WE AWAIT YOU, DIANA

Lucier examined the note.

"What does it mean?" Beecher asked.

"I'm not sure what the crescent moon and star symbolize," Lucier said, "but 'We await you, Diana,' is clear enough, don't you think?"

Diana lifted her gaze from the paper. "Ernie, remember a few weeks ago I told you that Diana was the Goddess of the Hunt, and you said she was also the Goddess of the Moon?"

"Yeah, I remember."

"The crescent moon is a symbol of Diana, but it's something else too—a symbol of witchcraft."

Lucier fixed his gaze on Diana, unable to hide a frown. He turned to Cash, the unit's closest answer to a computer geek. "Google Diana, Goddess of the Moon and Diana, Goddess of the Hunt. See what comes up."

Cash settled at Lucier's laptop. Pages of sites filled the monitor. This article says the city of Byzantium was dedicated to Diana. That's Constantinople, right?"

"If I remember my history," Lucier said.

"They called her Diana, Goddess of the Hunt," Cash continued. "Then it says the crescent moon was a symbol of her, so she was called Diana, Goddess of the Moon too. It also says she was a fertility goddess and a...a virgin." Cash's face flushed. He kept his eyes on the monitor. "People everywhere practiced witchcraft, sorcery, and magic in her name."

Diana tilted her head back and closed her eyes. "This just keeps getting better."

Cash pointed to the computer screen. "Lots of stuff about God and Satan. And Jesus. Wait, get this—" he turned to Diana and Lucier—"seems there's a link between Diana and Lucifer himself."

An uneasy feeling rose in Lucier's gut. He rested his hand on Diana's shoulder. "Until we know what we're dealing with, keep your doors and windows locked. When you visit the children's ward at the hospitals, I don't want you to go alone."

"Aren't you overreacting?" she asked.

No, he thought. No. Diana lived alone, vulnerable to those who'd want to hurt her. He wanted to live with her, to protect her. But she wasn't ready. He didn't push even though he was.

It had been eight years since an auto accident took the lives of his wife and children. He'd survived the grief, the endless days of work and sleep and more work. Diana had breathed new energy into him. She wanted him to cherish the memory of his former life and the woman with whom he shared it. He loved Diana for that. He'd never forget that life, but Diana was a different woman not a replacement, and their life together would be a different life. He couldn't lose her. He wouldn't.

"No. 'We await you, Diana' doesn't sound good to me. In fact, it sounds like someone is eager to make your acquaintance."

"They're capitalizing on the publicity. Someone's trying to put a scare into the psychic, that's all."

"Yeah, well, he's putting a scare into the psychic's boyfriend." Lucier realized what he said in front of his men. "You guys didn't hear that, okay?"

Beecher zipped his lips but couldn't hide the smirk beneath. Cash snatched the newspaper and hurried from the room.

Diana's smile brightened her face. "I like the sound of that, Lieutenant. I've never had a boyfriend before."

"What are you laughing at?" Lucier snarled at Beecher, who took the hint and left. Lucier stroked his fingers across Diana's cheek. "I don't want to be your first boyfriend and your last."

Chapter Six
The Offering

The man with the red beard stepped into the bedroom. The walls were painted bubble gum pink, and the sun shone through the Victorian leaded-glass windows, creating facets of dancing light across the room. Pausing by the empty crib, he remembered the baby who had occupied its place. She was a beautiful baby, he recalled. Always hungry. It was a pleasure watching her feed. He lamented that he had to give her up so quickly, but that's what they wanted. The babies only stayed for a short time before they were transferred. They'd probably have to stop for a while or a pattern would emerge. Maybe the FBI had already found one. He walked to the second crib and looked down at the small figure wrapped in pink.

"Good morning, Lilith." He stroked the baby's cheek. "I'm so sorry you must leave me soon. I wish I could keep you longer, but it's not to be." When he reached the third crib, he leaned down and picked up the new arrival with the same care her mother would have, given the opportunity. "You are a beauty," he said. "What shall I name you? Ah, Persephone, a fitting name."

He brought the baby to the young woman with long blonde hair, sitting in a rocking chair, and placed the infant in her arms. She unbuttoned her blouse and unsnapped the panel of the nursing bra. Cradling the baby in her arms and cooing softly, she guided the hungry infant to her chest. Persephone placed her tiny hands on each side of the woman's breast, as if to squeeze every drop from its overflowing bounty, and suckled hungrily. After a few minutes, the young woman changed sides and the baby drank until she fell asleep. Then she put the sleeping infant back in her crib and covered her with a soft pink blanket.

The man with the red beard watched Persephone sleep. "You will be a special gift. But the ultimate offering will be Diana herself, Goddess of the Moon."

Chapter Seven
Into the Mythological Realm

Willy Cash carried the printout into Lucier's office. "Here's the lowdown on the babies snatched in the past year, Lieutenant. Two from hospitals like the one here, but different M.O.s for the other. Besides the Seaver baby and the girl in Mobile, one baby went missing in Atlanta." Cash flipped to another sheet of paper. "A few other reports of missing babies from around the Southeast were parent abductions, and the police found both the parents and the babies.

"Halloran and I studied the tapes from the hospitals where the other kidnapped babies were born. Our man is in all of them."

"We got ourselves a suspect," Lucier said. "Now who the hell is he?"

Lucier's phone rang. Diana. He shot a pleading glance at Beecher. "Give me five, okay?" Beecher left, and Lucier turned his chair around to answer the call.

"Will you make it here for dinner?" she asked. "I'm trying my hand at pot roast. Even I can't screw up that."

"Yeah, but I don't know what time," he said, curling around the phone. "Might be late."

"I'll wait," she said. "And guess what's for dessert?"

"I give up. What?"

"Me."

Lucier broke into a huge grin. "I'll be right there." Her

wonderful, full-throated laugh never failed to excite him. "Keep dinner warm, and—" he lowered his voice—"don't let dessert get cold. I like my psychics warm with a little whipped cream. And I'm starved."

He hung up, turned around, and noticed Cash standing near his desk, looking almost as embarrassed as Lucier. *Shit.* He hated when his men caught him in a personal moment. "What?"

"Um, we showed the picture of our suspect to the hospital staff. Even though the face is obscured, one of the janitors recognized the jacket. Our guy's another janitor, named Dudley Reems, and he hasn't shown up for work since the kidnapping. Here's the hospital picture. No record we can find."

Lucier examined the picture. "Unless that's not his real name. Any other record of employment?"

"Not under that name. The same janitor that recognized the coat said Reems didn't talk much, but overheard him on the phone once mentioned the Sunrise Mission here in New Orleans."

"Doesn't that mission take in the homeless, give them a bed, and help them find jobs?"

"That's the place. They've been written up several times in the papers. People claim the place saved their lives. Maybe Reems stayed there."

"Did you find out who runs it?"

"Yup. It's under state control, but it was the idea of a guy by the name of Brother Osiris."

"Osiris. What the hell kind of name is that?" Beecher asked, slipping into the office.

Lucier did a double take. "You're kidding, right?"

"Nope," Cash said, brows raised, mouth twisted in a

smirk. "That's his name, at least to everyone who enters his domain."

"Sounds mythological. Find out Brother Osiris's real name and the mythology, Willy."

"I'm ahead of you. Real name is Edward Slater. Forty-one, unmarried, no kids, not according to this, anyway. In the late eighties and early nineties he was picked up on drunk charges a few times, and last year he was questioned after a woman filed a complaint that he swindled her."

"What happened?" Lucier asked.

Cash flipped the pages of his notebook. "Slater produced a signed letter that she'd willingly donated $25,000 to the Sunrise Mission. She didn't deny signing it and then dropped the charges."

"Sounds like a con man to me," Beecher said. "Hits on the ladies before they know what they're doing."

"Sure does, but you know as well as I that if someone wants to leave all her money to her cat, there's not a damn thing anyone can do about it. Remember that hotel heiress? What did she leave to her dog? Twelve mil?" Lucier scanned the sheet on Slater. "I assume you've already checked the mythology angle?"

"Yeah, and you're going to love this. I'll give you the abridged version." Cash carried a computer printout and started reading. "Osiris was an Egyptian fertility god, sometimes called god of the underworld. He was married to Isis and slain by his brother Seth, who then cut his body into fourteen pieces and cast them to the winds. There's another story that says his body was cut into twenty-six pieces. In both, Isis gathered up all the pieces except the phallus and healed the body. She magically restored that little baby 'cause she conceived Horus, who is often portrayed as a babe suckled by his mother.'"

"Jeez," Beecher said.

"Hey, I just wrote what I found. You couldn't make up this stuff."

"What does it all mean?" Beecher asked.

"He takes the name of a god whose member has been severed and restored," Lucier said. "Maybe he's saying he can overcome anything, or maybe it's a validation of his virility."

"This is too deep for me," Beecher said. "Sounds like the guy's a whack job."

"Could be. It'll be interesting. Is he always at the mission?"

"Figured you'd ask, so I took the liberty and called. He's there all day, every day. Gets in about nine."

"Good work. I want to take Diana to meet with this fertility god. Maybe she'll pick up some vibes."

* * * * *

That evening, Lucier filled Diana in on the case, including the Sunrise Mission. The weight of not finding the missing baby weighed on him. No ransom note, so money wasn't the object. Then what was?

She opened a bottle of pinot noir and poured two glasses. "Sounds like a front. Osiris, Jesus. One of the fertility gods."

Lucier sipped his wine, stopping at Diana's statement. "How do you know that?"

"Mythology interests me. Kind of overlaps into psychic phenomena."

"How so?"

"They're both mystical in different ways. Mythology is folklore passed down through civilizations, with their own deities and heroes. Zeus, Apollo, Aphrodite—they're all from mythology. A lot of comic book and movie heroes are based on the mythological warrior."

"Hmm, Aphrodite, the love goddess. Why does that spark excitement?"

"Can't imagine." Diana winked at Lucier as she placed slices of pot roast on two plates and spooned a mixture of roasted potatoes, carrots, and onions in gravy on the side. "No one understands psychic phenomena. I'm not even sure I do, but it's real enough to those of us who have the gift. Same with mythology. Some cultures pray to different gods for rain or for a good harvest. That's a form of mythology."

"Sounds logical when you explain it."

"Almost logical, like religion. You have to believe, Ernie, because if you thought too long, most of it doesn't make sense." She sipped her wine, then placed the glass on the table. "Let's eat."

"Right, I almost forgot. I'm starved."

"You said that hours ago."

Lucier forked a piece of meat but stopped before he put it in him mouth. "I keep thinking about the baby. Where is she? Why was she stolen?"

"No word?"

"Nothing. Every case has been a dead end. What are you doing tomorrow?"

"Nothing special. Answer some email, pay a few bills. Why?"

"Will you go with me to the Sunrise Mission?"

A smile brightened Diana's face. "Brother Osiris? Wouldn't miss it for the world."

Lucier put the pot roast in his mouth. "Hey, this is damn good."

"Is it? Really?"

"Absolutely." He proceeded to polish off his dinner.

Studying his empty plate, he said, "Hmm, I seem to recall you mentioned something about my favorite dessert."

"Warm with whipped cream—coming up."

Chapter Eight
A Magnetic Attraction

The next morning when Lucier got to the station, Beecher followed him into his office. "Name of our suspect isn't Dudley Reems, it's Ridley Deems. No record, but he has a warning for soliciting a fourteen-year old—a runaway, most likely. The girl screamed and caught the attention of a beat cop. She bolted, and they couldn't hold Deems without her, but the cop wrote him up. We checked his last address, but he's slipped under the radar."

Lucier took the sheet. "We'll check if the name and picture mean anything to Brother Osiris. Diana's meeting me for lunch, and we're going to the Sunrise Mission together. Maybe she'll have a take on this creature from mythology."

* * * * *

Diana and Lucier arrived at the Sunrise Mission at two. Situated on the fringe of downtown in what appeared to be an old cotton warehouse, the mission offered the homeless a bed and hot food for those in need. It reminded Diana of a children's shelter where she spent the afternoon while on tour some years ago.

"We're here to see Brother Osiris," Lucier said to the woman sweeping the entry floor. "We have an appointment."

"You must be Lieutenant Lucier, and you, of course, are the famous Diana Racine. Your reputation precedes you." It was a man's voice that answered. The speaker was a tall, lean man in his mid to late forties, with olive skin and prematurely gray hair.

His face, though handsome, was etched with the crags and creases of life's hard fought battles. A man who'd seen it all was Diana's first impression. His piercing blue-gray eyes lasered right through her. He wore a long-sleeved, dark red polo shirt, blue jeans, and rubber-soled loafers. He offered his hand to Lucier but not to Diana. She retrieved her outstretched hand and stiffened at the slight.

"I'm Brother Osiris. Don't be put off by the name. The Brother is to make people comfortable, and Osiris speaks of a man who, though cut in many pieces, had the good fortune to be repaired. A little mythology, a little philosophy, a lot of hope. Real name is Edward Slater. You can call me whatever you want. Come into my office and tell me what this is about."

Well, Diana thought, raising eyebrows to Lucier, *he took the phony right out of that, didn't he?* She wondered if Slater's reluctance to shake her hand meant he feared touching her. Considering all the published accounts about her sensitivity to contact, she found the action, or lack of it, significant.

"Somehow I thought you'd greet us in a long, flowing white robe," Diana said. "I didn't expect anyone so down to earth."

He laughed out loud as he led them through a large dining area with a half dozen harvest tables, each seating twelve. Basic condiments and napkin holders anchored the ends of the tables.

"Sorry to disappoint you," he said. "That would be a little over the top, even for me. As you can see, this is our dining room, and these are the sleeping quarters."

He held open a swinging door, and they passed through a large room with cots on each side of a narrow aisle. Satchels and plastic bags stuffed with the occupants' worldly goods filled the floor beneath the cots, some schoolbooks littered the tops.

"Until Katrina, we had enough to satisfy the demand, except on cold nights," Slater said. "Fortunately, this old brick building weathered the storm. Other than some missing roof shingles, we came out okay. We did our best to accommodate as many people as possible, but there just wasn't enough room. It was a nightmare. Much better now."

Diana and Lucier exchanged shrugs. She didn't expect this level of disclosure, and she could tell Lucier didn't either.

"Over here is what we call The Closet. All donated items. Clothes, shoes, and whatever else someone less fortunate requires to give them back a modicum of dignity. All we ask is that no one takes what he or she doesn't need. Some clothes are new, most are used but in good condition. There's a recreation room with a TV, a communal bathroom, kitchen, and nursery."

"And all this is donated?" Lucier asked.

"Everything, and those working are either volunteers or people staying here pitching in their share."

People scattered throughout the facility tended to different tasks, one worked in The Closet—a room the size of an average bedroom—a couple of others prepared food in the kitchen, and still another did laundry at a large washer/dryer. All the workers were women. A few children in the television room played, watched TV, or read. Diana assumed the men were out either working or trying to find work.

"Do you live here?" Diana asked.

"No, I'm afraid the state would frown on that. There are shifts of employees who work on the premises and take care of the daily business. I eat my meals here, but I have a room in a nearby boarding house. Just a bed and dresser." He turned to Diana with a crooked smile. "Oh, and a closet to keep my flowing white robes."

After years of suffering the sarcasm of audience hecklers, Diana was seldom embarrassed. But Edward Slater had turned her own words back on her, and she felt small and petty. Her cheeks burned with discomfort. "Touché," she said, forcing a smile. "I deserved that."

"Then we're even." He opened a door and ushered them inside. "This is my office. Please, have a seat."

Nothing in the office boasted of wasted money—a simple wooden desk and four slat-back chairs, two four-drawer file cabinets, and a six-foot bookcase crammed with books of a spiritual nature, from Buddha to Confucius to the Bible to the Bhagavad Gita, tomes on mysticism, mythology, parapsychology, and the psychology of Jung and Freud, among others. A locked cabinet on one shelf roused Diana's curiosity.

Everyone took a seat, and Lucier slid Deems's photo across the desk. "Do you know who this man is?"

Slater looked at the picture. "Yes, Dudley something or other. He sleeps here on occasion. In exchange for the bed, he offers his services as a janitor/handyman. He comes and goes, as do many of our residents. Why are you looking for him, and why here?"

"His real name is Ridley Deems. He mentioned your mission to one of his co-workers. We'd like to talk to him."

"Has he committed a crime?"

"He's a person of interest in a case we're working on. When was the last time you saw him?"

"I don't recall," Slater said. "What do you think he did? What case?"

"A baby was kidnapped from her home last evening."

"I read about that in this morning's paper." Slater slid back in his chair. "And you think Ridley's involved? He was always so helpful. Didn't strike me as the type to do such a thing."

"People say that about a lot of criminals, after the fact. Anyone here who might know something about him?"

"The secretary might. I'll go find her and bring her here."

Diana started to say something after he left, but Lucier motioned her to keep quiet. A slight shift of his eyes indicated a small light inside the vent high on the wall facing the visitors' seats. Diana's almost imperceptible glance confirmed Lucier's discovery, and her instinct cautioned a camera probably meant a recording device. Maybe the surveillance had its purpose, but until they knew for sure, she wouldn't say anything.

Slater returned with a beautiful young woman who looked to be about twenty. Diana couldn't help notice her voluptuous figure, small waist and hips, with breasts out of proportion to her frame. Her dark auburn hair fell past her shoulders. She wore no makeup, but her Madonna-like face required none.

"Ms. Racine, Lieutenant Lucier, this is Brigid. Maybe she can help you."

"Do you know this man?" Lucier asked, showing her the picture.

The girl stole a glance at Slater as if she were asking permission to speak. He nodded. "Yes, that's Dudley," she said in a soft voice. "He sometimes helps out here. In return for a bed, many men offer their services. I haven't seen him in a while, though."

"Do you have an address for him?" Lucier asked.

"I doubt he has one," she said, "which is why he comes

here."

"Check with the others, will you?" Slater said. "See if anyone knows more about him."

She nodded again at Slater and left the room.

"Beautiful, isn't she?" Slater said when she left. "A runaway. She showed up here a few months ago, pregnant and alone. Her father sexually abused her. The child was his. Fortunately, or unfortunately, depending on your point of view, she miscarried. She stayed on, grateful to have found a safe place. She's smart and efficient."

"And obviously quite devoted to you," Diana said. "Do many young girls in her condition come here?"

"I don't know about devoted, but my staff and I treat those who come here with kindness and respect. Women like Brigid respond. We have an open door policy. Most women who come here seek refuge from abusive lifestyles. Others have fallen on hard times and have no place to go. We give them meals and clothes, ask no questions, and offer no counsel other than a sympathetic ear. When they're ready to face the world, we help them find work. We hope those abused women won't go back to their former lives, but many do."

"How do you get your contributions?" Lucier asked.

"As I said, donations. They're a matter of public record, but I bet you're referring to Jeanine Highsmith."

"Who's she?" Lucier said.

Slater smiled. "Ah, Lieutenant, I'm sure you checked me out before you came here and learned of the lawsuit slapped against me and the mission last year. Ms. Highsmith made that donation of her own free will, and I gratefully accepted. We used the money to purchase more beds, food, and supplies. For some reason, she accused me of defrauding her. Nothing could be further from the truth. She later dropped the charges."

"You seem to know my mind, Mr. Slater," Lucier said. "Don't tell me there are two psychics in the room."

"Hardly. I just know how people think. They assume places like this are fronts, and that people like me pocket the money and one day disappear into an early and comfortable retirement. I assure you that's not the case here. Sunrise Mission was my idea, but the state monitors us closely. I solicit donations and, along with the overseer, recommend how the money should be allocated. But I don't handle it."

"Have other girls come here in the same situation as Brigid?"

"You mean pregnant and victims of incest? No, and we don't save all those who do. Not that I'm in the savior business, but we do what we can."

Brigid came back into the room. "I asked around. No one here has any idea about Dudley, Lieutenant Lucier. Is that all, Brother Osiris?"

"Yes, Brigid, that's all. Thank you." A slight bow of her head and she was gone.

Diana watched her go. "And you, Mr. Slater, mentioned being broken into pieces and put back together like your mythological counterpart. What's your story?"

"Oh, I'm afraid it would bore you. Let's just say that I've seen hell, and it made a huge impression on me." He paused. "Anything else I can help you with?"

"No, I don't think so, but if Deems shows up, I'd appreciate a call." Lucier handed Slater his card.

Slater turned to Diana. "If you don't mind my asking, are you officially involved in this investigation? I seem to recall that after your shocking experience recently, you said you were leaving the entertainment business and would no longer assist the police in finding missing persons."

"That's true, but I could hardly ignore the disappearance of an infant. I haven't been much help locating her, but I don't give up easily."

"I wish you success."

"Thanks," Lucier said.

Diana stopped in front of the bookcase on the way out of the office. "I see you're a student of religion. Are you a devotee of one in particular?"

"I follow no religion but am interested in all of them. I'm a disciple of faith and reverence. I've seen some dreadful things in my life. Things that make me respect the power of evil. One must never be complacent. It is only then that the soul is damned."

"What happens then, Mr. Slater? What happens when the soul is damned?"

The electricity in the room crackled. Diana and Slater traded stares, neither surrendering the stage. Lucier stood silently to the side.

"Why, you go to hell," Slater said, maintaining the intensity of his visual focus.

"Ahem, um, I think it's time leave, Diana. I'm sure Mr. Slater has other things to attend to, and I have to get back to work."

But the two people remained locked on each other until Slater broke contact.

"It's been very interesting," Diana said, her outstretched hand ignored. She smiled. Slater was afraid of her touch. "Maybe one day we can continue this conversation. I'd love to discuss mythology with you, considering your obvious fascination with the subject."

"It would be my pleasure. The goddess Diana is an

important presence in mythology, with threads to nature and fertility, as is Osiris, I might add."

"She's also Goddess of the Hunt."

Again, the sparks ignited, and a small smile played across Slater's lips. "Yes, she is," he said. "A versatile and talented figure. Are you in the hunting business, Ms. Racine?"

"I hope not, Brother Osiris."

When they left the building, Lucier showed his irritation. "What the hell went on in there? I felt like I was watching a stage play, with you two in the lead roles and me without a script."

"I'm not sure, Ernie. You noticed he wouldn't touch me, didn't you? I think he was afraid of what I'd see."

"And did you see anything without the touch?"

"No, but I sensed Edward Slater is a very conflicted man. I'm not sure whether he's the real thing or a blatant charlatan, a do-gooder or an opportunist, but he has a magnetic charisma, and he knows how to use it. He's smooth as silk."

"Did you see the girl? She wasn't his secretary; she was his disciple. There's a difference."

"More his slave, I think. The way she looked at him before doing anything. A young nubile thing like that can hardly be ignored by a virile man."

"I didn't notice," he said.

She laughed and punched him in the ribs. "Get out, you did too. I saw you staring."

"Just a quickie. I am a virile man, you know."

"You sure are." She latched on to his arm and snuggled beside him. "I'd love to know what's behind those locked doors on the bookcase."

"A first edition, some valuable signed version of a manuscript or publication, or maybe it's not a book at all."

"Maybe, but somehow I think the secret to Brother Osiris is in that office."

As they walked to the car, they exchanged glances when a slim young woman headed into the mission, her angelic face framed by straight blonde hair that blew slow motion in the breeze like a diaphanous curtain. Diana placed her age in the late teens. The buttons of her white blouse strained across her woman's chest.

Another runaway, or another disciple?

Chapter Nine
The Pink Room in the Pink House

"Anything on Deems, Sam?"

"Nothing. He's disappeared off the face of the earth. Could be he's off kidnapping another baby. The feds are issuing a news release with his picture."

"Good," Lucier said. "Janitors come and go. It'd be perfectly natural for him to cruise the corridors without raising suspicions. He probably used different names and disguises."

"None of the babies have turned up, and no ransom notes either."

"Sam, can you get me a list of contributors to the Sunrise Mission? Should be public record. And dig deeper into Edward Slater, alias Brother Osiris. A complete profile. I wish the hell we could get his fingerprints."

"Why? Do you think he's involved in this?"

"Probably not, but my gut tells me there's something fishy about our do-gooder. Diana thought so too."

* * * * *

That evening when the doorbell rang, Diana checked to make sure it was Lucier before she opened the door. He would have chewed her out if she hadn't. She kissed him on the lips. "You look tired." She pointed him to the sofa. "Relax, I'll get you a beer."

"I am tired. It's been a long day."

She handed him the beer, then curled up next to him. He

leaned back and took a long swallow. "Tastes good. Aren't you having one?"

"I promised myself I'd cut back."

"I thought it was just until you fully recovered. You're recovered."

"I know, but it won't hurt to take it slow."

He put his arm around her and pulled her close. "When was the last time I told you I love you?"

"Last night, in the throes of passion. That's okay, I'll take those words any way I can get them." She took his beer bottle from his hand and leaned into him. "You know what they say when a person stops drinking?"

"What?"

"That they need something to take its place."

"Really? What did you have in mind?"

"Sex."

He lifted her onto his lap. "Come here."

"If I get any closer I'll fit you like a glove."

"Exactly what I had in mind."

He moved her hair aside and put his warm lips on the back of her neck, alternating between kissing and licking.

"Hmm, that is so sexy," she said.

Still kissing her neck, he moved his hands up under the front of her shirt and brushed over her breasts, barely touching but touching enough to send her nerve endings into spasms. She closed her eyes and released a soft moan. "Oh, God, Ernie, I'm so in love with you. Love me like you've never loved me before."

"Loving you like that will take a long, long time." He removed the back sofa cushions and threw them on the floor. "Maybe all evening."

"I'm not going anywhere." She lifted her mouth to his and

whispered in his ear.

He broke into a raucous belly laugh. "I love when you talk dirty, as if I needed more encouragement."

He moved his kisses to her ear and nibbled on her lobe while he ran his hands up under the back of her shirt and unsnapped her bra. "You don't really need this."

She stopped unbuttoning his shirt to glare at him. "Thanks for reminding me."

"I didn't mean it that way. The size of a woman's breasts means nothing to me. What matters is who they belong to. For me, yours are perfect. I only meant I can't feel these getting hard through the fabric."

These were her nipples, and between the warm kisses on the back of her neck and the delicate touch of his fingers on the tips of her breasts, she thought she would scream in pleasure.

"You have pants on and nothing's stopping that weapon of yours from doing the same thing."

"I can't help it. You turn me on in ways I can't describe. Everything about you, your head full of curls, your lips, your perfect little body,"—he nuzzled into her neck—"the delicious, sweet scent of you. When I thought I'd lost you, I knew I'd never survive. I'd gone through it once. This time I would have died a slow death."

He pulled her shirt over her head and slipped her bra straps off her shoulders. He got up and took off his clothes, never removing his gaze from her. Diana loved his body, his tight muscles and strong arms that lifted her like she was nothing more than a puff of air. She loved his coffee-colored skin against her white, his gold-flecked hazel eyes, and the imperfect overlapping of one of his front teeth. She loved everything about him, especially now that he was taking off the rest of her clothes in the slow, methodical way he always undressed her, as if he delighted in revealing every naked inch of skin.

He reached for her hand and raised it to his lips, kissing each finger, nibbling on the tips, never taking his gaze off her. The tender action sparked every nerve ending, inciting her need of him in ways she couldn't explain. A playful smile crinkled the corners of his eyes as he moved into a slow, gentle kiss while he worked his fingers into the mass of curls, caressing, massaging the base of her skull, causing shivers of delight. His lips moved to her cheek and into her ear, his tongue curious, his breath hot, then down her neck to her shoulder, part kiss, part gentle, erotic nipping.

"I never thought I'd be blessed with love again," he said. "It's totally different the second time. One takes the first time for granted. Mid-twenties, you fall in love, get married, and have kids. You don't give it much thought. It's all in the timing. Then when everything crashes, you realize how much you lost. The second time is sweeter because you know how fleeting life can be and how important it is to make every moment count." He moved toward her and kissed her forehead. "I appreciate you more than words can say."

Diana's heart went into double rhythm. "Thank you. That's about the nicest thing you could say, because it wasn't said in the heat of passion. Well maybe a little passion. Sweet passion."

"I know we're not ready to live together, but it's nice to know there's someone waiting, especially after a week like this. I hope you feel the same way."

"I do. I love being part of your life. Even the cop part. Makes me feel like I'm not completely retired."

He took her into his arms. "I can't wait much longer."

"Then don't," she said.

* * * * *

After, they lay still for a long time. Diana enjoyed the warmth of his arms around her, the touch of his skin next to hers, the unmistakable scent of sex. "I know how difficult this week was."

"The Seaver kidnapping is eating at my gut. The longer the baby's missing, the less likely she'll be found."

He was right. The missing child ate at her too. "Anything on Brother Osiris?"

"You mean Edward Slater? Grew up in Dallas, both parents were teachers, good student, went to Brite Divinity School at TCU, but he dropped out before graduating."

"Any reason why?"

"Nothing on the record except a later problem with drugs and alcohol. Got picked up a few times. Then around 1993, he disappeared from sight until seven years ago when he showed up here as the driving force behind Sunrise Mission."

The missing block of time must be why Slater avoided her touch. What was he afraid she'd see? "What would make a divinity student drop out and turn into a drug-addicted drunk?"

Lucier's face scrunched as if in deep thought. "I couldn't find anything else that suggested the hell he said he experienced. Whatever it was must have happened during that ten-year period.

"The only complaint against him is from the Highsmith woman, and she recanted when he produced the papers she signed. Perfectly legal.

"I wonder why she turned on him."

"Maybe they had something going, and after he got the money he dumped her," Lucier said.

Or maybe it was something else. "Have you talked to her?"

"She teaches psychology at LSU. I'm seeing her tomorrow between classes at ten."

Chapter Ten
The Devil's Room

Dr. Jeanine Highsmith was not what Lucier expected. Tall, elegantly dressed, and attractive, she didn't appear to be the type easily conned into parting with her hard-earned money by some smooth-talking swindler.

"Thank you for seeing me, Dr. Highsmith," Lucier said.

She directed him to a chair in front of her desk. "What's this about, Lieutenant? I thought everything concerning the Sunrise Mission was settled. I had no case; I withdrew my complaint."

"We're investigating the disappearance of the Seaver baby. Maybe you read about it."

"Yes, of course."

"There's a person of interest who's spent time at the Mission, trading a bed in exchange for doing odd jobs."

A curious expression flashed across her face. "You don't think Edward had anything to do with that, do you?"

"No, but you're one of the volunteers who spent time there other than the few employees and the women seeking refuge. We've questioned all of them with little success. None of them paid this man any attention. I'd hoped you might remember him, even chatted with him. Any information you could give us is more than we have now."

Highsmith examined the photo of Deems, and Lucier watched her expression.

"The only person I recall who even resembled this picture didn't have a beard. This man looks, I don't know, scruffier and darker."

"He changed his appearance."

"It could be him. I don't know. I wouldn't want you to depend on my identification."

"Without invading your privacy, why *did* you bring suit against Edward Slater after willingly donating money?"

Highsmith leaned back in her chair, eyes on Lucier. She was obviously weighing whether to answer his question, and if so, deciding if she'd tell the truth.

"Let's just say the action stemmed from the weakness in a woman's vanity. I mistook Edward's interest in me as more than that of a benefactor. It wasn't. I'm embarrassed to say my pride was hurt, so I retaliated where it hurt him the most—in his pocketbook. I'm not proud of what I did, Lieutenant. I offered to pay his court costs, but he declined."

Highsmith's answer took Lucier by surprise. "Thank you for your honesty. I'm sure you're not the only one to have been deceived."

She shook her head. "You don't understand. Edward never deceived me. It was I who misinterpreted his feelings. Oh, there's something mysterious about him to be sure, but he never made an improper advance or gave me reason to think we enjoyed anything more than friendship. He might be gay, but he seemed rather, how shall I say, more asexual."

"What do you mean?"

"I'm not an unattractive woman, Lieutenant. That may sound immodest, but one knows into which category one falls. You, I'm guessing, couldn't help knowing you're a good-looking, sensual man. You carry that appeal in the same way you carry your badge—with confidence. I have no trouble attracting men. If I show interest, they usually respond. I found Edward captivating. A handsome man with no ego except in regard to his intelligence."

Focusing on a sheaf of papers on her desk, Highsmith picked at the corners, but Lucier could tell her thoughts were elsewhere. She smiled, as if remembering something pleasant.

"We enjoyed long discussions about philosophy and religion, about mysticism and mythology. I have a doctorate in psychology, so that entered into our discussions as well. He's very into that sort of thing. He's an atheist, so we spent hours discussing our beliefs. But no matter how he tried, mine were too strong for me to be swayed."

"Did he try to sway you?"

"Not overtly, but I always felt if I bent even a little, he would have considered it a conquest. The women who pass through the mission would do anything he asked. He was kind but not effusive. Believe me when I say I tried everything to tempt him into a more amorous relationship, but he never yielded. The more he resisted, the more I tried. It became something of an obsession for me. He never rejected me openly—he was too much of a gentleman for that—but he avoided my overtures as if I were infected with the HIV virus. You know the rest. Like I said, I'm not proud of what I did. He is the most intellectually stimulating man I've ever known and one of the most enigmatic."

She was telling the truth, Lucier concluded. No woman lied about being rejected. "He mentioned he'd chosen the name Osiris because, like the figure in mythology, he was cut into little pieces before—how did he put it—having the good fortune to be repaired. Do you know what he was referring to?"

"A traumatic experience darkened Edward's past.

Whatever happened, he chose not to share it with me; and even if he had, I wouldn't betray his confidence." Jeanine Highsmith pushed the papers on her desk to one side, leaned toward Lucier. "It seems, Lieutenant, that you're far more interested in Edward than in finding this kidnapping suspect."

"Just covering all my bases, Dr. Highsmith."

When Lucier left the professor's office, he wondered what it was about Edward Slater that gnawed at his gut. Highsmith saw it, even pointed it out. Was it Slater's smooth above-it-all demeanor or the way he focused on Diana, drawing her in, inviting her to discuss subjects of mutual interest? Subjects out of Lucier's realm of experience. Did he detect a chemistry between them? Is that why he was searching for clues to involve Slater, or Brother Osiris, or whatever the hell his name was? Clues that any good cop knew weren't there.

He answered his cell on the way back to his office.

"A patrol cop just picked up Deems near Audubon Park," Beecher said. "The cop followed for a while to make sure he had the right guy. Deems had shaved his beard and head but he wore the brown jacket. The cop didn't want to make a mistake, but he didn't want to let him get away either. Said he was willing to make a wrongful arrest."

"Good man. Where's Deems now?" Lucier asked.

"Interrogation. He's not saying a word and hasn't lawyered up. And Ernie, he's very strange."

"I'm parking now." Lucier hurried inside and went straight to the interrogation room. He was stoked. If they could get Deems to confess, they might break up this babynapping ring. He spied through the one-way glass. Deems, face and head hairless, sat with his eyes closed and arms folded across his chest. He didn't move when Lucier entered. The odor, though faint, hit Lucier immediately.

Almonds.

Cyanide.

"Son of a bitch." He ran to the door. "I need an EMS team," Lucier shouted. "STAT! Tell them we have a cyanide poisoning." Touching Deems's neck, he detected a slight pulse. He moved the body to the floor and started CPR. Putting his handkerchief over Deems's mouth to protect him from the poison, he began mouth-to-mouth and alternated with a series of chest compressions.

Within a few minutes the paramedics arrived, one older, one barely shaving. The older medic quickly broke an ampule of something between two pads of gauze and placed it over Deems's airway while the younger medic administered an intravenous solution. After thirty seconds, the first medic removed the gauze.

"Amyl nitrate," the paramedic told Lucier.

"Can you save him?" Lucier asked.

The medic didn't answer for a minute. "Doesn't look good. His pulse is fading."

The two men worked feverously. "Sometimes high doses of oxygen can—shit, he's convulsing!"

The other paramedic gave him an injection, and Deems stopped jerking and lay still. "Nothing's working," he said.

"Move over. I'm going to give him CPR."

Lucier watched for ten minutes as medic worked feverishly, pumping his chest. The other guy administered a second shot. When Deems didn't respond, he rested his hand on his partner's shoulder and spoke softly. "He's gone."

"Damn," Lucier said. "Damn, damn, damn."

Within a few minutes, the two men hoisted Deems onto a gurney and covered him. "Sorry," the older medic said. "Stuff works fast. He was a dead man the minute he bit down on that capsule." They rolled the dead man from the interrogation room.

"You did your best," Lucier said.

"We emptied his pockets and patted him down," Beecher said when they left. We thought he was clean."

"You couldn't have known. Who walks around with a cyanide pill in his mouth?" Lucier rubbed the back of his neck. "What the hell do we have here, Sam? A guy steals a baby, then commits suicide rather than be interrogated. He didn't steal this baby for money. No ransom, no calls. Nothing. I want to go over his personal effects. Maybe we can find something that'll lead us to the babies." Lucier rubbed his chin. "Son of a bitch."

He picked up the bag with Deems's belongings. A wallet, no driver's license or credit cards, six dollars and change. And a key. He called Diana, told her what happened. "There's a key in his personal effects."

"And you want to see if I get a reading."

"Yeah, I do. Maybe it will lead us to the house you saw in your vision."

"Are you sending someone to pick me up?"

"Stay there. Cash will come for you. I'm still worried about that note."

"I'll be ready by the time he gets here."

* * * * *

Diana's heart pumped a few extra beats when Cash ushered her into Lucier's office. He had that effect on her from the first time she saw him. After a quick smile in his direction, she took her usual seat. The key sat on the desk in front of her. She stared at it.

"What do you think?" he asked.

"Only one way to find out. You know I might not get any

reading at all, don't you?"

"I know. Feel no pressure."

She laughed. "No, of course not. It's just a baby." She gingerly picked up the key. "Does the captain know I'm doing this?"

"He said he's going to have to put you on the payroll."

"That's an idea. I'm out of work."

"Not lately." He clicked on a tape recorder, identified himself, and gave the date. "Diana Racine channeling a key found on Ridley Deems."

She wasn't sure she liked the word *channeling*, but what else could he call what she did? Glancing at Lucier, she tucked the key in the palm of her hand and made a fist. "Here goes." She drew a deep breath and closed her eyes. A few minutes passed before she spoke.

"I see a large Victorian house with a turret covered with decorative shingles. The house is pink with white trim, and there's a black wrought iron fence, the kind with spear-like tops." The vision clarified. "Brass numbers 107 are on the right side of the front door." Before long, she opened her eyes. "That's all I see, Ernie. I don't know if it's the same house with the pink room." She replaced the key on the desk, but she couldn't shake the ominous feeling the vision generated.

Lucier patted her back. "Good work, Diana." He flipped his intercom. "Willy, Deems was near Audubon Park, right?"

"Yeah, on Charles Street."

"Pull up all the addresses in the area with the number 107."

"I'm on it," Cash said.

Lucier turned to Diana. "If he finds anything, will you go with me to check it out?"

"You know I will."

After Cash came back with half a dozen hits, Lucier and Diana, along with Detectives Halloran and Cash and crime scene protective wear, set out to see if one of them was the pink house. They started with the address closest to Charles Street and hit pay dirt when they drove up to a pink Victorian with a shingled turret, enclosed by a black wrought iron fence.

"This is it," Diana said, craning to look out the window.

The house sat at the end of a cul-de-sac, a few blocks from Audubon Park, and the afternoon sun reflected off brass numbers on the door—107.

Halloran waited with Diana while Lucier and Cash scaled the few steps to the front door. Lucier rang the bell. Nobody answered. He banged on the brass knocker, shaped like a crescent moon. Still no answer. He glanced at the key, turned toward Cash, shook his head, and returned to the car.

"No way am I going to screw this up," he said. He called Beecher. "Sam, get a judge to issue a search warrant. I don't want evidence tossed later because we entered without proper authority. The words kidnapped babies should do the trick." He gave Beecher the address.

"What's the matter?" Lucier asked Diana when he disconnected the call.

"I feel uneasy. I don't know why."

Halloran made a coffee run. They drank while they waited for Beecher. He drove up with the warrant an hour later.

Lucier cautioned his men to don latex gloves and booties. "You too, Diana. I don't want this place compromised before the crime scene unit goes over it."

Diana donned the booties and gloves and waited at the car while Lucier tried the key in the lock. It fit. He waved her forward, but she was frozen to the spot, unable to move past the gate.

Lucier descended the stairs as the two detectives slipped inside. "What's the matter?"

"Something's not right."

"Lieutenant, we've found something," Cash called from inside.

Lucier took her hand and led her to the opened gate. "I'm not leaving you out here alone. Come on."

With every step, a sense of foreboding intensified. "There's evil here, Ernie."

"What do you mean?"

"Just what I said. This house is evil." Her grip on Lucier's hand tightened.

"Up here, Lieutenant," Cash said.

She stopped.

Lucier touched her cheek. "You're with me. Nothing can happen."

Though his words meant to reinforce she was safe, she still couldn't shake the darkness that filled her heart. As much as she wanted to flee from the house, her curiosity drew her forward, up the stairs to where Cash stood at the doorway of a baby blue bedroom. Two cribs sat empty. The only other furniture was a rocking chair and changing table.

A strange force beckoned her across the hall to a room painted cotton-candy pink, with the same furniture as theblue room. She took in the high ceiling and the leaded glass windows. The room was the identical to the one she'd seen in her vision. Halloran's call from down the hall broke her concentration.

Then Lucier was beside her. "Same room?"

She nodded.

"Come on. Let's see what Halloran found."

"Looks like a bunch of symbolic stuff, like from witchcraft,

Lieutenant."

Diana stepped inside the room, unable to hide a shiver. Drawings covered one wall. The room started to spin, and a queasy sensation roiled inside her. She leaned heavily on Lucier.

"Are you all right?" he asked.

"This is the evil I felt downstairs. Those are symbols of devil worship, the adoration of Lucifer." She turned to face Lucier. "This place is home to a Satanic cult."

Chapter Eleven
A Mixture of Purity and Evil

Lucier phoned Captain Jack Craven and filled him in on their discovery.

"We need to keep the satanic element quiet, Ernie. If this gets out, all hell will break loose." Craven paused. "Pardon the pun."

"Agreed, Captain. I'll make sure everyone keeps a lid on it." He broke the connection and found Diana standing in front of the drawings.

"The aura in this house is mixed," she said. "Yes, evil exists but so does purity." She pointed to the inverted star inside the circle. "The sigil of the Baphomet, the principal symbol of Satan. Could the babies be some sort of ritualistic offering to Satan? Sacrifices?"

"No one sacrifices babies, not even Satanists. Animals, maybe, but not humans."

She squinted at the wall. "Why else would they steal infants?"

Lucier didn't answer, because he didn't have one. In light of the investigation's direction, neither mentioned the ominous note Diana received with the picture of the star and the crescent moon. Whoever was behind this had targeted Diana. Was he trying to draw her in or scare her off? If the latter, he didn't know who he was dealing with.

"Do you feel the babies were harmed?" he asked.

She wrapped her arms around herself and shivered. "If they were, it wasn't in this room."

"The CSU is here, Lieutenant," Halloran interrupted.

Lucier wiped a smudge of mascara near Diana's eye. "Come on, let's grab a bite to eat while the unit does its job. Then I'm taking you home."

"Time is important."

"I know. A team's checking out the neighborhood, and we're running a check on who owns the house. Whoever it is chose this location because it's set off from the others on the street. Hopefully, someone saw Deems and others too, because more than one person is involved."

* * * * *

The next day in Lucier's office, Cash said, "The house is owned by a corporation doing business out of the Caymans. Agent Stallings said he'd look into it."

"Caymans, huh? Why am I not surprised? The feds have better resources to untangle corporate shenanigans. He running the prints too?"

"Yup," Cash said.

A few hours later, Special Agent Ralph Stallings popped his head into Lucier's office. "I was in the neighborhood, Lieutenant. Hope you don't mind my dropping in."

"Not at all. Wanted to talk to you anyway. Have a seat."

"I wanted to let you know that Deems's prints were all over the house, along with eight other sets." He sat down and took his time before unloading the bombshell. "The most interesting is Silas Compton."

The name took Lucier by surprise. "The industrialist?"

"The same. His prints are on file because he's worked on government projects. My guess is that Compton owns it, but proving it quickly won't be easy unless he fesses up. He's been on our watch list for years. He's anti-government but doesn't have a problem taking government contracts."

"A lot of people have no problem criticizing on one hand while grabbing all they can with the other."

"Well, Compton's taken his share. He complies with what he has to, but he owns a battery of lawyers to keep his private life private and his money hidden. If an employee breaks his confidentiality agreement, he's fired, and Compton pays so well that rarely happens. He controls his empire from a building he owns in the business district. Next to him, Howard Hughes looked like a publicity hound."

"Any indication of religious deviation?"

"You mean the satanic symbols on the walls?"

"Yeah."

"No, but he sure as hell wouldn't make it public if he did."

"What about other prints?" Lucier asked.

"We're still checking."

"Agent Stallings, now that your tech people are finished, do you have any objection if Diana Racine goes back into the house?"

Stallings shook his head. "None. With her track record, I'll be interested to see what she comes up with. We couldn't legally act on her impressions, of course, but we could…check them out."

Lucier extended his hand. "I'll keep you informed. Oh, and I'm glad you're running the case. About time we put our heads together without a turf war."

"Whatever it takes when the lives of children are at stake. Just as long as we both keep each other in the loop."

* * * * *

Diana stood in front of the pink house, acclimating herself to its aura. "Do you mind if I go in alone, Ernie?"

"You sure you'll be all right?"

"I know what to expect. I'll be fine."

Lucier pointed down the street. "When Halloran checked that house, the people who live there weren't home. There's a car in the driveway now. Maybe I'll have better luck."

"Hope so."

She waved him on and walked tentatively through the gate. When she got to the top of the stairs and put the key in the lock, she turned around. Lucier stood watching. She smiled, opened the door, and went inside.

As soon as she entered, a chill hit her like a gust of arctic air. Strange, because the air conditioner was off and the house was closed. She rubbed her arms to warm up. The crime scene unit left everything as they'd found it, but their presence might contaminate her perceptions in the same way carelessness contaminates a crime scene. Taking it slow, she wandered the ground floor.

In the kitchen, she checked the refrigerator and pantry. Empty, except for a few cartons of instant soup. The drawers contained towels and silverware, and an assortment of pots, pans, and dishes filled the upper and lower cupboards. She pulled out a chair and sat at the kitchen table, her hands palms down on top. She closed her eyes. "Talk to me," she said.

A strong sensation told her that people had eaten there in recent weeks. After a few minutes, she rose and strolled through the rest of the rooms on the first floor. No impressions. Nothing.

Climbing the stairs to the upper level, she stood for a long time outside the room with the drawings. The air was thick and heavy, and she found herself gasping to fill her lungs. Her pulse throbbed in her throat. She inhaled deep breaths before venturing inside, avoiding the wall with the diagrams. A small bed covered by a light blanket hugged the far wall. She sat down and closed her eyes. Someone had occupied it recently, maybe two people. Could they have slept in shifts?

The wall beckoned her. She cast her gaze on it, mesmerized by its satanic symbols. Diana's interest in the supernatural evolved as a natural extension of her psychic gifts. As a child, she'd been labeled a witch and a collaborator of Satan because of her uncanny abilities. People found it easier to associate her powers with the black arts than to believe they were a gift bestowed by a higher power. Even though she'd led police to missing persons—some living, some not—and her finds offered closure for the respective families, a few still claimed she was a conduit of Satan. The accusations inspired her to delve into the occult, if for no other reason than to disprove what they said about her.

She studied the drawings: the Sigil of Baphomet, the official insignia of the Church of Satan; the upside down cross, symbolizing the mockery and rejection of Jesus; and the pentagram, used in occult rituals to conjure up evil spirits. The sensation of malice enveloped her like the devil's cape. Dark impressions had been commonplace as a child, but the atmosphere in this room triggered an unprecedented reaction, as if fire seared her skin.

Get hold of yourself, Diana. Don't lose focus. They're just drawings.

With forced purpose, she viewed the other signs defacing the wall: the seeing eye, believed to be the eye of Lucifer—control it and you control the world's financing. The goat's head, mocking Jesus as the "lamb" who died for our sins. And last, the hexagram, a potent image of darkness and magic. There were more symbols, she knew, grateful they'd been omitted.

At age seventeen, when she expressed an interest in the occult, her parents thought she'd crossed over into another realm, that her psychic gifts had become rooted in the netherworld. Her father considered an intervention to release whatever evil spirit had entered her body, but he dismissed the idea when he thought of the publicity it would garner. Diana's fascination passed, but not before she'd immersed herself in the history and culture of the mystical.

Ultimately, she determined her visions were granted for a reason. Now, shrugging off the visceral effects of the symbols before her, she thought of the past, thought of the present. Of the babies. And she knew why she was there.

She turned her back on the symbols and walked across the hall into the blue room, then the pink, with their cribs and sunlight and colorful mobiles floating over where babies once had lain. The babies in these rooms were fed and nurtured and yes, loved. For what? An offering to Lucifer? A donation to the god of darkness?

She sat in the rocking chair, and a sense of innocence overwhelmed her. Before long, she was rocking back and forth, embracing a weight so light it barely kissed her skin. She felt her breasts as never before, hard and full, and when she looked down, damp rings stained her blouse. Tears filled her eyes and fell down her cheeks. In the pure room. In the evil house.

Chapter Twelve
Transformation

Lucier rang the neighbor's bell and waited patiently until a teenage boy answered. In the middle of his asking if the boy's parents were home, a middle-aged woman came to the door.

He flashed his badge and asked about their neighbors in the pink house without mentioning the reasons for his interest.

"I'm Marjorie Wilton," the woman said. "Come in." Her husband joined them and Lucier listened as the two people related what went on in the pink house.

"I'm not a busybody," Mrs. Wilton said, "but ever since that house sold—what, Stan, a year ago?"

"Give or take," Mr. Wilton said.

"Ever since, weird things have been happening over there. Not all the time. Maybe twice a month."

"Like what?" Lucier asked.

"They're not close to us, and you have to be outside to hear the sounds. Chanting, wouldn't you say, honey?"

"Sounded like that to me. Cars on the street and in the driveway. Expensive cars. Cadillacs, Mercedes, Lexus, even a Rolls once or twice. That's how we knew something was going on."

"Don't forget the girls," the boy said.

"What girls?" Lucier asked.

"Two of them. I tried to talk to one once, but she wouldn't even look at me. Both of them were really pretty."

"I've seen them too," Mr. Wilton said. "They come and go at different times, like they're swapping shifts."

"What did they look like?"

"Built," the boy said without hesitation.

"Jeff!" his mother scolded.

"Well, they were. You couldn't help noticing. They were older than me. The younger one had long blonde hair and the other dark red. Both of them had big, you know, big—" He cupped his hands in front of his chest. "Really big. You'd have to be blind not to notice." He looked at his dad, who bit his bottom lip and turned away, embarrassed.

Oh, yes, Lucier thought. You'd have to be blind. "Did you call the police about the noise?"

"No. Like I said, you couldn't hear it in the house, and I didn't want to get involved. They weren't bothering anyone. It was just curious, that's all. I did ask the only man I saw during the day what was going on in there, and he said they were playing cards. When I asked about the singing, he said they listened to Gregorian chants. He apologized if they bothered us and assured me they'd lower the volume. He seemed nice, not at all threatening."

"What did he look like?"

"Red hair and beard, about five-eight, always wore a brown jacket. He and the girls were the only ones I saw on a regular basis. The others came during their get-togethers."

Lucier flashed the picture of Ridley Deems. "Is this the man?"

The father and son nodded. "That's him," Mrs. Wilton said. "We've been on vacation the last week. What's going on there, anyway?"

"Nothing now. Anything else unusual?"

"No, but I don't make it a habit to spy on my neighbors."

"Of course," Lucier said. "Did you happen to notice a tall, good-looking man coming or going? Middle aged, graying hair."

"Nope, just the bearded fellow."

"And the group, would you recognize any of them?"

"Not in the dark. Their card games started late, around ten, sometimes later. They never put on the outside light."

"Any license plates stick in your mind?"

"I never paid attention. I'm sorry."

"What's this about," Stan Wilton asked.

"We're not sure, Mr. Wilton, but whatever's been going on there is over."

"I'm glad," Marjorie Wilton said. "The whole late-night thing was strange."

"If you think of anything else, or if someone turns up in the middle of the night and you happen to see, here's my card. Call."

"I will."

Lucier left the house sure what the Wiltons had described, and he'd bet the meetings took place during specific moon changes. Who would make that connection?

He sauntered back to the pink house. Diana wasn't waiting in front, so he went inside. An unearthly silence greeted him.

"Diana?" She didn't answer. Fear shimmied down his spine, and he drew his gun. Heart pounding, he cleared the first floor.

She must be upstairs. I should never have let her come in alone.

"Diana? Where are you?"

He scanned the room with the symbols on the wall, then moved stealthily toward the pink room, stopping at the door. Diana sat in the rocking chair, her arms crossed over her chest.

He wasn't sure whether she was in a trance or asleep. His heartbeat thudded louder.

"Diana?" He crept closer and spoke softly, careful not to alarm her. Leaning down, he saw that she'd been crying. He touched her face. "What's the matter?"

She lowered her arms, revealing the circles of dampness over her breasts. "It started when I sat in this chair."

A lump rose in his throat. "I should never have involved you in this. It's too soon. You're not fully recovered."

She looked at him, her expression questioning. "This doesn't happen, Ernie."

He slipped his hand around her arm and lifted. "Come, I'm taking you home."

"Those girls were here. Brigid and the other girl we saw going into the mission. They were here and breastfed the babies. They're wet nurses."

This case was taking turns he didn't understand, and because of its bizarre nature, he wasn't sure he wanted to. "I know. The people next door saw them. Deems too. I'll explain everything on the way home."

She stood in front of him, arms still crossed over her chest. Lucier took off his jacket and draped it over her shoulders. She slid her arms into the sleeves.

"I need to get you out of here," he said.

"I couldn't stop the flow. It kept coming, and I couldn't stop it." She wrapped the jacket around her more tightly. "Don't tell anyone about this, please."

He took her in his arms. "I won't, sweetheart. I promise."

Chapter Thirteen
A Truth Stranger than Fiction

This time Lucier didn't announce his arrival at Sunset Mission. A woman asked him to wait, left, then returned to usher him to Slater's office. The director sat behind his paper-strewn desk. He smiled when he saw Lucier.

"Lieutenant, what a pleasant surprise." Slater rose to shake Lucier's hand. "Have you come to donate time or money?"

"Neither," Lucier said. "I needed to ask you a few questions."

"Ask away." Slater gestured Lucier to a seat, then leaned back in his chair with the same natural confidence he exhibited on their first meeting.

"Do you know anything about a house at 107 Parkside Avenue." News about the house hadn't been released, so he watched Slater's reaction. There was none.

"I don't even know where Parkside Avenue is, let alone a particular number."

Undeterred, Lucier pressed on. "When Ms. Racine and I were leaving here the other day, a beautiful young blonde girl went into your Mission. She was identified, along with Brigid, as frequenting the Parkside address."

"Sounds like Nona, but why would her whereabouts interest you?"

"Is she your employee?" Slater frowned, and Lucier

thought he'd end the interview.

"No, she stayed here for a while. Another story of incest, I'm afraid. She gave up the baby for adoption and left when she got a job—don't ask where because I don't know. She helps out here when she has time." Slater moved forward and folded his arms across the desk. "I raise donations here, Lieutenant. I see that the money is well spent. It would be inappropriate for me to get involved in the lives of women who've been abused. Many are suspicious of men and rightly so."

Liar. But Lucier couldn't call him that to his face with nothing more than a cop's gut instinct. "The house in question is home to a satanic cult."

Slater jerked in surprise. "That's impossible. Voodoo I understand, but Satanists?" But when Lucier didn't argue, his brow furrowed. "Are you sure?"

"Positive. Satanic symbols covered the walls, and Diana sensed the presence of the kidnapped baby or babies. Those two young women nursed them in that house."

"Let me get this straight. Are you accusing Brigid and Nona of collaborating with Deems in kidnapping a baby from the hospital, or are you accusing me of being involved? Since all three connect to this mission, it sounds like the latter."

This was the first time Slater displayed anything other than an irritating calmness. Lucier hated himself for his perverse feeling of triumph.

"I'm doing my job, Mr. Slater," Lucier said. "That connection is the only lead I have."

"I assure you, Lieutenant, if you're looking for a fall guy, you're in the wrong place. I don't know Nona very well, and Brigid may be young, but she's too smart to be involved with a satanic cult."

"Nevertheless, I'd like to talk to her. Would you mind calling her into the office?"

"This is impossible," Slater said. "Those girls have gone through hell. They'd never hurt a child. Nona gave up her baby, and Brigid's was stillborn. Neither breastfed, which leaves what you're saying an impossibility."

"Then Brigid doesn't have anything to worry about if I ask her a few questions, does she?"

Slater was now in full annoyance mode. He spoke after a long moment. "I'll ask Brigid to step in here, but if I think her rights are being violated, I will end your interrogation and call one of our attorneys. Fair enough?"

"Absolutely."

Slater left the room and Lucier took the opportunity to look around. He tried the doors on the bookcase. They were locked. Then he remembered the camera, turned, and saw the red light glaring at him from the vent. *Damn.*

Slater came back into the office and took his seat. "She's not here. Strange, but now that I think of it, I haven't seen her all day."

"How convenient."

Slater's narrowed eyes bored into Lucier.

"I don't appreciate your sarcasm, Lieutenant. I've been perfectly willing to cooperate, but you seem determined to involve me in something I know nothing about. If you want to make a formal charge against me for whatever you perceive is my crime, make it. I dislike people beating around the bush. I have too many things to do and not enough time to do them."

Slater's forthrightness took Lucier by surprise, and he wondered why he was being so aggressive. He knew the reason, and he liked himself less when he forged ahead anyway. "Do you know a man by the name of Silas

Compton?"

Slater didn't bat an eye. "Of course. Everyone knows who he is."

"I mean personally."

Slater rocked in his swivel chair. "Mr. Compton is a generous contributor to the Mission. In fact, his money funded us in the first place, and he's been impressed enough with its success to continue his charitable donations. I'd like to think he's a friend, even though I'm out of his league. Now, what has he got to do with this investigation?"

"He owns the house where the cult meets."

Slater stiffened but recovered quickly. "I'm sure he owns many properties in the city. He's one of the wealthiest men in the country. As far as his politics or religion, I don't get involved. I'm only interested in helping people who need help."

"And Deems?"

"I told you, I barely knew him." Slater stood. "This has gone far enough. I have things to do, as you can see by the work on my desk."

"Why do you have a camera in the vent, Mr. Slater?"

Slater shook his head and released a long sigh. "After the incident with Jeanine Highsmith, I thought it best to protect myself. All financial transactions take place in this room. The tape activates when someone is present. I don't want a case of he said/she said. If money is donated I have a visual and audio record."

Lucier eyed the camera. He'd love to get his hands on those tapes, but he had no legitimate reason to requisition them. What would he find? Slater was too smart to conduct illegal business and record it.

As if Slater read Lucier's mind, he said, "You'd need a

court order, Lieutenant, and you have no reason to ask for one. Besides, the tapes only go back to the time after Ms. Highsmith made her accusation. Oh, and Silas Compton makes me shut it off whenever he's in my office."

Was that a look of triumph on Slater's face? "I'd be careful, Mr. Slater. If what went on in that house connects to Mr. Compton, the FBI might be interested in your mission when they find out he's the financial backer."

"It would be like the government to go after Mr. Compton, since he's an outspoken critic of the way things are done in this country. I'm apolitical, but I don't believe in biting the hand that feeds me."

"Are you a devotee of Satan, Mr. Slater?"

Slater laughed. "That's what I like, someone who comes to the point. No beating around the bush this time, huh, Lieutenant?"

"No, not this time."

"I've made no secret I'm an atheist. I lost faith in God many years ago. My philosophy, however, is personal—meaning it's none of your business."

"You didn't answer my question, Mr. Slater."

Slater walked to the door and opened it. "You can apply any interpretation you want. Now, if you'll excuse me." Lucier was halfway out of the office when Slater said, "And how is Ms. Racine? When you came here, I'd hoped she was with you. I'd like to meet with her again. She's a fascinating lady, but I'm sure you know that."

"Yes, I do. I'll tell her. Thanks for your time. I'll ask Ms. Racine to drop by and see you."

"Excellent."

But not in my lifetime.

* * * * *

After swearing he wouldn't tell Diana about his visit to the mission, let alone Slater's disappointment she wasn't with him, when he got to her house he told her anyway. He could have written her response beforehand. She never disappointed.

"I want to go."

"No way. I didn't tell you that to encourage a visit. I'm only reporting what happened."

"I know, but maybe I can get something out of him."

"That's what I'm afraid of." *Damn right, that's what I'm afraid of.*

Diana arched one brow. "You're not jealous, are you?"

Lucier turned away, unwilling to look her in the eye. He could usually hide his feelings, but not where she was concerned. "Don't be ridiculous."

"Really."

It wasn't a question.

"I heard the panic in your voice when we were in his office," she said. "You couldn't wait to get me out of there."

He turned to face her. "You're right. The man's probably a Satanist, a baby kidnapper, and a serious sex addict, considering all those beautiful young girls who furnish a constant supply of infant nourishment. Who knows? Maybe he keeps them pregnant. You saw the look on Brigid's face. She worships him. Tell me that didn't enter your mind."

Diana let out a long breath. "I thought of it. Slater is a handsome, sexy man who'd have no trouble enticing young women to be his sex slave."

Lucier didn't like Diana's description, because he couldn't be objective where Slater was concerned. He was allowing personal feelings to interfere with a case. It was wrong and unprofessional.

"I remember the way Brigid looked at him," Diana continued. "And guess what it says about *Nona* in the mythology book. She's the goddess of pregnancy."

Lucier slapped the sofa. "What did I tell you?"

"Okay, so you might be right."

"Those two women are long gone. I told Ralph Stallings about my meeting with Slater. The feds questioned him too, but they came up as empty as I did."

"Let me go, Ernie. Slater's curious about me. I think he's afraid I might read him, but on the other hand, he's willing to tempt fate. He can't help himself."

"I won't allow it." The minute the words came out of his mouth, he knew they were a mistake.

"You can't stop me."

"Could I ever? Once you've made up your mind, you'll do what you damn well please. I recall you going off to meet a man who was hell bent on killing you."

"I knew you'd bring that up." She sighed heavily. "This is different. This is…intellectual."

Lucier didn't like that response either. "Fine, go. But I'll be nearby. In case."

"I wouldn't have it any other way," she said.

He hoped she couldn't decipher what he said under his breath.

* * * * *

Diana debated whether to drop into the mission or to call first. She decided to play it straight and phone. Slater claimed he was delighted to hear from her and asked if two that afternoon suited. She said it did.

She arrived at exactly the appointed hour, and one of the women cleaning up after lunch ushered her into Slater's office.

"Thanks for seeing me, Mr. Slater."

"It was I who asked to see you, Ms. Racine. I'm surprised the lieutenant told you." He still didn't offer his hand, nor did he take hers when she held it out.

Diana stared at her empty hand and grinned. "You still refuse to touch me. Why?"

"I find your gift fascinating but not enough to let you glean anything from my touch. You may be able to anyway, but I'd rather not make it easy."

"Are you afraid I might see what you're hiding?"

"Of course. We all hide things, don't we?"

His honesty always caught her off guard. "Oh, not me. My life's been an open book for twenty-five years. Everyone knows my story."

"I researched you before you came. I'd give anything to have your talents. Not for entertainment but for the insight to help people."

Diana made a circle of his office, stopping in front of the bookcase. "Is that what you're all about, Mr. Slater? Helping people?"

"Not all. I hope there's more to me than that."

She ran her finger across the book bindings, scanning the titles. "I'm sure there is." Turning, she said, "You're interested in the metaphysical, the abstract, and the unexplainable. A man searching to find his way in life." She flicked a finger at a familiar book, one she'd read long ago. "You have a particular attraction to Jung."

Slater stood by his desk, clearly watching her every move. "Yes, he's my favorite."

"Mine too," she said.

"Really. His interests were very eclectic. Besides philosophy, he was into mythology and religion. Mystical stuff as well. Alchemy and Kabala."

"I came across his interest in mythology during my own studies."

"A fascinating man." Slater rubbed his chin. "He dreamt about the dead and interpreted it as representing the unconscious. Not the personal unconscious that defined Freud, but a new 'collective unconscious.'"

"The kind of knowledge we're all born with without being directly aware of it. The reservoir of our experiences," she added.

He pulled out a chair for her, but she remained standing. He edged around the desk and sat. "When you have a vision, how do you feel? Do you think it's part of your collective unconscious?"

"I don't know. I don't intellectualize my gift. That part is out of my control."

"Hmm." He trained an almost hypnotic stare on her. "Intriguing. I can only imagine what that's like."

Diana forced a break from his visual intensity by momentarily focusing on the camera light. "It can be very scary and invasive to both me and my sitter." She brushed her hand down the spine of the Jung book, feeling nothing but the heat of Slater's gaze. Nothing from the book. Nothing from the room. His voice broke her concentration.

"Sitter—that's the person you're reading?"

"Yes. Sometimes I see and feel things I don't want to, like in the house on Parkside Avenue."

A smile curled Slater's lips. "Is that the reason you came here? To connect me to whatever went on there?"

Slater read her perfectly, but mentioning the house was a dead giveaway. No point in stopping now. "Those two women breastfed the babies there. Stolen babies, Mr. Slater."

"Both girls came here pregnant: Brigid first. She's the

older. Her baby was stillborn. Nona came after. She gave up her baby for adoption. The girls are sisters. Their father was the father of both those babies."

Diana gasped.

"Frightening, isn't it," Slater said. "That those girls should suffer the sins of their parents. I say parents because apparently their mother knew and did nothing to stop her husband's abuse." He drew a deep breath, hissed it out. "After they had their babies, they were never pregnant again." He kept his gaze riveted on Diana. "I'm not the most attentive man, but I'm sure I would have noticed that."

The thought going through Diana's head was something she'd rather not think, but she brought it up anyway. "Because a woman loses a baby or gives one up for adoption doesn't preclude her nursing after. That's what wet nurses do."

"Are you implying those girls nursed stolen babies from the end of their pregnancies to the present?"

"It's a possibility," she answered.

"That's preposterous."

"Unless you're holding back to protect them."

Slater frowned. "Why would I lie?"

"To protect yourself."

His chair squeaked on its hinges as he leaned back. He steepled his fingers under his chin. "For what reason? Do you think I impregnated them?"

Now it was her turn to stare him down. "The thought entered my mind."

Slater's skin paled, and he didn't flinch except for a small twitch in his cheek. "Would that I could."

The response stopped her. "What does that mean?"

"I don't have a penis, Ms. Racine."

Chapter Fourteen
The Descent into Hell

Diana gasped for the second time in as many minutes. Shocked and confused, words failed her. No psychic revelation prepared her for this. She slunk down in the chair, aware of Slater watching her reaction.

"I was twenty-one," he said." One of the rarest forms of cancer, and even rarer in one so young. Almost unheard of, in fact. It started with a small lesion at the base of my penis when I was in divinity school. I wasn't a virgin. Not that I was promiscuous, but I'd discovered sex and liked it—a lot. I assumed I'd contracted herpes and bought some over-the-counter cream, but it didn't clear up."

He stopped and gazed across the room, then back at Diana. She felt the heat on her face, saw the pain on his.

"Finally, I went to a family practitioner. He prescribed a pill and more cream, but the sore still didn't clear up; in fact, it got worse. I went back to the doctor and he prescribed a more potent pill. By the time I went to a urologist, the cancer had spread to the lymph nodes in the groin. I won't bore you with the chemical torture other than to say nothing worked. My penis had to be excised or I would have died. Surgery was the only way to save my life, and against the odds, I'm still alive. Ironic, because I spent the next ten years trying different ways to kill myself. It would have been a lot easier and less painful had I let nature take its course." Slater's voice came out flat, his statement a matter-of-fact explanation of a condition he'd long since suffered and accepted.

Flashes of heat pulsed through Diana's body, her heart thrummed. When she realized she sat as rigid as a statue, she made a point of relaxing. But the gesture must have seemed as phony to Slater as it felt to her. His story shook her, and he knew it.

"I'm...I'm so sorry. I don't know what to say."

"That's why I didn't want to touch you. I was afraid you'd sense something."

She didn't think she was capable of such a vision, of so shocking a revelation. "So, the name Osiris was a literal interpretation. Cut into little pieces and put back together, except for the phallus."

"Exactly. I thought you might figure it out."

"Who could possibly connect mythology with reality and come to that conclusion? Those ten years you spoke of, where were you?"

"Reconstructive surgery, not to create a penis as Isis succeeded in doing, although I wear a prosthesis to create the illusion, but surgery that allows me to urinate. Then more chemo, radiation, drugs, alcohol, and three suicide attempts. I've been to hell and back, Ms. Racine. I'm sure there are worse things than losing your manhood, but to be honest, after what I've been through, I can't think of one. And don't say that one's manhood isn't all between his legs. Try telling that to a woman who thinks she loves you, until you tell her you're missing a crucial part of the love-making process."

Diana nodded, then wondered how she would feel if she learned that about the man she loved. She shook off the thought. "So you lost faith in God."

"No benevolent god could allow such a travesty. Believe

me, being a divinity student put my faith to a test. My faith lost."

"Hence, all the studies, the psychology and philosophy. You were looking for answers. You must have come to terms with your situation. You seem at peace."

"In many cases, radiation kills sexual urges, but not in mine. So I had myself castrated. It was the hardest thing I've ever done, but it relieved me of feelings I couldn't engage in and lessened my torment."

So that's why he didn't follow through with Jeanine Highsmith. He couldn't.

"Why are you telling me this, Mr. Slater? Obviously, you've kept this from everyone. You refused to touch me, so why tell me now?"

"Because we share a sense of mysticism. In that realm, I am normal."

"So you became a mythological figure, explaining, if only to yourself, a situation you couldn't face as Edward Slater."

He sucked in his bottom lip and closed his eyes for a minute. When he opened them, he stared at Diana. There passed between them a brief connection so strong it was as if a spark ignited. She couldn't explain the sensation, nor did she want to as a picture of Lucier flashed in front of her eyes, but her heart raced.

"Something like that," he said, still staring.

A moment later she found her voice. "What took the place of your faith?"

"I'm an atheist. That's renouncing belief in a supreme being. I never said I relinquished my faith. On the contrary, if you remember when we first met, I said I was a disciple of faith and reverence. It's not faith in God. Nothing radical, I assure you, but it entails a long story, which I'll save for another time. I'll probably regret telling you what I've already told you."

"Did you tell Jeanine Highsmith?"

"Jeanine was seeking something I couldn't give her. She possessed an exceptional intellect, but she clearly had other things in mind—carnal pleasure, for one. And I…well, I'm not in the market for that and never will be."

"You still could have pleasured a woman. Not with penetration but certainly with other methods. Before castration you had physical cravings."

"Which only made me more aware of my deficiency—no pun intended. I read something of Kierkegaard once. I've kept it as a kind of mantra because it applies in so many ways. 'There are two ways to be fooled,' he said. 'One is to believe what isn't so; the other is to refuse to believe what is so.' It took me ten years to face reality and come to that conclusion. If I were going to live any kind of life, I couldn't live as half a man, feeling sexual desires without the goods to follow through. That's worse than torture. So, I made my decision to live in a way I understood, and God wasn't part of it. Granted, my way isn't for everyone, but it makes sense to me. I certainly don't bandy about my atheism, especially here."

"Who saved you?"

"As I said, another time, and I hope there will be another time. Maybe I'm holding back the rest of the story so I'll be sure we meet again. You're intellectually stimulating, and we've barely scratched the surface of subject matter."

He got up, walked around to the back of her chair, and pulled it out. "You can tell your lieutenant to relax. I have no designs on you sexually." He smiled and looked at her as a man would look at a woman who holds for him sexual interest. "Would that I could."

* * * * *

"He what?"

Lucier and Diana finished dinner and curled up together on the sofa. His exclamatory question was in response to a chronicle of Diana's day, which ended with most of her conversation with Edward Slater.

"You heard me," she said. "The man is incapable of being a sexual predator or impregnating those women." Diana decided not to break Slater's confidence by telling Lucier the true nature of his condition. She inferred Slater was gay. How could any man understand the choices he made or comprehend living without his manhood? "He couldn't possibly be a Satanist. One of the primary characteristics of a Satanist is carnal pleasure, and Edward Slater isn't interested in those women."

"So maybe it's carnal pleasure with men. It works both ways, you know. Pleasure is pleasure. Depends what floats your boat."

"He didn't impregnate those two girls, and I don't believe he's involved in the disappearance of that baby, any baby. The man's been through hell, Ernie. Drugs and alcohol brought him down as low as a man can go, and he's rebuilt his life, devoting himself to helping people. At worst, someone is using his mission to prey on the women who wind up there, for whatever reasons."

"You're losing your objectivity."

"He's not a Satanist," she said louder than she intended.

"Then what's so secret about his faith or religious persuasion?"

"I don't know—something he's devised to make sense out of his life. All I know is that Edward Slater hasn't got the perverted character to be involved in what went on in that house."

"And he told you this, or is it something you *felt*?"

She noted his sarcasm but chose to ignore it. "Why are you so negative concerning him?"

"Because I think your feelings about our good Brother Osiris are way off track." He rose from the sofa. "It's been a long day. I'm going home before one of us says something we'll regret later."

He pecked her on the forehead and walked out the door, leaving her confused and—dammit—angry at him for being so stubborn and shortsighted.

Then she wondered if she had indeed lost her objectivity. Had she become a victim of Slater's charismatic spell?

Chapter Fifteen
Hacker Extraordinaire

Diana sat in the dim light alone, stung by Lucier's accusation. Was his opinion of Slater colored by his love for her? He judged Slater as an adversary and as a suspect rather than how she saw the man—as a victim. But then she knew his story, or part of it. There was more. He as much as told her so.

She couldn't share Slater's secret with Lucier or anyone else. She'd be betraying a man who'd been betrayed, rightly or wrongly, by the greatest force in his life: his God. No, she entered into a tacit agreement, and she wouldn't break it without good reason.

In questioning Lucier's motives, she had to ask about her own. What made her so sure Slater was telling the truth? This time, to reinforce her intuition that she wasn't being conned, she needed outside help. She'd deal with the residual guilt later.

At age twelve, Diana could no longer bear the pressure of leading police to missing people, most of whom were dead, so she said she'd lost her psychic gifts. Because her father was unwilling to give up the notoriety and the money his daughter generated, he devised her act. Her performances employed assigned seating, and a series of computer hackers matched the information culled from the credit card payments to the people she called onstage. Though using most of her researcher's material to avoid giving herself away, she couldn't resist incorporating a tidbit from her psychic impressions that, despite raised eyebrows, she logically explained away.

Computer hacker Jason Connors was the latest in a line of techno geeks employed first by her father, then later by her. They all signed a confidentiality agreement, and to date no one had cashed in on what would surely be a juicy story. She picked up the phone, punched in Jason's cell number, and felt a wave of nostalgia when she heard his enthusiastic greeting.

"Wow, Diana," he said, "I never expected to hear from you."

"Why not, we're friends, aren't we?"

"Yeah, but now that you've retired, I didn't think you'd have any need for me."

"Ah, surprise. I do need you. How's your new job?"

"Boring computer crap. Nothing like the excitement of working for you, but it's a job that pays the bills."

"I've got an assignment for you. I want you to research a guy by the name of Edward Slater. I need to know everything about him, especially medical records. Also, while you're at it, do a number on Silas Compton. When you finish, send me a bill."

"Compton, the billionaire?"

"Yeah. I know you'll find a lot of anti-government dogma, but it's his religious views I'm most interested in. I don't want the standard Googling; anyone can get that. I want what isn't attainable."

"He's gonna be tough. From what I've read about him, his privacy is guarded like Fort Knox. I doubt I can break into his system. It's probably tighter than cracking the Pentagon, and that was the hardest crack ever."

Diana chuckled. Jason *had* hacked into the Pentagon to see

if he could do it. Fortunately, hackers who knew what they were doing also knew how to use backdoor programs to cover their tracks, and Jason was one of the best.

"I know, but for you it should be a snap. Start with Slater first." She gave him all the basic information she had. "There are ten years when you might not be able to find anything on him except some drunk charges. Those are the years I want. See if you can find out where he was during that time. He tried to commit suicide a few times, so there should be records."

"You don't make it easy."

"If it were easy, I wouldn't need you."

* * * * *

Because of the warning note Diana received in the mail, Lucier begged her to be careful when she went out. After an hour and a half of performing at the children's ward of the hospital, she picked up some groceries, then locked herself securely inside her house, made lunch, and settled on the sofa with a book. No matter how hard she tried, her thoughts wandered back to her bizarre experience in the nursing chair, knowing that the incident frightened her but acknowledging, in a sliver of reality, it also intrigued her. She still felt the phantom hardening of her breasts, the sensation of nursing a baby. Her hand unconsciously moved to her chest, and her fingers caressed her sore nipples. She smiled at the maternal feeling it generated—until she thought of Edward Slater.

If that strange and wondrous event occupied part of her thoughts, Slater dominated the rest. His confession confirmed her original impression of a conflicted persona. There were rare times when she couldn't separate intuition from her highly receptive sensory channels—those things she envisioned—as one overlapped the other. Slater confused her because emotions got in the way. Even though he'd come to terms with his situation, she felt sorry for the life he didn't have and for the torture he'd endured.

In the past, her psychic abilities connected her to missing persons, audience participants looking for fun, or wealthy patrons planning their lives by what she sensed in their futures. With the exception of relating to a death, rarely did those associations delve any deeper or develop into anything more personal.

Slater wasn't a subject, not overtly, and he'd been careful not to put himself in that position. Nevertheless, he confided in her as one would to a close friend, and that touched her deeply. She thought of what he'd gone through, and before long she was sobbing like a baby, while scolding herself for becoming emotionally involved.

* * * * *

"Silas Compton, for all his notoriety, is a hard man to get a handle on," Jason said when he called back a couple of days later. "He hasn't given an interview in over twenty years, only statements, and every article about him is pure research on the part of the journalist. He never even comments on them. His financials are off limits because his holdings are privately held. Because Compton International has the resources to do what few others can, his bids on government contracts are the only bids. Everything is in the control of the Compton family. No shareholders. Forbes estimates his to be the largest privately held company in the States, maybe the world, and Compton to be one of the richest men."

Diana held the phone to her ear and circled the room, walking off the tension that had her strung tight. "What else?"

"That's the easy stuff. You know, Diana, I can usually hack into anything, but his computer system is ironclad. I got what anyone with minor hacking abilities could get."

"Give me what you have. I doubt anyone else could do better."

"Okay, here goes. I know you asked for Slater first, but I'll start with Compton, because he's more complicated. Born in Oklahoma to dirt poor farmers in 1950. He worked his way through the University of Oklahoma in the engineering program and got a job with Barton Oil and Petroleum. Before long, he was running the place. When he tendered his resignation ten years later, he was a multi-millionaire. Then he started Compton International. A few years before, he purchased a parcel of land in Southern Oklahoma. Compton perfected new methods of deep drilling, making him a billionaire a few times over and one of the most powerful men in the state. Behind the scenes, he backs political candidates who promote his agenda—fiscally right, socially left, and he'll ruin anyone who gets in the way of his business. If he could start his own government, he'd be God and Master."

"How'd he get to Louisiana?"

"Offshore drilling, oil, and gas. Made him billions more and expanded his political clout. Of course, all the dollar amounts are supposition because no one really knows his worth."

"What about religious affiliations? Any contributions to any particular church or religious organization?"

"He's covered every base into heaven," Jason said. "Donates to all of them: Jewish philanthropies, Christian charities, even Muslim awareness programs. Not millions, mind you, but enough to build allies against government's intrusion into an individual's personal business, more specifically, his personal business. Those donations are a matter of public record, so no way he can hide the information. If he's funded other organizations, he's done it under the radar through a PAC, because I couldn't find them."

Diana marveled at Compton's ingenuity. He'd made sure everyone was on his side. Hard to go against someone whose deep pockets fill your coffers.

"He's a strange dichotomy," Jason continued. "Against government. Thinks social work should be the domain of the private sector and that people need to raise themselves up by their bootstraps like he did, without the help of government handouts. 'Course, he forgot that he went through college on government loans, but that's another story."

"That seems to be a common occurrence these days. I got mine; you're on your own, kid. What else?"

"He's publicly condemned the IRS as a tool of government waste and feels that people should be free to invest or spend as they see fit. I'm sure he's finagled his taxes to pay as little as possible, all legally, of course. Probably stashed money offshore, where the government can't touch it."

"I'm sure he's not the only rich guy doing that."

"You do that, Diana?"

She laughed. "No. I don't have that much money, and if I did, I wouldn't stash it. I believe in government. Keep going."

"Here's what I meant about the dichotomy. He's made comments that label him socially liberal. Doesn't care who marries whom, believes in a woman's right to choose, and is in favor of a separation of church and state."

"Interesting," Diana said. "Not the average right-winger. What about family?"

"Married in 1971 to Eliza Fannon, daughter of Gault Fannon."

The name struck a familiar note. "The senator?"

"Same. She and Compton had three children, two girls and a boy. The boy was retarded. He drowned in the family swimming pool at age five. Shortly after, Mrs. Compton committed suicide. The articles written at the time implied the guilt was too much for her. Nothing suspicious, but that didn't stop tongues from wagging."

"What do you mean?" Diana asked. "Did the articles imply that Compton had anything to do with his wife's suicide?"

"No, but not long after he appeared in the society columns with Selene Crane, daughter of Phillip Crane. Name mean anything to you?"

Diana whistled through her teeth. "I'll say. Looks like Compton knows how to pick the women in his life. Crane's a multi-gazillionaire."

"Yup. His grandfather struck oil. Crane was raised in enormous wealth, as were his children, and both he and his father increased the fortune tenfold. He's not only Compton's father-in-law, they're best buddies."

"This is getting more interesting by the minute," Diana said.

"When they married, Compton was thirty-nine, Selene Crane twenty-one, with a degree in philosophy from Harvard. Early photographs show a beautiful young woman. Reading between the lines, Phillip Crane brokered the marriage."

"Why do you say that?"

"Tabloids show the three of them before Compton and Selene were married. If his daughter marrying a much older man bothered Crane, it didn't show in the photographs."

"Hmm, this is getting better with every revelation. Do these two have any children?"

Jason hesitated. "Um, I don't know."

"What do you mean? Do they or don't they?"

"The second marriage is where Compton's private life gets

really private. Selene is rarely seen in public and there's no record of any children."

"How does he manage to keep that under the radar? They'd have to have social security numbers and all that."

"There's a doctor on staff. Maybe everything happens *in house*, so to speak. I don't know, but if they have kids, he's found a way to keep their existence secret. Researching unearthed plenty of Comptons, but none traced back to Silas, other than the two daughters from his first marriage.

"What about them?" Diana asked.

"Maia and Dione. Both graduated from LSU, but while there, they returned to the Compton compound every night like good little girls. Compton keeps his family close. The daughters are said to be smart, beautiful, and unmarried. They hold positions in his companies but still live at home, except for the times they travel as troubleshooters for their father's business. They go overseas for months at a time to take care of foreign investments, both in the Middle East and Europe."

"Boyfriends?" Diana asked.

"Not that I found. Compton owns houses all over the world, and they're like fortresses. State of the art security systems keep out trespassers. Compton International maintains a fleet of private jets, so he never avails himself of public transportation."

"So no one sees the wife or knows anything about offspring?"

"Selene Compton does a lot of charity work. She ventures out occasionally, mostly to a play or an art exhibit, an occasional shopping spree in Europe, but she's not the social butterfly she was before she married. I dug up a recent picture of her at the symphony, alone, by the way. It's pretty grainy, but she's still a knockout."

Diana was always amazed at how much information Jason unearthed. Whatever floated around in cyberspace or in someone else's computer, Jason would find a way to access it. If he couldn't get the information, no one could.

"Good job, Jason. Now Slater?" He was the one she was really interesting in.

"You were right. Those ten years were tough to research. Shortly after dropping out of divinity school, he stacked up major medical bills. I hacked into the hospital accounts, but his personal records are probably on microfiche in the hospital's archives. Even though he was still insured by his parents because he was in college at the time, the bills were astronomical. I hacked into the insurance company but like the hospital, records that old aren't accessible."

Diana knew what cost so much, and she couldn't ignore what it must have been like for Slater to go through that.

Jason went on.

"I found half a dozen arrests, drunk tank stuff, nothing violent. Also a drug possession charge. They held him for a few days and Mr. Anonymous bailed him out."

"No name?"

"Uh-uh. Nothing after that until he started the Sunrise Mission eight years ago using the name Brother Osiris with money from, guess who?"

"Silas Compton."

"Bingo, among others. How'd you know that? Don't tell me you've got a psychic thing going with him."

"No. Slater told me yesterday. Besides, that's public record."

"They get backing from the state, but most money is raised through donations."

"Did you find out anything unusual about Slater? Love

interests, friends?"

"Nothing. The guy's a monk. Good-looking monk from the picture on his driver's license. His mug shot, not so good. Looks wasted." Jason detailed Jeannine Highsmith's lawsuit against the mission, and Diana told him what Lucier had found out. "Plenty of recent articles in the paper, all praising his work. The Brother Osiris moniker is a bit pretentious, but, hey, whatever works.

"Okay, Diana, what's the story? You wouldn't be checking into this if something damn interesting wasn't going on. Wanna fill me in?"

"Not yet, because I have no idea what all this means. When I know, I'll get back to you. Fair enough?"

"Sounds good. Now my interest is piqued."

"Thanks for the info. Send me a bill. I emailed you my address, didn't I?"

"No charge. My pleasure. Besides, I don't think I got anything you couldn't have gotten yourself."

"I doubt that. Besides, you do it fast and thoroughly. Send me the bill, Jason. I mean it. I may need you again, and I don't want to feel like I can't call on you because you won't charge me."

"Okay, if you insist. I'll fax you everything I found on Compton, credit card charges, etc. Those things go to his accountant." Jason laughed. "His computer was tough but not impenetrable, except I couldn't access Compton's tax records. His accountant must remove them from his electronic database. Most everything else is tangled in that big shell game I mentioned."

"What about Slater's money?"

"The man doesn't even own a credit card. The Mission does, but not Slater. Most of the charges are for supplies, food, like that. He draws a yearly salary of eight thousand dollars and doesn't spend much of it. He rents a room in a boarding house, eats at the mission, and I suppose spends money for clothes. Looks like the way he lives, he must have some money in an account, but I couldn't find it."

"Thanks, Jason. You know I love you."

"Yeah, like a friend. I know."

Diana tapped her phone shut. Why would someone like Silas Compton fund the Sunrise Mission? What was in it for him, and what the hell did it mean?

Chapter Sixteen
The Invitation

Lucier picked up the phone in his office.

"Lieutenant Lucier, Ralph Stallings here. Thought you'd be interested in one other set of prints we found at 107 Parkside besides Compton's."

"You bet."

"Another big Louisiana name: Fernando Reyes."

Lucier's head went into a spin. "Another multi-millionaire. What's going on here?"

"Haven't a clue. What do you make of it?"

"Has he ever been connected to a fringe religious group or cult?"

"Not that we can find. When we asked both men what their prints were doing in that house, Compton divulged that he and Reyes were the owners, saving us a lot of trouble unraveling the mess of paperwork. He said they went to look the place over before they bought it. Their plans fell through, so they hired an agency to rent it out. Only knew of Deems by name. Never met him, they said."

"How could Deems afford a house like that on a janitor's salary?" Lucier asked. "And if he rented it, why was he trading off a bed at the mission for work? It doesn't make sense."

"The guy offed himself before anyone had a chance to ask."

"Damn. I suppose Reyes didn't know anything about the drawings on the wall."

"Right you are. Compton received no complaints from the agency. The renter paid on time, and that's all he cared about."

"Sorry, but that doesn't ring true. Satanic meetings went on there, and Compton knows about them. Deems didn't have friends with the expensive cars parked at the house during what he called their *card games*."

"Why would a guy like Compton be involved in the black arts and kidnapping babies? If he is, we'd sure like to know. He's a major thorn in the side of government. My bosses in Washington are salivating to get something on him. I don't suppose Ms. Racine would go with you while you interviewed Compton, would she? I know she stopped helping law enforcement long before that serial killer debacle, but maybe if she met him, she might tune into things we can't. We can't use anything she comes up with, but it might give us an edge."

"I don't know. I've been worried ever since she got that note. *Diana, we await you.* Someone wants her involved in this investigation, and they're doing everything to draw her into it. They must know she has the curiosity of the proverbial cat." Lucier knew, though. Diana was nothing if not predictable. "Besides, you guys have already interviewed Compton. Why would he agree to one with a New Orleans cop?"

"Two words. Diana Racine. The man's got a hard on for famous people. I guarantee he'll want to meet her."

"Hmm. I'll ask her, but I already know the answer. Any idea how to incorporate her into the meeting?"

"Compton doesn't forget anything. Just say your name clearly. He'll know you were the cop who saved Ms. Racine's life, and sorry, Lieutenant, but everyone in town knows you two have a thing going. He'll ask you to bring her along."

Everyone in town? Had they been that obvious? "You play the ponies?"

"How'd you know?"

"Sounds like you're a betting man."

Stallings laughed.

"Any luck tracking those two women?" Lucier asked.

"Not a whisper. One of our agents checked back at the Sunrise Mission, but no one there has seen either one of them. Slater was upset that the girl Brigid hadn't shown up. 'Course it'd help if we knew her real name. The one on her employment record is a phony, at least the last name is. Those places expect a number of false names from people who don't want to be found. She stayed there for room and board. He paid her a small amount for her services out of a miscellaneous fund. I hope those girls don't wind up like Deems."

"Me too." He remembered Deems gasping for breath, the pungent almond odor sharp in his nose. "What about other properties Compton owns under the dummy corporation?"

"Try conglomerates. We've got our Corporate Crimes Division untangling them, but his people are good. We're still trying. That man has his fingers into more pies than Sara Lee, with lawyers and bankers in his pocket to protect his interests. He's made a lot of people rich, and you can bet your pension no one's talking.

* * * * *

Lucier was relieved to see that Diana had either forgotten his sharp exit the other night or she chose not to bring it up. She curled up next to him on the sofa, coffee cup in hand, legs tucked beneath her, and listened to what he learned earlier in the day. She looked like a teenager.

"Silas Compton, huh?"

"Stallings said when I make the appointment he's bound

to connect me with you. Hell, the story was in the news for days. Did you know that people around town think the two of us are an item?"

She tilted her head, flaunting a half smile. "We are."

"Yeah, but I didn't know we were common knowledge."

"Does that bother you?"

Lucier noted the edge in Diana's voice. *Better tread lightly.* "Not really, but you've been in the public eye since you were a child; I'm not used to being *common knowledge.* Makes me feel like something I'm not."

"You had to know this would happen."

"Guess I didn't think that far." She smiled, and his heart rate ticked up. "I'll get used to it."

She jabbed a playful finger in his arm. "You better, buster, cuz I'm here to stay."

He leaned over and kissed her. "I wouldn't have it any other way."

"Good. Got that straight. Now, what else did Stallings say?"

"That Compton's like Francine Marigny—obsessed with famous people. If my name doesn't ring bells, Stallings said I should say something about you finding the house from the key in Deems's pocket. He'll want me to bring you along." Lucier drained his coffee and put the empty cup on the cocktail table. "That's if you want to go."

"You're kidding, right?"

Predictable as the sunrise. "That note you received would have spooked nearly everyone else off this case. Everyone but you. Anyone following the hunt for a vicious killer knew that."

* * * * *

The next day, as Stallings predicted, the mention of Lucier's name sparked Compton to ask about Diana. He followed up with an invitation to bring her along and to meet at his home rather than his office.

If Compton is behind any nefarious activities, his predictability quotient will work against him. Lucier stayed at Diana's that night, something he was doing more often, and by ten the next morning they started out for the Compton home in the French Quarter.

"Compton has homes all over the place—New York, L.A., even Paris, but this is his in-town residence," Lucier said. "I've heard it's spectacular, so thanks for taking me along."

She socked him gently in the arm. "Wise guy."

"If he wasn't anxious to meet you, I'd have met him at his office. Now I'll see a part of New Orleans only a chosen few have seen."

"Why at his house and not his office?" Diana asked.

"To impress you, my dear."

* * * * *

Diana knew residential treasures existed in the French Quarter, but she'd never have noticed this gem solidly hidden behind elaborate iron gates, which parted like the Red Sea to let them enter. The guard on duty nodded to Diana and asked for Lucier's identification, which he handed over. No impostors welcome. After checking his clipboard, the guard indicated where Lucier should park. A middle-aged man waited to open Diana's door. The dark suit couldn't hide the bulge of a weapon or his Mr. Olympia physique.

"Mr. Compton is expecting you in his study," he said. "This way."

Diana leaned over and whispered in Lucier's ear. "You think? Photograph comparisons, waiting butlers, or is this hulk a bodyguard? I'm almost flattered."

"Maybe Compton's panting to meet the hero cop," Lucier teased.

She laughed, but the tension inside didn't ease until she stepped out of the car and into a lush tropical garden surrounding an elaborate fountain. Perfume filled the air, and the mist from the fountain felt almost therapeutic. Instead of the bronzes of gods and goddesses she expected, the sculptures were surprisingly contemporary. She felt like she'd just entered Wonderland.

The old brick walkway led to the entrance where a maid ushered them into a large mahogany paneled room. A fancy gilt-framed landscape adorned the wall opposite a massive fireplace bordered by hand-painted Portuguese tiles, chosen, Diana assumed, to match the painting. A quick glance at Corot's signature confirmed her suspicion of an original old master. She saw Lucier scan the room, probably searching either for cameras or some connection to the occult. A few classical bronzes of gods and goddesses were evident in the artfully arranged bookcases but nothing she'd consider satanic.

Compton rose from an ornate desk and walked eagerly toward them with long strides. He stood as tall as Lucier, with a golf-course tan and piercing blue eyes that studied his visitors with intelligent curiosity. His features were classic and masculine: straight nose, square chin, and a broad forehead under a head of thick, graying hair, cut short. He wore knife-creased slacks and an open-collar, striped dress shirt with a monogram on one of the cuffs.

"Lieutenant Lucier, Miss Racine, this is indeed a pleasure."

His *pleasure* clearly targeted her when he lowered his head to kiss her hand, European style. She flashed Lucier a cutesy shrug and smiled, but when she looked down, she gasped at the sight. Her hand, still in Compton's, had morphed into a skeleton, charred as black as coal. She blinked a few times, and her hand appeared normal again. Swallowing hard, she hoped the savage drumbeat thumping in her chest wasn't visible through her blouse. Neither man seemed to notice anything odd about her hand or strange in her behavior. Still, she couldn't erase the memory of the vision.

"Delighted to meet you, Mr. Compton," Diana managed to respond with a smile. She noted Lucier returned Compton's greeting with an energetic handshake.

Surely the macabre sight was a hallucination, a mirage. She'd been under a lot of stress lately. Maybe Lucier was right. It was still too soon. She hadn't fully recovered. The satanic symbols, the incident in the rocking chair, and all the talk about cults must have had more of an effect on her than she realized. After a moment, the throbbing in her head receded and allowed Compton's words to filter through.

"I don't entertain many guests, but I'm a big fan of yours, Ms. Racine. Unfortunately, I missed this year's performance. I saw your show last year and was quite impressed. All that hoopla recently with that serial killer—my goodness, amazing. I admire that kind of fortitude, especially in a tiny package as yourself."

Diana forced a smile and a thank you even though she found his remark condescending, as if *tiny packages* were too insignificant to pack a punch. Common sense prevailed over the urge to comment. No point incurring his wrath before getting what she came for. So far the only reading she'd received had been her own.

Compton directed his two visitors to a sofa in his office, and he took a nearby chair. "I think it's a shame you're giving up the entertainment business. Not many like you around."

"We all have to retire sometime."

"Not me. I'll die behind my desk. Can't help it. There's too much going on, and I'm having way too much fun."

He crossed his leg and relaxed his shoulders, gestures of nonchalance, but Diana detected the movements were calculated. Silas Compton was about at ease as a coiled rattler, ready to strike.

"Now, what can I do for you?" he said. "You mentioned you had some more questions about my house in Audubon Park, Lieutenant. I don't know what I can add to what I told Agent Stallings, but I'd be happy to go over it again." Then a change in attitude confirmed that Compton was no fool. "I'm curious, Ms. Racine, did you accept my invitation just to see if you could get a reading on me? Maybe tell if I was lying or not?"

Diana raised an eyebrow. "I get sensations about people through psychic readings, Mr. Compton. I'm not a mind reader, and I certainly couldn't tell if you're lying. I'm sorry if you think I came here as a tool of the police department, but you extended the invitation to me. I was honored you asked me to accompany Lieutenant Lucier, pleased that you wanted to meet me." Diana tilted up her chin. "Now I feel unwelcome."

Compton's face reddened, and he bowed his head to his visitors. "I sincerely apologize to both of you. I'm embarrassed. The world has turned me into a cynic." He focused on Diana. "Let me be clear. I did want to meet you. Very much. Reading anything else into your acceptance is ungracious of me. I hope you'll forgive me."

"Of course." Diana decided to return the compliment. "Who wouldn't crave the opportunity to meet one of the world's most famous men? As I said, I'm honored."

Compton smiled, but everyone in the room knew the game being played.

"Now," he said, "if apologies are accepted, down to business. No one understands that better than I. Ask your questions, Lieutenant."

"Ridley Deems, Mr. Compton," Lucier said.

Compton sat up straight, squared his shoulders, but his eyes rarely left Diana. Hard and intense and penetrating. His words said one thing, but she sensed his objective was something else.

"I didn't know him, other than by the name Ridley Deems. I assumed my rental agency did the necessary checks on the man. I didn't know he had any connection to the Sunrise Mission."

"How could someone like that afford to rent a house at, what was the rental fee?"

Compton, a smile twitching his lips, answered without hesitation. "Three thousand dollars a month." He turned to Lucier. "I have no idea, but he paid the agency six months in advance, plus the same amount in a security deposit. I'm a businessman, Lieutenant. That was good enough for me. Wouldn't it be for you?"

"Yes, sir, it would."

"I recognized his name when I read the article in the paper. Other than losing a tenant, I had no feelings about it one way or the other. I was glad the article didn't mention the alleged goings-on in the house. It'd make renting it again harder." Compton shrugged. "Like I said, I'm a businessman. Even if I'd noticed him at the mission, I'd never have made the connection, because I never saw the man who rented the house."

"I see," Lucier said. "Who else had access to the house?"

"The agency, of course, Fernando Reyes, and myself. We found the situation disconcerting. Imagine, satanic symbols in one of my properties. As soon as we get the all-clear from the authorities, the management company will have a cleaning service in there to scour the place down, then repaint. Good thing Mr. Deems paid in advance. His money will help defray the costs of repairs."

Businessman, indeed. Or was that part of the act?

"Your prints and the prints of Mr. Reyes were all over the house."

"We checked out the house thoroughly before we purchased it. Even at foreclosure prices, a million is a lot of money. Fernando and I purchased it with his wife in mind. She's an interior designer, and he thought an exclusive bed and breakfast would be an interesting project for her. The property is on a cul-de-sac, making it a perfect location. But shortly after we bought it, she contracted a huge project that would keep her busy for quite a while. So we rented it out. Besides, property is a good investment right now. We considered the house was a bargain."

"Would the agency have a photocopy of Mr. Deems's canceled check so we could see what bank it was drawn on? If we could track the account, we might find out who financed the rental."

"Good point. I'll ask them to send it over to you. Now, if you'll excuse me." He rose. So did Lucier and Diana.

The two men shook hands. "I appreciate your time, sir," Lucier said.

"No problem." Compton turned to Diana with a fawning smile. "It's been a pleasure, Ms. Racine."

He took her hand again. She held her breath, but her hand didn't transform into an atrophied claw, black with foreboding. "I'm sorry we met under these circumstances."

"Maybe we'll meet again," he said.

"Thank you for inviting me," she said as a reminder. "In spite of the situation, I enjoyed the opportunity to see your beautiful home. The Lieutenant said it was rumored to be one of New Orleans's showplaces. From what I've seen that wasn't an exaggeration. It's magnificent, and incredibly large. How many of your family live here?"

Compton, his smile in place, answered, "All of them." His outstretched arm moved them toward the door. "I'd like to invite you back and show you around. You too, Lieutenant. Would you consider giving me a private reading, Ms. Racine, if you still do that sort of thing. I'd be happy to pay double your professional rate."

"That's not necessary. A tour of your lovely home would be fair exchange."

Compton's smile cracked, and he missed a beat, imperceptible to most, but not to Diana, who'd spent a good part of her life studying people's nuances.

"Settled then. I'll be in town for the next two weeks. Give me a day or two to check my schedule and I'll call you, if that's all right."

Diana wrote her number on a card she pulled from her purse. "This is my cell phone, or you can always get Ernie at his office. Either way, I look forward to seeing you again."

"And I you," he said.

Compton saw them to the door, and the two men shook hands again. The doorman waited by the car and opened the passenger door. When they both got inside and closed the doors, Lucier asked, "Well, what do you think?"

Diana recalled the black handshake, and the memory made her queasy. "Drive out of here first." She didn't know why, but she wanted to get as far away from the house before revealing her experience. She spoke when they were into French Quarter traffic and out of sight of the house. "When we first got there and I shook his hand, did you notice anything strange?"

"No, why?"

"Because for a fraction of a second, my hand turned black and skeletal."

Lucier started to laugh but stopped cold when he glanced at Diana. "That's—"

"Go ahead. Say it. Sounds crazy, I know. But he offered his hand to see if I'd pick up any vibrations from him, and he must have seen I did. I tried not to react, but I couldn't help it. It's not every day I see my hand a charred mirage before my eyes." She held her hand up in front of her face. "Silas Compton lives on the edge."

"So you're saying what?"

"I'm saying he's evil." Lucier didn't say anything. He probably thought that stress had finally tipped her over the edge, and she needed a month in an ashram to restore her sanity. *Yup. He thinks I'm losing it.*

He drove her home and planted a chaste kiss on her cheek before they got out of the car. At the door he picked up the newspaper. A slip of paper fell from its pages. On it were written five words: Diana, we still await you.

Chapter Seventeen
A Question of Genes

Ralph Stallings knocked on Lucier's office door. "Hope I'm not interrupting anything."

"No, no. Come in. Good to see you again, Agent Stallings."

"Call me Ralph. We've talked to each other on the phone and met enough times to dispense with formalities."

"My experience with your coworkers hasn't always been as pleasant," Lucier said. Stallings frowned. "Sorry, but that's been the case."

"It happens. Can't seem to get through to some of our guys that working with local law enforcement has advantages."

"What've you got on the note?"

Stallings scanned the room. "No coffee?"

"How do you take it?" Lucier asked.

"Black."

"Be right back." Lucier left the office and returned a few minutes later with a mug he set down before the agent.

"What, no one to fetch?" Stallings said, blowing on the liquid before sipping.

"I wouldn't like someone asking me to *fetch*, so I doubt anyone else would either. Now if one of my men asks if I want a cup or if he brings me one, I won't turn it down. But I don't ask."

"Nice boss."

"Bad history."

Stallings nodded, took a gulp, and placed the cup on the table. "Note's just like the last one. The paper is common variety sold in almost every chain store, and the envelope is self-stick. No DNA. The message was typed on a computer and printed on a laser printer. No prints, nothing traceable."

"What I expected."

"How's Ms. Racine? I can't imagine she spooks easily, considering her former profession."

"She's taking it in stride. This is nothing compared to what she went through recently. At least I hope that's the case"

"Since I was sidetracked by the note, I never asked about your visit with Compton. Did Ms. Racine get any vibes?"

"She had an interesting experience when they shook hands, but nothing tangible. Call it psychic channeling or telepathy or clairvoyance—whatever—but when she gets those feelings, she's usually right. I've seen it firsthand."

"Man, I'd hate my wife to have that talent. How can you stand her knowing what's in your mind all the time?"

"She only does it through touching someone she's reading."

Stallings stopped in mid-sip and peeked over the rim of his cup.

Lucier shrugged. "She says not. At least I hope not. I wouldn't want her to know what I'm thinking during—hmm, better not. I don't know you well enough."

Stallings laughed. "'Nuff said. She's an attractive lady. I saw her show this year for the first time, before the killings. Now I wish I'd seen her every time she performed in New Orleans. Very entertaining."

"Compton asked for a private reading."

"Is she going to do it?"

"Yes."

"Gutsy. And Slater?"

"She's clearer on him than I am. Something about the guy irks the hell out of me. Did the Bureau turn up anything on him that's not out there for us mere mortals?"

"Nothing federal, just the drunk charges in Texas years ago. He's cleaned up his act since then. As far as we can tell, Sunrise Mission is the only association he has with Compton. They don't exactly travel in the same circles."

"Compton admires Slater's work. Maybe Diana will find out more when she reads him."

The two cops drank their coffees and discussed the still unbelievable prospect that some of the richest men in the state—in the country—were involved in a satanic cult. After a lot of headshaking, Stallings left.

Cash passed the agent as he barreled into the office. Beecher followed. "Lieutenant, I got an idea and did some checking."

"Go on."

"I wondered if the babies had anything in common. Five babies. Why those particular ones? I checked their families' backgrounds. Except for one, both parents of each kidnapped infant are brainiacs. They're either scientists, mathematicians, or doctors, each renowned in his or her field." Cash put his findings in front of Lucier. "Those babies were chosen."

Lucier flipped through the five histories. "For their genetic makeup?"

"Yeah, that's what I think," Cash said. "Why else? Deems worked at each hospital on average of six weeks. He was waiting for the perfect babies before he snatched them and disappeared, which means if I'm right, the babies are probably still alive."

"And what about the fifth baby?" Beecher asked.

"Working class parents. Neither finished high school. The baby was returned with a ten thousand dollar check."

"Sounds like someone made a mistake," Lucier said. "Did you follow up with the other parents?"

"No, I wanted to see what you thought first."

"Do it. Damn good thinking, Willy. You might have something. Sam, catch Stallings before he leaves the building. We'll check out the parents in New Orleans; he can check out the others. Now all we have to do is figure out if they really are targeting these babies. And if they are, why?"

* * * * *

Lucier made an appointment to meet Dr. Jennifer Reese and her husband, Charles Seaver, at their home. Reese, a striking woman in her early forties, put off having children to pursue a career as a molecular biologist. She and her husband, a nuclear radiologist, were anxious to talk to Lucier and help in any way to aid in the return of their daughter. Lucier showed them a series of computer generated pictures of Deems in different disguises, from: bald and clean-shaven, red-haired and bearded, to combinations of both with different colored hair.

"If he was on the floor of the birthing center, I don't recall seeing him," Dr. Reese said.

Her husband studied the photo. "Nor do I. Why would someone do this?"

"To be honest, we're not sure, but your daughter is one of four babies, maybe more, taken from parents with superior intellectual credentials. We think that's why they were chosen."

"Four babies and maybe more? This is the first I've heard of that," Jennifer Reese said.

"The abductions were in different states, spread apart in time. We just made the connection when we found the work records of the man we think took your daughter at the other hospitals. Unfortunately, the man is dead, so we can't get any information to verify if we're right."

"Chosen. That would mean they're alive," Seaver said. "Otherwise it wouldn't matter who their parents were, would it?"

"We think so. Of course, it could be a coincidence. I wouldn't want to get your hopes up. Whether or not they were chosen for a specific reason, we still have to find them. If our theory is correct, they'll all be together."

The two people clutched each other. Lucier sensed their desperate optimism.

"Do you have anything to go on?" Dr. Reese asked.

"We're working on some ideas but nothing concrete. I wish I could tell you otherwise."

"I understand Diana Racine is helping," Dr. Seaver said. "Is that true?"

"She has offered impressions."

"Impressions of what?"

"I'd rather not say right now. I assure you we're doing everything possible to find your daughter."

* * * * *

Lucier walked through the tourist crowd on Jackson Square on his way to meet Ralph Stallings. The historic site teemed with artists and musicians, creating its unique flavor. On occasion he'd bought artwork that hung on the iron fence to support the talented artists, some famous, who had populated the square for generations. He'd seen plays at Le Petit Theatre, eaten Creole cuisine at the many excellent bistros dotting the area, and even tipped back a few at one of the bars in the old

Jax Brewery building, followed by sobering up with *café au lait* and beignets at the Café du Monde. The electricity in the square was what he loved about New Orleans—a city like no other.

It was at one of those small bistros where he'd arranged to meet Stallings for lunch. The air was thick and humid. He thought the exercise would do him good, but by the time he arrived, sweat glued his shirt to his back. He found Stallings at a table near the window, nursing a glass of iced tea.

"It's like a sauna out there," Lucier said, grateful for the air conditioning. He pulled a handkerchief from his pocket and wiped the sides of his face.

"You walked?"

"Thought I needed to get off my ass. Now I not only need a shower, but it's clear I need to get back into a regular fitness routine." Lucier caught the waitress and ordered iced tea with extra lemon. He turned to Stallings. "What've you got?"

"None of the other parents remembers seeing Ridley Deems at their respective hospitals. Good work by your detective, Ernie. The theory that the babies were taken because of their genetic makeup gives us hope they're still alive. From our investigations at the hospitals, Deems kept to himself. Janitors are part of the scenery. No one notices them. When they fail to show up for work, the employment office fills the vacancy. Deems worked third shift. Quiet time. Perfect for stealing a glance at records, see enough about the mother to run the name through the computer and find out all he needs to know—papers, conferences, whatever.

"So we have four babies taken, all—how did one of my sons describe the smartest kid in class—*genetically enhanced*?"

The memory of his dead son stopped Lucier cold. Those times from his past life still shot arrows into his heart. He noticed a strange look on Stallings face and wondered if the sadness showed on his own.

"Right. The fifth seems like a mistake, wouldn't you say?"

"That's what I thought. I don't get it. A kidnapper and sexual predator who'd rather commit suicide than talk to us, a satanic cult, a billionaire, two young women who've disappeared and who possibly tended the babies, and payment to return an erroneous abduction. What else?"

"Isn't that enough?" Stallings asked. "This is one of the weirdest cases I've ever worked."

"What's Deems's background?"

"Born in Alabama, raised in an orphanage. Mother gave him up at birth, but that's all we know about his parents. He had good grades in high school but dropped out. Worked a series of odd jobs, mostly as a laborer or janitor. The only time he got in trouble was when he hit on the girl."

"Maybe he was soliciting young runaways for the cult."

"Could be. Guys like him prey on young girls."

"Any religious activity?"

"Not that we can find. I doubt he'd broadcast he was a devotee of Satan."

The waitress put Lucier's iced tea in front of him, and he took a long swallow. Sugar sweet, lemon tart, and icy cold. The drink felt good after his sweaty walk. Both men ordered a grilled fish sandwich and side salad. The waitress refreshed their glasses.

"One link ties three of the things I mentioned," Lucier said.

"What?"

"The Sunrise Mission. Deems worked there, both girls had an association, and Silas Compton is the main benefactor."

"Didn't you say Slater wanted to meet with Ms. Racine

again? That they had some kind of psychic connection? I know you're worried about the note, but she might be our only entrée into the Mission without a warrant, and we don't have probable cause."

"She received a second note yesterday. This one said they were still waiting for her. I'm more spooked than she is. The note has a purpose."

When they finished lunch, Lucier speed-walked back to the station, not only because of the brutal heat, but because the note now weighed heavily on his mind. What was its purpose? A scare? A warning?

He called Diana as soon as he got to his office. No answer. He called her cell. Still nothing. When he arrived at her house, her car wasn't there, and neither was she.

Chapter Eighteen
Ascent from Hell

Slater met Diana at the door of the Sunrise Mission and ushered her to his office, still refusing to let her make contact. "I was delighted to hear from you, Ms. Racine. Frankly, I didn't think you'd call."

Ernie will be furious I did. But curiosity prevailed because Diana was anxious to get inside Slater's head.

"Why is that, Mr. Slater?" She focused on the red light of the camera above Slater's desk and made sure he saw her doing it.

"Call me Edward."

"Or Osiris?"

His smile emphasized the crinkles around his eyes. Steel gray, penetrating, unnerving. Diana pondered whether she found him charming or arrogant.

"If you wish," he answered.

"I think I prefer Edward."

"May I call you Diana?"

"Of course."

Their formal banter reminded her of a tennis match, with the ball trading sides of the court. She was struck by the man's charisma. He was as handsome as any leading man. The wrinkles etched on his face only made him more appealing. The hard-drinking detective in a noir film, struggling to stay on the wagon. The lone gunfighter taking on the bad guys, squinting into the sun. She understood how a woman like Jeannine Highsmith became obsessed.

Diana didn't have to touch Slater to sense the mass of contradictions. A man who claimed he wanted nothing sexual, yet he exuded a raw sensuality, a powerful magnetism, as if drawing in a woman were on his agenda, but it clearly wasn't, as in the case of Highsmith. Was he still trying to prove his maleness? There was no denying his allure. Diana disliked the effect he had on her.

He leaned over and extracted two bottles of water from a small fridge next to him and offered her one. When she nodded, he placed it on the desk. She smiled at his continued reluctance to touch her and noted he kept a barrier between them. He looked relaxed and comfortable in jeans a light blue button-down shirt, sleeves rolled up.

"You were going to tell me why you didn't think I'd call," Diana said.

"Obvious. Lieutenant Lucier, of course. You two are together, aren't you?"

"Yes."

"I don't think he likes me very much." Slater waited, letting a long moment pass before speaking. He wore the same half-way smile. "You and I have a connection he's not part of, or didn't you notice?"

He drove straight to the point, and the point made Diana even more uneasy. "I wouldn't put it that way, and I wish you wouldn't either."

"How *would* you put it? He's not comfortable in certain areas. Higher planes of thinking, for instance. Your lieutenant may be good at what he does, but I think he's out of your league."

Diana forced a smile. "Why, Edward, you're an

intellectual snob." He didn't refute her, and she figured he probably agreed. "We all have different areas of expertise. You must judge yourself above mere humans? Has the mythology of the gods gone to your head?" Diana noticed a crack in his composure. Did she strike a nerve?

"My pursuits are entirely philosophical."

Diana wanted to contradict him, but it would be like fueling a fire that burned out long ago, with no chance of reigniting. Still…

"You came here because you're curious about me. You wanted to know what it's like to go to hell and back."

Again, to the point. The man didn't waffle. "Yes."

"Mine is just one experience. Hell is different for everyone." He didn't flinch. "Have you been to hell?"

Dozens of pictures flashed through her mind. Visions she hoped had been filed away forever. Images of carnage she wasn't supposed to see but sometimes did. Visions her father failed to protect from her.

"Yes, many times through someone else, and one time recently through my own experience. Certainly not as intense as what you've been through, nor as constant, but hell nevertheless."

"Yes, that must have been a terrible experience."

Diana thought back to her captor's Adonis-like face, not unlike the man before her, and picked up on her inadvertent reference to another mythological god. "Yes, I looked in the face of evil, and I'll never forget it. But sometimes evil is developed through personal history. Others made him the way he was. I doubt he was born that way."

"Interesting. What about the other times?"

"My journeys took me into people's minds. Places I didn't want to go, but I had no choice."

Slater leaned across the desk, closing the space between them. "Could you have stopped if you wanted?"

His scent, Patchouli, she thought, wafted off the heat of his body, and the room suddenly felt as if all the air had escaped. Rattled, she leaned back in her chair and squirmed from the situation in which she'd put herself. "No, not once I found a connection to the missing person."

"Did you always locate that person?"

She shook her head. "No, regrettably."

"But most of the time."

"I revealed clues that led to their discovery. Is that why you don't want to touch me?"

"I'm not lost," he said. "Not anymore."

"But you want me to know about you. Why?"

Slater's expression hardened, his mouth rigid, and for the first time he took his eyes off her. "Because I've never been able to talk about it. You don't strike me as judgmental."

"Why would anyone judge the course you took?"

"It's ugly." Now Slater tensed, his jaw a series of clenches. He slunk further back in his chair and closed his eyes. "Remember, I was twenty-one, brought up in a rather restrictive atmosphere. I'd discovered women and they me. I have some wear and tear on me now—life has a way of showing, doesn't it?—but at the time I was considered quite good looking. I had no trouble attracting women."

Slater paused. There was nothing innocent about the sensual way he looked at her, whether he meant it or not. Diana felt the heat rise to her cheeks, the thrumming of her heart. The moisture in her mouth disappeared. No, Edward Slater would have no trouble attracting women. Even now with the *wear and tear*. If he noticed her discomfort, he didn't let on.

"I doubt I would have pursued a career in the ministry. I loved God, but I loved other things too. Things that would have conflicted with the life of a preacher."

Again he stopped and studied her. She forced herself to sit still, eager to hear the rest of his story.

"I began to think about teaching philosophy and decided to change majors when my whole world came crashing down. That disease." He stopped for a long moment, took a deep breath. "It couldn't be happening to me, I thought. There must be some mistake. Penile cancer is an old man's disease, not the curse of a twenty-one-year old. My choices weren't very appealing. I had the surgery. I lost weight, my hair fell out, and I was in tremendous pain, both physically and psychologically. I wanted to die, to disappear off the face of the earth." He sat statue still, the only movement a slight tic at the corner of his mouth. "So I did."

She tried to ignore the effect of his penetrating eyes, and for the first time questioned whether she should have come. "Where did you go? I mean, you had family. I'm sure they were concerned."

"All I could think of was that everyone knew I wasn't a man anymore. I couldn't look anyone in the eye. I started drinking to avoid facing reality, and before long was heavily into drugs. Heroin, crack, meth, anything I could get my hands on, and I'd do anything to get it. Fortunately, I had money—a nice inheritance from an uncle. I doubt I could have sold my body to pay for my drugs, unless I sold myself as a freak. I don't think I did," he said almost apologetically, "but I'm not sure. Some time shifts are vague.

A shiver spiraled down Diana's spine. She had wanted to hear this, but now she'd become a reluctant voyeur into Slater's life.

"It's astonishing how many people eagerly help you descend into that dark place called hell. My fall was precipitous. Not even my parents knew what happened, only that I'd disappeared. They searched for me, but I didn't want to be found. Actually, half the time I had no idea where I was."

Diana listened, trying to picture the nightmare Slater related. She couldn't. "Didn't you seek help?"

"For what? I'd lost my manhood. No doctor could restore that, and Isis wasn't available."

"So you tried to kill yourself."

He nodded. "In the slowest possible way."

She thought she saw dampness in Slater's eyes, but in the next moment his eyes were clear and cold and steady. "How long did this go on?"

"Six very messy years, give or take. I weighed one thirty at the time. I'm six-two and weigh one eighty-five now, so you can imagine what I looked like. My total concentration revolved around getting the next fix. I don't know how I managed to last as long as I did."

"Maybe you didn't want to die as much as you thought."

Slater shrugged. "I wasn't thinking much at all then, but I suppose the natural instinct for survival won out."

She couldn't get her eyes off him. "And God?"

"What God? God was no longer an option for me. Before my diagnosis, I thought He ruled the universe, and He let me down. At least that's how I felt when I was lucid enough to feel."

"So what happened?"

"The last I remembered I was in Mexico nursing a major heroin habit. I don't how, but I wound up outside Tulsa at a shelter run by an old Osage Indian. He treated those from the reservation who suffered from alcoholism. There are a lot of them, you know. George tried to get them back on their feet, give them a place to recover.

"He'd never seen anyone like me. I hadn't had a fix in a while and was going through the stages of withdrawal. I'd been rolled, because I had no money left. Don't think I'd eaten in days, but I managed to get my hands on some liquor to ward off coming down. I'd wet myself, a common occurrence, I might add."

Slater showed no embarrassment. He was a man who'd come full circle, from wanting to die to helping others survive.

"While cleaning me up, George saw what he said caused him to throw up. When he got over the shock, he secured me to the bed and helped me get through the next few weeks. He enlisted the help of what we'd call a medicine man, or faith healer. He didn't look like an Indian and didn't live on the reservation. In fact, he was whiter than me, but he said he was of Indian heritage. The two of them took care of me like a baby while I retched and spasmed and screamed till I thought my lungs would burst. I remember begging them to let me die, but they wouldn't."

Slater stopped and drank some water from the plastic bottle. He ran a moistened tongue over his dry lips. For the first time, Diana saw his vulnerability. A twitch in his cheek, a quiver in his chin. She knew on some level this was tearing him apart and wondered why he chose her to confess his tragedy to. Maybe it was nothing more than expediency, someone to listen. Sitting quietly, she waited for him to continue.

"The healer took me to a place after I recovered enough to know what was going on. He didn't live there but came often. He applied traditional Indian healing methods along with alternative medicines to aid my recovery. I stayed there with his disciples for four years. I had no idea where he went when he left, and I never asked, but I looked forward to his frequent visits. He and his people taught me respect for the earth, the wind, the trees and," he pointed, "that table over there."

"Animism."

Slater kept his eyes on her. He seemed surprised. "You know about Animism?"

She nodded. "Yes. I came across it during my curious period. The idea that a soul or spirit exists in every object, even an inanimate one, appealed to me."

"To me too. Animism is one of man's oldest beliefs, likely dating to the Paleolithic Age. The men taught me that life exists not only in man but in everything, and that all life is sacred, with no distinction between the spiritual and material, sacred and secular."

"Mediums claim that Animism may be the unconscious fabrication of a spirit, and that he or she is actually channeling that spirit."

"Yes."

"I'm not a medium."

"I know, but your gift suggests you've reached a higher plane of thought. I've never told anyone this. The only ones who know were involved."

"And the castration?"

"I couldn't control the sexual urges. My transformation as a eunuch was complete."

Diana's skin prickled at his revelation. "You did what you had to do to live without torture."

"Only to a point. The desires are gone, but the reality is still torture. Women like Jeannine Highsmith and others have shown interest over the years, and I still find beautiful women desirable, maybe not sexually, but visually and intellectually.

"You, for instance. Were I so inclined, I would find you a most appealing partner. I feel liberated in saying that because I know you will take it as a compliment, with no ulterior motive."

Diana's heart rate increased to what seemed a dangerous level. "I'm flattered." But was she? Edward Slater had an unusual effect on her, as if he emitted a mesmerizing pheromone. "But also uncomfortable."

"Please accept my apologies." He bowed his head. "I don't want to embarrass you in any way. My honesty often gets me in trouble. You see, because of what I've gone through, when I quote that hackneyed expression, 'life is short,' I mean it as a personal truth. My life may be shorter, because I could face a recurrence of cancer at any time. It's not unheard of, and I have no illusions. For that reason, sometimes I say what I feel without thinking. Again, I apologize." Then, his eyes steady on Diana, he said, "But I don't take it back."

Heat surged through her, and her body burned as if she were in a sauna. How could she let him get to her? She sought to change the subject and hoped her voice remained steady. "Did you reunite with your parents?"

Slater smiled as if he realized Diana's deliberate shift in conversation. "My mother died during my disappearance. She never knew what happened to me. I regret that more than anything; to have put them both through the uncertainty is unforgivable. My father was happy to see me alive. I told him little of what I'd gone through. He didn't need to know. He's since died."

Slater drank from his water bottle. "So you see, Diana, I could no more hurt a child or subscribe to evil than I could impregnate a woman. If I've been blind to certain things, it's my failing. Maybe I should have paid more attention to Brigid and Nona and noticed something wasn't right."

"As a student of mythology, didn't their names ring any bells?"

"I knew what they meant, and I knew they were phony, but I assumed they chose them because of their history."

"Why didn't someone file charges against their father?"

"They wouldn't, nor would they let me. They told me their last name was Fulceri. I searched the internet for their father. Maybe he was molesting others, but I couldn't find any trace of the name."

"A phony?"

"Probably, but I wouldn't pry. The sisters ran away because they were afraid of him. I wouldn't do anything to put them in harm's way."

"Fulceri," Diana repeated. "Interesting name." She was about to elaborate when Silas Compton opened the office door without knocking.

"Oh, sorry," he said. "I didn't know you had company."

Slater stood. "Not a problem, Silas. Come in. I believe you know each other."

Compton offered his hand to Diana. "A pleasure to see you again, Ms. Racine."

Diana took his hand and held her breath. Nothing. "The pleasure's mine. I won't keep you two from your business. I was about to leave anyway. It was nice seeing both of you."

Compton held on to her hand. "Nonsense. No need to rush off. I just dropped by to give Edward this check. It's from a client who respects the work you do to help the people in this great city of ours."

Slater took the check and peeked at it. He let out a whistle. "This is most generous. I'll have to call and thank him."

"Do that," Compton said. "Again, sorry to interrupt." He

started for the door and turned to Diana. "By the way, Ms. Racine, are you free right now? I have a few hours off. How about that reading you promised me? My car and driver are right outside."

"I drove," Diana said. "I—"

"Not a problem. After the reading, my driver will bring you back to your car. I won't take no for an answer." He tucked her arm into his. "Ciao, Edward. Call Stanford. He's worth a bundle and could be a continuing donor."

"I will," Slater said. "I can't wait to hear all about your reading, Silas."

Diana hesitated. "I really shouldn't. Ernie won't know where I am."

"Call him from the car," Compton said. "Unless you have to check with him for everything. He does keep you on a short leash, doesn't he?"

Diana thought about that. Did Ernie have the same control over her as her father had all those years? No, and she wouldn't let him."

"Okay," she said. "I guess now's as good a time as any."

Chapter Nineteen
To Sleep, Perchance to Dream

God, what is that sound? Diana clamped her hands over her ears, but the noise inside her head pounded like a hammer. She forced her eyes open. At first, she didn't know where she was. It took a moment to recognize her own bedroom and the insistent buzzing of the doorbell. She checked the read-out on the clock—seven a.m.

Go away. But the racket continued. *Shit.*

She swung her legs off the bed to sit on the edge and realized she was still dressed in last night's clothes. *What the hell?* The room spun in circles, and she steadied herself on the footboard. Nausea rose from the pit of her stomach into her throat. She'd suffered hangovers before, but she didn't remember drinking. This felt different. Worse. She strained to stand, firmly gripping the bedside table.

"Coming, coming." She shuffled to the door, dragging sluggish legs and squinted through the peephole. Lucier. He knew where the key was. Why didn't he use it? Then she realized the door was double bolted and chain latched. She didn't remember doing that. She unlocked everything and turned the knob. Lucier barged in.

"I've been calling you all morning. Why haven't you answered? I've been out of my mind with worry." He stopped his rampage and put both hands on her shoulders. "What's wrong? You look terrible. Are you sick?"

He led her to the sofa and she fell into the cushions, curling up in a fetal ball. He sat down beside her.

"I'm fine." She wasn't, but she didn't want to tell him that because she didn't know why she felt so bad. She rubbed her eyes, but it made everything fuzzier so she closed them.

"I don't want to seem like an overprotective parent—God, one father like yours is enough—but frankly, if you weren't here this morning, I would have put out a BOLO. I called you the whole day, then there was an ugly murder in the Quarter last evening, and I didn't finish up until the wee hours of the morning. By then, it was too late to call or come over."

"I'm sorry, Ernie. I went to the Sunrise Mission yesterday, and while I was there Silas Compton came in. He asked if I had time to do his reading. After that everything happened so fast."

"Jesus, Diana, what the hell's wrong with you? Do you always have to tempt fate?"

"I didn't think it would turn into a whole day and evening. And please don't yell at me. I feel like I've been in a train wreck."

"I'm sorry, but you've received two warning notes, and no matter what you think, that mission connects to four people we're investigating, including Silas Compton, who might very well be the head of a satanic cult. Doesn't any of that make an impression on you? And don't even mention Brother Osiris, a man you seem to trust because he fed you some bullshit about his tragic past that you're determined not to tell me about."

Her cheeks burned at Slater's name. She didn't know why unless than she had a fever. "Stop. I can't have this conversation right now."

Lucier got up and paced the floor in a short circle. "Well, that's tough. I need to know what happened. This is serious."

She'd never seen Lucier so mad or speak with such force, even when she took off after a serial killer on her own. He'd always been steady and calm.

"I'm sorry. I didn't think it was a big deal at the time. And yes, I do trust Edward. I'm convinced he's incapable of anything evil. He's only trying to make his life count."

Lucier bristled, his topaz eyes flashed in anger. "So now it's Edward. Getting chummy, aren't you?"

"Stop this, Ernie. You sound like a jealous schoolboy."

He looked as if he'd been hit with a foul ball. "Jealous? I'm not jealous. I was worried, and now I'm pissed." He got up from the sofa. "I'm going back to the station. I don't like where this is going. I'll hear all about Compton after we've both calmed down."

"Fine. Go. I'm tired anyway. You woke me up."

"Sorry. That's what happens when you stay out all night with the big dogs of society. Go back to bed."

The sound of the door slamming left Diana wondering what just happened. She really wanted to tell him about Compton's reading. She wanted to, but she couldn't remember anything after getting into his limo. Not even how she got home or into bed, which is exactly where she was going now to ease the pounding in her head and soothe a stomach that churned like she'd eaten road kill.

* * * * *

The room, bathed in red light, spun around as dozens of dark eyes stared at her naked body. Murky faces, featureless and unrecognizable in the shadows, chanted strange, unintelligible words in an a cappella staccato drumbeat, worshipping as if some divine creature lay supine before them. She understood only one word in a repetitive drone: Diana…Diana…Diana.

She tried raising her head to protest, but her voice locked in her throat, her numb body the immobilized object of voyeuristic concentration. The slightest sensation tickled her desensitized skin as hands groped from out of the darkness and took turns caressing her breasts and abdomen and hips. She knew their final destination, felt it.

A naked figure hovered above her on all fours, straddling her body. His face, transformed by either makeup or a mask, darted back and forth, eyes squeezed shut in rapturous ecstasy. The chanting increased, monotonous sounds with no melody.

Gibberish words.

Louder and louder.

She uttered something unrecognizable, then a hand cradled her head and another placed a glass of liquid to her lips. She drank greedily to moisten her dry mouth, then she fell back. Her body disappeared into oblivion. She couldn't move. Not even her little finger.

* * * * *

Diana jerked awake, feverish, sweat oozing from every pore, plastering her clothes to her body. Tendrils of hair clung to her damp face and neck and back. Gasping for air, she struggled to breathe. What was happening to her? She looked around, panic subsiding as she recognized the familiar room and the comfort of her own bed.

Where was Ernie? Why did she drive him away? Her first impulse was to call him, to apologize and tell him what happened. But what *had* happened? A bad dream. That's all it was.

Her body tingled, nerve endings retaining the memory of unwanted touches slithering down her torso. Sweat turned icy on her skin. Uncontrollable shivers. Her head pounded with excruciating pain, pulverizing her thoughts into worthless powder. Then nausea swept over her. She ran to the bathroom and collapsed onto the floor with her head hanging over the toilet while she purged black bile. The foul sight shocked her, but she couldn't concentrate for the infernal beating inside her head. She needed a shower. Needed hot water pouring down on her to wash away the sickness.

As she mustered her strength to rise from the floor, the dizziness overwhelmed her, and she slumped back onto the cold tile floor. Her head hit the side of the tub and she slid into unconsciousness, silencing the drumbeat in her brain.

* * * * *

Lucier spent the next two hours alternating between being mad and feeling like a shit. He called half a dozen times to apologize. No answer. Guilt took hold and he raced back to her house first chance he was free. He'd acted stupidly, and yes, he was jealous without good reason.

He knew where she kept a key, but he was unwilling to take that liberty. Not when she'd been so angry. He rang the bell. Again, no answer, so he pounded on the door. Frightened now, he snatched the key from its hiding place and slipped it into the lock.

"Diana." The small house answered in deafening silence. He hurried through the living room to the bedroom and found her lying naked on the bathroom floor, vomit in the toilet bowl. Her skin was so pale he thought she was dead. He swore his heart stopped beating.

No. You can't be.

He got down on his knees and touched his finger to her throat, relieved to feel the strong pulse. She was soaked in sweat. He picked her up, laid her on the bed, and covered her with a blanket. Then, hands shaking, picked up the bedside phone to call an ambulance.

Her eyes fluttered open. "Ernie?"

"Yes," he said, sitting down by her side. "I'm here."

She reached out her hand and he took it. "Don't leave."

"I'm not going anywhere. I'm getting you to the hospital."

"No. No, please. I felt nauseated and fainted. I must have hit my head on the tub. I'll be all right. Really."

Lucier considered the situation. Diana didn't need another high profile incident to call attention to her. She'd endured enough of that. But he wouldn't chance risking her health because of publicity. "What happened?"

She tried to raise herself up but collapsed on the bed. Lucier wedged a pillow behind her back and helped her sit. Her voice came out in a raspy croak. "I don't know. I honest to God don't know."

"I'm going to phone a doctor friend of my father's. He'll make a house call for me." Lucier called Dr. Reginald Haley and explained what happened over the phone. Haley promised he'd be there within the hour. Lucier got on the bed next to Diana and held her while she dozed. He hoped he was doing the right thing.

Dr. Haley arrived and performed the usual procedures: blood pressure—a little low, heart rate—a little high. Neither in the danger zone. He took a blood and urine sample, and bagged a sample for analysis of whatever she vomited to eliminate the possibility she'd been poisoned.

"She'll be all right, won't she, Reggie?" Lucier asked.

Before he could answer, Diana said, "I'll be fine. Did you see the vomit?"

"Yes, what did you eat?"

"I don't remember eating anything. Certainly nothing to cause me to vomit black liquid."

Lucier and Haley exchanged glances. "There was nothing black in the toilet, Diana," Lucier said.

"Ernie, I…I vomited something black. You saw it, didn't you, Doctor?"

"I didn't see anything unusual, Ms. Racine."

"I swear it was black." She tried to get up, but again fell back onto the bed. "It was black when I threw up. I'm not crazy."

"Black vomit is usually associated with yellow fever, my dear, or with excess blood in your stomach. I feel certain you have neither. My guess is that you caught a virulent stomach virus. Those things can put you down and pass just as quickly once you've flushed out your system."

"You were delirious," Lucier said. "You probably thought you saw it."

"I'm not crazy," she said, tears filling her eyes. "I know what I saw."

"I'm going to give you an antibiotic shot," Dr. Haley said, "and I'm leaving you something to take for your stomach. You should feel better in a few hours. You have a low-grade fever and you're slightly dehydrated from vomiting. I'll send the samples I took to the lab as soon as I get back to the office and let you know if there's anything to worry about. I doubt there is."

"Thanks, Reggie," Lucier said. "I appreciate you coming over so fast."

"Nothing I wouldn't do for the son of Remy Lucier. Your father was a fine doctor and a great man. I wish he were still around."

"So do I."

Lucier accompanied Haley to the door and returned to Diana's bedside. She looked pale and confused. "I'm going to make you a cup of tea."

"No, I don't think I could hold it down."

He took her hand. "Okay then, do you want to tell me what happened?"

She skipped the part about Lucier keeping her on a short leash. Compton had played her perfectly. "That's just it, Ernie. I don't know. I remember getting into Silas Compton's limo at the Sunrise Mission, and that's all I remember. I'm sure I gave him a reading, but I don't remember that either."

"Did you drink anything? Anything at all."

"A Coke. He snapped open the can and poured the cola into a glass from the bar in back of the limo."

"Do you remember arriving at his house?"

"I told you, everything's a black hole." She pinched the bridge of her nose and looked up as sad-eyed as a sick child. "How is that possible?"

"Have you ever heard of date rape drugs?"

"Yes, of course. You don't believe Silas Compton drugged me, do you?"

"The three biggies, Rohypnol, GHB, and Ketamine, are virtually undetectable: tasteless, odorless, and colorless. The lab would have to run a special test to detect them. You'd be rendered unconscious but responsive. And guess what?" He touched his lips to Diana's forehead. "Most likely, you wouldn't remember a thing."

"I don't understand."

"Nor do I." Lucier called Reginald Haley on his cell and told him to run a test for any of the known date rape drugs and fast. He also asked him to return with a rape kit.

"You think Compton would be so stupid to drug and rape me?"

"I don't know what to think any more. Men like Compton think they're above the law, that they can do anything they want and get away with it. I sure as hell don't want to find out you were violated, but if you test positive for one of those drugs or if you've been sexually penetrated, I'll get a warrant to search Compton's house so fast, he won't know what planet he's on."

Even as he spoke the words, getting a judge to issue a warrant to search the house of a multi-billionaire wouldn't be easy. And searching for what? Compton wouldn't have anything incriminating in his house, especially on the word of a woman who didn't know where she was the day before or who she was with.

Diana rubbed her temples. "There's something else, Ernie." She looked almost apologetic. "I had a dream. At least I think it was a dream. It might have been a memory."

She told him about the red room, the eyes in black faces, the chanting, and the hands running the length of her body. "After I woke up, I got sick."

Lucier pulled her into him. It sounded like stories he'd heard of satanic rituals, and the thought scared the hell out of him. Now he was more worried than ever.

"You're not going anywhere alone from now on, do you hear me? And stay away from Edward Slater."

"I'm sure Edward's not involved. If Compton did what you think, he did it without Edward's knowledge."

"You're sure?"

"Yes. I'm going to tell you a story, but you have to promise not to break my confidence."

"Depends."

"Promise or I won't tell you."

When he promised, Diana told Lucier the story of Edward Slater. She left nothing out except his oblique reference to his interest in her.

"Jesus," Lucier said when she finished.

Chapter Twenty
Back into the Lion's Den

"And how are our little ones today," Silas Compton asked.

"They're so beautiful and hungry, but Persephone is the hungriest of all, I think, don't you, Nona?"

"Oh, yes. Look how plump she is."

Wrapped in a pink blanket, the infant suckled at Brigid's breast. Nona did the same to another baby, months older. Both women's long hair fell over their bare shoulders. Neither wore blouses or bras and their breasts protruded full over slim midriffs.

Compton stroked each woman. "How flush with milk you are. These babies will never go hungry, my fertility goddesses."

Brigid smiled. The compliment assured his approval. They'd do whatever he desired to make him happy. He was their god and it was their pleasure to serve him.

"Mr. Deems is no longer with us, and with the media attention and the interference of the police in our business, we will curtail our searches, for now. I know how difficult it is to find the perfect women to expedite our long-term plans, but you must stay away from the Mission. Do not see Brother Osiris or any of the women you befriended while working there. Of course, the house on Parkside Avenue is off limits forever. Too bad. It was the perfect location— close to Sunrise Mission and an excellent intermediary facility." He cooed again at the newborns. "Needless to say, we can't keep the babies here."

"It was such a lovely house," Brigid said.

"Yes, well...I must send you both to the compound to be on the safe side. I can't risk having either of you recognized and picked up by the police."

"Whatever you wish," Nona said.

"Will the Goddess Diana be back?" Brigid asked.

Compton drank in the beauty of the two women. "Oh, yes, she'll be back. She doesn't know it yet, but she will. Unfortunately, we couldn't keep her this time. Too much attention has been focused on our project because of Mr. Deems's carelessness. Next time we'll take the Goddess Diana to a higher level. I'm betting one of her progeny will have the same psychic makeup as the mother. Imagine, having a baby even more special genetically than the ones we have."

"More special than yours?" Nona asked.

"All my babies are special, my loves."

* * * * *

Later that day while Lucier was still at Diana's house, Reginald Haley called. "The lab found no trace of semen or of any date rape drug. Doesn't mean much, Ernie, Those chemicals leave the system quickly."

"Thanks, Reggie. I figured as much. I'd appreciate if you'd kept this quiet."

"Of course. Call me if anything changes, but I think Ms. Racine will be fine after she gets some rest. Make sure she has plenty of liquids. Ernie, do you mind if I ask what this is all about?"

"I'm not sure, and neither is Diana. The hallucination could have been a dream, or a memory of what really happened. I have no proof to follow up. The people involved aren't the kind you make false accusations against. They'd slap me with a harassment suit faster than I could say sorry."

Haley left with his question unanswered, because Lucier didn't have one. He tiptoed into Diana's bedroom. She appeared to be sleeping, but when he turned to leave, she called his name.

"Don't go, Ernie."

He claimed the edge of the bed and kissed her cheek. "You're awake."

"I couldn't sleep with all those thoughts floating around in my head."

"Are you willing to go over it again, from the time you got to the Mission?"

Diana nodded and began, answering his questions as best she could. She recounted the time with Slater without hesitation, but after the drink in Compton's limo, everything went blank.

"The only thing I remember with any surety is the black night and the red eyes. Or was it the red night and the black eyes?"

"In your dream, how many sets of eyes did you see? How many people?"

"I called it a dream, but there was nothing dreamlike about it. More like a nightmare, where the red planets in the sky were staring down at me." She closed her eyes, as if conjuring up a vision. "I'm not sure. There could have been a dozen or two dozen. I just don't know."

"I'll tell you what I think. Your subconscious relived your experience in a dream or a nightmare, whatever, and I think you got sick from a knockout drug, which is a common side effect. Your hand turning black and the black vomit is a sign of evil only you can see because you're highly sensitized to those things. How does that sound?"

"Scary as hell because I don't think you're far off." She massaged her closed eyes with her fingertips, then kneaded her temples. "Where do we go from here?"

"Since you can't remember anything, I haven't got probable cause to get a warrant for Compton's house. Not to mention he's Silas Compton."

"I could follow up on his reading."

"No way. You're out of this."

She laughed. "You know that's not possible. He's targeted me. I'm Diana, Goddess of the Moon, for God's sake. I don't have to go there; I can call. He must know I don't remember anything. That was the whole point of the drug. It'd be natural for me to question the reading, don't you think?"

* * * * *

Just as Diana mentally prepped to make the call, one eye on a questioning Lucier, the phone rang. She mouthed Silas Compton with a waggle of her brows.

"Miss Racine. I hope I haven't reached you at a bad time."

"Not at all. How are you, Mr. Compton?"

"Well, thank you. My wife and I are having a few friends over for dinner this evening and would like to invite you and Lieutenant Lucier to join us. My friends heard about my reading yesterday and how on target you were. They're anxious to meet you. Why, you might even contract to read some of them. I know it's short notice, but I hope you can find time in your busy schedule."

"The Lieutenant is here. Let me check if he's free." She covered the mouthpiece and relayed the invitation to Lucier. "It's perfect. Say yes."

"It's too soon," he said. "You're not up to it."

She knew he was right. "Really, I feel fine. Not perfect, I

admit, but good enough. I'll take another of Dr. Haley's magic pills before we leave. I might not eat a lot, though."

"I don't like it, but it would be a good opportunity to get inside his house. Besides, what can he do in front of his invited guests?"

"Exactly." She uncovered the mouthpiece. "Thank you, Mr. Compton, we'd love to come."

"Nothing formal. About seven, for drinks."

"We'll see you then."

"If you wish, I'll send my car for you."

Diana glared at the phone. *As if!* "No, thanks. We'll drive. See you at seven." She placed the receiver on the cradle. "He asked if we wanted him to send a car for us. No way. I'd walk to his house before getting in his limo. He spiked my drink, the bastard."

"Beecher will know where we are. As far as I'm concerned, this is police business."

"You don't think he'd try anything, do you?"

"Honestly? I have no idea, but I don't trust the man, with good reason."

She took an extra long time to get ready to show Compton that whatever he gave her hadn't put her under. "How do I look?"

Lucier nuzzled his face into her neck. "Good enough to forget about dinner at the Comptons. Sure you want to go?"

"Wouldn't miss it for the world."

In order to conform to Diana's well-known costume color code—black, white, with an occasional touch of red—she wore a black above-the-knee skirt with high-heel slingbacks, white silk blouse, and a red pashmina shawl embroidered in black over her shoulders. Around her neck hung a mother of pearl quarter moon pendant on a black silk cord.

He fingered the pendant. "Tempting the gods, are you?"

"I don't want to disappoint. Besides, it's much more apropos than pearls."

"Well, at least you're not wearing a satanic symbol around your neck."

"Now would I do that?"

He smiled. "You know damn well you would if you owned one."

She sighed but didn't answer, because he was right.

When they arrived at Compton's residence, the guards waved them through the gate without stopping them for identification.

"Guess we're on the A-list now," Diana said.

The burly weightlifter greeted them at the door, offering to take Diana's shawl. She opted to keep it to provide a dramatic flourish, and the red added color to her more-than-usual paleness.

She'd noticed the magnificent Lalique cactus table in the foyer on her first visit. The one she'd seen in Paris some years before cost close to a hundred grand. Fitting it should grace the home of one of the world's richest men. This time she stopped to admire its graceful lines.

"Beautiful, isn't it?"

Diana was stunned by the speaker's staggering beauty—smooth, translucent skin, clear blue eyes, ebony hair pulled straight back off a face that could have been painted by da Vinci, and the body of a porn star.

"Yes, I saw a Lalique at an exposition in Paris a few years ago."

"So good to see you again, Diana." The woman turned to Lucier and offered her hand. "I'm Selene Crane Compton, and you must be Lieutenant Lucier."

Diana barely heard their exchange—Lucier saying to call him Ernie, Selene Compton extending the same permission—so bewildered by the comment that she and Silas Compton's wife had already met. To her recollection, she'd never before set eyes on the woman.

Never.

Chapter Twenty-One
A Game of One-Upmanship

"Come, our guests are anxious to meet you."

Selene wore a low-cut black knit dress that accentuated her reed-slim but curvaceous figure. Working Vegas, Diana had seen enough silicone to know Selene Compton's assets were the real thing. They bounced, and she bounced them. Tiered strands of jade encircled her neck, cascading down the front of her dress, highlighting here exceptional cleavage. Diana assumed Compton kept the women in his life on the same tight leash he implied Lucier kept her. Selene Crane Compton was not a woman restrained.

She and Lucier followed her down a different hallway from the one that led to Compton's home office. This one opened into a massive living room, tastefully furnished in shades of moss green and buttery gold. A hand woven silk Oriental rug covered the center of the dark wood floor, and a grand piano dominated the far right corner. Eclectic and expensive-looking accessories decorated tables and bookshelves. People Diana had never seen before occupied three large sofas that didn't make a dent in the vastness of the room.

Silas Compton rose from one of them to greet the new arrivals. "How good of you both to come."

All eyes centered on Diana. *This is no different than standing in front of a sold-out crowd, Diana.* She consciously made an effort to relax.

Selene began the introductions. "You all know the famous Diana Racine, and this is her friend, Lieutenant Ernie Lucier of New Orleans' finest." She turned to them. "Thank you both for coming on such short notice. May I introduce our other guests: Sophia and Fernando Reyes, Rhea and Jeremy Haynesworth, Anastasia and Martin Easley, my mother and father, Cybele and Phillip Crane, and my stepdaughters, Maia and Dione Compton."

Even though his daughters were from his first marriage, they were every bit as beautiful as Selene. Diana felt almost boyish in the midst of a roomful of women who all looked like they descended from Aphrodite.

The obligatory handshakes generated the same queasiness she experienced earlier in the day, though it passed quickly. She received a particularly eerie feeling from Martin Easley, but something was off with the whole group, though she couldn't figure out what.

"You've met Edward Slater," Selene said.

Slater entered from a hallway and nodded his greetings but didn't offer his hand to either one of them. He sat in a chair he had apparently occupied before leaving the room, because he picked up a drink off the table.

"I feel like a fifteenth wheel," he said, "but I couldn't resist the invitation. At least I'm not unlucky thirteen."

"Nonsense," Selene said. "Your perspectives always add to the conversation, and who says thirteen is unlucky? It's my lucky number. Besides, if it weren't for you, we wouldn't have the pleasure of our two guests. Silas is grateful." She addressed Diana. "He's an unabashed admirer ever since he saw you during one of your standing-room-only performances."

"I'm flattered," Diana said. "Nice to see you again, Edward."

"Same here," Lucier said. Slater smiled but kept his seat.

Two people shifted into chairs to open up a space for them to sit down and join the group clustered around a large coffee table. All had drinks—some wine, others with tumblers or highball glasses.

"What can Juan get for you to drink?" Selene asked, as the butler waited.

"Bourbon and water for me, please," Lucier said, "and a Coke for Diana."

"No," she said. "Tonight is special. I'll have a Scotch, on the rocks." She detected Lucier's frown but refused to acknowledge him. This *was* a special night, she thought, and she didn't want her mind diluted by Coke, especially since the last one she drank had such a devastating effect.

The memory of yesterday surfaced. Surely she and Lucier were safe drinking in front of all these people. Not even Silas Compton would risk doing something so foolish.

She laughed inwardly at her rationalization. When Lucier finally caught her eye, she whispered, "Just tonight." She turned back to the group and noticed Slater's sly smile. She assumed he resisted the lure of spirits, given his history.

"You must still be recovering from your ordeal with that psychopath," Sophia Reyes said. "I followed the whole thing. I can't imagine going through something like that and keep my sanity."

"I'm not sure I have," Diana said. The room grew quiet, then they all chuckled, figuring in unison she was joking.

Fernando Reyes sat forward. "And Lieutenant—"

"Call me Ernie."

"Okay, Ernie, how did you ever track that man down?"

"Good teamwork."

As Lucier fielded questions about the capture of the man who wanted Diana dead, she studied the people in the room. All the women were extraordinarily beautiful and at least twenty years younger than their husbands, except for Cybele Crane, who had to be sixty but looked a couple of decades younger. She was an older version of her daughter but no less beautiful, with fine features the very rich seemed to inherit with their money. If she'd undergone cosmetic surgery, it was deftly done. Even the delicately etched lines on her face enhanced her beauty. Diana assumed the May/December couples were second marriages, as was the Comptons'.

Maia Compton appeared to be in her late-twenties or early thirties and seemed reserved, as opposed to her younger, more-outgoing sister, Dione. They complimented Diana's act, which they saw opening night during her last engagement. Interacting politely, if unenthusiastically, with the rest of the guests, Maia and Dione eventually settled into conversation with each other.

"...and Silas reported your reading was quite on target," Jeremy Haynesworth said.

Diana, caught in her observances, barely heard the address. "I'm sorry, I guess my mind was somewhere else."

"I was just mentioning Silas's evaluation of his reading."

"What did he say about it?"

"That you told him things no one could possibly know."

Diana turned to Compton. "Did I? I don't recall. In fact, much of the afternoon is a blur. I intended to ask you about it."

"That's odd," Compton said. "You acted fine when you were here."

"Yes, I thought so, too," Selene said.

"I have little recollection after getting into the limo until I woke up this morning." A quick visual exchange among the couples added a moment of tenseness.

Selene glanced at her husband. "I hate to bring this up as a possible reason, but you had a few drinks before and after the reading. Scotch, wasn't it, Silas?"

"Yes, scotch," Compton said. "I fixed them myself. Quite a few, in fact."

"Three or four, and you downed them as if you the world was ending, and this would be your last chance for a drink. I remarked to Silas after you left that you possessed an amazing tolerance for such a tiny person."

Selene's account of yesterday left Diana breathless, and she struggled to maintain her composure.

Liar.

She wanted to defend herself but chose not to give anything away. Yet. "Well then, that must have been what happened. After my near catastrophe a while back, I drank a little too much, then quit until I was sure I had a handle on it. I guess I started back too soon."

"You blacked out," Phillip Crane said. "I remember a few of those from my younger days, don't you, Cybele?"

"I'm loath to confirm that," Cybele said. "I finally made him cut down." A chorus went up among the men admitting to those *wild days when they were young*.

"Now, at my age," Crane said, "I have two drinks, and that's quite enough."

Diana debated pursuing the line the conversation had taken and decided to forge ahead. "I did have a rather unusual dream, however, and when I awoke, I became rather ill. Result of the scotch, I imagine."

"Tell us about the dream," Sophia Reyes said.

Diana caught a warning eye from Lucier but acted once

more like she didn't see him. "It was very strange. Either the room was going around or I lay on a revolving platform, naked. The room was bathed in red light and people congregated around me, staring, touching me. I couldn't see their faces because they wore masks." She watched the couples fidget as she spoke. Martin Easley looked especially uncomfortable, focusing his attention on Lucier. Sweat beaded on his upper lip, and he wiped it away with a handkerchief. Edward Slater's slow shake of his head sent a warning, but she ignored him too.

Everyone in the room reacted. *How many sets of eyes leered down on me? Ten? Twelve?*

"What an odd dream," Rhea Haynesworth said. "But then I suppose a lot of your insights appear in dreams, don't they? Like that television show where the psychic always wakes up with some premonition or vision or whatever they're called."

"Actually, no. If you've ever seen one of my shows, you'd know that my insights materialize through contact with an article from the person I'm reading or the person himself. Sometimes an unsolicited impression develops, something so invasive it's impossible to ignore, but that's rare."

"That's how you did my reading," Compton said. "We sat at that table over there, and you took my hands in yours. You made me take off my wedding ring and close it in my hand."

The thudding beat of Diana's heart increased until it was so loud in her ears she feared everyone heard. That's how she read a private client. How did he know that if she hadn't read him? Of course. She'd mentioned her method in dozens of articles over the years. He probably read it.

Silas Compton probably knew everything about her.

Fernando Reyes interrupted her thoughts. "Do you think your dream was one of those? I mean, you didn't have something in your hand when you were sleeping, did you?"

She could hardly get out the words. "I—I did wonder what the dream meant," Diana sputtered. "It sounds otherworldly, doesn't it? More like a scenario from *The Exorcist* or *Rosemary's Baby*." A few of them exchanged glances. Diana almost questioned whether she'd translated an ordinary nightmare into an imagined interpretation. Then she remembered the sickness and the black bile.

"Are you implying your dream contained satanic overtones?" Selene asked.

Right out in the open. She looked at Selene. Calm, self-assured, smiling. She was goading Diana, and it pissed her off. But then she was goading the group. She didn't meet his gaze but felt Lucier's stare bore into her. "I don't know what the dream meant. I guess my overindulgence yesterday affected me more than I thought."

"Or maybe—" Selene stopped.

"What?"

"Well, our driver mentioned you were so unsteady he walked you to your door."

"Well, that does it then." Diana tapped her knee. "I was sloshed. Serves me right for drinking so much. No wonder I had a nightmare."

She caught Lucier scanning the room. Maybe he wouldn't chew her out for bringing this up after all. She worked the group the same way she worked an audience. Throwing tidbits at them, reading their responses, measuring their body language. Did he see something she missed, because she received nothing from anyone in the room except Slater? He sat cross-legged trying to appear relaxed, but he was as tense and coiled as she now felt, and he fixed on her the steely stare of his blue-gray eyes.

Silas and Selene were lying through their teeth. She would never request a scotch before a reading and would never get drunk after one. Never. Diana passed out before returning home, and they knew it. Worse, one of them had taken her home, told her to lock the door, and go to bed. She wanted to tell them that, scream it, but for once, she curbed her candor. She'd gone too far already.

The butler brought Diana and Lucier their drinks. "Maybe I shouldn't have this after all," she said. "What do you say, darling? Should I?"

"I'll make sure you don't overdo it." He held up his glass. "A toast. To good company and interesting conversation."

They all raised their glasses. She noticed Selene nodding toward Lucier. The smile she beamed at him was more than from a hostess to a guest. It said, here I am, come get me. Even before this blatant come-on, something about the woman made Diana want to smack her well-chiseled face. Was it because Lucier smiled back?

She reminded herself this was all part of their strategy to befriend the enemy. Then she thought—whose strategy? *Befriending the enemy* worked both ways.

At the dining table, Selene conveniently seated Lucier next to her, and they engaged in animated discussion. Diana held the seat of honor to Compton's right, with one of his daughters on her right, and Compton's mother-in-law, Cybele Crane, a woman his own age, to his left. Polite conversation ensued throughout dinner.

And what a dinner. Compton had lured a renowned New Orleans chef from a famous restaurant into his employ, so the cuisine reflected what one would expect from the kitchen of a man in wealth's stratosphere: crawfish bisque followed by pan-seared scallops and grouper with champagne sauce, with an appropriate wine accompanying each course.

Dinner guests paired off. Compton, his fascination with the famous well documented, monopolized Diana while Selene applied her abundant charms to Lucier. One would have to be blind and deaf not to see and hear her compliment his heroic exploits in the capture of a killer, and a man would have to have one foot in the grave not to react to her fawning over his every witticism. Lucier responded like the very living, breathing, virile man he was.

Damn him.

Diana finished her wine, and the attending waiter refilled her glass. Her face flushed with annoyance. Why, Lucier barely looked at her all evening, but then Silas Compton never relinquished her for a second. The Comptons were carrying out a planned divide-and-conquer strategy. Slater spoke in hushed tones to Sophia Reyes, his eyes shifting toward Selene and Lucier, then in Diana's direction. Their gazes met, and she interpreted his apparent amusement at Diana's forced restraint. She covered her wineglass when the server offered a refill.

After dessert, the party retired to the main living room. At the other end of the room, Lucier fell into deep conversation with the queen witch, as Diana silently began referring to Selene. Diana latched on to Compton's arm, and a slight wave of dizziness hit her. Then poof! It was gone. What was it about his touch that rendered her lightheaded?

"Come," he said. "I want to show you my art collection. Oh, don't worry about your man. Selene will take good care of him."

That's what I'm afraid of. She shook off her uneasiness and joined Compton, arms linked.

"I couldn't help overhearing, Silas," Slater said. "You've

promised to show me your art collection, and so far I haven't seen it. Mind if I tag along?"

A flash of irritation sparked Compton's eyes, but being the good host, said, "Of course not, Edward."

Slater offered an almost imperceptible nod in Diana's direction. She breathed a sigh of relief, glad he'd forced his way into their company.

Compton led the way through his house, pointing out the museum-worthy collection of two Picassos and one each Miró, Kandinsky, Cezanne and Van Gogh. A few paintings by artists with names Diana didn't recognize covered the walls throughout. A small Degas pastel of a horse race caught her eye.

"Degas is one of my favorites," she said.

Compton moved closer to Diana. "I bet you'll like the next one then."

He led her to a framed pastel sketch of ballerinas hanging above a small settee in a sitting room off the main hall. From the feminine décor, Diana assumed the room was Selene's private domain.

"Yes, it's beautiful." Diana examined the loose sketchy quality of Degas' later works, as his eyes failed. She'd viewed collections in museums around the world where she performed, but seeing this private collection provided an extra thrill.

"Degas is one of my favorites too," Slater said. "Though I prefer his horse scenes."

"A difficult choice," Compton said. He concentrated his tour on the first floor, by-passing the stairways to the upper and lower levels and making no excuses for doing so.

"Are there more treasures in the rest of the house?" she asked.

"A few less valuable pieces. The crown jewels are on the main floor. Only people who interest me are invited to my home, Diana, and I'm quite selective when extending invitations. Maybe I'll include a codicil in my will to show the collection as an exhibit, but I'm not quite ready to die, so I choose not to project such negative vibes."

"It's a beautiful collection," Diana said.

"I'm blessed to be able to afford it. As you may know, I acquired my wealth the old-fashioned way: I worked my ass off."

Diana smiled at the comment that brought to mind an old TV commercial. "I'm honored you're allowing me to see them. After all, we've just met."

"You're special," he said.

Compton's touch on Diana's arm gave her the willies, almost as if he were trying to hypnotize her. She moved closer to the pastel, freeing herself from his hold.

"I came from a poor family in a restrictive Catholic environment," he continued, "but I questioned the dogma when I became more exposed to the outside world. I'm always seeking answers to questions that have no definitive answers."

"Some things have no answers," she said. "I speak from personal experience."

"True. That's what so challenging about the fascination with mysticism Edward and I share. We've spent many evenings of deep philosophical conversations. He mentioned you have similar curiosities."

Was Compton feeling her out, and if so, in what capacity? She'd been right. He liked living on the edge; otherwise, why would he risk exposure? Because he thought himself above everyone, with no boundaries, able to pursue whatever he wished.

Diana decided to play his game. He wanted to determine if she'd be amenable to his dark philosophy. She glanced at Slater, now expressionless. A slight doubt crept over her, like a fleeting cloud obscuring the sun. *Am I playing the game with one person...or two?*

"When I was younger," she said, "I became interested in the occult. Certain things are almost a rite of passage in the young—reincarnation, preoccupation with death, belief or disbelief in God. Maybe that's why I was so sensitive to the goings-on in your house on Parkside Avenue, Mr. Compton." She walked farther into the room, taking in the expensive accessories, searching for anything to shed light on the Comptons' dark side. She saw nothing. "When I saw the symbols on the wall, I felt the connection. My childhood was out of the ordinary, but I still went through the stages of curious exploration. The occult seemed like the next step."

"What do you mean? The next step to where?" Slater asked, his face bright with interest.

"Obviously, I possessed a gift apart from the perceptual or intellectual, with direct access beyond the external world, a subjective force, if you will. I wanted to explore it more thoroughly." She couldn't decipher what she saw in Compton's face—curiosity, anger, or was it smugness?

"What happened?" Compton asked.

"I found the study interesting but never a path into the spiritual world beyond. No witches or magic. No resurrections. Most discoveries fell into the realm of hoaxes—charlatans sucking their poor marks into paying a small fortune to see their dead husband or child, phony séances. No, Mr. Compton, I'm afraid there is no other side. At least no portal I can enter."

Compton's face froze into a smile, disturbed only by a

twitch at the corner of his mouth. Slater's furrowed brow now sent a clear warning.

"So you believe the occult is hogwash," Compton probed. "That there is no dark force?"

He's forcing a response. How far can I go before I push his warning buttons?

"Oh, there is a force, something unexplainable. I'm a perfect example of that. And, yes, sometimes it is dark. Times in my past I've been burdened with feelings so black I couldn't breathe. But is it the work of Satan? I hardly think so. One must believe in Satan, and I don't. Do you, Mr. Compton?"

Compton broke into a broad grin, but there was no mirth in his eyes. "No, Diana, I don't. If I didn't know better, I'd think you were trying to connect me with the satanic cult operated by the man who rented my house."

"Not at all, sir, but you do seem inordinately fascinated by my abilities."

Slater stepped forward. "I'm sure Silas's curiosity is more about the mystical aspects of your gift, Diana."

His voice sounded tense and cautionary. Diana sensed he intervened to redirect the prickly dialogue between her and Compton.

"Ah, *gift*. Such an elusive word. Many times I thought it more a curse than a gift. Remember," she said, trying to smooth things over, "I was very young and idealistic. Most of all, inquisitive. Why did I have this *gift*? I couldn't imagine the force that created it. I still don't understand why or how it works. Sometimes people have difficulty separating my psychic powers from the mystical. As I told Edward, I stopped intellectualizing my abilities long ago, gave up searching, and let things fall into place wherever they landed."

"You're a fascinating woman, Diana. I'm honored to know

you. I hope we can delve more deeply into these subject at a more convenient time." Compton paused, but his eyes never left hers. "Just the two of us."

A darting glance toward Slater revealed nothing. "It would be my pleasure, sir," she said. They started toward the main hall. "Is your wife interested in mysticism, Mr. Compton?"

"Selene is interested in everything. That's why I married her. She's much like you, without the psychic ability."

"Only taller," Diana said.

They all laughed, but when they got to the main room, Compton left them to tend his guests. Slater blocked her way and spoke in hushed tones. "Don't provoke Silas Compton. It's unwise."

"Is that what I was doing?"

"You know damn well you were. He's not an idiot."

"What's going on here, Edward? What do you know?"

"Not now."

"When?"

Selene approached, Lucier on her arm. She clung to him like rooted ivy.

"Diana, you have a very interesting friend. He's kept me entertained while you got the grand tour. I hope we get to see more of you both. I'm so wrapped up in my boards and charities and foundations I forget everything else. Do let's make plans for another get together."

"Sounds terrific," Diana agreed, hoping she sounded like she meant it. "Let's."

Selene squeezed Lucier's arm and flashed a smile sensual enough to ignite a forest fire. Diana felt her own fires burning, and she hoped the steam wasn't shooting out her ears. Selene lingered on Lucier a moment longer, then moved away with the grace of the Degas dancer in the pastel that hung in her sitting room.

Bitch.

Chapter Twenty-Two
Break Up or Make Up

Lucier read Diana's anger, but he wasn't sure he understood it, and he sure as hell didn't know how to approach her sulk on the ride home.

"Okay, let it out," he said. "You're pissed because Selene Compton was all over me while you were sounding out her husband. And if you're listening, I said *she* was all over *me*."

"You didn't have to enjoy it so much." Her words were clipped and she kept her eyes straight ahead.

"Aren't you the one who accused me of being jealous of Edward Slater?"

"Edward's…different."

"Well, I didn't know that at the time. Even though I have two advanced degrees, he made me feel I wasn't smart enough to be in your conversation. You don't have to be sexually attracted to a woman to be interested. An intellectual connection can be just as powerful."

Diana didn't answer.

If she's going to be that way, let her. Two can play the same game. He pulled up in front of her house, put the car in park, but didn't shut off the engine. He waited for her to get out.

"Aren't you coming in?" she asked.

"We've both had a trying day," he said. He kept his words as tight as hers, faced front. "Get some rest. I'll call you tomorrow."

She didn't move. A few moments passed. "I'm sorry." Another minute. "Don't go."

Lucier turned to her. "I love you, Diana, and a woman who means absolutely nothing to me flirting for one night isn't going to change that, not even your childish reaction to something so insignificant."

"I've never been jealous before."

"I don't play games. Yes, I was upset about Slater because you reacted to him. He's a damn attractive man, and he has a connection to you I don't have. I wish I did, but I don't."

"Selene Compton isn't attractive? She's drop-dead gorgeous, and she clung to you like flypaper. Edward is attractive, and yes, we share things in common, but I'm in love with you."

Her hand stroked his arm, and a ripple of need skittered through him.

"Turn off the car and come inside," she said.

"It's been a long time for me. Eight years long. I told you once that I'm just an ordinary guy with no extras. I didn't know about Slater's problem, but he hit me where I'm the most insecure. As far as Selene, I was playing her game. Isn't that what this evening was about?"

"Yes. I'm wrong, you're right, and there's nothing ordinary about you. Now shut off the car and come in, or I'll really get mad."

"You really know how to get under my skin."

"I know. I'm a brat. You can spank me." She grinned and he shook his head.

He turned off the ignition. When he got around to the other side and opened the door, she took his offered hand and led him into the house. A low light glowed from a lamp in the living room. She didn't turn on another.

"Stand there and don't move," she said.

"But—"

"Don't speak, either." She threw her shawl on the sofa, then proceeded to unbutton her blouse.

He reached for her, but she danced away.

"I said don't move."

He watched her slip each button through the buttonhole and slide the blouse off her shoulders. She unbuttoned her skirt, letting it fall in folds at her feet. Stepping out of its confines, she kicked it and the blouse behind her before removing her underwear, leaving only the high-heeled sandals her only ornament.

Lucier felt the swelling in his groin. He reached again, but she waved her finger no. "I don't know how long—"

"Didn't you hear what I said? Quiet."

He visually traced her naked body. Her skin shone incandescent in the dim light; blue highlights shimmered off her black curls. He stood, fully clothed with an erection primed to bust his zipper. How much more could he take?

She started undressing him in the same methodical way she'd taken off her own clothes. First the jacket, then the tie and shirt. She ran her hands over his chest, before unbuckling his belt and letting his slacks fall to the floor. She left on his boxers and pressed her naked body against his bare torso. Heat shot through every part of him, and he visualized him levitating from the pleasure.

"Have I ever told you I love the color of your skin, the smoothness of it?" she said "Your smell, your taste?"

"Diana—"

"Shh. That was a rhetorical question." She bent down, took off his right shoe and sock, then picked his foot up and out of his trousers. She did the same with the other foot. He never realized how much desire hurt until now.

"You're moving."

"That's because I'm not dead. I'd have to be dead to stand still while you're running your hand up my leg." The moan rose from deep inside. "Enough."

"If you move, it's over. I'll lock myself in the bathroom and you'll be forced to jerk yourself off."

"This is torture worse than waterboarding." Christ, he was begging the woman to stop pleasuring him. He must be deranged. "Have pity."

"No pity. Don't move." She kissed her way down his chest until she got to the waistband of his shorts.

"Fuck it! That's enough. You've proved your point. I accept your apology." He picked her up. She weighed almost nothing, a tiny perfectly-formed woman, skin like cream velvet.

"You didn't let me finish," she teased.

"Look at me. I'm finished. You finished me. If you kept going there'd be nothing left for you."

She burrowed her head into the crook of his neck. "I thought a tough guy like you could go all night, and then some."

"Not this one. Not if you kept doing what you were doing." She laughed. God, he loved her laugh.

Then he kissed her all the way to the bedroom as if she were dessert. She tasted sweet, like honey, and smelled deliciously spicy. "I love the scent you wear."

"It's Opium. The perfume."

"No wonder they named it after a drug. It's intoxicating."

"You weren't supposed to do this, you know," she said. "I had plans."

"So do I. Very special plans."

She bit his neck. "Remind me to pick a fight with you more often."

Chapter Twenty-Three
The Never Retractable Word

The next morning, Diana arrived at the Sunrise Mission without advance notice. She wore black jeans, a white blouse, and her hair pulled into a high ponytail. Slater was sitting at the entrance desk looking over a sheet of paper when she entered. He didn't seem surprised to see her. His longish hair was damp from his shower, and he wore khakis with a gray short-sleeve polo shirt that matched his eyes. His arms were tanned and well-muscled. The place smelled of fresh coffee and maple syrup.

"I suspected you'd drop in today," he said, "but after lunch—*after I called*." He emphasized the last comment to make a point. "I'm running late. Just got here myself." He carried a steaming cup of coffee. "You're an impatient woman, Diana."

"Yes, I am. I wanted to know what you meant last night."

"Coffee's in the kitchen. Wait in my office. I have a few things to attend to."

Diana looked around. The mission was busy. Breakfast food still covered the sideboard, while one woman cleaned the table and set new places. When she scooted around the tables and into the kitchen, another woman was putting dirty dishes into a huge dishwasher. An industrial-sized coffeemaker sat on the counter next to a plastic-wrapped stack of waffles. Still another woman opened the oven to check on two large pans of macaroni and cheese that Diana assumed comprised part of the lunch menu.

As people sauntered in, a server asked them not to take more than they could eat because waste left someone else hungry. A good philosophy for every home, Diana thought. She poured a cup of coffee and made her way to Slater's office.

The papers and folders on his desk were arranged in neat stacks. Edward Slater was an organized man. The red light in the vent verified the active camera. She remembered Lucier saying it activated when someone came into the room. Damn. She would have liked to try the cupboard to see whether it was locked, but she dared not. Instead, she perused the book titles in his library. For an atheist, he owned a good many books on religion, including the Bible and St. Thomas Aquinas's *Summa Theologica,* which she pulled from the shelf.

"A great philosopher, some think second only to Aristotle," Slater said.

"I wouldn't know. Religion is not my strong point. I was raised in the hellfire and damnation philosophy. Do bad things and God will get you. You don't study that, you accept it. Later, I drifted into the curiosity phase of my life—which my father seriously frowned on—and finally settled into the "I don't know" period. Even though my gift points to a higher force, I'm still there."

"I've always found agnostics take that stand to hedge their bets on getting into heaven rather than take a stand against the apocryphal God."

Apocryphal. I guess that would be a good word for an atheist when discussing God. Diana thought about that one and agreed. She'd seen too much to discard the theory of a supreme being, but no matter how she tried, she couldn't buy into theocratic ideology.

"I didn't come here for a philosophical discussion, Edward. I came because I want to know what Compton is up to. Why is he interested in me?"

"Compton is fascinated by your powers, but he's put off by your arrogance. He knows you think he's involved in a satanic cult. You're not very subtle."

"He is involved." She told Slater about seeing her hand turn black and skeletal when Compton held it. "He's evil, and you know it."

"I don't know it. Your psyche is controlling your visions, and they're off base. Silas is a generous mentor. Why would he jeopardize everything to embrace Satanism? It doesn't make sense. I'd be a more likely disciple."

"Are you?"

He took the book from her hand and slid it back into its place on the shelf. "No."

She sensed his irritation. "I know what I saw."

"Silas Compton, for all the good he does, can also be a formidable adversary. I would think long and hard before screwing with him. And that dream you announced to everyone in the room? You described a satanic ritual of which you were the offering. You don't have to be a Satanist to get the picture."

"It wasn't a dream. It happened. Compton drugged me and served me up to his group. I'm not crazy, Edward."

Slater shook his head and let out a long breath. "That didn't happen, and you'd be unwise to broadcast it. Silas can do you a lot of good. You heard him. You gave him an outstanding reading. One word from him and you'll have a second career one could only dream of."

"I don't want a second career. I've already had two. And I don't remember one second of my supposed reading with

Compton. Not one word. I can't be bought, can you? Is his evil money that important? Surely you've made enough connections now to support your mission without Compton."

"First of all, his money isn't evil. You've gotten that into your head, and you're wrong. Secondly, am I bought by money? You're damn right I am. Do you know how much it takes to run this place? Food, beds, electricity, rent, and a hundred other expenses to keep it going? We get a pittance in federal money. Without Compton's funds and a few other generous benefactors, the people who come here would be sleeping in boxes on the street and scavenging in Dumpsters. Yes, I need his money, and I won't do anything to throw a monkey wrench into my relationship with him. Including my relationship with you."

Diana froze at his words. "I didn't know we had a relationship."

"Yes you did. You know and so does your cop. He doesn't like it either."

Blistering heat circled Diana's neck. What was it about this man that both irritated and attracted her? He was so sure of himself. So goddamn sure. Well, she didn't like someone taking for granted who she was or wasn't in a relationship with.

"What do you think we have, Edward? The same kind of relationship you shared with Jeanine Highsmith? Are you looking for a donation?"

Slater looked stricken. Diana wanted to take back her words, but words spoken can never be retracted. They hang in the air like an endless echo in an empty room.

"I don't need anything from you, Diana," he said calmly. "You're the one still searching." He went to the door and opened it. "You'd better leave. Please make an appointment with my new secretary if you need to see me again." He avoided looking at her as she passed by.

"I'm sorry," she said. "You didn't deserve that."

"You're right. I didn't. Good-bye, Diana."

Diana left feeling like a slithering bottom-feeder. What possessed her to insult him? It was as if she had no control over her words. Edward Slater never mentioned money to her. Was his manipulation more subtle by implying a relationship? Or did they have some special symbiosis she refused to acknowledge. Lucier said that intellectual relationships were just as strong as sexual ones. Maybe, but despite what she knew about Slater, he emitted vibrations that were far more than academic. Could it be her imagination? Every time she was in his company, he never let her touch him more than a passing brush of her hand. What was he afraid of? If he was holding something back he didn't want her to see, he'd buried the secret deep in his soul. Now she'd never get the chance to find out.

Chapter Twenty-Four
When Dreams Become Reality

That morning, when Lucier arrived at the station, Beecher was waiting at the back entrance. "We've got a situation."

"What kind of situation?"

"Two guys say they broke into Silas Compton's house to steal his paintings and were attacked by a group of monsters."

"Are they high on meth, coke? Drunk?"

"Nope, just scared shitless."

"How in hell did they get into that compound? It's guarded like the White House."

"That's the interesting part. They said one of Compton's daughters, Maia, drove them in while they hid in the back of her car. She told them which paintings to steal. Said she had a buyer."

Lucier shook his head. "Impossible. I've met Compton's daughters. Neither one would defy her father. In fact, I doubt anyone does."

Beecher tucked his persistently unruly shirt into his pants. "Just telling you what they said."

Confused, Lucier headed toward his office. He made a mental inventory of the case file and added the two cryptic notes targeting Diana, who was sure everything tied together into one evil package because of a bad dream. He wanted to add Edward Slater and the Sunrise Mission into the mix, but he wasn't sure the green-eyed monster didn't have something to do with that.

In crime fiction, the cynical hero cop always says he doesn't believe in coincidences. Lucier did. Coincidences happen, but in this case they stretched credulity. Everything seemed to connect, only he didn't know how.

Yet.

"So allegedly, Maia Compton drove them in," he said. "Did she drive them out too?"

"Here's where it gets a little fuzzy. They vaulted the fence and sprinted to a car they'd parked somewhere on the street, put the metal to the pedal, and took off."

"Where was the guard?"

"Apparently, he didn't notice them until they were over the fence. He's more concerned with people going in, not going out."

"So who brought them in?" Lucier asked.

"A patrol car caught them tearing down Canal Street toward Convention Center Boulevard like they had a jet engine under the hood. When they started ranting about Compton, the officer brought 'em here."

"Where are they?"

"Interrogation. They're so psyched both are going to need tranquilizers. I can't understand what they're trying to tell us, but their story sounds like they've seen aliens from outer space."

"Shit. I've had enough of Silas Compton, his wife, and Brother Osiris to last me till I'm on Depends."

Lucier peeked through the one-way glass of the interrogation room.

"The older one's Johnny Meade," Beecher said. "He's got a few marks, mostly mischief, a couple of drunk charges. Nothing serious. The jitterbugger is Antony Hall. He's clean."

Meade hunched motionless over the table, his head buried under a tangle of long, stringy hair and arms, one of which was decorated with a barbed-wire bracelet tattoo. Hall, a smorgasbord of Louisiana ethnicities, fidgeted in his chair, every part of his scrawny body in motion—tapping or rocking or jerking. Both men snapped to attention when Lucier and Beecher entered.

Meade catapulted off his chair. "You've got to protect us," he said. "There are freaking monsters in that house. They came after us."

Hall jumped at Lucier at the same time, grabbing his shirt and pulling him close. "Yeah, brother, put us in protective custody, witness protection, or something. I ain't going out there again."

Lucier wanted to assure them that breaking into Compton's house guaranteed they wouldn't be leaving anytime soon. "Okay, calm down. Tell me what happened."

Both started talking at once.

"Hold on. Meade, you go first." He pointed Hall to his seat. "You'll have your chance after." Hall opened his mouth, but one look at Lucier and he clamped it shut.

"I met Compton's daughter in a bar. She—"

"Which daughter?" Lucier interrupted.

"Maia. She came on to me like I was Brad Pitt or someone. The—"

"What bar?" Beecher asked.

"Juno's in the Quarter. A lot of hot women go there after work."

Beecher snickered.

Lucier took a seat on the other side of the table. "Was she alone or did she come in with someone."

"She always came in alone, ordered that pink drink.

What's the name of it?"

"Cosmopolitan?"

"Yeah, that's it."

"Okay, go on."

"This woman is blonde, beautiful, and built. I didn't know who she was, I swear. She never told me her last name until later. Shit, I didn't care. When a broad like that hits on you, you don't ask questions. You go with the flow, know what I mean?"

"You mean like how come a gorgeous babe would hit on a skank like you?" Beecher said.

Meade jerked his head back and stuck out his chin. "Hey, I don't need the insults. A lot of women come on to me. I got sex appeal."

Beecher snorted, glanced sideways at Lucier.

If this concerned anyone other than Compton, Lucier might have found the humor. But it did, and he didn't. "She came on to you and then what happened?"

"We got to talking. I couldn't get my eyes off her…you know. She kept pushing those babies in my face like I was supposed to do something with them. I wanted to, you know." Meade looked at both cops as if he expected agreement. "Anyways, we met a few times at the same bar, and one day she brought up her father's art collection. She said she hated her old man—something to do with her mother—and this was the best way to get at him because he loved his paintings more than his kids. It was worth a fortune and she knew someone who'd pay a lot of money for whatever she could get her hands on. Oh, Jesus."

Meade ran his fingers through his greasy hair while he kept his eyes steady on Lucier. Sweat trickled down his sideburns to his neck and onto his tee shirt, already ringed with dark underarm stains. "Look, before we say anything more, if we tell you what we saw, you'll give us a deal, right? I mean, we didn't do nothing. You can't put people in jail for *thinking* about doing a crime, can you?"

Hall bobbed his head in agreement, muttering something under his breath.

The two didn't have half a brain between them, Lucier thought. "Depends on what you tell us, and if Ms. Compton backs up your story." But why would Maia Compton admit to robbing her father? Two facts bolstered their story. First, the two jerkoffs couldn't have passed through the gate without help. And second, why would anyone admit to attempted robbery unless they were telling the truth? Logic told Lucier that Maia Compton did what they said, but why? The security tapes might shed light on the answer. If he could get his hands on them—which he seriously doubted.

"Start from the beginning," Lucier said.

Hall pushed Meade aside. "The woman, Maia, said no one'd be home. We got inside, and while Johnny checked out the paintings, I thought I heard music coming from the basement. Not music, really, but like the music I heard in church when I used to go, but different."

"Different how?" Beecher asked.

"Like, I don't know, like chanting kinda, but not the same thing."

Lucier and Beecher exchanged glances. "What happened then?"

"I opened the door and went down the stairs. It was dark except for red lights, like a brothel." He caught himself. "N-n-not that I've ever been in one." He rubbed the sweat off his forehead. "When my eyes adjusted, it looked like fucking Halloween down there. People with masks like monsters. They were in a circle around something in the middle. I couldn't see what. Shit, I didn't want to see; I just wanted to get the hell out of there. I started to creep back up the stairs when one of 'em saw me. He pointed and everything stopped. I spooked and leaped the stairs three at a time, yelling to Johnny to let's get the fuck out of there."

All during Hall's version, Johnny Meade sputtered and stuttered, waiting his turn. "I thought he was kidding. Then one of the monsters burst through the door after Tony. I didn't wait another second. I shot out of there like a cannon and even passed Tony."

"Yeah, almost pushing me to the ground."

"Calm down," Beecher said. "We got time."

"Did anyone say anything? Yell at you to stop?"

Both men ranted at the same time. Words ran over words into a cacophony of confusion. Lucier couldn't keep track.

"Yeah the guard yelled something like stop or I'll shoot," Johnny said, "but I don't think he had a gun. Anyways, I wasn't about to turn around to find out. We just ran the hell down the street."

Then both said different versions of "I've never been so fucking scared in my whole life."

"Okay." Lucier stepped in between them, hands raised in a cease-fire. "One at a time. How many people would you say were there?"

"I don't know," Hall said. "A dozen, maybe. It was too dark, and I wasn't about to count heads."

"Where was Maia during this?"

Sweat dripped off Meade's nose and on to his soaked T-shirt. Both men reeked, and Lucier thought he would retch from the smell.

"I don't know. One minute she was standing right beside

me, but when Tony came running and yelled about monsters, she disappeared. I wasn't gonna hang around to see where she was neither."

"Me either. I was too busy running for my life," Hall said. "The guard in the gatehouse was facing the street and didn't see us until we'd climbed over. He tried to stop us, but we were gone."

"I'd never run so fast in my life," Meade said. "You can't let them get us. Them people in there are crazy."

Lucier would have thought their story fantasy, except for the red lights and the chanting. The image eerily mirrored Diana's dream. He'd filled Beecher in on the dream and caught him nodding as he recognized the same scenario.

"You said you went there in Ms. Compton's car. How did you get away without a car?"

"Johnny went with her. I followed in his car. I don't have one." He stopped at Lucier's expression. "I have a license, though, in case you're thinking I don't."

"Driving without a license is the least of your problems," Beecher said. "Keep going."

"I parked his car a couple of streets over in the Quarter," Tony said, "then got in hers. We hid in the back seat, hidden by the dark windows."

"Okay, guys, sit tight," Lucier said. "Someone will be in shortly to take your statements. Tell him everything you told us, without the hysterics. What the people looked like, the music, everything. Understand? I'll be back later."

"You're not gonna let us go, are you? We need protection."

"Oh, don't worry. You're not going anywhere."

They were still yammering when Lucier closed the door. He and Beecher stood at the glass and watched the two men.

He flicked on the speaker and heard them rant about monsters and chanting and the double-crossing Maia. He shut it off.

"What do you think?" Beecher asked.

"They saw what they saw. They're too scared and stupid to make that up."

"They walked into a satanic meeting?"

"Sounds like it. Bottom line is that Silas Compton is free to have any kind of meeting he wants in his own house. That's a right guaranteed by the First Amendment of the Constitution. We might not like what he practices, but he has every right to practice it."

"Yeah, I see what you mean."

"I have to approach this need carefully. I don't want the department slapped with a harassment suit." Lucier shook his head in disgust. "Diana just about accused Compton of complicity in a satanic cult the other night, and that implicated him to the kidnappings. He wasn't happy then; he'll be pissed when this lands on his doorstep, especially with these two involving his daughter.

"What do I say to him? 'Um, excuse me, Mr. Compton, but does your daughter hate you enough to hire two nitwits to steal your paintings?' Can you imagine what Compton's lawyers would do with those two? By the time they finished questioning them, they'd be ready for a padded room." Lucier headed toward his office. "There's only one way to clear this up."

"What's that, Ernie?"

"Maia Compton."

Chapter Twenty-Five
The Age of Defiance

Maia Compton stared straight ahead, avoiding the glaring eyes of her stepmother. She hated Selene even more than she feared her. She hated Selene's parents, too, the king and queen of evil who spawned the princess witch. And she hated her father for being so weak. Hate worked both ways. Selene hated her. The feelings had been mutual from the beginning. Dione felt the same way, but she kept her loathing private, playing the role of obedient daughter.

Both had been indoctrinated into the "culture." Maia conformed, contributing to the group's master race—until she found out about the kidnappings. Now her unforgivable acquiescence tore her apart. She'd rebelled by needling her father about her brother, a retarded child who died in a tragic accident. So much for the Comptons' superior bloodline. The petty provocation left her feeling more guilty than victorious.

"What the hell were you thinking?" Selene said.

"No one was supposed to be home," Maia replied.

"That makes it right? Bringing two outsiders into the house is against all the rules, and for what? To steal millions of dollars of your father's art collection. What happens if they go to the police and bring you into their story?"

Maia kept silent. Her father's fury showed red on his face, and his jaw worked as he clenched his teeth, but he spoke not a word. Selene ran the show, as always, even before the day her mother, in a desperate state of depression, threw herself out the window of a sixteen-story hotel. Silas had never been discreet. How much did his betrayal contribute to her mother's suicide?

As soon as Silas's public grieving subsided, his relationship with Selene went from gossip to front-page news in the society section. Silas possessed all the attributes the Cranes sought, primarily a brilliant opportunist who'd do anything to get what he wanted. They tempted him with more riches than their young, beautiful daughter. Silas didn't stand a chance. What man would? Even Diana Racine's cop lover fell under Selene's spell. Five minutes alone with Lieutenant Lucier in the bedroom, and Selene would have him panting for more. The psychic saw it too.

Maia looked at her father and thrust out her chin in defiance. Silas Compton personified the iron man—the big Libertarian industrialist and philanthropist. If people only knew that Selene had his dick tied around her little finger and tugged him along like a lap dog. To Silas's credit, if she went too far, he stopped her, creating a tug-of-war control game that appealed to them both. Selene used sex to get what she wanted, from whomever she wanted, whenever she wanted, and Silas got his rocks off watching. From the moment she became Mrs. Silas Compton, she taught Maia and Dione to do the same. Her own children, secret to the world except for the group, didn't stand a chance. Selene and her parents taught them from birth, then sent them off to the compound. But Selene couldn't get rid of Silas's young daughters as easily. They were a known fact of life.

Maia closed her ears to Selene's verbal lashing. Silas sat tight-lipped. Maia braced herself for when he calmed enough to speak.

Why didn't she go to the police the moment she learned about the first kidnapping? Why enlist Johnny and his twitching friend to do something so stupid? Even now she couldn't believe it had ever entered her mind.

Now what? She'd certified her own exile. They would send her to the compound and put her through a series of indoctrination exercises. Only this time they'd keep her there, like Martin Easley's son, Cal, and like Anat, the only one of Selene's daughters with an independent streak. How Maia envied their courage and wished she were like them. She'd have her chance now, because she'd be with them, ostracized from society.

Silas would explain her absence by saying she was troubleshooting his business problems. That's what he did whenever Maia and Dione went to the compound. Why not? Who would Silas send if not his own daughters? Both women were brilliant, knew the business inside out, and favored by the Middle Eastern men with whom Silas did business.

Maia tuned back in. Selene moved to Silas, ran her fingers through his thick salt and pepper hair, and whispered something in his ear. Then she spoke loud enough for Maia to hear. "We must send her away, Silas? After what she pulled, what's to stop her from exposing us?"

"How could you, Maia?" Silas said, speaking for the first time. "You leave me no choice, especially now with the Racine woman and her police lieutenant in the picture."

"Not to go over this again, darling," Selene said, caressing his shoulders, "but you should have listened to me. Drugging Diana Racine before she got to the house was stupid. She'll never come for another reading now. I told you to wait until—"

"Shut up, Selene. She'll come. She's too curious not to."

Bristling at Silas's tone, Selene quickly recaptured her composure. "Yes, but not without the cop. She—"

"I said, shut up."

This time Selene froze, cheeks flushed. A momentary wave of triumph filled Maia when her father showed some balls. It wouldn't last. Not after Selene unzipped his pants. Her stepmother knew what to do. She eased her body into his, rubbing, undulating.

"She goaded us in front of my parents and everyone else. They didn't like that."

"Tell her, Maia," Silas said. "Tell her you won't say anything."

"I won't say anything."

Selene glared at Maia but held her voice steady. "At least speak with some conviction, *dear*. What will you say when the cops come to the door and ask about the two men you invited to our home, huh, Maia?"

She should have said it with more assurance, but she couldn't. The thought of begging to Selene made her stomach turn over. She'd rather be banished. "What men? It's their word against mine, isn't it? Who'll believe two street bums over Silas Compton's daughter?" She purposely didn't say Silas and Selene Compton's daughter. She wasn't Selene's daughter. Never was.

"This is a question for the group," Selene said. "She put us in jeopardy. We all should decide what to do."

Selene nuzzled her face into the crook of Compton's neck and ran her hand down his torso and over his crotch. She smiled smugly at Maia and left.

Silas, his face flushed, seemed flustered, then rallied his self-control. "Why, Maia? You have everything you could possibly want. Why endanger the group like that?"

"You really don't know, do you? You're so blinded by that woman you can't see what you've done. What did Phillip Crane offer you all those years ago besides his daughter, Father? Was it money or sexual pleasure that made you drive my mother to suicide and sell your soul and the souls of your children? Tell me, because I have to know."

The strike across her face came swiftly and forcefully, knocking Maia into the table and onto the floor. Her stinging cheek brought tears to her eyes.

"You will never speak to me like that again, do you understand?"

Compton approached her, offering his hand to help her up. She shrugged him off.

A pained expression twisted his face, and he stepped back. "I've never told you this—you and your sister were just children at the time, toddlers—but your mother was a disturbed woman, unable to handle the pressures and guilt born along with a retarded child. From the moment we found out Crane wasn't normal, she blamed herself, thinking she'd done something during her pregnancy. She slowly sank into a far-off place, unable to give you and Dione the attention you deserved."

Maia didn't remember her mother's slide into depression. She remembered her mother's touch, her smell, her warmth. Silas was right. She and Dione were babies, but her memories were strong nevertheless.

"I couldn't reach her," Silas said. "Maybe I should have been more understanding, but compassion doesn't come easily for me. In fact, until I met Selene I never felt much of anything. Work was my lover, ambition my driving force."

Maia pulled herself up, her face still searing from the brutal slap. "Oh, and Selene taught you how to love? How touching." She went behind the bar and poured a vodka straight, drank it, and poured another. "Did she teach you to love or to fuck so you could father her babies, my half-sisters, all of whom she spirited away to the compound as soon as she drilled the basic teachings into them? The Cranes picked a brilliant man, eager to do anything for money, and you willingly became her sex slave."

"You don't know what you're talking about," Silas said, pointing his finger and speaking in the tone that had always paralyzed her with fear. "Selene gave me a reason to live, to love. I'd been numb to everything before then."

She let out a strangled snort. The vodka burned her throat. A welcome burn, as if the scorching pain might erase her years of acquiescence. Maybe if she drank enough she'd be like her father was, before, and wouldn't feel anything, remember less. She added ice and sipped the drink.

"How wonderful for you, Father. All during that time, you never gave one thought to what Dione or I wanted from our lives. Selene mesmerized you to ignore that she was pimping us out to the sons of the group so we could bear their children to populate your so-called new order. No different than Hitler's vision of a master race." She paced the room, staring at the floor. "Why didn't I see what was happening? Why didn't I stop it?"

"Because it's right," Silas answered. "Not for everyone, I admit, but it is for us."

No, it isn't. She'd already said enough to seal her fate, still she couldn't stop. "And you covered up our pregnancies by sending us away on phony business trips. Dione and I have five children between us, and after we gave these innocents nourishment, after we bonded with them and loved them, they were taken from us as if we were unfit mothers." Her head spun, but she took a long swallow of vodka anyway.

"They're your grandchildren." Hot tears flooded her eyes as she remembered the warmth of the babies she cradled in her arms. "They're not even being raised by their own blood."

His voice softened as if he needed to convince her in a sane manner. But he wasn't sane. Silas Compton had lost all sanity the day he met Selene Crane and her parents.

"You make it sound ugly. We're not creating a master race. We're not killing anyone. We're only separating ourselves, evolving into a culture of intellectually gifted men and women, steeped in spirituality and sexual pleasure, without the restraints of God."

"But with the tentacles of Satan."

"Not tentacles, Maia. Liberation."

Chapter Twenty-Six
A Little Twist of the Knife

"I waited until today because of the holiday, Captain," Lucier said as he took a seat in his captain's office. Jack Craven was a fair and honest boss in a city wracked with problems. After Diana's ordeal, he'd forced Lucier to take time off—time he'd refused when he lost his family.

Lucier proceeded to explain what Meade and Hall claimed had happened yesterday at Silas Compton's house in what the department now secretly called the Satan Baby Kidnappings Case.

"There'd be hell to pay if that codename ever got out," Craven said.

"Bound to leak sooner or later. This place is like a sieve. Jake Griffin must have someone on his payroll to get the stories he writes for the paper."

"If I ever find out who, there'll be hell to pay."

"I wanted to check with you before I question Maia Compton. Her father is not a man to treat lightly. I don't want to bring the wrath of his lawyers down on us."

"You have to talk to her, Ernie, Compton's daughter or not. Those men made an accusation, and even though it sounds hokey as hell, they weren't on drugs. You said yourself their story meshed with Ms. Racine's. We can't ignore the connection.

"Furthermore, they admitted they planned to steal

Compton's paintings. Why would they implicate themselves in a theft if they weren't telling the truth? Maybe they thought they saw what they said, maybe they saw it. Either way, a meeting in a private residence is not illegal. Still, if she lured them into a robbery, you have to follow up."

Lucier leaned back in the visitor's chair and blew out a breath. "That's the way I see it. I'm sure this will be a case of he said, she said."

"Be careful. Call the daughter first. Make an appointment."

Lucier got up, headed for the door. "Will do."

"Hanging out with some pretty lofty company, huh, Ernie?"

"Me? I'm too low on the totem pole. They're interested in Diana. I just tag along."

"Compounded with the house on Parkside Avenue, this is beginning to sound like Compton and his gang might be dabbling in the black arts. What's your read on this?"

"If he is, like you said, it's none of our business. If he's involved in kidnapping babies, it sure as hell is." He started for the door and turned around. "Do you believe in coincidences, Captain?"

"Yeah, I do. I've seen too many of them not to. But I still like to check them out."

"Me too."

Lucier decided to do more than check. Holding a list of names in front of him, he called Diana. "You think Jason might do a little more digging for you? For me, really, but I don't want to run the search through the department. Man like Compton might have someone on the payroll."

"You mean a cop on the take?" Diana asked.

"Not necessarily. A little under-the-table appreciation

wouldn't be unheard of, though. Money talks, or haven't you heard? Will Jason help us?"

"He'll jump at the chance. He's bored stiff at his tech job."

Lucier read off a list of names he wanted Jason to check, beginning with Phillip and Cybele Crane. "Also, see what he can find out about Compton's first marriage and his wife's suicide."

"What's going on, Ernie?"

"I don't know, but this is more than some rich people dabbling in the occult. Maybe Maia Compton can clue us in. She seemed willing to get at her father for reasons known only to her. How far will she go?"

"I'll call Jason," Diana said and hung up.

When Lucier called Compton International, Maia Compton's secretary said that she left two days before on a troubleshooting assignment out of the country and probably wouldn't be back for at least a month. How could Maia Compton have invited those two bozos into her house yesterday when she'd supposedly left the country?

He cradled the receiver and let out a long breath. This was becoming more complicated by the minute. Beecher tapped on his door and came in without waiting for an invitation.

"Doesn't your wife check you out before you leave the house?" Lucier asked, pointing at Beecher's disheveled shirt. "Look at you. You're falling apart."

Beecher gazed down at himself. "I don't know, Ernie. I don't look like this when I leave in the morning. Something happens during the day. A poltergeist must be following me around, messing me up."

Lucier laughed while the big man smoothed his shirt into the waistband of his pants.

"What are we going to do with those two from

yesterday?" Beecher asked. "We can't hold them without charges, not that they're anxious to leave."

"We've got time. Have they lawyered up?"

"Not yet, but when they stop shitting their pants, even those two will think of it."

"Let me know when they do." Lucier rubbed his temple and leaned back in his chair. "I tried to make an appointment with Maia Compton, but her secretary said she left on a troubleshooting assignment the day after Diana and I met her at Compton's and probably wouldn't be back for a month. That means she couldn't have set up those two idiots to steal the paintings because she wasn't in town. Convenient, wouldn't you say?"

"Well, ya. Shouldn't be hard to confirm. All we have to do is check the airline manifests."

"Compton International has its own fleet of jets, remember? They can go anywhere they damn well please."

"They still have to file a flight plan. Every plane does."

"Don't think a man like Silas Compton can't make things look like he wants. One of his planes could have flown to the Mid-East that day. Who's to say Maia Compton wasn't on it if he wanted her to be?

"Meanwhile, I'll make an appointment to see Compton. Wanna bet his family was at a July Fourth get-together yesterday and no one was at home? And wanna bet a dozen people will swear to it."

*****

Diana got up that morning, made coffee, and sat down to read the paper, but her mind wandered hopelessly. She felt rotten about her last meeting with Slater. So rotten, in fact, she resisted telling Lucier, because she was at a loss to explain her reaction. Not to him. Not to herself. So when Slater called,

Diana couldn't contain her surprise.

"I overreacted," he said. "I was presumptuous and totally out of line suggesting we had a relationship of any kind. I don't know what I was thinking."

"No, it was my fault." She almost said she had hit below the belt and caught herself before she turned a common idiom into an indignity. "I was the one out of line. I guess after thirty years of my father telling me what I think, I rebelled when you told me what I supposedly knew."

"You were right. Tell me, do I come across as an arrogant charlatan?"

"The Brother Osiris bit might be a little much, but I can relate. Remember, you're talking to someone who's spent the last twenty years of her life entertaining to make a living. We use whatever works."

"I hope I don't rise to the level of entertainer—no offense intended—but I hope I'm a bit more subtle. That covers the charlatan part; what about arrogant?"

"How much truth can you handle, Edward?"

"Now I'm afraid to say anything you might misconstrue, but your opinion matters."

Diana couldn't help smiling at how cautiously both she and Slater measured their words. She always prescribed to the idea that if someone asked her a question, they deserved an honest answer.

"Okay, you're very sure of yourself. I don't know if that rises to the level of arrogance, but it's close. Lately, I've been right there with you. My behavior to Silas Compton the other night made you look like an amateur. You called it. I was baiting him. If that's not arrogance, I don't know what is." Diana paused. "Let's change the subject. You're sorry; I'm sorry. We have a lot in common, and if we have any relationship at all, how about calling it a budding friendship? I'm not interested in anything more, and neither are you. You're an interesting man, and you've confided in me, as a friend, personal facts about your life. We'll go from there."

"Sounds good. How about I invite you to the mission for lunch to make amends? I've hired a new cook who does a mean down-home meatloaf. Best I ever tasted. It isn't Emeril's but it doesn't cost as much either. Besides, I have something to tell you, something to show you, and something to give you."

She could hear the smile in his words and found herself smiling in return. "Sounds like triple intrigue. What time?"

"Noon? And don't worry, we'll have lunch in the office."

"Eating family-style wouldn't bother me. I've done it plenty of times. See you at noon."

Diana hung up and debated calling Lucier. He didn't see Edward Slater objectively. She wondered if she did.

* * * * *

Lucier made an appointment to meet Compton at his downtown headquarters, situated on the top floor of a fashionable high rise. He was greeted by an attractive secretary who announced his presence to Compton, then ushered him into the industrialist's office.

Lucier expected antique furniture, Oriental rugs, and gilt-edged leather books, but instead found Compton's office decor elegantly contemporary. Taking up most of the floor's area was a rug designed to co-ordinate with the vibrant painting on one wall. He checked the signature. Kandinsky. A brushed steel sculpture braced the front of a massive desk with a glass top that seemed to float over side panels of exotic wood. Two modern chrome and leather chairs faced the desk that held a laptop computer. Nothing else. Not even a sheet of paper. Light filtered in from a picture window that showcased the magnificent view of the Mississippi and the twin spans of the Crescent City Connection bridges.

Nice to be king.

Compton was on the phone. He waved Lucier inside and extended a waiting finger. When he hung up, he rose and held out his hand, which Lucier took.

"Lieutenant, what a pleasure. Have a seat."

"Your desk puts me to shame," Lucier said, sitting down. "I can barely see the top of mine for all the papers."

"That's because I have a secretary who's an OCD neat freak. I give the orders; she does the work." He walked to a banquet where a silver coffee service sat on a matching tray.

Lucier recognized the distinct set from an art exhibit some years before. He couldn't remember the designer, but he remembered the price tag, which was more than many yearly wages. He figured a famous artisan created the sculptured desk, but he didn't know who.

"Coffee?" Compton asked.

"No, thanks. I've had my two cups already."

"You don't mind if I do?"

"Of course not."

Compton poured coffee into a plain white china mug, decorated with the company logo, and sat down.

"You're probably wondering why I'm here," Lucier said.

"It crossed my mind, Ernie. May I still call you Ernie, or is this an official visit?"

"Ernie's fine, and it's semi-official. About your daughter."

Compton didn't blink. "Which one?"

"Maia. Two men leveled a rather bizarre accusation against her, and I can't seem to get in touch with her to clear it up. Her office said she was out of the country."

"That's right. I sent Maia to placate one of our Saudi

associates. Something about construction on a complex he wasn't happy about. She's my best negotiator when it comes to this particular sheik. He likes her manner and blonde hair. I'm not above using her attributes to smooth things over." He trained a steady gaze at Lucier. "Now, what accusation did these men make against her?"

Lucier returned Compton's pause with one of his own. "Can you tell me when she left the country?"

"The day after our get-together," Compton said, as if anticipating the question. "I've answered all your questions. I'd appreciate if you'd answer mine. What accusation?"

"The two men in question said she invited them into your home yesterday to steal your paintings, and they interrupted a meeting in the lower level of your house. A rather strange meeting, they said."

Compton emitted a deep belly laugh before he spoke. "Really. And this was supposed to have taken place yesterday, July Fourth, you say?"

"That's what they said."

Compton's face lightly flushed, but he kept his composure. "Maia had already left for the Middle East, and because we had the day off, we were at the lake home of my in-laws. You've met my daughter, Ernie. Does she seem the type who'd invite men into our home? *Into my home?* Hardly a likely scenario, don't you think? Who are these liars?"

"Some locals looking to cash in. I guess they picked the wrong story to tell. To clear up this nonsense, which flight did your daughter take out of the country?"

An involuntary twitch rippled Compton's cheek. He didn't like being questioned, but he covered his irritation well, burying the tic under a cold smile.

"She flew overseas on one of Compton International's

private jets. I can give you the flight time and you can check with the airport, which is surely your next request."

"I'm being thorough, Mr. Compton. This is one of those times when my job puts me in an awkward position, but that's what I'm paid to do." Lucier stared unblinkingly at Compton. "Your tax dollars at work. I'm sure you understand." *Yeah, taxes you find every possible way to avoid.*

He nodded agreement, but his eyes grew narrow before he glanced down and tugged at something hidden behind the desk. *So that's where the drawer is.* Lucier marveled at the innovative design and concluded one advantage of being rich is having articles designed and made especially for you.

Compton caught his interest. "Clever, isn't it? This desk was designed by Sophia Reyes. I mentioned she's a designer, didn't I?"

"Yes, I believe so."

"The sculpture is by a local artist. Sophia devised a drawer in back to hold a few pads of paper and writing utensils. It's hidden by the panel of black glass fused to the desktop. A work of art in itself."

"Absolutely."

Compton took out a card and handed it to Lucier. "My pilot's number is on this card. You can call him and verify the flight plan. If that isn't enough, you can check with air traffic control at the airport. They'll confirm the plane left two days ago for the Middle East. Long before those hoodlums decided to taint my daughter's good name."

Lucier read the card. "Thank you. I'm sure his confirmation will clear this up."

"As if my word wouldn't?"

The icy tone of Compton's voice sent a sharp chill through Lucier. He didn't say anything but met the man's stare with one of his own.

"Did you really think one of my daughters would devise a plan to steal my paintings?"

"No, sir, I didn't. But like I said, I have to check out these allegations. In fact, I asked my captain if I could come here personally. As uncomfortable as it would be for me, when I learned your daughter wasn't available, I thought you'd find being questioned by an acquaintance less awkward."

Only Compton's lips smiled. "I appreciate that consideration, Ernie. I do."

Lucier didn't know why the familiar use of his name from this man bugged the shit out of him. They'd spent time in a social atmosphere, but Compton had never invited Lucier to address him by his first name, as if he wasn't quite good enough to be on a first-name basis with a man as exalted as Silas Compton.

"Is that all?" Compton asked.

"That'll do it," Lucier said, rising. He offered his hand. "Nice to see you again, *Silas*."

Chapter Twenty-Seven
A Tangled Web

Lucier questioned why dropping Compton's first name at the end of the meeting gave him such a vicarious thrill. Childish, he thought. So what? It was worth the stunned look on Compton's face.

He returned to the station and his cluttered desk. His cell phone rang before he could get down to work. Private number, the readout said.

"Morning, Lieutenant," Jason Connors said.

"How'd you get my cell number?"

"Um, that's what I do."

"Of course. What was I thinking?"

"I knew the info Diana requested was for you, so I cut out the middleman."

"Glad you called my cell."

"Even if I called the station directly, there'd be no way to trace the call. I use a routing number. If anyone decides to check, they'll come up empty."

"Maybe I should put you on the payroll."

"That'd be great, Lieutenant. Beats the hell out of writing computer code."

The kid's computer talent was way over Lucier's head. "What have you got?"

"Not everything. Haven't had enough time, but I thought you could use what I have now. I'll get back to you with the rest as soon as I get it."

"Go. I've got a pen and pad ready."

"So far, the connection for Compton and the rest is Phillip Crane. The two men go back to when Compton first started at Barton. One article about Crane claimed he put Compton in the driver's seat at Barton. Crane's company is the leader in oil drilling technology, and Haynesworth and Easley hold high positions. Crane inherited the company from his father. It's publicly traded, or else he'd probably be as secretive as Compton."

"What about Reyes?" Lucier said, cradling the cell phone on his shoulder to take notes.

"He headed the engineering department at Barton. When Compton left to form his own company, Reyes went with him. So did many of Barton's customers. Eventually Barton went under. The five men have stayed tight. Crane retired a few years ago. He turned the company over to his oldest son, but he's on the board of directors. He's probably on Compton International's board, too, but I haven't gotten that far yet. That information, like everything else in Compton's life, is private."

"Hmm," Lucier hummed. "Seems you got a good chunk of off-limit information."

"Digging is what I do, Lieutenant."

Lucier didn't want to know that Jason did some digging for Diana's act. He knew, but he didn't want to. "Still doesn't explain why Crane took an interest in Compton."

"Might be because of Compton's first wife," Jason said. "More specifically, her father, Gault Fannon, the senator."

"You mean votes for contracts?"

"Nothing proven, but a huge government contract went to Crane's company with a push from Fannon in the Senate."

Lucier wondered what Crane had on Fannon or his daughter to force him to back the bill. Or maybe Compton found the smoking gun. "What about Compton's first wife?"

"Socialite, beautiful, rich, much richer than Compton at the time, which is before he met Crane. He went after Ms. Fannon like a hungry lion looking for his next meal. Pictures of them filled the society pages. The man was moving up, and she was the top rung on the ladder."

"Any gossip about either the senator or his daughter that would lead to blackmail?"

"Haven't found any. If I found the link, the congressional committee investigating the contract would have found it. There's something that Crane or Compton had on Fannon personally that'll never see the light of day. But that's only a guess."

"I think you're right."

"Even without proof, when Compton hooked up with Crane, the blowback from Fannon's vote blackened his name. No one proved he was on the take, but a cloud hung over him from that point on. He never ran for re-election and died shortly after of a heart attack."

"What about Compton's children with Eliza Fannon?"

"Maia and Dione were originally named Susan and Meredith.

"Why would Compton change their names?"

"That would take more talent than I have to find out. However, the current names are from mythology, if that means anything."

"It might, if I knew anything about mythology. The name changes are one more bizarre aspect of this case." What case? Lucier thought. There was no case, only suspicion. "What else?"

"A son, Crane, followed a year after the birth of Dione. Interesting name, don't you think?" Jason didn't wait for an answer. "He was severely retarded. Eliza Compton shut herself off from everything to stay with the boy. His nanny wasn't paying attention one day, and he drowned in the swimming pool. A year later, depressed by the death of her son, Mrs. Compton jumped out a hotel window. A few sensational days in the media and the story faded into oblivion, until an unauthorized biography of Silas Compton dredged it up again. The author claimed Compton cheated on his wife with Selene Crane, in addition to a few other assertions that painted an ugly picture of the man. Shortly after the book came out, the author, Donald Stanton, was killed in a hit and run accident. They never found the driver."

Lucier wrote everything down. The information piqued his curiosity. Fannon and then Stanton, both dead.

"So Selene Crane entered the picture before Eliza Compton's death."

"So buzzed the gossip rags. The son named after Phillip Crane gives you an idea."

Mega-rich company presidents, senators on the take, beautiful women, adultery, back-door deals. The story teemed with elements of a potboiler movie script. But nothing connected these people to the occult, except the word of two losers with a far-out tale no one in his right mind would believe, along with an always-questionable vision by a psychic.

"What about Crane's offspring? Who besides Selene?"

"Thought you'd never ask. The Cranes had five other children. I mentioned the oldest son who runs Crane Corporation. He's equally as private as Crane. Selene has a younger brother Seth and three sisters. Guess who they are."

"You're kidding."

"Nope. Sophia, Anastasia, and Reah. Those are their birth names too."

Lucier exhaled a long breath. "Jesus." Now that he thought about it, he saw the resemblances.

"I already mentioned I couldn't find any record of Compton and Selene's children, but I did for the other second marriage liaisons. Interestingly, all their kids were home schooled, all took the state tests and passed with exceptionally high grades, and all went to a small private college in Pennsylvania, Middlebridge.

"The oldest offspring of the first wives head up divisions in Crane and Compton's businesses, like Maia and Dione Compton, and are groomed to take over the top spots in the company."

Lucier detected a pattern evolving, but he didn't know what it meant. "Tell me about the college. Is it a religious school? Who funds it, and where do the kids go when they graduate?"

"That's what I'm working on, but so far they might as well be on a different planet. Except for the ones employed by their fathers' companies, the others are gone for months at a time, sometimes longer, to either represent the Crane/Compton international businesses or to do humanitarian work for one of their foundations. The latter sends them all over the place. I'd have to break into the Treasury Department and pull up their passports to find out where."

"Can you do that?"

Jason's nervous laugh echoed over the phone line. "Man, that's tricky. If I got caught, they'd haul me off to someplace like Gitmo, and no one would ever hear from me again." He cleared his throat. "Unless it's a matter of national security and someone higher up on the food chain is asking—no offense, Lieutenant—I'd rather not. I have a feeling this doesn't meet the requirement."

"No offense taken," Lucier said. "Forget I asked. I'm over the line with this as it is. I'd hate to get you in trouble, and I'd hate to explain what I'm doing, especially since I'm not sure I know."

Jason's laugh came across full-throated. "I'll call you when I get the rest of the information."

Without putting down the phone, Lucier tried calling Diana again. No answer. He couldn't force her to stay home, but she seemed to enjoy flying in the face of danger. He wished she took the two threatening notes seriously. Lucier guessed where she was, which was why she didn't answer her phone. He marshaled all his willpower not to go to the mission.

* * * * *

Diana sat at the now-cleared table in Slater's office, demolishing the platters of food one of the women brought in. "You're right. This meatloaf is delicious, and I'm not a big meatloaf fan." Diana mixed the meat with mashed potatoes. "The corn pudding is excellent."

Slater heaped a spoonful of the yellow mixture onto his plate. "You'd think a man wouldn't beat on a woman who cooks like this but beat her he did. She has a restraining order on him. They don't work. If a man wants to get a woman bad enough, he'll find a way. She's safe here for the time being. Problem is most women go back for more. Don't ask me why."

"I won't because there's no logical answer." Diana wiped her mouth and sipped her iced tea. "You've piqued my curiosity with your lunch invitation, Edward. Three times. What will you start with, tell, show, or give?"

Slater laughed and said, "Show." He stacked the dishes and took them to the kitchen.

She looked around, noticed the camera again. Annoyed, she wished she could turn it off. Was she finally going to learn what Slater kept behind the locked cabinet door?

Upon returning, he wiped down the desk with a cloth he kept in the bottom drawer. "Don't want to get crumbs on my treasure," he said. Unfastening the key ring hooked to the belt loop of his jeans, he unlocked his bookcase.

Yes.

Slater brought out what looked to be a very old book and gingerly placed it on the desk as if it were bound in eggshells. "This is a first edition of Edward Burnett Tylor's *Primitive Culture*, published in 1871." His smile faded when he saw Diana's face. "You don't know what this is, do you?"

Diana shook her head. "No, I don't. Other than it must be valuable, I have no idea who Tylor is or what this book is about. Should I?"

He sighed. "I thought you might, considering your interest in mysticism and religion, the spiritual in general. Tylor was a cultural anthropologist who reintroduced the ancient theory that the soul is the origin of the belief in spirits: animism."

"I'm sorry to disappoint you. I've only dabbled in mysticism, a cursory education. I never studied it in depth." She assumed Slater showed his treasure to Jeanne Highsmith and that their conversations were far more comprehensive than any he could carry on with her.

He pulled out the top desk drawer and extracted a paperback. "Now you can read it at your leisure. It's the same book, though obviously not a first edition, printed in 1958." He handed it to her, careful to avoid her touch. "Don't worry, I won't test you. I just thought you'd be interested."

"Of course. I don't know what to say except thank you. I look forward to reading it."

A first edition tome behind the cupboard doors was not what Diana expected. Was she relieved or disappointed? What had she anticipated? No question about her host, however. Disappointment etched his face. He expected more of her.

"I've let you down, Edward. You gave me too much credit."

"Not at all. I tend to assume things sometimes. Why would you know of this book? It's not as if you had time to study this field in depth, always on the road. Your strengths are far more esoteric, more unexplainable than any written word. I apologize. You could never let me down."

"Thank you. I look forward to reading this." She carefully tucked the book in her purse. "Now, you mentioned something you wanted to tell me."

"Oh, yes, I almost forgot. Brigid and Nona Fulceri came by yesterday."

Chapter Twenty-Eight
Hidden Meaning

It took a moment for Diana to comprehend what Slater said. When she did, words failed her. She finally found her voice. "Why didn't you call the authorities? Those girls are wanted for questioning. They were in that house, nursed the kidnapped babies."

Slater leaned forward in his chair, his arms folded on the barren desk. "You don't know that. The police have no proof other than your impression from a vision. From a vision, Diana. Besides, the Fulceris said they weren't there."

His voice was so persuasive she easily envisioned him convincing people to donate money to his worthy cause.

"These girls have been through hell," he said. "They trusted me when they came here to explain."

"You may not put credence in my visions, but I found that house, and then those young women disappeared. A man killed himself rather than talk about what went on there. Doesn't that resonate with you?"

"Obviously not in the same way it does with you. Both those girls were raped by their pedophile father from the time they were old enough to understand what he'd do to them if they told. I'm sorry, but I wouldn't turn them over to the police and their interrogation methods. They need counseling. I made an appointment with a psychologist. I begged them to go, but I forced them. Not because I believe they had anything to do with Deems, that house, or those babies, because I don't. I want them to straighten out their lives."

"You made a judgment call. I don't agree." Diana rose. "Thanks for the lunch, Edward, and for the book. I'll read it."

"You're upset with me again," he said, standing. "I push your buttons, don't I?"

"You impeded a police investigation. If I'm right about those girls, and I am, they might have helped us find the kidnapped babies. There's something evil going on, and you're purposely ignoring it, first with Compton, now with the sisters."

"If I were involved with the house on Parkside Avenue or thought the Fulceri sisters were connected in any way, would I have told you about them coming here?"

Slater made a good point, but she was still angry at his duplicity. "I don't know what I think anymore."

"I suppose you'll tell your lieutenant about this."

"I suppose so."

"I understand. Still friends?"

"Of course, Edward. Still friends."

* * * * *

Diana waited until she and Lucier finished dinner and were settled in her small den with the remainder of the bottle of wine to tell him about the Fulceri sisters. He reacted exactly as she anticipated.

"I have a good mind to arrest your Brother Osiris for aiding and abetting," he said. "And you—I'm at a loss for words."

Diana barely looked up from her notepad to say, "He's not mine."

"You're not listening." Lucier huffed and sipped his wine. "First you go to the mission without telling me—didn't answer your phone either—then you report that those two women popped in there to say *ciao* and inform Slater they didn't know anything about the missing babies. Now you sit here and ignore me while I make the case that Slater is in this up to his handsome neck."

Diana stopped doodling to focus on Lucier. "Am I supposed to tell you everything I do? Maybe you should get one of those GPS things and strap it to my ankle so you can track me every minute of the day. Put me on house arrest, why don't you?" Her eyes filled with tears. "I can't live like that, Ernie. It's taken me twenty-five years to break from my parents and acquire a measure of independence. I won't get into a relationship where someone's telling me what to do all the time and hovering over me like I'm a child. I've lived that life. I don't want a repeat."

Lucier set his glass on the coffee table and leaned over to kiss her forehead. "I worry about you. I can't help it. I'm a cop. Cops worry about the people they love. If anything happens to you, I don't know what I'd do. It took me a long time to find you, and I almost lost you once already. I don't want to go there again."

"This isn't always about you." She brushed her hand across his cheek. "You won't lose me, Ernie. Ever. But you can't tie me to you. That's not a relationship, that's control. We can't make this work to suit only your needs. I have needs too, and they don't include a bodyguard."

He pulled back.

"I wanted to tell you I was going to the mission, but you've been so overprotective and irrationally opposed to Edward, I decided not to."

"Okay, I concede being overprotective, but not on Slater. You seem blind to the possibility that he's involved. He's protecting those girls, and you don't see it."

Conceding, she said, "I do, and I'm torn between what I felt in that vision and Edward's faith in those girls. Maybe I'm wrong. I didn't specifically *see* them in my vision, only that someone nursed in that chair." She pulled Lucier toward her and told him the girls' history, then kissed his cheek. "I'm sorry. I got pulled into their story. Edward didn't want them to go through a police investigation. I was very verbal in my opposition, if that makes you feel any better."

"Good. You're not completely oblivious to his manipulations." He pulled a sheet of paper from his pocket and unfolded it, letting her see what was written on it. "I found this stuck in your door when I came looking for you." Drawn on the paper was a crescent moon and the printed words, "A crescent moon is near."

Diana read it, held it in her hands and closed her eyes for a long minute. "No vibes," she said when she opened her eyes.

"Nothing we can trace either," Lucier said.

"What the hell does it mean?"

"It means on the day of the crescent moon I'm not letting you out of my sight, even if I have to lock one of those GPS tracking devices on your ankle, and even if you never speak to me again."

"When is the night of the crescent moon?"

"The new moon is in a few days. A crescent moon is a couple of days after that. I checked."

"Weird things are supposed to happen on the full moon, not a crescent one."

"The crescent moon is the symbol of the goddess Diana, or have you forgotten?"

"No, I haven't. I wish now I were back in the days when they called me Diana, Goddess of the Hunt. At least no one was sending me scary notes."

"From the new moon on, and with your permission, madam, I will stick to you like glue." He nudged his way next to her and studied the pad of paper she was doodling on. "Now, do you mind telling me what you're doing?"

"Check this out. Brigid and Nona's last name.
~~FULCERI~~ ~~CERIFUL~~ ~~FURLICE~~ ~~LICUREF~~ LUCIFER

"Jesus," Lucier said. "Remove one letter and it spells my name too, straight out."

"I didn't notice that," she said, "but you're right."

Chapter Twenty-Nine
Irresistible Magnetism

When Maia arrived at the compound from New Orleans, Nona and Brigid were already there. She hadn't seen her half-sisters in a couple of years. She remembered their transition into young womanhood. Brigid had developed early, and Maia remembered how the young girl relished the attention and flaunted her attributes with no inhibitions, as her mother taught her. Now, as Maia sat in the nursery watching them nurse the babies, she realized how perverted the group's ambitious project was. She'd spent the last two days kicking herself for carrying out the pitiful act of revenge against her father instead of going to Lieutenant Lucier and exposing the whole operation.

Instead, she'd been reprimanded and escorted to one of the Compton planes, flown to the compound, and confined.

Do not pass go. Go directly to jail.

She'd been allowed to see her half-sisters, but nothing she said to them countered the lifetime of programming they'd sustained.

Maia marveled at their startling beauty. Phillip and Cybele Crane's sons and daughters produced perfect, brilliant, and beautiful offspring, exactly as Maia had. What she saw now was different. Her half-sisters were nursing not their own children, but babies stolen from the warmth of their birth mothers' arms.

Brigid was pregnant, and not for the first time. A baby bump swelled under her clothes, her figure fuller, breasts heavier. Maia remembered the feeling well. Although she was well endowed, she couldn't compare to Selene's obedient daughters. Raw sexuality comprised part of their genetic makeup, inherited from a great beauty and taught by the best of all teachers. Maia didn't realize until now, looking at the two women, that Silas was nothing more than a pimp with a stratospheric intelligence, and that all his children were nothing more than pawns in the group's egotistical ambition to populate their fantasy world with their genes.

She pulled up a chair to face the two women. "You know what you're doing is wrong."

Brigid switched the hungry child from one breast to another. "How can this be wrong, Maia? Look at them. They're beautiful."

"But they were kidnapped—taken from their natural parents who are grieving. Doesn't that mean anything to you?"

"This is for a greater cause," Nona said, cradling her infant. "We love doing this. Father says we're giving these babies part of us. We want to please him."

"He's using you," Maia said. "You're nothing more than sexual objects to him." Both women stopped, frowned at Maia, and the worst feeling she ever had in her life shuddered through her. Bile rose to her throat, and she pushed the obscene thought from her mind, unwilling to think the unthinkable.

They, like all the young women here, had been brainwashed by lessons taught from birth. Little girls were created to be goddesses of fertility, boys their gods, and pleasure their destiny. For the longest time, she and Dione did what Silas expected of them—yes, to please him—but they lived different lives than the others. As daughters of one of the world's richest men, they couldn't be hidden away and trained as courtesans, like the rest of the women born of the group. They maintained important positions within their father's companies. They were written about, photographed, admired. Their trips to attend Compton business were covers for the time they spent at the compound to give birth. They nursed their babies, held them, and loved them. Then Maia and Dione returned home to carry on with their lives, leaving their babies to be raised by others. Home to Silas and Selene, the queen bitch—or witch. She was both, but one thing she was not and never would be—she wasn't their mother.

Maia and Dione saw their children when Silas allowed. By then, the babies had bonded with others who lived at the compound, teaching and indoctrinating them. They'd bonded with her half-sisters, Maia knew, and it caused a jumble of emotions, none good.

Sure, Maia thought sardonically, let's keep it in the family. Now their babies had grown into toddlers and kindergartners and school age, and Maia and Dione hardly knew them.

The only sister their children didn't bond with was Anat, Selene's first daughter. They didn't because Anat rejected Selene's teachings, refused to be a wet nurse, scorned the Crane god, and turned her back on the growing community of sexual hedonists. Anat was here somewhere, segregated. Maia didn't know where, but she would find her.

The babies suckling at the breasts of Nona and Brigid weren't family. They were stolen to enrich the genetic pool of the group and nursed by strangers.

She had learned about the kidnappings only a few days ago and couldn't comprehend the impossible. Whatever she'd been taught—all her indoctrination—paled to what she now knew.

This must stop.

How long could her father explain her absence? He could say she died overseas and keep her here forever. Then they would force her to bear other children. No lack of willing sons. One especially. She would fail to reproduce, but they didn't know that.

No one in the outside world knew about Selene's three daughters. Anat had always been a thorn in the side of her parents. Now, with the twisted turn of kidnapped babies, Maia could only imagine Anat's rebellion.

Maia needed to find a way out of the compound. She had a vague idea, but the area was huge, bordered by rivers, mountains, and barriers of trees and guarded by men who were paid to keep everyone inside. The only way out was by air, difficult without the children, hopeless with them.

Her father never invited outsiders to his home. Diana Racine was not an ordinary person susceptible to group tactics. What was the group planning?

She heard the key turn in the door, locked only to keep her inside. She hadn't seen him in a while, and as hard as she tried to rein in her reaction, her heart pounded when he entered the room. Still handsome, even with fine lines etched around his eyes and mouth. Still with the sexiest, self-confident smile.

"You're a foolish woman, Maia. What were you thinking?" he said, locking the door behind him.

"Hello, Seth. Or have you changed your name? Maybe to Apollo or Adonis, perhaps?"

His smile broadened, as if he found her taunt amusing. "Since we've been intimate, you can call me Seth. I find name changing pretentious."

Maia's full-throated, cynical laugh woke one of the babies.

"Now see what you've done?" Brigid said. "He was in dreamland and you've awakened him."

Seth exchanged the baby sleeping peacefully in Brigid's arms with the crying baby in the crib. Brigid cooed and cuddled the infant, and she quickly found peace at her breast. Seth stooped in front of the sisters. "You shouldn't have gone to the mission," he said. "What if someone was watching?"

"They weren't," Nona said. "We checked."

"If the police had that place under surveillance, you wouldn't have seen them. Now you have to stay here. It's too dangerous for you to leave. You could expose everything. Whatever the cops suspect, they can't prove a thing." He curled his index finger under Brigid's chin and lifted her head. "Do you understand?" he said in a knife-thin whisper. "No more."

"We would never say anything," Nona said.

He alternated his attention between the two women, his tone firmer. "Do you understand?"

"Yes, Seth," they said in robotic unison.

"Besides," Brigid said, "Father told us we'd be here for a while."

"True," Seth said. "There's plenty for you to do here." He patted Brigid's stomach and smiled, then rose and took Maia's arm. "Come with me."

She looked back at her half-sisters, cooing over their charges, and shook her head. They were nothing but automatons. What will happen to them when this compound comes to the attention of the authorities? Where would they go?

Maia followed Seth, noticing he didn't lock the door after him. Why should he? Brigid and Nona weren't being held here against their wills. "Where are you taking me?"

Seth stopped, fixed his black eyes on her. "You haven't eaten anything since you arrived late last night. You're hungry, aren't you?"

He must have heard the rumblings in her stomach. "Yes."

"I thought I'd have the cook prepare you something to eat."

"As long as you taste it first."

"Maia, Maia, don't you trust me?" Seth's patronizing tone always infuriated her, but she needed to be smarter now than in times past.

"Not long ago my food contained something that knocked me out. Nine months later I gave birth to a bouncing baby boy."

"That's because the third time you were difficult. You left me no choice."

So it was Seth. Part of her breathed a sigh of relief; the other part felt sick. "There's always a choice."

"I'm the father of all your children," he said, "but making love is much better when it's consensual." He opened another door and held it.

When she started through, he blocked her way, coming so close she breathed in his scent, the same spicy fragrance she remembered, filling her senses. He cupped his hands over her breasts and massaged them. She felt them tighten, nipples protruding hard in his hungry fingers. She stared at him as if his contact meant nothing, even though her body quivered inside. She didn't remove his hand. It had been a long time since he'd touched her intimately, and he still wielded the same sensual power over her.

"Don't fight it, Maia. We were meant for each other." He nuzzled into her neck and murmured in her ear. "You're still the most beautiful, you know, and at your peak of childbearing years." He drew back, smiling. "Admit it, you wanted me as much as I wanted you, and from what I'm feeling under your blouse, you still do."

She brushed his hand aside. "You wish."

She'd loved Seth Crane, then and now, and he knew it. She remembered that summer after the end of her home schooling. Her father consented, with a hundred caveats, to her wish to attend the fall semester at Tulane. First, however, she must spend the summer at the compound.

When barely a teenager, and she first set eyes on Seth, she felt an inexplicable pull. She tried to ignore the attraction because he was Selene's younger brother, and she hated Selene. But his olive skin and black eyes mesmerized her. His strong muscled arms held her, hands stroking her body, while his mouth covered every inch of her skin, giving her pleasure she'd only dreamed about. He teased her, played with her for hours, bringing her to the height of excitement. When he entered her, the world exploded in unimaginable ecstasy.

The summer turned into more than a year when she got pregnant, which was the group's plan all along. She put college on hold to have Seth's baby. Such a beautiful baby boy, with Seth's dark skin and her bright blue eyes. After a few months, they took the baby from her and she went back to school. A repeat performance the summer before her junior year produced a daughter. She couldn't resist Seth's magnetism.

"I want to see our children."

"They're beautiful," he said, "especially the girl. She looks like you."

He moved into her, so close his hardness pushed against her. "Come here to stay, Maia. I've missed you."

The words were empty platitudes, but he made them sound believable. She had loved her babies and had loved Seth in earnest, not realizing at the time that to him she was just another incubator for the new generation.

One of his many incubators.

Chapter Thirty
Gods and Goddesses

"You asked for a rundown on the progeny," Jason said when he called Lucier back, "but first, you asked about the college the group's children attended."

"Give," Lucier said, grabbing a pencil from atop his desk and readying a pad of paper. "I'm taking notes."

"No need. I'll fax you everything when this call is finished."

"Better," Lucier said.

"Middlebridge's endowment is huge, and the biggest benefactors are Crane Corporation and Compton International. It has a small student body and promotes a basic liberal arts curriculum, and I do mean liberal."

"Explain please."

"You wanted to know if it was a religious college. I didn't find any courses in religion, but the curriculum covers just about everything else—literature, art, mythology, world cultures, even erotica. The tuition is double the top private colleges, which keeps the elite enrollment small. Besides the group's offspring, children of others in the same financial stratosphere as Crane and Compton's go there. Excellent avant-garde and progressive professors in the artsy subjects, and only one has a direct connection to our man. He used to teach an abstract reasoning course at Oklahoma, where Compton went to school. He's old now but still considered a giant in his field. The sons and daughters of our subjects graduated with very high GPAs."

"I would have thought there'd be a right-wing lean, but it doesn't seem that way."

"Not so sure," Jason said. "The political science professors tend to be Libertarian and Conservative, but, as I said, the other courses lean socially left. Go figure."

"Interesting but not surprising. What happens when they graduate?"

"Here's where it gets strange, because I haven't been able to fill in the blanks."

"What do you mean?" Lucier asked.

"Some of the sons and daughters are supposedly off doing humanitarian work overseas for the family foundations. They've filed IRS forms, but their income is listed as stock dividends or interest from inheritances, and their addresses are the same as their parents. They have no records of employment, credit cards with no charges, and are without debt. Nothing more I can track."

"I see what you mean."

"Of the six progeny of Phillip Crane, Seth is the only one I can't account for. He's one of the out-of-the-country people. You know about the Crane women, and the oldest son, David, runs Crane Corporation. He's married, has three children, all grown, oldest in the business; the other two are in the missing column. The other families follow the same pattern. Martin Easley's son Cal is the only other child of a first marriage I can't account for."

"What the hell's going on?"

"I'm just the messenger, Lieutenant," Jason said. "I'm curious about the answers myself. My fax will contain an exact breakdown of the family trees, their history, et cetera. But the only second marriage with no traceable children is Silas and Selene Compton."

"Which makes Selene an oddity of the group."

"Yeah. An article about Jeremy Haynesworth said his son and daughter were off doing humanitarian work overseas. That's the same story the others say when asked."

"Damn, I'd love to get my hands on their passports. See whether they've really left the country. I doubt they have."

"Why? Where do you think they are?"

"Damned if I know, but my gut instinct says they're not where they're saying they are. I've used up my supply of hunches lately." He tapped his pen on the empty pad of paper. "Is that it?"

"For now. I'll let you know if I find out anything else."

"Hey, thanks a lot. Great work. I'm just not sure what to do with it."

"Can't help you there. You're the cop. I'll fax this to Diana so it doesn't go through your office. Is that all right?"

"Perfect."

"Tell her I love her."

"Wait in line, buddy."

"As a friend, Lieutenant. Wish I were competition."

Lucier laughed and hung up. He leaned back in his chair and scratched his head. What the hell.

* * * * *

By the time he arrived at Diana's that evening, Jason had faxed his report and Diana had read it.

"This is major strange," she said, "especially about the name changes. Which got me thinking." She handed Lucier the pad of paper she had in front of her.

"More crosswords?"

"No, research. Look at these names. Cybele, Selene, Maia

and Dione. I went online and typed in the names. Are you ready? Cybele—a fertility goddess, mother of the gods; Selene—moon goddess, known for her countless love affairs; Maia—impregnated by Zeus in the dead of night while all the other gods slept; Dione—the mother of Aphrodite by the big guy again, Zeus. These women are all named for mythological figures."

"Jason figured that out, but it made no sense to me. Maia and Dione—you're not thinking Compton, a very Zeus-like character, did the dirty with his own daughters, are you?"

"Nothing would surprise me anymore. Compton's a megalomaniac. I wouldn't put anything past him. Did you see Maia the other night? Not the most outgoing, is she? And the deal she pulled with those two hoodlums. She hates her father, and Selene, too. Again, why? There's more here than meets the eye."

"There's no indication that Compton did anything with those women. Selene isn't a woman who'd share her man with his daughters."

"Selene's either a sexual predator or she's a big tease. I'll go with my first impression. Selene and her sisters are all gorgeous and not as dumb as they wanted us to think. My father would call them stacked. Not a bad description either. Like the two girls, Brigid and Nona." Diana tapped her pencil. "Oh, and I mentioned Nona is the goddess of pregnancy in Roman mythology, but Brigid is the goddess of childbirth. Now doesn't that ring your bells even a little?"

Lucier scanned her notes more carefully. "So we have disappearing people, satanic elements, stolen babies with IQs that will probably soar off the charts when they're grown, lots of voluptuous women, and mythological gods and goddesses." He fell back into the sofa's cushions. "This is way over my head. What do you think?"

"I don't know, but it's not good."

"I'd need a hell of a lot more to question Silas Compton than your mythology research."

Diana pointed to the names in the notebook. "Don't you see? Mythology is all mixed up in this."

"That proves my point about your Brother Osiris. Another mythological name."

"Would you stop saying he's mine. You know why he picked that particular name."

"Yeah, because he has no—"

"Stop! Don't say it. He had cancer, for God's sakes. It's not like he chose the name without reason. And the name Seth, Crane's son and Selene's brother—the one who's supposedly doing *humanitarian* work overseas? I remembered what Cash found at the beginning of this case and looked it up. Seth was the brother of Osiris, the one who killed him."

Heat prickled Lucier's skin. Rubbing his scalp, he said, "I want you to leave New Orleans and go to South Carolina to stay with your parents."

She jerked back and scowled. "Don't be ridiculous. I wouldn't miss what's going to happen for the world."

"We don't know what's going to happen."

"That's exactly why I wouldn't miss it. Besides, Silas Compton called. He wants to set up a time when I can read the group."

Lucier's breath caught. "I hope you said no."

"I did at first. Then he said he'd donate a million dollars to any hospitals or charities I chose." She shrugged, a mischievous glint in her eyes. "I couldn't turn that down, could I?"

Chapter Thirty-One
Temptation

Maia sat at the dining room table reserved for the elders. No point in being stubborn. She was starved, and she ate with unabashed relish. "Great food, as always," she said. "Healthy and plentiful."

"Why did you do it, Maia?" Seth asked, fixing his magnetic eyes on her. "You had to know what would happen."

Avoiding his gaze didn't relieve the unnerving effect of his penetrating stare. Steeling herself, she faced him. "Those babies were kidnapped. How can you condone that?"

"I don't, but my father says we need other genetic material. We've tried to keep certain of the youth apart. I've segregated some of them because there were…problems. Even a—" Seth turned away, either unable or unwilling to look at her.

"Even a what?" Maia asked.

"A brother and sister—"

"Oh, my God," Maia said, cutting him off. Her food, delicious just moments before, now rose in her throat like spoiled leftovers. She stood and paced the perimeter of the room. "What are we doing, Seth?"

"I stopped them before it happened a second time. Fortunately, nothing…took." He looked at her apologetically. "Animal attraction is difficult to control."

"If anyone should know that it's you. I'm the perfect example."

"I know you'll find this hard to believe, but you're the only one I've impregnated. Oh, I've engaged in other sexual liaisons. I am human, after all. But my only children are your children."

Did she believe him? Did it matter? "Yes, and the last time you drugged me. I'm not a baby machine. I didn't want another child taken from me as soon as I'd given it sustenance. You can't imagine how painful that is." Tears flooded her eyes. *Damn.* "You raped me, Seth." She brushed the back of her hand across her cheek to wipe away a tear.

"I'm sorry." He brushed away another tear.

"Your job may be to make babies; it's not mine."

Seth didn't speak for a while. "After you left—after the last time we were together—I've been only an organizer because my sperm didn't take with anyone else. They even harvested it, but nothing happened. There's nothing wrong, but…" his gaze locked on Maia's, "I can only succeed with you."

Heat engulfed Maia's body as if flames licked around her, searing her flesh. "This has to stop. You must know that."

"We're in too deep. Our culture has been taught from birth, drilled into us. Rejecting everything we know is going against family. Against my father and mother, against my sister—your mother."

Maia bolted to her feet. "Selene is not my mother. My mother threw herself out a window because life was too unbearable, and *your sister* waited in the wings with her talons sharpened to drag my father into this abomination. It's the old story of Faust, isn't it? Sell your soul to the devil for riches. But this story has a twist—sex. Then one day the devil calls in his marker. Am I my father's marker, Seth? Am I?"

"Stop!" Seth tipped over his chair when he got up. "This compound can't be exposed. The world wouldn't understand our ways."

"Do you understand? I grew up in it too. Not from birth like you, but early enough to be indoctrinated. I bought into the whole package until I was forced to have a third child. Then I found out about the kidnappings. It's one thing to keep our ways within the group, quite another to destroy the lives of others by stealing their babies. Don't you see how wrong this is?"

Seth raked his fingers through his hair. Frustration etched his handsome face, the lines deepening. But he kept silent.

"I know the agony of having my baby torn from my breast. Now we're doing it to innocent people. People who weren't brought up like we were. They're in pain and we're the cause. We must put an end to this."

"Don't say that to anyone else, Maia. As much as I'd like to keep you here, I want you to stay because you want to, not because the leaders forbid you to leave."

"You'll tell what I said because duty is burned into your brain, just as fucking is. They'll never let me go. Not unless you help me. The kidnapped babies must be returned to their parents."

"I need time to think."

He's wavering. Could he finally see the evil?

"They'll do whatever it takes to stop me. Even my father." Seth snorted. "Especially my father. Once I break the code, everything's over. For everyone. You know as well as I that sex and riches are powerful incentives. Incentives my father and his father before him used to recruit the others."

"People literally sell their souls to the devil, don't they? Just like we did."

"We had no choice. Besides, Satan is no different than any other god. Instead of guilt, we have pleasure. How can that be wrong? How can love be wrong?" He moved toward her, traced his fingertips around her nipple. "It wasn't wrong between us, and you know it."

Her skin tingled from his touch, excitement shimmered down her spine. "No," she said, pushing him away. She couldn't do this, but she was already limp in his presence. She mustn't fall under his spell again. "Please, Seth, no. I can't."

"I know you want me," he said, moving even closer. "I hear your heartbeat, feel the tremors when I touch you."

His hot whispers in her ear sent pulses to her sex. *I have to resist him.* "I can't. Please stop," she begged. "Please."

He backed away, the hand that caressed her frozen in midair. "I want to make love to you more than anything else in the world."

Seth always had power over her, ever since they were children. She wanted to believe him, but he was a trained seducer, like his sister. "I suppose you'd keep me here forever, making your babies."

"It would be my pleasure, but only if you want to. I won't force you again. I promise."

"I can't do anything until the stolen babies are returned. I won't."

He shook his head, but said nothing.

"What about Anat?" Maia asked. "Will you keep her locked up forever? She's your niece, Selene's daughter, my father's daughter, my half-sister. She and Cal were the only ones who fought the evil from the beginning."

"There was no evil here until the new babies. Just love. As for Anat, she's well cared for. She has everything she needs, and she has her baby."

"What?" Maia said, her voice pitched high. "Did you drug her too?"

"Honestly? I don't know how it happened or with whom. I told her with her beauty and brilliance she'd have to conceive sooner or later. She has visitors. I'd say Cal Easley, but I don't think so for other reasons. If she knows whose baby it is, she's not telling, and her visitors say she didn't have sex with them. One of them is lying." He turned to her. "Maybe you can find out."

Even if she found out, Maia wouldn't tell Seth. Anat, beautiful Anat. So different from Maia. "Let me see her, and I demand to see my children." She paused. "Our children."

* * * * *

Selene sidled next to Silas into the cushy down of the sofa and flung one long leg over the other. "Do you really think Maia will behave, Silas? She hasn't been herself lately."

"What do you want me to do? Lock her up like Anat and throw away the key?"

She coyly twirled a strand of hair around her finger. "It's an idea."

Selene's tone indicated she was joking, but Silas knew her too well to be taken in. "A month or two at the compound will do the trick."

"If Seth can't handle her we might have to resort to something drastic. He's the only one who holds sway over her. She can't resist him."

"That's because the Cranes are irresistible, my dear, but even Seth may have trouble this time, like last. She doesn't want another child. Not even with your baby brother."

"Wait and see."

"I can't keep her locked up. I won't. No one knows about Anat and the others, but Maia has a job. She has a life, such as it is. Dione's sister will ask questions. Do I tell my other daughter her sister won't be coming back?"

"What if some nosy reporter starts digging? Not to mention Diana Racine and her cop lover, especially after that fiasco with those two street thugs. They could blow everything to bits. We can't allow that to happen. We have to control them."

"We will, but first things first."

"Is that why you're arranging these readings?"

"Of course. She's Diana, Goddess of the Moon, daring and curious, unable to resist tempting fate. It's as much a part of her as her gift. Besides, your father wants her."

"I don't know why. She's such a puny little thing with none of the attributes to make a man happy."

"Phillip doesn't want her like that. Your mother would never consent to another woman." He slid his hand into the warm notch between her legs. "Is that all you think about?"

"Yes. Pleasing a man has been my destiny since the day I was born, just like my mother from her birth. I don't hear any complaints from you, considering your hand is in my crotch."

"Because you're irresistible."

Selene inched closer until she was almost on top of him. She unbuttoned his shirt and eased her hand inside. "If Daddy wants Diana Racine, he shall have her. And I shall have you. Isn't that what you want, darling?" She buried her face into his chest, nibbling his nipples, biting hard until she drew blood, which she sucked with unabashed delight.

"Oooh, yesss," Compton murmured, pain stimulating the swelling in his loins. "Angel of Darkness, what you do makes me crazy."

She stood up and slipped out of her skirt and blouse, revealing skin the color of rich cream and breasts that swelled over a low-cut lacy black bra. She wore no panties. "Relax," she purred, "and let me pleasure you."

"You're so cruel. I'm about to burst, but you know that." Compton's eyes closed and his head lolled back in ecstasy. "You beautiful witch," he said, reaching around her back to the snaps on her bra. Her skin felt like the velvet touch of an orchid petal on his fingertips, and he caressed her back in long strokes as he inhaled the sweet scent of sex. She pulled back, as she always did, teasing him into desiring more. Leaving him breathless.

"I saw the way that cop looked at you the other night. I saw his hard-on. He couldn't resist you any more than I can."

"Hmm, I'm not so sure," she said, stroking herself. "I think he was playing the game."

"You found him attractive, didn't you?"

"Yes. The color of his skin, his strange, exotic eyes. He's an incredibly sexy man. What's more irresistible is he doesn't seem to know it."

"And you wanted him."

"Yes. I liked the way he moved, like a cat. I imagine he'd be an excellent partner in bed. Does that turn you on?"

"Thinking of you with a man outside our group has an erotic effect on me. I could watch you fuck him, but then I'd have to kill him. I couldn't let anyone live who had taken you." He drew her near, put his lips to her breasts, then his tongue, then his teeth. Her moan hinted of pain but also pleasure, and he felt himself grow harder.

"The thought of you killing someone over me makes me want you more, because no one satisfies me the way you do. Am I not enough for you?"

He took in the beauty of her form. "You're worthy of the gods."

She stood and stretched him on the sofa, tugged off his trousers, and tickled her fingers over the length of his now naked body. Teasing his erection, she watched him shudder. He reached for her. "Not yet, baby."

She strolled to a chest against the wall and opened the top drawer. Along with a pair of handcuffs, she extracted a ring-like contraption and a flogger. She smiled at the look of anticipation on his face when she turned him over and cuffed his wrists behind him.

"Now I'll make you forget everything else, including your wayward daughter." She began what would take hours to finish.

Chapter Thirty-Two
The Agenda

"I'm not surprised the reading will take place on the night of the crescent moon," Lucier said, placing a bowl of vegetable pasta in front of Diana. "The obvious timing seems more like a warning to stay away than a temptation for you to go."

"Why?"

"I don't know, but if you insist on going, you're not going without me."

"Don't worry. I wouldn't."

Lucier emitted an under-the-breath scoff.

Spearing a wedge of zucchini, she said, "I know what you're thinking."

"Right. You trotted off before without backup. Twice. That hardly makes you trustworthy."

"Not fair. I had good reason."

"What about getting into Compton's car?"

"That…that—"

"Exactly."

"These people have already tricked me. It won't happen again."

"Damn right," Lucier said. "I don't suppose Slater will be there, will he?"

"I didn't ask, but I wouldn't count him out. He'd never let me read him, though. He's never let me touch him."

"I thought you told me you did. You lied."

"A tiny white lie so you'd leave him alone." Diana caught Lucier's furtive glance. He was jealous of Slater, and her fib didn't help. A moment of guilt fluttered through her for deceiving him, but another part of her thought his reaction kind of sweet. She'd never been jealous before she met Lucier, and no one had ever been jealous over her.

"You think if I touched him, the same thing that happened with Compton would happen with him, don't you?"

"You mean you'd see your hand turn black and skeletal? I don't know, but I bet he'd pass something to you, which is why he's stayed out of your reach."

"He'd have to let down his defenses."

"Compton couldn't have wanted to transmit to you, yet he did."

Was Compton so arrogant he'd passed his evil to her on purpose? "Maybe he forced the image into my mind to observe my reaction. No law officer in the word would or could act on an image or vision, nor would a judge or jury accept them as fact. My so-called nightmare? I'd have the courtroom in stitches."

Lucier swirled linguine onto his fork. "I'm going to try to talk to Dione Compton. She and her sister are close. If she's convinced something's happened to Maia, she might talk."

"Don't bet the farm. She's more afraid of Silas than she is of harm to her sister. Or…"

"Or what?"

"Or maybe it's Selene she's afraid of." Diana sipped her iced tea. "Something about that woman gets under my skin."

"She was the perfect hostess."

"Yeah, to you. She ignored me."

"So she's a man's woman. Lots of women are."

Diana kept her silence. Lucier was right. What man

wouldn't respond to a woman who threw her lean, shapely body at him like Selene did to Lucier. If she said anything, he'd call her jealous again. She almost laughed. These were devious people, and they brought out the worst in Lucier *and* her. Jealousy, suspicion, subterfuge. If they were playing Compton's game, they were sure learning fast.

"Besides," Lucier continued, "Compton lassoed you as soon as you got through the door."

"I think they followed a divide and conquer agenda."

"They won't the next time. When you're not reading one of them, I'll be right by your side."

* * * * *

Getting through to Dione Compton was like tracking down the President of the United States on his Blackberry. Lucier convinced the operator at Compton International that he was an old friend from Tulane in town for the day and wanted to surprise Dione. She took the call.

"Very sneaky, Lieutenant." Dione said when Lucier identified himself.

"Sorry, I didn't think it was a good idea to leave my name."

"That depends. What can I do for you?"

"I'd like to talk to you about your sister."

A beat of silence. "Maia is in the Middle East taking care of a problem for the company."

"I don't believe she is, and I don't believe you think so either."

"I really have to go, Lieutenant. I shouldn't be talking to you. If you think Maia is in trouble you need to speak to my father."

"You know that's exactly who I shouldn't speak to, Ms. Compton. Maia's life could be in danger."

A longer silence. Lucier thought she hung up.

"Café du Monde, nine-thirty tomorrow morning."

The line went dead.

* * * * *

Lucier strolled through Jackson Square, teeming with tourists even at the early hour. He arrived at the Café du Monde before the arranged time, took a chair outside, and ordered coffee and a beignet. After dusting off some of the powdered sugar and sinking his teeth into the doughy confection, he spotted Dione Compton striding toward the café. She was a little shorter than her sister and possessed the same good looks—long blonde hair, lovely figure. The man following her never let his eyes wander from his prey. Lucier tossed a bill on the table, sprang up, and headed in her direction to ward off any obviously planned contact.

He spoke loud enough for everyone to hear. "Why, Ms. Compton, how nice to see you again." Without changing expression, he said sotto voce, "You're being followed. Say hello and go inside the restaurant as if nothing unusual happened. Don't turn around. I'll be in touch."

"Nice to see you, too, Lieutenant…Lucier, isn't it?"

"Yes." He tipped his head. "Time to go to work. Bye now."

"Goodbye," Dione said, and went inside without missing a beat.

Lucier clicked a mental photo of Dione Compton's shadow. Six feet, thinning hair, average looks, medium build, off-the-rack suit—nothing to set him apart from hundreds of others. Unfortunately, there was nothing average looking about Lucier. His mixed-blood skin, hazel eyes, and light brown hair left an image easily remembered. The Shadow returned the same scrutiny as he passed.

Damn. The last thing he wanted was to get Dione

Compton in trouble. Best to go on the offense. When he got back to the station, he called Silas Compton.

Lucier's name must have been on a list of acceptable callers because the operator transferred him to Compton's private line.

"Lieutenant, what can I do for you?" Compton said.

"I wanted to make sure you were okay with me accompanying Diana to your house for the reading. Between you and me, she's been a bit clingy since her nightmarish experience. I'm sure you understand."

Compton let his prolonged silence answer. No, he didn't understand. More specifically, he didn't like someone trapping him, but he wouldn't say so.

"Of course," Compton said, "although I can't imagine why she'd be uptight around us. Actually, I assumed you'd be with her. Since each reading will be private, you'll have plenty of company. If the men bore you, Selene will see you're entertained."

I'll bet. "Great. Thanks. Is Edward Slater coming?"

"I invited him, but he declined. Even though Edward's interests are eclectic, he'd never let himself be exposed in that way. He keeps his life pretty close to his vest."

Lucier presumed that Compton executed a complete background check on Brother Osiris before he parted with his money.

"Oh, by the way, I bumped into your daughter this morning at Café du Monde. You have two beautiful daughters, Mr. Compton. You must be pleased with their accomplishments. I'm sure you rely on them."

"I do. They're exceptional young women. I'm proud of them."

"Any idea when Maia will return?"

"She's still in negotiations. Maia hasn't taken a vacation in a couple of years and mentioned traveling a little after she settles our business. She may be gone for a few months. Dione will take care of her duties."

"I see," Lucier said. "I never asked, and if I'm out of line, just say so, but I don't recall you and Mrs. Compton mentioning children. Do you have any together?"

Compton's voice lowered. "My wife miscarried a few times. We decided not to pursue trying further due to the risk on her health. It's our greatest regret. Any children of Selene's would be quite special."

"I'm sure. She's a beautiful woman."

"And an incurable flirt. I hope you didn't take her attention too seriously."

"I was flattered, but Diana is enough for me to handle."

Compton laughed. "We both have strong partners, Ernie, but doesn't that make life more interesting?"

"Most definitely."

"Until the fifteenth, you take care of yourself."

"In my business that's the best anyone can hope for. See you on the fifteenth, *Silas*."

He did it again, called Compton by his first name. It was as if a little gremlin inside his head took over, and he couldn't help himself. The man was as slick as black ice.

Now if he could only secure a meeting with Dione Compton without her father's tail.

* * * * *

"Let the two boys go, Sam," Lucier said. "We've kept them here too long. They don't want to leave. Why should they? Three squares and a bed. We can charge them with unlawful entry, but they're the only ones claiming they entered Compton's house unlawfully. Even the guard who supposedly pulled a gun had no idea what I was talking about when I questioned him."

Lucier made a sound that crossed a whistle with a sigh. "Without Maia Compton we can't get them for anything more."

"Betcha even if she was here, she'd say she never saw them before," Beecher said. "It was a sting gone bad, and these two con artists were the dupes."

"Right, and if I pursue the matter further, I'd be calling Compton a liar. He said Maia left two days before this happened, and I have no doubt he could prove it. I hate to think money can buy anything, but that's the way it is, isn't it? The rich get away with murder."

"Kidnapping babies, too," Beecher said.

Lucier hated to agree. If Compton hosted a satanic gathering, it was over twenty seconds after those two so-called art thieves fled the scene. "As abhorrent as the idea of a satanic ritual is, it's not illegal. We need to connect Compton and his group with the kidnappings. The key is Dione."

Lucier tried to get through to her again, using the old school chum front, but Ms. Compton wasn't taking any calls today from anyone, her secretary said. Sorry. He hung up the phone feeling trapped.

The fifteenth was a few days away. Whatever they had planned for Diana and him, he'd better be one step ahead.

Chapter Thirty-Three
A Tearful Reunion

Maia clutched the three children in her arms while Seth watched. In less than six months they had grown and changed.

"They're more beautiful than I remembered." Phillip, named for his grandfather, held back, reserved. Why wouldn't he? He hardly knew her. A few times a year for a couple of days was a second in time to a ten-year old. He was a clone of his father—tall for his age, with eyes as black as onyx, olive skin and black hair. She spoke to him, but he answered in one-syllable words. When she pulled him close, he resisted.

"Have you forgotten me already?" she asked.

He looked toward his father, as if asking permission to speak. "No," he said softly.

"You're not afraid of me, are you?"

Again, a furtive glance at Seth. "No."

That's all she could get from him. He backed away, but he didn't go to Seth either. He stood as if disconnected from all the others. It wasn't shyness but something else. Something she couldn't put her finger on. Her heart broke.

Iris responded more effusively. At six, she was a heartbreaker, with slightly lighter coloring, blonde hair, and eyes that matched her name—a combination to make hearts flutter. She was all girl, and Maia could see the indoctrination in full nurture. She played her father like a woman, batting her long lashes and cajoling to get what she wanted. Oh, yes, Iris was the perfect little temptress.

Three-year old Leo—a mixture of both parents, had the blackest hair and bluest eyes and Maia's pale skin. She named him Leo because he fought with the strength of a lion to be born, in spite of her fighting against his conception. Unlike the others, he clung to her fiercely, and she held him, caressing his soft velvet skin, breathing in his little boy scent.

Maia's eyes filled with tears from the emotional response, which convinced her even more that the stolen babies must be returned to their birth parents.

A beautiful young girl around the age of twelve came into the room and beckoned the children to follow for their lunch. Maia knew she was the granddaughter of Martin Easley. The rule was never before sixteen, so this adolescent, already showing the buds of puberty, would enjoy a few years of innocence before she was with a child of her own. Still too young, unless, in desperation, the rules had changed. Maia had been nineteen, Dione eighteen before they gave birth the first time. Brigid and Nona were younger. She clung to Leo as long as she could before he was tugged away. Tears now fell without shame as she crouched empty-armed.

She needed her children to be part of her life.

Seth came up behind her, lifted her, and pulled her close, cupping her breasts. He spoke, breath hot in her ear. "Seeing you with the children convinced me you belong here, with them and with me. Can't you see how right it is?"

She literally fell back into his arms, weak with despair. Everything here was so far from right. Why had she never seen it before?

Seth turned her around into his arms. She felt safe with his strength wrapped around her. How could she find comfort with him? But she did. She always had. He pressed against her, and the ache of need overwhelmed her. She tightened her hold.

"I want you so much, Maia. Just breathing you in fills my senses." His lips covered hers.

She parted them to let his tongue touch hers at the same time he unbuttoned her blouse and reached around back to unsnap her bra. As much as she wanted to fight against him, she couldn't ignore the sparks his caress ignited. Gently, his fingers grazed her body. Desire filled her. This was what she was groomed for, willingly or not, wasn't it? she asked herself as he led her to her room, to her bed. She was a fertility goddess in his hold, without choice, without will.

"You're still the most beautiful." He undressed her as if she were made of fine porcelain, removing each article of clothing with tenderness, stroking her skin. Free from her restrictions, her training took over, and she caressed herself because she knew it made him want her more. He shed his clothes in the golden light, his dark skin glistening, a man whose confidence rippled in his lean, muscular body. His erection pressed hard against her thigh as he lay down beside her.

From the beginning, Seth's control amazed her. She'd never been with another and could make no comparisons, but her sister spoke of other men's eagerness. Seth always took his time, pleasuring her first before satisfying himself. He fulfilled his training, too, for men were taught to give as much as they received, lest a woman wouldn't respond.

He kissed her neck and bit the lobe of her ear. "I'm sorry about the last time, Maia. At risk of sounding like a wartime underling, I was only following orders. I hated taking you and fought against the deception, but it was your fertile time. Will you forgive me?"

"I'll never forgive you for not standing your ground, Seth. It was beneath you."

"I know now. Forcing you changed me forever. Please believe me."

"I believe you because it makes no sense for you to lie. You have me in bed, where you want me."

"Let's put the past behind us. This is another time. I love you, Maia. I always have."

She flung her leg around his middle, moving into his power. "Make love to me, Seth."

Yes, she loved him, but she would never bear him another child. She'd made sure of that.

Chapter Thirty-Four
An Unthinkable Conclusion

As much as Lucier tried to concentrate on his work, all he could think of was Diana. The desk phone's ring brought him back to the present, to his office and the ongoing cases strewn across his desk.

"I'm calling from my cell phone, Lieutenant," Dione Compton said. "I don't believe my father fell for your story of running into me at Café du Monde because I'm still being watched."

"Can you lose your tail?" Lucier asked.

"Not without raising suspicion. Ever since Maia pulled that stunt on July Fourth, I've been chauffeur-driven. My father is treating me like a child and I don't like it. Not at my age."

Did she realize she just verified the break-in? *Forget it, Ernie. She'd deny she said it.* "Is only one person following you?"

"I think so. He's the same man you saw the other morning. Do you think any harm has come to Maia?"

"You know your family better than I. What do you think?"

"She's not on a business trip. She would have told me."

"Any idea where she is?"

Dione hesitated. "Um, yes…and no."

"What does that mean? You either know or you don't."

"It's more complicated. I'll have to think about this. If my father finds out I've talked to you, I'll be sent away too."

"Sent away where?" Lucier persisted. She didn't answer. "What they're doing is wrong, Ms. Compton. Practicing the occult is one thing; kidnapping babies is something else entirely."

"Oh, God."

"Ms. Compton?" He waited.

"I knew nothing about the babies. They've been suspicious of Maia for some time, and because we're close, they've excluded us from their plans. Now, because of what she did, they're circling me like buzzards over road kill."

"Your father is looking at a long prison sentence. So is everyone else involved."

A long silence hung in the air before Dione Compton spoke. "My father isn't in charge."

"Then who? Your stepmother?"

"I've said too much already. Give me time to think. I'll tell you this. Something is in the wind. Watch out for Ms. Racine."

Lucier's nerve endings went on full alert. "What? What are they going to do?"

"I don't know."

"Can you find out?"

"I'll try, but I doubt I'll be privy to the information. They don't trust me now. That's evident by my bloodhound."

"If you feel you're in danger, I'll pick you up and put you in protective custody."

"Not yet, Lieutenant. Let me see what I can find out. I'll get back in touch."

"Ms. Compton."

"Yes?"

"I'm going to give you my private number. Memorize it and then empty the numbers in your cell."

He did, and she clicked off.

* * * * *

"Don't leave the house, Diana," Lucier said when he called. "You're on Compton's agenda, but Dione doesn't know what the agenda is."

"We'll find out in a few days, won't we?"

"I'll be over after work."

"I'm trying out a new recipe. Pork chops, apples and sweet potatoes."

"Sounds, um, interesting. Like I've always said, home cooking is better than a frozen dinner."

Diana hung up the phone and went back to the kitchen. Except for a couple of minor tiffs, she and Lucier fit together like two pieces of the same puzzle. She loved having him around, loved their intimate moments.

The only drawback was whether she'd transferred from one over-protective man to another. From the shelter of her parents to the safety of Lucier. She'd never experienced true independence. Love came along and she'd have been foolish to cast it off for…for what? Being alone? Is that what independence was? Why would she? She'd done everything she wanted. Traveled the world, experienced things few women, single or partnered, had the opportunity to experience. What more was there?

She laughed out loud when she faced the two sweet potatoes on the cutting board. Learning to cook, that's what. Number one on her personal list of things to do. Hopefully, she wouldn't poison her lover in the process. She picked up the peeler and attacked the rough skin of the sweet potato with single-minded determination.

Hmm, the doorbell. *I'm not expecting anyone.* She wiped her hands on the towel and fingered open the window blind. Her heart rate accelerated. She opened the door.

Edward Slater held out a small bouquet of flowers. "Peace offering?"

Chapter Thirty-Five
A Little Background Music

Lingering over coffee at the dinner table that evening, Diana noticed Lucier's distraction. Something was on his mind he seemed unwilling to share. She didn't prod. He'd get to it eventually. When he read the fax Jason sent with the information about the group's backgrounds, he did.

"Everyone in the group other than Crane grew up poor as dirt. Fernando Reyes's parents were migrant workers who came over the Texas border from Mexico; Martin Easley was raised by his mother after his father was killed by the police in a botched arrest; and Jeremy Haynesworth's father was a drunk—his mother cleaned houses to eke out an existence. All of them were brilliant and found a way to pay for college—their way out of hell."

Out of one hell and into another, Diana thought.

"They all worked for someone else and made their bosses a lot of money with their ideas or patents," Lucier continued, his brow furrowed in thought. "Not one reaped financial benefits personally until they hooked up with either Compton or Crane."

Diana listened. Coming from humble circumstances herself, she found the background stories of those climbing the ladder of success interesting.

"Compton's story is similar. Poor but hardworking parents. He had a head for business and driving ambition. He also married well—twice. His first wife's father, Senator Gault Fannon, wasn't rich, but he enjoyed a spotless reputation. What he had were connections."

"There's a switch," Diana said. "An honest politician. Or is that an oxymoron?"

Lucier played with the remainder of a sweet potato on his plate, seemingly oblivious to her remark.

"So Compton married well," she said, trying to get him back on track. "What happened?"

He looked up as if he suddenly remembered she was there and continued to explain the gossip about Fannon and the votes for the government contract that put Compton on the map. "Married well, but not as well as marrying into the Crane family." Lucier related the phone conversation he had with Dione Compton. "She knows more than she's willing to tell right now."

"Once she does, the whole thing will be out in the open. I can't imagine she'd expose her family unless she fears for either her life or her sister's."

"Compton sent Maia somewhere," Lucier said. "Ralph Stallings is trying to unravel the properties owned by Compton's conglomerate, but there's so much corporate finagling it'll take awhile. I'll update my request to include Crane's holdings."

"You know, Ernie, the property could be in the name of one of the others or their wives. Since they're all related, it might be joint property."

"Dione said her father wasn't the one in charge. That leaves Crane, the granddaddy of the group, and I bet his holdings are more convoluted than Compton's. These guys know how to tangle business so you can't find what they don't want you to find. We'd be hard pressed to uncover the mystery location before the night of the crescent moon or before Dione Compton disappears if they find out she's talked to me."

"Can't you pick her up?"

"She said no protective custody. Not yet. She's not ready to turn herself over to us and expose her family's shenanigans until she finds out more. There may be more children involved than just the kidnapped babies."

"You mean all the kids from the group's second families who are *working overseas*?"

"Exactly," Lucier said. "Cal Easley and Seth Crane are the only ones missing from a first wife, and Cybele Crane is the only first wife still around."

"Maybe they're in charge of wherever they are," Diana said. "All these sons and daughters working out of the country doing humanitarian work is a little much."

"If they have kids, the numbers could be more than we first thought."

"Have you checked passports?"

"Stallings did. Their passports confirmed they're where they said. Destinations all over the place—Africa, Asia, in the most remote places. Crane's and Compton's foundations do valuable work overseas—no doubt about that—so the state department doesn't find any of this strange. The question is, are these sons and daughters where they're supposed to be. I don't think so. These companies have private jets and enough money to bribe officials, especially in third world countries."

"What if those people really are out of the country doing good deeds?" Diana asked.

"Then I'm wrong, but I don't think I am, and neither do you. The fear in Dione Compton's voice told me she knows enough to be in serious danger." He pushed aside his plate. "I hope she cleared her cell phone like I told her to."

"Even if you're right, Ernie, why the disappearing acts?"

"I'm not sure, but Crane is behind it. He picked those men. Offered them more riches than they could ever attain and daughters who'd make any man come just by looking at them. In exchange, they had to embrace his philosophy." Lucier pinched the bridge of his nose and shook his head. "Maybe he never mentioned the word Satan until later, calling it something else."

"Slater mentioned animism," Diana said. "A spiritual philosophy nothing like Satanism, but it might have worked as a stepping-stone to gently release those men from their own beliefs."

"I don't believe a man like Reyes, who must have been brought up Catholic, would chuck his religion and divorce his wife just like that. Not without a major case of guilt. Yet, that's what he did. Reyes, Haynesworth, and Easley all divorced and remarried a few years after going to work for either Crane or Compton."

"There has to be more." Something popped into Diana's mind. "This might be crazy, so hear me out. Question: what did all the kidnapped babies have in common?"

"Besides being taken by Deems or someone like him? They were all from super intelligent parents."

"Yes, and what else?"

"I don't want to play twenty questions. Just tell me. What?"

"I'm not sure where I'm going with this, but don't stop me until I finish." She got up from the table and paced. "Crane recruits brilliant men, right? All good-looking men too. Harder to notice when you're around their wives, but I noticed. He partners them with his beautiful, brilliant daughters." She reversed her pacing, barely noticing the quizzical expression on Lucier's face. "They create beautiful, brilliant children who scatter to different places, ostensibly to do good works."

The idea formed as she spoke, and the more she thought about it, the less crazy it sounded. She must have gone deep into thinking mode because the next thing she knew, Lucier was calling her name.

"Ego. It's all about ego." She pounded her fist into her palm as her thoughts gelled. "Listen. Besides wealth and beautiful women, what if Crane promised the men that their superior genes, joined with those of their brilliant, gorgeous wives—his daughters—would be the basis of a new society, first through their progeny, then through subsequent generations."

"You mean he's creating a master race? Didn't someone already try that?"

"Yes, but Hitler weeded out what he considered the less pure; Crane is creating the race from scratch. He chose those men for their intellectual and physical attributes. Compton was a no-brainer. He'd already proved he'd do anything to get ahead by marrying his first wife. Crane recognized that characteristic. He had his pick of the best and the brightest from both companies, mated them with his own offspring—daughters raised to please—ego again, then he mixed in the worship of money and uninhibited sex instead of God. When things didn't develop fast enough, he tossed in a few extra genius babies for good measure, and voilà, his own master race—a new culture, created with Crane genes."

Lucier scoffed. "It's too far-fetched. Those four women couldn't produce that many babies, and wouldn't they all be cousins or something?"

"Cousins removed with carefully distant inbreeding. Then

he employs surrogates, offers them money and a good life, and implants his daughters' eggs. Why not? Tell me what's wrong with the premise? Think what's happened over the last week or two. Remember, money is no object. Crane has geneticists in one of his companies. Scientists can be bought just like anyone else, especially if they can work on special projects. I'm hypothesizing. Tie it all together and it's diabolically plausible."

"A real stretch, Diana. Even if you're right, why Satan?"

She plopped down into her chair at the table. "I don't know. Something to bind them, a powerful feeling of belonging. That's what most religions offer. Maybe at first he explained it as their personal religion, without the demon aspect. In the end, the men rationalized to embrace guiltless hedonism and all the money they could ever want."

Lucier lifted his water glass and took a sip, his eyes focused on Diana. "He raised his daughters to seduce from birth, with Cybele as teacher. Even at sixty, she's competition to her daughters. I never had Jason check her history, but I bet her roots are similar to Crane's, and their small family affair turned global."

"Now they've taken a different path—a futuristic one," Diana said. "Maia and Dione went along because they didn't have a choice. Cults don't give you choices, and that's what this is. They've been brainwashed to become willing members, everything within the group, with no repercussions to outsiders. " She stopped, and both said the next sentence together…

"*Until the kidnapped babies.*"

"Maia bucked the system," Diana said, "now Dione Compton is scared because she's contemplating following in Maia's footsteps and going against everything she's been conditioned to believe. Whatever rituals the group participated in, whatever practices they followed, until those babies, they never broke the law."

"The root of all evil," Lucier said. "Then pleasure."

"Not so simple. To embrace Satanism, you first must deny God."

"Jesus," Lucier said.

"Him too."

Neither seemed interested in their food any longer. What if her hypothesis was correct? The thought frightened her, and for the first time since the Seaver baby disappeared, she understood why she'd interest Crane and Compton. Her genes. The unique gift for which she had been either blessed or cursed.

"The captain would laugh me out of the office."

Diana nodded in silent agreement. Who would believe such a radical idea?

"As far-fetched as I think your theory is, I can't ignore it," Lucier admitted. "Now to figure out what to do."

They cleared the table, took the dishes to the kitchen. Lucier's attention wandered to the coffee table. "Pretty flowers," he said. "Where did you get them?"

Diana glanced across the room. How would Lucier interpret Slater's visit? He was already suspicious where Slater was concerned. Besides, nothing happened but a mystical conversation. "One of the neighbors brought them from her garden. Wasn't that nice?"

Chapter Thirty-Six
The Seed of a Plan

Seth escorted Maia up the elevator to the fourth floor. Anat's building was one of two multi-storied structures in the compound, and she was the only occupant in it. He unlocked the door, and they stepped inside Anat's suite, outfitted with everything one needed for a comfortable imprisonment. Sofas covered in chintz, bookcases overflowing with reading matter, a complicated-looking sound system playing Mozart, and an in-house gym. Anat Crane lay stretched on a chaise on a large balcony, her arm curled around a beautiful toddler on her lap. She read to the child from a large picture book. Both acknowledged their guests with a smile.

Maia's half-sister was even more breathtakingly beautiful than she remembered. She saw her last a little more than a year ago. Anat favored Selene, only her features were softer, where Selene's were angular and sharp. She inherited the knockout body, though. Long and lean, with curves in all the right places, skin gleaming like burnished bronze from the sun.

Anat emerged from the womb with a streak of independence and defiance not acceptable to the group. She fought everything from the time she learned to speak. No one, not even Silas, could tame her mind. Gifted with an intelligence far exceeding those around her, she met every persuasion with a cogent and logical antithesis. Religion in general sapped the individual of reason, she said, and offering oneself to Satan to rationalize sexual pleasure was the height of perversion. No matter what indoctrination techniques they used, Anat resisted. She even drew some of the younger ones to her side, but she was quickly plucked from their presence. When she was no longer controllable, she was *separated*—a euphemism at the compound for luxuriously imprisoned, but only if you were a Compton, Crane, or from one of the main families. Other less important members in the group's tentacle-expanding assemblage received a month at *camp*. Just the threat of ostracism and the tactics used to bring one back into the fold squelched any potential uprisings.

Maia breathed a sigh of relief. Anat was too smart not to play along, as long as it served her purpose. She understood control because she'd been taught by the best.

Wearing shorts and a tank top, Anat swung her long legs off the chaise and placed the child in a playpen. The little girl picked up a book and opened it, pointing at the pictures and cooing words that were almost intelligible, never once with a whine on her lips. Anat patted her daughter's hair, then walked slowly toward Maia and threw her arms around her.

Maia kissed her and whispered in her ear, "How are you?"

Anat glanced at Seth and whispered back, "Bored, except for Chloe. Even though they forced the pregnancy, I can't imagine life without her. She's my beacon of light."

Maia stood back and studied her half-sister, ran her fingers through Anat's long sable hair. "You're beautiful," she said, then walked out to the balcony and crouched in front of the toddler, who lifted big blue eyes and grinned wide enough to show the few teeth poking through her gums. "She's a beauty, Anat."

"Smart, too." Anat turned to Seth. "Can we have some

time alone, please? I haven't seen Maia in a while, and I'd like to speak to her without you looking over our shoulders and listening to everything we say."

Seth shook his head. "You know I can't."

"Please, Seth," Maia said. "Don't be the obedient soldier for once."

"Maia, I—"

She locked gazes with Seth. "Please."

He bit his bottom lip. "Okay. For a while."

He left. Maia heard the key turn in the lock.

"Come onto the balcony," Anat whispered in Maia's ear and tugged her outside, closing the sliding glass door behind her. "There might be hidden microphones, but I haven't found them. Still, you can't be too careful. No camera, though. I've checked thoroughly. They hide cameras in the compound so they don't intimidate the children. They're afraid a Big Brother attitude might spawn another me." Anat grinned and walked to the balcony railing. She pointed to the vast forest. "A long-range camera could be aimed at the balcony." She waved, taunting the possibility. They settled into two chairs. "I play their game as best I can, Maia, and give them as much trouble as I can too."

"Even if there is a mike, there's no one for you to talk to."

Anat shrugged. "People visit. They need an okay from the boss, and they can only stay an hour, but they visit. Sometimes we write notes, like when I want something I'm not supposed to have."

"Like what?"

"Later. There are those here who help me when I ask. I don't do it often, because I don't want to get anyone in trouble. They let me keep Chloe because I swore I'd jump off the balcony if they didn't. Silas would never allow that. Nor would Selene, even though she doesn't understand how she produced such a genetic malfunction. Of course, I'd never jump because I'd be leaving my child to be raised like we were. That's unacceptable."

The large balcony jutted out twelve feet over a steep canyon of jagged rocks and white water rapids. A panorama of lush verdant hills and trees surrounded the compound. If there was a way down, Anat would have found it.

"What do you do all day?" Maia asked.

"Read, study, exercise, listen to music. I paint and write short stories too. I keep busy, and sometimes I don't know where the day goes. And most importantly, I play with Chloe." Anat looked at Maia. "Why are you here? Did you come to—"

"No," Maia said, shaking her head. "No more children." The reality of Anat's words settled hard in Maia's mind. Was this going to be her life too? Confined to living life in a vacuum? Anat had made the best of it. Could she?

Anat got up and leaned over the railing. Her voice brought Maia back from a place she didn't want to be. "Then? No, don't tell me. You finally spoke up and they shipped you off. It'd have to be you. Everyone else is incapable of making decisions for themselves." She looked off. "Except Cal. You know, Cal Easley. His suite is on the other side of the compound. Unlike me, he can roam freely. They don't think he has the guts to cause an uprising."

"How is he?"

"I see him at meetings they make us attend, and sometimes he visits. He works out and looks good. When I knew they were going to force me to have a child, I said I'd mate with Cal, but I guess they thought any offspring of ours would be worse than the two of us put together." She gazed at

Chloe. "Cal's gay, you know."

Maia rose and joined Anat. "No, I didn't."

"He's the smartest person here, but they won't harvest his sperm for fear *the gay,* as they call it, will be passed on. They must be pissed to pass on such rich genetic material."

Maia chuckled.

"Cal gets a perverse pleasure knowing that," Anat said.

"How strange, because I've never known the group to care if people are gay."

"No, as long as they're not part of *our* society."

Maia put her hand on Anat's arm. "Whose Chloe's father? Seth says you won't say."

"I won't. I don't want anyone using this baby against the father. There are a few of us with a remnant or two of independence. Please don't ask, Maia. Especially if you intend to tell Seth."

She'd never tell, but Anat didn't know that. "I wouldn't. I understand."

"Thank you." Anat offered a loving glance at Chloe. "What did you do to wind up here? Must have been a beaut."

"I almost blew the whole thing wide open, but I don't want to talk about that now. I should have done things differently. Better." Maia lowered her voice to a whisper. "Do you know about the kidnapped babies?"

"Yes. At first it was just gossip, a whisper. I didn't believe they'd do something so stupid. Then someone confirmed it. Cal tells me what's going on when he visits, as do others. I can't imagine anything worse. They're spitting in the face of the law because they don't think the law applies to them, that they're above it. Whose idea was that? Do you know?"

"Phillip's, of course. He's the Grand Master, and he's getting old. Time to speed things up. Dione and I didn't know anything about it until one of father's dutiful lapdogs got caught. Do you know about Deems?"

Anat nodded. "He killed himself rather than face kidnapping charges."

"Or be forced to tell on the group. I don't know how far they'd go to protect themselves these days. They've lost focus."

"Isn't that what happens with megalomaniacs?" Anat asked. "Damn. This has to stop. I'd do it, but I'm a little tied up. Even if I weren't, I have no idea where the hell we are. Someplace in Oklahoma, I think, but I'm not sure."

"They've done well keeping this place secret. I've tried to figure it out—two-hour plane trip, no ocean, mountains, but that could be a zillion places. When I learned about the babies, I should have gone to the police. You would have. Unfortunately, I'm not as brave. Now I won't have the chance because they won't let me go."

"Maybe they'll give you the suite downstairs," she said. "We could talk from the balconies."

"It's not funny, Anat. Our father is involved in something that could put him and the others in prison for life."

"Good."

Maia was taken aback by the hatred in Anat's voice.

Anat drew a deep breath and let it out slowly. "Have you seen what he's doing to Brigid and Nona, with my mother's blessing? They're nothing more than genetic material and wet nurses. And Silas, our…father, I wouldn't be surprised if—"

"If what?"

Anat clasped her hands around her neck and shook her head. "Never mind."

After Maia saw what her two half-sisters were doing, she banished those theories too perverse to give credence. She bet

Anat thought the same thing now.

"What about Dione?" Anat said. "Is she still the obedient servant?"

Anat hadn't handled her imprisonment as well as Maia first thought. Resentment colored her tone, not that Maia blamed her. "Don't be so hard on her. We can't all have your courage. Dione's coming around. Still, I don't think she has the nerve to go to the police."

Anat signed. "Too bad."

"Cybele is a bitch," Maia said with more venom than she intended, "and she spawned a bitch—four bitches—all with their husband's dicks wrapped around their little fingers." She paused and caught Anat's eye. "I've asked Seth to help get the babies back to their parents."

Anat snorted. "Don't count on him. He's their number one soldier and master organizer. He's sterile except with you."

One part of her hoped Seth had lied. Then he'd be easier to forget. But he'd told the truth. "I didn't believe him."

"Yup, his little swimmers sank every time. He sure made beautiful children with you. He brings them here often. I hate what they're doing to them, and I worry about Phillip."

Maia's nerve endings pricked to attention. She found it hard to draw a breath. "Phillip? Why?"

"He's withdrawn and shy, complicated. I'm not sure—" Anat stared out over the balcony. "I'm not sure something hasn't happened to him."

"Like what, Anat? Tell me."

Her sister spoke so softly, Maia strained to hear her over the roar of the water below. "I'm not sure. Something isn't right. I've asked, but no one's telling."

Maia paced the balcony. "Phillip did seem unnaturally quiet." Peering over the side, she looked down at the raging rapids scrambling over the glistening rocks, splashing foam into the air. For a brief moment the rocks came toward her, as if she had plummeted over the side in a feverish attempt to avoid what she didn't want to face. The vision seemed so real. Did her mother see the pavement coming toward her when she threw herself out the window, or did she close her eyes until she splattered to her death? Had her guilt about her retarded son, Maia's brother, been the cause of her death?

Her own guilt churned inside her. How many times had she wanted to steal her children and run away? Except where was the compound? Each time she came by company jet, she relinquished her cell phone so the GPS couldn't reveal the location. Seth knew because he flew in and out on occasion, even though this was his home, and he rarely left.

She'd failed her children miserably. If they were damaged, she blamed herself. She was no better than the others, probably worse. "We need to get out of here. Send the authorities. Something, Anat."

"Cal and I have had a plan for years," Anat said, "but we couldn't carry it out alone. We need Seth. With him on our side, we might have a chance to stop this madness. You're our only hope."

Chapter Thirty-Seven
Who's Watching the Children?

Lucier pushed aside the papers on his desk to answer the phone.

"You were right, Lieutenant," Dione Compton said. "My father took my phone and checked the numbers in the data bank. He found nothing, thanks to you. I would never have thought of doing that."

"Did you find out anything about your sister?"

"No. After I asked about Maia, everyone clammed up more than usual."

"What's your honest opinion?"

"I'm almost sure they've sent her away."

"Do you know where?"

A long pause hung on the line. "Hmm, yes…and no."

What the hell did that mean? "Your father's group is on the verge of being exposed. I'd hate to see you caught in the crossfire." Lucier could almost hear Dione Compton wrestle her conscience.

She remained silent for a long moment before she spoke. "I can't. You don't understand. I'm afraid. Terrified."

"I do understand, Ms. Compton. Without satanic ritual abuse, worshipping Satan in itself is not a crime. Five babies, maybe more, have been stolen from their parents. Whatever justifications your father and his friends gave, kidnapping *is* a federal crime."

Dione didn't respond. The telephone line crackled with the silence of fear. Was he getting through to her?

"Maia and I didn't know about the babies until that kidnapper was caught," she said softly. "Oh, God, please, what should I do?"

"If you believe in God, you'll make the right decision. It's not too late."

She sniffed, and Lucier thought perhaps he'd finally broken through. "Are you familiar with two young women who call themselves Brigid and Nona Fulceri?"

Dione Compton hung up.

*****

Maia spent the afternoon in her quarters with her children. She was no psychologist, but she agreed with Anat. Her older son Phillip was abnormally withdrawn and remote. He'd suffered something traumatic, and he wouldn't confide in her. In fact, he only spoke in one-word answers. Leo, the youngest, clung to her and didn't want to let go. She sensed that he, too, was on the way to having problems. Only the girl, Iris, acted like a girl her age should act—if she were raised within the confines of the group.

"What happened to Phillip?" she asked Seth later when they were alone.

He looked at her quizzically. "What do you mean?"

"Something's wrong. Haven't you noticed?"

"He's a quiet kid."

"How much time do you spend with him?"

"I see him every day," Seth said. "I see all of them every day."

"Not see them. Spend time with them."

"What are you getting at, Maia?"

"Do the boys stay with you at night?"

"You know all the kids stay together."

"Who watches them?"

"The leaders take turns. What's this about?"

How could she phrase this without proof? "I think Phillip has been sexually abused."

Seth started to laugh but stopped when he realized Maia was serious. "Don't be ridiculous. The pleasuring here is strictly heterosexual, and a strict hands-off policy is in effect until the kids reach a certain age. You know that."

"What about Cal Easley? Does he spend time with the children? Could he have been with Phillip alone?"

"Cal? He spends time with all the children, teaches them math and science and art. Every subject imaginable. The kids love him. Cal's the most gentle person here. He'd never touch a kid. He may be gay, but I think he's more, I don't know, asexual. Sex with either gender doesn't seem to interest him. He's always been…different, an anomaly, ever since we were children. He does pretty much what he wants, and no one pays attention. Cal shouldn't be here," Seth admitted. "If he could find his way out, he'd be gone. Cal is instrumental in the intellectual cultivation of the next generation, but a sexual predator? No. Not Cal. Not anyone."

Maia felt ashamed to suspect Cal because he was gay. Child predators were a special strain of deviant. "I don't believe this." Maia paced the floor of her suite. "Don't you care what happens to the children? To your children? Your sons have all the characteristics of troubled psyches, and you choose not to notice." She fell into a chair. "It's as much my fault as yours. I've been a pawn in all this. Silas said go, I went. Silas said stay, I stayed. Silas said fuck, I fucked. My children have been raised by others when I should have raised them. But not here. Not in this place. I want both worlds and I can't have either."

Seth knelt down before her. He gently brushed away a tear crawling down her cheek. "I'll talk to Phillip. If something bad has happened, he'll tell me. I'll find out, Maia. Promise."

"I need to talk to the group, Seth."

"Not until you go through…counseling. Those are my instructions."

"You don't mean counseling, you mean a dozen sessions of brainwashing. It won't work. It didn't work on Anat, and now it won't work on me."

"Then you'll never leave here. That's the word from the counsel, which is okay with me. Nothing would make me happier."

Never leave? Even though she'd brought up the possibility herself, hearing the words from Seth turned her stomach into a tornado. Had she made another mistake? Screwed up again? Why didn't she just keep her mouth shut and go along until they let her go? Then she would have blown the whole thing wide open. Instead, she was caught in a web of her own doing.

Her sons needed counseling, outside the compound. There was no time to lose. Anat's plan, as difficult as it would be, was the only way.

Chapter Thirty-Eight
The Night of the Crescent Moon

After the abruptly ended conversation with Dione Compton, Lucier finished up his work and headed to Diana's house. Dinner there had become a routine. She practiced her cooking, he ate. He couldn't have cared less about the food. He loved being with Diana.

Tonight she ordered a pizza, which was fine with him. They devoured it in record time. He patted his belly. "Good dinner. Pizza from Gino's Grotto is my favorite."

"I didn't feel like cooking tonight. Hope you don't mind."

They were sitting on the sofa. An empty pizza box took up most of the coffee table, along with paper plates, soft drink cans, crushed red pepper, and the remains of freshly grated Parmesan.

"Once my belly's full, doesn't matter whether I've eaten a gourmet meal or a peanut butter and jelly sandwich." He moved closer and nuzzled his face into the crook of her neck. "Actually, my needs are more primal. Food is survival. Making love is soul food."

"I love soul food," she whispered in his ear, "but I want to hear more about Dione Compton."

"Riiight," he drawled, disappointed she didn't pursue the more amorous angle.

She gathered the crumpled napkins, tossed them into the box along with the paper plates, and brought them into the kitchen. Lucier carried the drink cans.

He gazed wistfully at the moist spot on her neck and sighed. "When I asked Dione if she knew where her sister was, she gave me a rather cryptic answer."

"Like what?"

"How did she put it? 'Yes and no.'"

"She knows but doesn't know the physical location?"

"That's what I thought."

Diana finished her Coke and tossed both cans in the recycle bin. "You haven't found possible properties?"

"A clever corporate attorney can tangle properties into all kinds of corporate mumbo jumbo. Neither Jason nor Ralph Stallings, with all the FBI's data, came up with anything. They're still trying."

"If they hadn't stolen the babies, we might never have known about this group."

"This is bigger than I thought. The idea gives me the creeps."

"Wherever this place is, it must be remote, and they go by private jet. What do the experts say? Ninety-eight percent of the population lives on two percent of the land? That leaves a big part of country from which to carve out their hideaway."

"Thanks," Lucier said. "I feel a whole lot better. Both Crane Corporation and Compton International have their own planes, but the pilots aren't around for us to interview. That leaves the airport and Dione. I bet Compton or Crane pays out enough money to the right people, who in turn will say whatever they're told to say."

"Will Dione be at Compton's the night of the crescent moon?"

"I doubt he'll allow it. Checking her cell phone means he doesn't trust her, and I'm sure he won't want her anywhere near me."

"Maybe if I say she asked for a reading. What do you think?"

"You'd be putting words in her mouth." Lucier stopped and weighed his words. He couldn't deny how uneasy he felt about their upcoming evening. "What if I asked you not to do this reading?"

She stopped wiping down the counters and raised an eyebrow. "What? Say that again. I must have misheard."

"You didn't. I asked you not to go to Compton's on the crescent moon."

"Why?"

"They've done everything to broadcast that something will happen on the night of crescent moon. Dione confirmed that you're in their plans. I have a bad feeling for good reason."

"I'm the one who's supposed to have those prescient feelings. Besides, it's tomorrow night. What can they do, Ernie? People will know where we'll be. Compton wouldn't dare do anything. If he was seriously planning something, why would he send notes and warnings?"

"Maybe he's not the one sending them."

"Then who?"

"I don't know, but I don't like it." Lucier's premonitions came shrouded in a black cloud. He couldn't shake it. Compton and Crane's wealth and power had insulated them. They flaunted their misdeeds in the faces of those they considered inferior and expected to get away with them. Lucier didn't know what they planned for Diana, but his job was to make sure nothing happened to her, both as a cop and a lover.

* * * * *

All the next day, Diana's thoughts focused on this night—the night of the crescent moon. She peeked out the bathroom window. Though still light outside, the pale sliver of moon hung low in the sky, one eye winking at her. Her heart beat a little faster, and a ring of heat circled her neck. She'd determined long ago that she had a screw loose somewhere to keep tempting fate. Now, she was about to do it again.

Lucier had gone home to change. She hadn't heard him come into the house, but she turned to find him leaning against the frame of the bathroom door with an admiring expression on his face.

"Are you ready?" he asked.

After a dab of her bright red lipstick, a quick fluff of her curls, and one last check in the mirror, she said, "Yup, ready as I'll ever be. Tonight's the big night. The night of the crescent moon."

"You're sure you want to do this?"

She drew a deep breath, let it out in a long sigh. "Positive. This is our chance to find out what's going on. Five men think they can hide their inner sensations. I'm betting at least one of them will give off vibes that exposes their plans, whether he wants to or not. That's all we need. Just one."

"I'm worried about 'Diana of the Moon, we await you.' They want to place you on an altar and worship you."

She snorted. "They've already done that."

"Except this time I'll be watching everything you put in your mouth. Drinks out of the same containers as everyone else; food the same way."

"They can't drug me without drugging you, and how can they do that when your men know we're there."

"We still have to be careful. These people think they're above the law."

"In their world, they are the law."

"I've planned a few things of my own." He put something in her hand the size of a dime.

"What's this?"

"A GPS tracking device. Tuck it in your purse. I put one in my wallet and another on the car. My people will know where we are at all times."

She shrugged and dropped it in her evening bag. "I feel like Mata Hari on some kind of spy mission."

He kissed her. "You're my Mata Hari. Come on."

They left in Lucier's car and arrived at Compton's French Quarter residence five minutes after seven. Since only the men asked readings, Diana wasn't sure the women would be there, but they were, minus Anastasia Easley, each in slinky dresses. So slinky and close to the skin Diana could tell none of them wore underwear. A quick exchange with Lucier told her he noticed too. She scanned the room. No sign of Edward Slater. She wasn't surprised but thought he'd be curious enough to show up.

Dione Compton wasn't there either.

Everyone greeted them like old friends. Both Diana and Lucier decided earlier not to accept drinks before dinner, and a series of knowing glances passed among the group. Diana thought the Easleys might be late, but when they didn't show after ten minutes, she said, "I thought I was going to read Mr. Easley. Is he not coming?"

"Ah, um, unfortunately, Martin and Anastasia had another engagement," Compton said, stumbling over the answer. "They send their regrets."

Strange, Diana thought. "Some other time."

"Definitely."

"Well, this is exciting," Fernando Reyes said.

He'd draped his hand over his wife's shoulder and was tickling the side of her breast. "Tell me, Diana," Reyes said. "How do you do this? Do we all get to listen while you read us, like in your performances, or do we lock ourselves in another room?"

"I'm sure everyone wants his reading in private, Fernando," Compton said. "I certainly don't want anyone to hear what Diana has to say about me this time. She's already told me things no one could possibly know." He chuckled. "I hope you don't blackmail me." Compton leaned close to her, pretending his words were out of earshot. "No telling what other dark secrets you might unearth."

"Your decision," Diana said, knowing in her heart there wasn't a past reading unveiling Compton's secrets. Her gaze wandered back to Reyes, who had finger-walked all the way to Sophia's nipple, pinching and tweaking as if daring Diana to react. A taunting smile played across Sophia's lips. Diana glanced at Lucier, who'd been trapped again by Selene and didn't notice.

This was a blatant, provocative act. She had a strong urge to grab Lucier and get the hell out of there. *Make some excuse, Diana. I've a stomach virus, I feel a migraine coming on—something. Anything. Just get up and go.*

But she'd committed to this reading. They were trying to throw her off her game. This was a job, nothing more.

She nodded to Reyes. "I've read both ways. My act is geared for audience participation; my private clients prefer their readings to be…private." She turned to Compton. "I don't recall anything scandalous in your first reading; I doubt you have anything to worry about now." Which was true. She didn't recall anything. "Even if you impart something you don't want to, I always respect my client's privacy."

"I expect no less," Compton said.

A conversation arose as to who would have the first reading. Fernando Reyes, drawing Diana's attention back to his dexterous manipulation of his wife's breast, decided to go first, Compton last. This time, when she caught Lucier's gaze, he furtively nodded to the Reyeses' exhibitionism. She responded with an almost imperceptible raise of her brows.

"No reading for you, Mr. Crane?" Diana asked. He sat like a king on the throne, surveying his flock. The man was a perfect specimen. Paul Newman eyes that hinted amusement, a face chiseled for Mount Rushmore. He wore no jacket, as if formality were beneath him.

"No, no," Crane said, waving her off. "I know where my life has been, and I'm old enough not to care where it's taking me."

"Surprising that none of the ladies are interested in a reading," Diana said. "Most of my clients are women. What about you, Mrs. Compton? Game?"

"Oh, no." Selene laughed, with a firm hold on Lucier's arm. "I'm embarrassed to say that I don't believe in psychics. They're fine as entertainment, but I can't imagine putting my future decisions in the hands of a seer."

Seer, indeed. An obvious put-down. "I've heard the sentiments before," Diana said. "Many times, in fact. Most people change their minds after one of my readings."

"Go on, Selene. Sign up," her mother said. "I want to see what she says about you."

"But not you, Mrs. Crane?" Diana asked.

"I'm with Phillip, my dear. Too old to care."

"I'll think about it during dinner," Selene said. "Speaking of dinner, what do you say we eat?"

Everyone agreed, and Selene called her servants to set out

the food. As if she expected Lucier and Diana to be cautious after Diana's inference about the drink in Compton's limo, Selene had directed her caterer to arrange the buffet on two sideboards in the huge dining room. A stack of fine china sat at one end, and everyone lined up to fill their plates with the same food.

Appetizers of shrimp and caviar. A salad bar section with dozens of items. Roast beef and salmon. Pork tenderloin and chicken breast. Trays of vegetable casseroles, rice, and potatoes. The presentation equaled those of expensive restaurants and grand hotels, rarely a private home.

She and Lucier exchanged almost imperceptible nods as they found their place cards at the table. This time, Diana sat between Phillip Crane and Jeremy Haynesworth, and Lucier's dining companions were Rhea Haynesworth and Cybele Crane. The butler filled the water and wine glasses from the same pitchers and bottles.

Silas Compton raised his glass. "A toast to our esteemed guests, Diana and Ernie. I hope this will be the first of many celebrations."

"Thank you, Silas," Lucier said. Compton's solicitous smile didn't hide the tic in his cheek. They all lifted their glasses. Diana sipped her wine. Delicious. Well, why wouldn't it be? Probably cost $200 a bottle. Before she knew, she had drunk half the glass and decided to sip or it might interfere with her readings.

"So, Diana," Rhea Haynesworth said from across the table, "my husband has been so looking forward to this. He's never had a fortune teller give him a reading before."

First seer, now fortune teller. No sarcasm crept into Rhea's tone, and Diana peered over her wine glass for any sign of condescension. She saw none.

"And he won't tonight, Rhea, because I'm not a fortune teller." Diana fought to keep her voice even at what she perceived an insult. Most people wouldn't distinguish the nuances that separated the different psychic channels. "Fortune tellers and seers predict the future. I read psychic energy. Psychic phenomena can embrace the past, present, *or* future of a person's life. I only absorb impressions the sitter transmits to me. Sometimes I receive nothing at all, so I hope no one is disappointed if that happens."

"Does one have to consciously transmit, or does it happen involuntarily?" Rhea asked.

"Yes, do tell us," Cybele said. "I've always found this sort of thing fascinating."

Diana sipped more wine, gazed from woman to woman, noticing their resemblance. How could she have missed that at first? It was so obvious. Then, as if she were looking at them under water, they all started to look wobbly. The voices in the room seemed to slow down, like a sound track on a lower speed. Even Lucier looked funny. He was acting funny too, his head drooping over his plate. He called her name, slowly, each syllable reverberating echolike in her head.

"Di—a—na."

Sounds faded into the background. The glass in her hand felt heavy, weighted, and fell from her grasp onto the table. Everyone was looking at her, smiling. Her hand fell into her food as all sensation left her body.

Why couldn't she keep her head up? It fell forward, down, into her plate of food. She smelled the salmon, the lemon too, right by her nose. Lucier slumped lower, his expression apologetic before he fell face first into his plate. Before she blacked out, she remembered what she thought when watching the Reyeses. They didn't care what her impressions were about their inappropriate petting, because she and Lucier weren't going to leave here.

Chapter Thirty-Nine
Fear, the Consequence of Truth

Beecher took Lucier's call on Sunday morning. Everything had gone well at the Comptons' Saturday night, he said, and he'd fill Beecher in on Monday. Lucier's voice sounded flat, his phrasing robotic. Beecher figured he was tired. Oh, to be young again, drink, and stay up all night.

When Lucier didn't show up for work Monday morning, Beecher started to worry. The tech said all three GPS tracking devices signaled from the area around and in Diana's house. Beecher called there. No response. He called Lucier's cell with the same result, then Diana's. Again, no answer. This was not like his boss. The only time Beecher remembered the lieutenant break the rules was when he saved Diana from the psycho who tried to kill her. Today, the inconsistencies set Beecher's nerve endings on full alert.

He drove to Diana's house, saw Lucier's car in the driveway, and the tracking device still in place. No one answered the door. He searched around, found the fake rock with the key inside, and entered—something he would never do except in this situation. The house was empty, as expected.

He sped to Compton's residence in the French Quarter. Even if he could have found a parking space on the tourist-crowded street, the iron gates to the house were locked. No guard.

An uneasy sensation roiled in Beecher's belly; sweat

sprouted on the back of his neck and hairline. The physical effects turned into full-blown anxiety. Considering what Lucier suspected about the Comptons, Beecher was scared shitless.

* * * * *

Lucier's head throbbed; his mouth and throat felt like he'd swallowed a bucket of sand. He tried to raise his hand to massage his temples but found his wrists shackled to an arm chair with plastic cuffs. Ropes secured his feet together, and a leather strap stretched tight across his chest. Stabs of pain shooting into every muscle woke his body from its numbness. Even a shallow breath sent tremors through his ribcage. His bladder verged on exploding.

Where was he? He rotated his head to view an unfamiliar large room with dozens of chairs lining the walls. Then the last image of Diana filtered through the cobwebs of his mind. Tremors intensifying, he tried to focus through the pounding in his head while tendrils of fear snaked through the hammering tension. Snippets of visuals flashed in his brain—Diana's face, beseeching, begging forgiveness.

His already-churning stomach revolted even more. He was the one who should beg forgiveness. He'd seriously misread the situation.

What was that? He turned at the abrupt sound, squinted. A silhouette emerged in grainy shadow, and Lucier blinked to clear his vision

"Ah, you're finally awake," the familiar voice said.

Was this a dream, his mind playing tricks? Then reality seeped into his memory, scene by ugly scene.

Compton's house.

Sitting down to dinner.

His own fading vision.

Darkness.

His stomach sank, and he struggled helplessly against his bonds. He coughed to clear the raspy croak that substituted for his voice. From his training, he knew the adrenaline pumping into his bloodstream would help disperse the fog in his head. Until then, he wouldn't give anyone the satisfaction of seeing him cower.

Seeing Slater standing in front of him, a smirk on his lips, didn't surprise Lucier in the least. "Where's Diana? I swear if anything's happened to her, there won't be any place for you to hide."

A derisive huff emerged from Slater's throat as he paced before him, his relaxed demeanor conveying his advantage. "His first words are for his lady. How noble. Brave, too, considering you're strapped to a chair."

"My men and the FBI know where we are. You won't get away with this."

"You mean those little GPS tracking devices you and Diana carried? They're beeping signals as we speak. At Diana's house. Did you really think you could pass through the security gate without alerting us of their presence? Your men couldn't find you now with the latest in satellite technology or with a team of champion bloodhounds.

"Besides, you called your man—what's his name? Beecher?—and told him you and Diana spent a lovely evening at the Comptons'. You even mentioned you found no evidence to implicate our group in anything more nefarious than unknowingly renting a house to a man who kidnapped a baby. Your detective must think the two of you took an extended holiday, when in fact you're hundreds of miles away from New Orleans, in our compound."

What call? Think, Ernie. But his mind was a black hole. He writhed against his bonds to free himself, caving limp in the chair as his weakened body collapsed. Even in full strength, he couldn't have shucked his bindings.

He'd been surprised Slater wasn't at Compton's house the night of the reading and concluded he'd been wrong about him. He chalked up his irritation at the man to a foolish emotion that colored his opinion from the beginning. Colored it green. Now he knew his innate sense of distrust had been spot on, and Diana, maybe for the first time in her career—her life—had missed Slater's evil core.

He should have trusted his cop instinct.

"Tell me," Lucier said, "is Diana okay?"

"She's fine. Why would we hurt her? She's what this is all about."

"What *is* this all about?" Lucier asked, forcing out the words.

"You'll find out soon enough."

Keep your wits. Find out as much as you can. "What day is it?"

"Monday morning. I'm afraid you've been out for quite a while."

Monday. At least thirty-six hours had passed. He'd probably been restrained all that time, which accounted for the stiffness. "I need to pee."

"Soon. We made sure you did your business. We wouldn't want you to mess yourself, but you do reek."

The thought that someone had seen to his bodily functions caused a cold spike down his spine. What drug had allowed them to put him under so completely? "When I don't show up for work and they can't find Diana, they'll come looking for us. They'll find us."

Slater arched one brow. "Hold the thought."

The ominous phrase chilled Lucier. Slater sounded so sure of himself. With the tracking devices useless, and if they were hundreds of miles away, how would anyone find them? Ralph Stallings said the combined properties of the group were a complicated mess.

"How did you drug us? I watched every morsel of food we ate, every drop of liquid poured into our glasses."

Slater's arrogant sneer claimed victory without words. "But not the drop at the bottom of the glass, *before* we filled it. Enough to put you under. We supplemented later, after you fell into your plates."

I was so careful, so prepared—so stupid. He should have switched place cards and changed seats. If he'd done that, the looks on their faces would have given them away. He should have checked the glasses. Should have insisted that he and Diana stayed home. Should have, should have. Didn't.

Too damn late now. He strained harder against the binding straps, but they only cut deeper into his skin.

"Sorry about the restraints. Letting you roam free didn't seem like a good idea."

"You son of a bitch," Lucier said, still struggling. "Where is she? I want to see her."

"You will. In a minute. She's quite something, you know. An amazing woman. I'd hoped she'd take to our way of life, but she's too strong-minded."

"Don't hurt her. She's been through enough. You of all people should understand."

"Are you appealing to my sense of justice?" Slater asked. Then his tone hardened. "Don't bother. I lost that years ago."

"What's this about, Slater? Why kidnap Diana? Why kidnap babies?"

Slater's mouth twisted into an ugly grimace. "I wasn't in

favor of the kidnappings. That was Phillip's idea. He judged it imperative to inject heightened genetic material for the future of the group: scientists and doctors. I grew to embrace the concept, however. As for Diana—how could we resist the opportunity? The name: Diana. Her exceptional psychic abilities. Coincidence? I think not. She insinuated herself into our sphere of interest when she found the pink house. Everything fit so perfectly."

These people were deranged. All of them. Lucier didn't realize the extent until now. "Crane? I don't understand."

"Phillip's great-grandfather is full-blooded Osage Indian. That's common knowledge for anyone doing the research."

"I suppose there's a connection between him and your Indian savior. Unless the holy man discovered the fountain of youth, he must have been a descendent."

A frown creased Slater's brow. "So, Diana betrayed my confidence. I wondered if she would. Such a juicy story. Yes, of course, a descendent—Phillip's grandfather. He and his people saved my life. The story gets better."

Even though Lucier tried to act disinterested, Slater's tease drew him in.

"Phillip's great-grandfather received an allotment of land through the Dawes Act, a noble experiment doomed to fail. Unlike many of his people, he was neither ignorant nor stupid. He took a nubile young white woman for his wife, over whom he wielded considerable power, and transferred his property to her name so the white man couldn't take what was his." Slater moved closer to Lucier, almost into his face. "The Crane magnetism goes way back, doesn't it?"

Lucier snorted, but now he was caught up in the story. Hopefully, Slater would tell him what Jason couldn't find out. Then he thought if he never left this place, knowing Crane's background wouldn't much matter.

Slater continued. "That worked well when he discovered oil in 1913. You see, the white man and his god would have taken everything from him, and his father's god allowed his tribe to live in the Dark Ages. So he elaborated on his Indian culture, veering from the script, and founded a new religion by transposing *god* into one of his own philosophy. Phillip's grandfather was a child at the time, but he learned how to live in two worlds—the very public white world when he took over after his father's death, and the other, as a simple man who helped his people. That's the man I knew. A man as white as me, like his mother, I presume, although he proudly claimed his Indian heritage. He was very old when I met him, but he had much to teach."

How far back did Jason go in Crane's history, and what would it matter if he'd discovered this? Who could tie it together? "Yeah, how to use what you had left to enjoy earthly pleasures. Sex 101: A million ways to get your rocks off without a dick."

Slater squinted, his eyes turning cold. Lucier braced himself for the inevitable fist, but Slater held back with the same cool above-it-all arrogance.

"Actually, you're right. That's exactly what he did, among other things, and I embraced his god in the process." He walked around Lucier's chair, checking his bindings to make sure his prisoner wasn't working free. "I concede you're not as dim as I first thought. I wondered what Diana saw in such mediocrity and figured it must be something you're hiding. Something I can't compete with."

Ignoring the bait, Lucier reeled in his fury to meet Slater's composure with his own. "Women don't fall in love with dicks, Slater. They fall in love with the man. Osiris, my ass.

You should have given yourself more credit instead of becoming a eunuch."

Lucier's comment had the desired effect. Slater's face bloomed with color.

"Below the belt, Lieutenant," he said through clenched teeth, "metaphorically speaking, of course. I'm afraid you're wrong, though. That was my one white lie, or should I say black lie. Why in Satan's name would I eliminate the one thing to give me sexual pleasure? Diana was right. Penetration was out of the question, but I can still pleasure a woman and, more importantly, a woman can still pleasure me. Pleasure is anything that transpires between two consenting adults." He paused, and a smile twitched his lips. "Even those non-consenting. I bet Diana does an excellent job pleasuring. What do you say?"

Slater was pushing all the right buttons. Lucier knew it and couldn't control himself. He fought harder, the sharp edge of the plastic cuff cutting deeper into his skin. Blood trickled down his hand to his fingers, leaving a telltale stickiness. He collapsed in fatigue, breathing hard. Sweat crawled down his back like liquid worms, soaking his shirt. He shimmied against the back of the chair to stop the slithering effect. "Diana wouldn't touch you," he said.

"Are you sure? You didn't see her when we were together. She's fascinated by me. I sensed it. So did you. I saw those cat's eyes of yours turn green. Ask her."

"I will if you bring her here. Let me see she's all right."

"Soon. You'll see her soon. Like you, she may be a little groggy, but she'll come around."

"If you've hurt her in any way, I'll kill you."

Slater laughed. "I admire your optimism. You see, Lieutenant, we use special tactics to incorporate people into our sphere."

"You mean cult, don't you, Slater?"

"If you choose to call it that, I have no objection. People crave affection. Other than Phillip, the founding males of our group, including Silas, pulled themselves up from dismal beginnings, some with parents who were so busy surviving they had no time for their children. The one thing those men shared was brilliance and a need to be loved and admired. And greed, of course."

"But not you. You were blessed with loving parents, belief in God. You had everything."

"Yes, until I got sick. You know the story so I won't bore you with the details. Suffice to say I slipped as low as a man can go and still live. These people offered me the love and passion I'd lost. They accepted me for who I am, or who I had become. A half-man."

"So the medicine man taught you what? All about Satan?" Lucier snorted. "Give me a break."

"Ever heard of love bombing?"

"No, and I don't want to hear about it now." Lucier wriggled in his chair. "Take off these restraints," he demanded.

Slater ignored him. "Too bad. I'm afraid you're a rapt audience. Love bombing takes many forms. It may be a session where the members hold hands, hug each other, and bond. Cults use the tactic. So do many successful organized religions, especially in fundamentalist and extreme churches. You've seen pictures on TV of parishioners touching and holding each other, while the preacher strokes their egos, boosts their pride and self-esteem. The method works extremely well with children from the earliest age and makes them dependent on their leader."

"No different than brainwashing. No different than the Nazis."

"Yes. The Germans did it well. Turned a whole country into their way of thinking. Our tactics are slightly different. They used hate to bring them together; we use love.

"You remember the polygamist groups? They use love bombing to keep their people in line—to convince them the world is an ugly place outside their confines. The technique does not promise unconditional love. In fact, quite the contrary. Love bombing is highly conditional. Love is tied to membership and participation in the group. If a member doesn't join or wants to leave, all love stops."

"You're justifying using young women like Nona and Brigid and turning them into baby machines to populate your so-called new order. Do you think drugging them to have sex against their will is love?"

"No one drugged Brigid or Nona," Slater said. "They were eager and willing to do whatever Silas wanted. He's their father, you know. Selene's daughters."

Lucier muffled his gasp, but his shock showed nevertheless. He watched the satisfaction on Slater's face as the man relished his surprise.

"You didn't guess, did you? No, I can see you didn't." Slater pulled a chair close to Lucier but out of his reach. "Those two women love sex. Each has produced one child, but Brigid's pregnant again. They were a little young, but they're Selene's daughters and very much like her. Not at all like their older sister, Anat. She's an untrainable non-conformist. Resisted our methods completely, so we were forced to resort to other techniques. We can't allow her to leave because she'd go to the authorities. She's content. Not happy, but content. All this is to create a superior race. A city wholly unto itself. Two or three more generations and we'll be there. Then we'll infiltrate the best of our group into society to begin the transformation on a larger scale. That will take many more generations, but it's doable."

The scope of Slater's acknowledgement sent ice through Lucier's veins. "This place will be found, your perversions stopped."

"Who's going to stop us, Lieutenant. Certainly not you, because you'll never leave here. Your prying awakened the authorities, so we've readied another place. Diana will join us there. In fact, she'll be the high priestess. Diana, Goddess of the Moon."

"Why the notes? You had to know they'd start an investigation. Why?"

"One of our members acted alone, thinking the warnings would scare you off. Unfortunately, they had an opposite effect. When we found out, we dealt with him."

Slater's explanation was so preposterous, so bizarre, that Lucier's stomach somersaulted. Could these people conceivably pull this off? Thinking of Diana as the offering to their so-called deity triggered another losing battle against his restraints. "You'll never tame her," he said, panting. "She'll never conform."

"You wouldn't like to bet on that, would you?" Slater rose and went to the door, beckoning to someone outside. A young boy pushed Diana in a wheelchair, a strap tight around her chest, her arms and legs secured to the chair. "Let me reintroduce you to our new goddess. With Diana's talents, we should be able to produce some special offspring, although genetics don't always follow the first generation. If not her children, maybe her grandchildren."

Lucier lifted his chair off the ground when he saw her, but

his feet were bound to its legs, and he almost tipped over before he righted himself. Thrashing against his restraints summoned power he didn't know remained. Her name left his throat like the wail of a caged animal, pleading for her to listen, but her blank stare focused on nothing.

"You bastard." Lucier hissed out the words with as much venom as he could muster. He rubbed sweat off the side of his face with his shoulder, trying hard to calm a heart that pumped so hard he thought it would explode inside his chest. "What have you given her?" Diana was in the drug's darkest throes. A date rape drug could result in long-term hallucinations or dissociative brain damage, and he'd bet that's what had rendered her helpless.

"Not so feisty now, is she? Our doctor is trying different combinations and doses. I heard she fought like a wildcat when she woke from the initial dose. She rejected our vision for her future, and I'm afraid he had to calm her down. Unfortunately, he gave her too much, and she lost her ability to walk. Actually, she lost all motor function and couldn't feed herself now if she were starving and a plate of food sat in front of her. She's so tiny he had a hard time judging the dosage, but he'll get it right. The wheelchair is a nice touch, don't you think? Even if we unstrapped her, she'd be unable to move, other than to fall to the floor. The straps are for her protection. We don't want her to hurt herself."

Lucier's head pounded, the result of drug residue and his futile attempt to break free. His stupidity in succumbing to the lure of the crescent moon left him in a state of despair. He'd underestimated these people and had only himself to blame for Diana's predicament.

Think, Ernie. Clear your head. No one would come for them. They couldn't, because no one knew where they were. With

Slater exposing the group's intent, Lucier would never leave there alive.

"She behaved beautifully Saturday night, though," Slater went on. "The night of the crescent moon. Of course, she couldn't do much else, considering her condition. She enjoyed the place of honor. Wish you'd have seen her. Diana, Goddess of the Moon. A glory to behold."

"You fuck—" Lucier fought the straps again, jumping the chair toward his tormentor until Slater moved back, clearly wary. But Lucier couldn't keep up his assault, and he collapsed once more. "What did you do to her?"

"Tsk, tsk. Calm yourself. You'll get sick. Too much action and those drugs can make you nauseous, and we gave you an extra strong dose. Don't worry. We didn't do anything to Diana this time. We were all in awe. Once she goes through some…reconditioning, she'll enjoy what happens."

Lucier found a new level of strength and screamed. "You'll kill her."

"I'm well acquainted with the state she's in," Slater said. "Been there, done that. For many years, in fact." He walked over to Diana and ran his index finger down the side of her cheek. "Don't worry. She doesn't feel anything, and she won't remember what's happened."

Lucier sensed the interview was ending. *Keep Slater talking*. Information was power, and he needed power. "People will search for us, and they'll keep searching. I'm a cop, for crissakes."

"Yes, that's the one issue that bothered Martin. Funny how different things bother different people. He wasn't in favor of kidnapping babies or even bringing Diana here. He wrote the notes, hoping to frighten Diana off, but she's not one easily frightened, is she? You knew, though, didn't you? Martin went along, but he fears cops. Didn't like you. Bad experience from his childhood. After the incident at Silas's house with those two idiots Maia brought there, he got cold feet. And when he found out you were accompanying Diana the night of the crescent moon...well, he made his objections public. Not good."

"Martin was right. You should be worried."

"There'll be speculation, no doubt. Did you and Diana run away together? Have an accident? The newspapers will have a field day, but they won't find either of you. Ever. Your cop friend will say you called and said everything went fine. It'll be one of the world's great mysteries. Like what happened to Jimmy Hoffa or Amelia Earhart."

Diana's body slumped pitifully in the chair. Lucier didn't care whether Beecher sent out the FBI, the CIA, or the Canadian Mounted Police. All he cared about was her. He had to save her from whatever indignities they had in store.

"You can't keep her like this."

"Oh, we won't," Slater agreed. "Not all the time. Only if she's a problem when we need her, like the other night. The dream she spoke of at Silas's house happened. She took center stage, lying on a revolving platform, naked for us to worship. Unfortunately, we didn't give her enough drugs that time, or she'd never have remembered the experience. Our error. It won't happen again, but I doubt we'll have to resort to that method forever. She'll fall in line." He gazed at Diana, a smile crinkling his weathered face. "She's the perfect offering."

Slater walked to Diana and ran his fingers across her chest. "Except for one thing. She's not made the way the men in our group like their women. Too flat-chested. We cultivate women here who have special endowments to aid in man's pleasures. Our doctor is experimenting with a growth hormone to ensure those who lack the gene get a little boost. Our men love the results. So do the women, by the way. Makes them feel more like women. We might try some on our little goddess here but, frankly, we're more interested in her eggs to perpetuate her unique talent."

The bastard touched her breasts. Lucier emitted a low growl as he jiggled his hands, wasting energy to stretch the plastic cord. Slater checked them from afar, giving Lucier no chance to come in contact.

"Fortunately, Cybele's well-endowed mother passed those enhancements to Cybele, a fact Phillip couldn't ignore when he chose the fifteen-year old beauty as his wife. She, of course, passed the genes to her daughters, who in turn passed them to theirs. The sensual beauty of his immediate family gave Phillip the idea to take the religion of his father and his father's father to a new level—one of hedonistic pleasure."

"Satan, sex, and pedophilia," Lucier said. "How did Crane convince all the men to embrace that?"

"Really, Lieutenant. You're joking, right? You've seen those women. They could make a priest forget his vows and genuflect before them."

"And the Sunrise Mission?"

"A repository of young women with low self-esteem, tossed away like garbage by the men in their lives. My job was to feel them out, ease them into the mindset. Not all the women responded, but most did. They trusted me, and when they were willing, they came here. No money worries, food prepared, education for their children. They think they've died and gone to heaven."

With an expression of self-satisfaction, Slater pranced in front of his captive. Lucier listened, sickened at Slater's words. "You're no different than the men who used them before."

"You're wrong. We've given them a good home and a purpose. Some act as surrogates and others, the beautiful, intelligent ones, are happy to procreate to help us avoid inbreeding, a difficult task at times. The young are so romantic. We've only experienced one unfortunate mating."

Lucier huffed almost under his breath. "My God, you're mad."

"A reaction of the unenlightened," Slater said.

This travesty must be exposed. They couldn't keep him strapped forever. They'd either have to kill him or untie him eventually. "And Jeanine Highsmith?"

"I tried. Subtly of course, but I never felt comfortable she'd embrace our goals. Too independent and confident. She didn't *need* us. That's what it's about. Need and acceptance."

Slater took a handkerchief out of his pocket. He moved closer to wipe the sweat from Lucier's forehead but must have realized he'd be vulnerable to an attack, even from a man tethered to a chair. He retreated.

"We never mentioned our religious persuasion with any of the women," he continued, "just love and affection. By the time the worshipping began, they were so happy, so loved, they didn't care if the devil showed up in his horns and cape and swept them away to Hades." He put the handkerchief back in his pocket. "By then, they needed us."

Lucier couldn't say anything. That was how cults worked. Lure in the weak, the outcasts. Make them feel they belonged.

"I find your lady appealing," Slater said. "She's highly intelligent with amazing sex appeal. Once she produces babies, she'll develop more interest in her sexuality. Between giving birth and her harvested eggs planted in surrogates with the chosen sperm, she'll produce enough offspring in the time left to her. She'll nurse them, and I guarantee the motherly instinct will take over. Maybe I'll keep you around long enough to witness that."

Lucier thought about the morning in the pink house, in the rocking chair—Diana's lactation and its effect. He saw his hands around Slater's neck, but it was only a mirage. His arms and hands were still strapped to the chair, his fists clenching and unclenching with the fury of a man poised on the threshold of committing murder.

Anyone could be brought to the point of homicidal rage, given the right conditions. He'd seen it as a cop, now experienced it as a man. He needed to save his strength until he found an opportunity. Unless they killed him shackled to the chair, he would.

"I'm sure I can interest her in me again," Slater said. "She is already—the tortured man, striving to find peace in his ruined life."

"Man?" Lucier sneered. "Hardly."

Slater ignored the sarcasm. "Enough of one to make a woman forget. I possess unique talents."

Lucier's stomach sank. They were going to turn Diana into a sex zombie. "What you're doing is not only illegal, it's immoral."

Slater's laugh was the most evil sound Lucier ever heard.

"I have no morals, Lieutenant. May I call you Ernie? I've never felt close enough to you till now."

"Fuck you."

Slater crouched in front of Lucier's chair, just out of reach. "Only weak men resort to cursing. I was weak once, but not now. Diana will find out. Of course, I'll share her with the others. All the men will want their time with the Goddess of the Moon. That's how it works here. Don't worry. Being a pragmatist, she'll grow to enjoy the adulation. No sense fighting what you can't change."

The scene resembled a bad horror movie. Slater had obviously lost his mind along with his manhood. They'd all lost their minds.

Diana looked pitiful. Her head lolled to the side, drool hung like a liquid thread from the corner of her mouth. Fighting the restraints only sapped Lucier of what little energy he had left.

Slater, the bastard, knew it too.

Chapter Forty
Return to the Comfort Zone

Captain Jack Craven knew Ernie Lucier as well as he knew any man. Before the deaths of his wife and children, his lieutenant never took off a day he didn't have coming, and he was back on the job the day after he buried his family. Craven had begged him to take time off, but Lucier refused. No way would he miss work for anything less than a calamity. Unless he were seriously hurt or dead, he'd have checked in.

Beecher's description of Lucier's automaton-like voice bothered Craven most. A no-nonsense boss, well-liked and respected by his men, he could sometimes be aloof. But no one would ever describe his speech pattern as robotic.

Beecher had brought Craven up to speed on Lucier's investigation. He'd checked the whereabouts of Compton's group. All were out of their offices this morning except Martin Easley, and none of the secretaries would confirm when their bosses would return. He'd called the Sunrise Mission, too, and the secretary said Edward Slater had left on a short, well-deserved vacation."

Coincidence? Craven didn't think so. He believed in coincidences. They happened all the time, but there were too many in this case to ignore. Lucier's disappearance might push the right buttons to search more thoroughly into Compton's hidden properties. He picked up the phone and called FBI agent Ralph Stallings to fill him in on the goings on.

"Any luck untangling the mess of properties owned by the men, especially Compton and Crane?" Craven asked.

"Our team of forensic accountants is working on it. The men's multiple corporations have a tangled provenance of ownership, most through shell companies and land trusts, some registered offshore."

"We're looking for someplace within a few hundred miles, I'd guess," Craven said. "Someplace a couple of hours by private plane."

"What makes you think that?"

"Nothing concrete. I'm hunching here, Ralph."

"Hold on."

Craven heard the rustle of paper. He waited.

"Sorry to keep you. I wanted to make sure I had all the facts. At least those we can confirm. Hmm, let's see."

More paper shuffling.

"Both Crane and Compton were born in Oklahoma. In fact, all five men are Okies. People often resort to their comfort zone when seeking a place to hide. In other words, someplace they're familiar with."

"Which would be somewhere in Oklahoma?"

"If I were a guessing man, yes, although I'd hate to hang someone's life on a supposition."

"What about Slater?"

"Born in Texas. Never had enough money to buy property. Not according to his tax returns."

"You have better resources than I do, Ralph, but go deeper into Crane's history. This thing may go back generations. He's the one I'm betting on, 'cause it's his seed money. He bought Compton and the others too."

"I'll get back to you," Stallings said.

"Thanks. Meanwhile, there's one last idea I want to

investigate."

Craven hung up and buzzed Beecher to his office. The big man entered, looking more put together than usual. With Lucier AWOL and B. D. Harris retired, Beecher was senior man. Today, he wore a pressed shirt tucked it into his pants, although they were still slipping down below his gut. Beecher and Lucier were close, and Craven saw the worry lines on his detective's face.

"Pay a visit to Martin Easley, Sam, and take Cash with you. Easley's the only one in town this morning and the only one you verified who stayed in New Orleans this weekend. I called and made an appointment. I wanted him to think about the reason you're coming. Think and worry, if he has reason to. I think he has."

"Why, Captain?"

"Something strange in his history makes me wonder," he said, referring to a folder on his desk. He opened it, riffled through until he extracted a sheet of paper. "In the late fifties, Easley's father was accused of raping and murdering a college girl in town. The cops went to his house to question him, but he resisted, claiming he was innocent. One overzealous cop knocked him around. Easley, Sr., fought back and they beat him so bad, he later died of a brain hemorrhage. Ten-year-old Martin witnessed the whole thing. Easley's mother filed a lawsuit, but no jury was going to convict two cops of killing a dirt-poor farmer. They got off, and later, another man confessed to the girl's murder."

No light bulbs seemed to be going off in Beecher's head. Maybe his idea was off the wall, Craven thought.

"What are you thinking, Captain?" Beecher asked.

"If Compton and Crane are masterminds of a group of baby-kidnapping Satanists—of which we have no concrete evidence—Easley's been involved. Until now. I think he opted out because his friends abducted a cop, and Easley has a deep-rooted, lifelong fear of the police."

"That's an awful lot of ifs, sir."

"Yeah, I know. But right now we have nothing else. Won't hurt to turn the screws and see his reaction. He said he'd be home at noon. Probably doesn't want the cops to go to his office. I'm hoping we got ourselves a weak link. God knows, we need one."

Chapter Forty-One
To Act the Part

Diana forced her eyes open. She lay on a bed in a strange room, unable to move. Not her hands or arms or legs. Not anything. It was if her body belonged to someone else. She wasn't dead because she heard her accelerated heartbeat pounding in her ears from fear. *Where am I?* Inching her head to the side to see her surroundings took every ounce of strength and left her breathless. The room equaled one in a five-star hotel—expensive furnishings, luxurious draperies pulled closed. She managed to turn to the other side and saw part of a marble-tiled bathroom. A fleeting memory attacked her consciousness.

This was no hotel.

Slowly, her fingers came to life, followed by her hand and arm. Next, her body regained prickly sensation, leaving her limbs heavy and weighted.

But she felt them.

Nausea moved up from deep in her gut. She needed to get to the bathroom. Sitting up sapped her energy, and she collapsed back onto the bed. The nausea abated but still smoldered in her belly like a fire's dying embers.

Flashes of memory hit her next—wavy visions and distorted sounds, Lucier's heartrending helplessness as his head sank into his plate of food, the pungent aroma of lemon and salmon, the soft cushion of the fish's flesh warm on her cheek.

The blackness from her own lapse into unconsciousness.

She closed her eyes now and more memories flooded into her mind.

Silas Compton stood over her with a welcoming smile on his face as if she'd be happy to see him. Another man, someone she didn't know, stood next to him.

"You're awake," Compton said.

Her throat was so dry, tongue like sandpaper. He held out something to drink. She shook her head violently. **Can't drink. Can't drink. Drugs.**

Compton handed the glass to the other man. "Welcome to our world, Diana," Compton said. "You will be happy here, I promise. You'll be worshiped and adored."

Her voice, shrill in her head, screamed and swore. She clawed at Compton. He jumped back. The other man stepped forward holding something in his hand she couldn't see. He brought it forward. A hypodermic needle.

She fought some more, but she weakened quickly. They held her down and the other man plunged the needle into her arm.

Diana bolted upright, fully awake now, but the room spun, and she once more flopped on the bed. How did the group trick them? She and Lucier ate the same food as the others, drank the same liquids. The answer mattered little. She was locked in a room in a place she assumed she'd never leave.

Where was Lucier? The group needed the Goddess Diana but they didn't need a New Orleans cop who could put them all in prison. Was he already dead?

No, no. She couldn't think that.

The possibility reignited, and sorrow clashed with anger. She squeezed her eyes shut, forcing tears that crawled down her cheeks. These people couldn't be allowed to get away with such things. She had to stop them.

She laughed at the brave words. Stop them? She could barely move. The fury inside her forced another attempt to rise. This time she succeeded with an extra surge of energy.

Okay, Diana, swing your legs to the side.

The room spun again, and the nausea returned, gathering force from deep in her belly, rising into her throat. She swallowed to stave off the sickness until she felt steady enough to get to the bathroom.

Deep breaths. In. Out. In. Out.

She sat up, saw the little red light high in the wall vent not unlike the camera setup in Slater's office. She didn't care. If watching her gave someone a thrill, let them watch. She saluted to the red light.

Scanning the room, she noticed clothes in the closet and a makeup case on the dresser. Everything a prisoner needed to make herself presentable. The clothes appeared to be the right size too. Compton had planned all contingencies. She checked the armoire for scotch. Nothing better to ease nausea than a shot of whiskey. Damn, nothing but a TV.

The dizziness returned. She held on to the footboard, waffling as her legs almost buckled beneath her. One step, then another. She would not let anyone see her vomit, so she shuffled to the bathroom, resisting the urge to flash her middle finger at the camera. She turned on the light and closed the door behind her.

Nausea and lightheadedness played tag as they surged and ebbed like ocean waves. Still weak, she lowered herself to the edge of the tub and waited for the sickness to either pass or erupt. Within a few minutes, she began to feel better. She searched the room. No suspicious holes in the walls, nothing in the vent. At least these people afforded their hostages a modicum of privacy.

What happened to her when she was out cold, helpless in the presence of the people who'd done this to her? She examined her body. It didn't seem as if she'd been violated. Rage grew within her that she even had to check, and she shrugged off her dark thoughts.

Toothbrush and toothpaste, towels, a robe. Yeah, they'd prepared for her arrival. How could she and Lucier have been so naïve? He'd warned her not to go, but she wouldn't listen. History repeated itself, and she ignored its lessons.

She brushed her teeth and splashed cold water on her face, dismissing the thought that her recklessness had endangered Lucier.

Concentrate on what to do to get out of this.

She was their prize, but they didn't need her cooperation. Drugged, she became the object of the group's adoration. Somehow, she suspected that wasn't all they had in mind for her.

She needed a shower to revive. *Deep breath, Diana. Let it out.* Opening the door, she went back into the bedroom and checked the dresser drawers. Lingerie. Black, silk, and lacy. No surprise there. Satan's women would never wear white cotton Jockeys. She looked at the camera, waved the underwear in the air, and disappeared inside the bathroom. She doubted Lucier basked in such luxurious accommodations.

Ernie. Guilt washed over her. She wanted to pray for his well-being, but years of tracking the horrors man perpetrated on other men and women and children had destroyed her faith. Maybe that's part of the bond she shared with Edward Slater. Their journey to the dark side left their blood-pulsing organs numbed. For Lucier, she said a silent prayer. *Please,*

God, if you're listening, protect him.

Diana opened the glass door of the marble enclosure and turned on the water full blast hot. Too hot. She adjusted the temperature and stepped inside. Streams of liquid pleasure pulsed from multiple jets, pelting her awake, massaging her body like tiny fingers. A gold shower caddy held everything a woman needed. Expensive shampoo and conditioner, French-milled soap, a brand new loufa wrapped in cellophane. They spared nothing for the Goddess Diana. The luxury was lost on her. How could she enjoy anything in this place?

She needed time to think. Time to plan an escape. But how? She'd bury her anger and rage and let things play out—see what happened.

She showered quickly. The hot water relieved some of her tension, though she still felt lightheaded. She left her hair to dry naturally, then put on the lingerie to find the group's one miscalculation in their perfectly orchestrated imprisonment. The bra was at least one size too big. She donned the terrycloth robe and stepped from the bathroom.

After a fleeting acknowledgement to the camera, she rummaged through the closet. The clothes were not at all to her taste. She favored tailored, simple lines, but the outfits in the closet were either ultra-feminine décolleté dresses of flowing silk or slinky black vixen numbers. Not a pair of slacks anywhere.

The key jiggled in the door. Diana cinched the robe tighter. Though scared witless, she'd be damned if she'd let them treat her without respect. After all, she was Diana, Goddess of the Moon, and she'd play the role to the hilt. Then she thought, this wasn't a game. Not one bit.

"I'm sorry, Miss Diana, but—"

The voluptuous blonde's hesitant tone gave her the clue

Diana needed. "You have no right to barge into my room…Brigid, isn't it?"

The girl nodded.

"Now get out!" Diana demanded.

Brigid turned bright red and stuttered, "It's just— just, um, that someone wants to see you."

"I said get out. If someone wants to see me, they can make an appointment. I will not have my privacy interrupted while I'm dressing."

"But—"

"Get. Out."

Brigid turned, flustered. The girl's baby bump showed now. Diana thought she was more beautiful than ever. Glowing, her ample breasts heaving from a low cut dress, Brigid backed out of the room.

Diana's posture carried her indignity, knowing the camera had recorded her temper tantrum. She had years honing her show business chops. She'd learned how to carry a scene.

Now if I can keep it up when I face someone higher on the food chain.

Chapter Forty-Two
Into the Lioness's Den

Maia deliberated on Anat's escape plan until it burned a hole in her brain. The scheme was dangerous. Could they pull it off? If they tried and failed, even their pitiful freedoms would be rescinded. Seth would be part of it—a means to an end, just like she had been to him. Did she have the guts to follow through?

She spent the morning in her suite with her children, making progress with Leo but not with Phillip. His reticence disturbed her. She asked which people he liked and who he didn't. The boy measured his answers to address some questions and added nods and shakes of his head for others. No matter what Maia did, she couldn't break through the layer of self-protection he'd constructed. The fact that a ten-year-old boy had erected a protective shield against any closeness warned her something bad had happened to him.

Iris plied her feminine charms like she'd been instructed to do. She fawned over Maia the whole time, touching her hair and tracing her fingers over her mother's face, calling her princess mommy. She tried to monopolize Maia, determined to keep her from connecting with the boys, and seemed resentful when she did. She'd learned her lessons well.

"Let me visit with Anat for an hour or two, Seth," Maia said when time came for the children to go. "I'm hungry for companionship."

"Aren't I enough for you, Maia?"

Maia had learned her lesson too. Truth got nowhere with Seth. Anat was spot-on. He was a company man, right down to the hard-on for her he carried like a warrior's spear. No matter how much he claimed to love her, his allegiance had always been to the family. She doubted Seth planned or condoned kidnapping other peoples' babies. That decree came straight from the top. Was he ready to buck the system?

"You're more than enough. You always were." Maia meant those words even if she used them to get what she wanted. Even if it meant giving in to the skilled hands now caressing her body, turning her nerve endings into firecrackers. She could no more resist his touch than she could cease breathing.

Over twenty years of brainwashing couldn't eliminate the group's obscene criminal offenses. They must be stopped. She'd turned against her own people, rejected their rituals and way of life, but as Seth undressed her, as he kissed and licked her naked body, she spread her legs and let him in.

* * * * *

Later, after Seth relented and allowed Maia to visit Anat, the two women sat on the balcony, huddled close, with only the sound of the rushing water breaking the silence.

Maia's determination held fast. If she didn't do this now, she'd never forgive herself. In the clear light of day, she saw her responsibility stretched beyond her personal well-being.

"Are you sure you're up to this?" Anat asked.

"I've thought about it, and yes. I have no choice. I can't let my children live here any longer, and you'll rot soon if you don't leave."

"I won't rot, but if I don't agree to bear another child, they'll do what they did to you. The only reason they didn't is because I got pregnant. They're dying to discover who the father is, but that's between me and him. The board, minus Seth, questioned everyone who's ever visited me." She gazed at Maia. "I do have friends here."

"Thank goodness." Maia shook her head. "I can't believe I went along all those years. What was I thinking?"

"You weren't thinking. If you're one of us, you're not supposed to think, just perform."

Her half-sister made a good point. "Why are you different?"

"A wayward gene." Anat's tone changed. "There's a bigger problem, though, one that might alter our plans."

"Like what?"

"Ever hear of the psychic, Diana Racine?"

"Of course. She's been at the house. Silas is fascinated by her. Why?"

"She's here, along with her cop boyfriend."

Maia's stomach lurched as if an earthquake had taken residence. A flash of heat zapped her. "What? How…how do you know?"

"A visitor. She was all excited and said they're going to keep her here. She called her Diana, Goddess of the Moon. Your father invited her to your house in New Orleans on the crescent moon, and she was the offering. She and the cop were probably drugged to get them here. All the elders attended except the Easleys. I don't know why."

Maia felt ill. The group was increasing their criminal activities. Did they actually think they could get away with kidnapping someone as famous as Diana Racine? "What about Dione? Was she there?"

"I'm not sure."

"I can't believe this. I heard whispers but not enough to

piece it together."

"They want Diana Racine's eggs in hopes her psychic abilities will pass to one or more of her children. My visitor thought bringing her here was the best thing ever. Can you imagine?"

"They kidnapped the lieutenant too? Unbelievable."

"I don't know what they plan for him. They can't let him go. He knows too much, and he's a cop."

Maia shivered in fear. "You're right. This changes everything. We must do something and fast."

"I thought Seth might have told you."

"Ha. Seth doesn't want anything to spoil his sex. That's all he cares about."

"He cares about you, Maia. I know he does."

Maia turned away with a shrug, biting her bottom lip. *Caring for her didn't stop him from doing his job.* "Maybe."

Anat gripped Maia's arm. "If this is none of my business, say so, but are you protected?"

"I have three children I hardly know. I'm not proud of allowing them to grow up in the hands of others. It won't happen again. If I ever leave here, they'll get the best medical and psychological care available, and I'll be with them every step of the way."

"Good girl. Okay then, let's get started." Anat went inside. She uncovered the diaper pail next to Chloe's crib and lifted out the bag with the used diapers. Digging down under a clean second bag she plucked a small zipper-locked plastic bag containing about a dozen pills and beckoned Maia back to the balcony. "You'd better take these now in case the plan goes bad and something happens to me."

Maia didn't like the tone of Anat's statement, but she took the bag. "What are these? Will they—"

"They'll just make him sleep. Don't worry."

"Why did you hide them?"

"They don't trust me, which accounts for the occasional room check. I don't know what they expect to find, but they don't find it. Part of the teenagers' duties is to clean the rooms. One of them comes in with a master key every afternoon to take out the trash and remove the dirty diaper bag. She never checks under the clean bag."

"Where did you get the pills?"

"I got them one at a time and squirreled them away for when I'd need them."

Obviously, Anat chose to hold things back, like who'd been helping her. Not even Anat trusted her. Maia understood her caution. She wasn't sure who to trust either. Maia swallowed and straightened her back. "I'm ready. Let's do it."

* * * * *

Maia's heart beat like a jackhammer. She played games, read, and watched videos with the children all afternoon. Even Phillip loosened up a bit, chatting and laughing. They ate dinner together, served in her room. She admired Anat more with each passing hour. This was her life, and she'd used the time to fill herself with knowledge, to learn and create and bond with her child.

Maia doubted she'd survive years as a captive, but she'd been raised in the public eye, not in the compound. Silas and Selene indoctrinated her and Dione into their religion—or better yet, their cult, for that's what it was. A cult that rejected God and worshipped the high priest of love and pleasure and fertility in His place, and damn anyone to Hell that got in the way.

When her half-siblings came along—Brigid, Nona, and three boys Maia knew only by name—they were shuttled off to the compound one by one, groomed to supply their precious genetic material to expand the population. Compton-Crane material.

Though she'd turned her children over to others, Selene visited frequently, returning to extol *her* offsprings' superior attributes. How could they be anything less than perfect, considering their parents?

For fear of being discovered, "Selene's children" were prohibited from going to Middlebridge College. Maia never understood why they were kept secret, but since Brigid and Nona slipped back and forth between New Orleans and the compound, she figured they enlisted new devotees without connecting the Crane and Compton families. She and Dione saw them when they gave birth, but it was far from a family reunion.

The thought brought Seth to mind. From the beginning, he was like a magnet, drawing her into him with his words and touch…until they took the second child, Iris, from her arms so she could return to the real world. Though she never lost her desire for Seth, she wouldn't allow another baby to be plucked from her breast and nurtured by strangers. In spite of her vow, it happened one more time—without her consent.

She checked herself in the mirror, dabbed on his favorite perfume. Where was he? He should have come by now. *Please don't let me lose my nerve—fall helplessly into his charms—and forget my mission. I must do this.*

A first-class chef was on call 24/7, and the food was outstanding. Meals were served in her suite. There was a mini-fridge for drinks, imported coffee beans, and tea, along with a few snacks. She made a pot of coffee, and the rich aroma filled the room. The jolt of caffeine would boost her energy level. It'd be a long night.

The coffeepot stopped gurgling. She poured a cup and waited, hoping her shaking hands wouldn't give her away—hoping she could entice Seth into a cup of coffee before they made love.

The key turned in the door and Seth slipped into her room. Her heart rate skyrocketed, not only because of what she intended to do, but because it was Seth. He was as predictable as the earth's rotation when it came to his nightly dose of sex. As always, he shut off the camera with a wink to the lens. Maia insisted on privacy from the start. She would not allow prying eyes to watch while they made love. Seth's acquiescence to her wishes made Anat's plan feasible.

Maia's heart fluttered at the sight of him. His roguish smile and flashing black eyes broadcast his desires, and she forced herself to concentrate on the task at hand. He kissed her neck, and she felt weak.

"You smell of coffee and cream and sugar," he said. "Good enough to drink."

"I wanted to be alert to enjoy you. I needed the stimulant. Have a cup while it's fresh." She poured the brew into a giant mug. "Then you can lap up every drop of me until the wee hours of the morning."

"Exactly what I had in mind," Seth said.

Chapter Forty-Three
Who's the Boss?

Beecher and Cash pulled into the circular drive of Martin Easley's renovated Greek Revival, in the heart of the French Quarter. Beecher eased out of the air-conditioned car into the oppressive summer heat. Within seconds, his shirt stuck to his back and perspiration beaded his forehead. He mopped his brow and tiptoed on the chevron-patterned brick walkway, puddled from the automatic sprinkler system. The spray drenched the flowering shrubs around the house, releasing a mixture of perfumed scents. Beecher muffled a sneeze. *Freaking allergies.*

"This place must be worth a couple mil, even in this economy," Beecher said.

Cash scanned the area. "You ever been in a house like this before?"

"Yeah, a domestic violence call a couple years back." Beecher pulled his collar away from his neck. *Damn crime to have to wear a tie in this heat.* "Not anything I usually respond to, but I was nearby. A neighbor called it in. Husband was a mean drunk. Beat the crap out of her. Wife wouldn't press charges. They rarely do, especially if they'd lose their cushy lifestyle. I've seen her in the society pages a time or two, without the black eye."

"No shit." Cash craned his neck to peek in the window. "This is my first."

"This isn't a social call, Cash. Don't forget, this guy's a Satan worshipper."

"Man, I don't understand tha—"

The door opened and a regal-looking black woman stood before them.

"May I help you?" she said.

Beecher crammed his handkerchief in his pocket. "I'm Detective Beecher, NOPD. This is Detective Cash. We have an appointment with Mr. Easley."

She moved back so they could enter, directing them to a large living room. "I'll tell him you're here. Make yourselves comfortable." Then she left.

"Jeez, will ya look at this place," Cash whispered. "It's like out of a magazine."

"Actually, it was," Martin Easley said, entering the room. "*Architectural Digest* featured the house after the renovations were completed last year. Sophia Reyes did the design. She's amazing, really. Martin Easley." He offered his hand to the two cops.

Beecher introduced himself and Cash. Easley motioned the men back to their seats. Tall and lean, almost gaunt, Easley wore slacks and a short-sleeve knit shirt sporting the polo-playing logo. His weathered look reminded Beecher of a lifelong mariner—tan, crinkled skin, sun-bleached hair. But instead of confidence, Beecher noticed shaky hands with nails bitten to the quick.

"What can I do for you gentlemen?" Easley said.

"We understand you were recently in the company of Diana Racine."

"Yes," he answered, eyes darting between the two cops. "Silas—Mr. Compton—invited Ms. Racine and her friend for a delightful evening a week or so ago. Why?"

"Ms. Racine's friend, Lieutenant Lucier, is our boss. They were invited to Mr. Compton's house again. Now they're missing."

Easley swallowed, his Adam's apple bobbing in his throat. "How strange. My wife and I were also invited to attend, but we had a previous engagement."

"Do you mind telling us where?" Beecher asked.

Easley seemed at a loss for words, but he recovered. "Does it matter? I said we weren't there. What's this about, Detective? Am I under suspicion for something?"

"No sir, but we haven't been able to connect with your friends. They've all left town for the weekend and haven't returned. We'd like to ask them some questions. The captain thought you or your wife might help us."

"I'd like to, but I haven't a clue where they are. We're good friends, but we're not joined at the hip."

Beecher found the temperature in the house to be on the chilly side, but Easley was sweating like he'd just run a marathon. "Is there someplace you all go on either Mr. Compton's private jet or on Mr. Crane's? Some place secret? A hideaway, if you will?"

"Are you accusing me of complicity in the disappearance of your boss and Ms. Racine? Because that's what it sounds like."

Easley ran a shaky finger across the top of his sweaty lip, glistening from the sun streaming in the bay windows. He acted nonchalant, but any idiot could see Martin Easley verged on falling apart. Beecher had never seen a thin man sweat so heavily.

"Do I need a lawyer present?" Easley asked.

"Any reason why you need one?" Beecher asked.

Easley squared his shoulders. "I know nothing about

where your lieutenant is, nor do I know the whereabouts of Ms. Racine. And since that seems to be what you're implying, I think you gentlemen should leave. If you have further questions, make it official and I shall arrange a lawyer to be present."

Beecher rose and stood face to face with Easley. "I'm sure the captain will find that satisfactory."

Easley stuttered a few unintelligible words, and was about to say something when Anastasia Easley sauntered confidently into the room. Beecher was struck by her classic green-eyed beauty. Her dark hair swept loosely into a topknot around her fine-featured face. A silk caftan cut low enough to expose two assets many women would pay good money for, clung to the contours of her body as she floated into the room. Beecher forced his focus away.

"There's no need, Detective," she said. "The fact is my husband is being gracious. We begged off Saturday because we really don't believe in psychics. It makes us uncomfortable. Even if Ms. Racine is on the level, I'm not interested in knowing what will happen in my life, and neither is Martin. I made up the excuse to Silas that we had other plans we couldn't break." She exchanged glances with all three men. "Silas doesn't like to be refused. Neither does my father."

"So you intentionally begged off."

"Yes."

"Do *you* know where your friends are, Mrs. Easley?" Beecher asked. "The dinner was supposed to be at the Comptons' on Saturday, yet no one was in town Sunday morning, nor are they at their offices today." Beecher paused. "The ladies are your sisters, correct?"

"Yes, but they don't tell me every move they make. Have you tried my father's lake house? Sometimes we go there on

Sunday for a barbeque."

Beecher shook his head. "Nope. We checked."

"Sorry we can't be more help, Detective. Now Martin and I must ask you to leave. If you have any other questions, we'll be happy to meet your captain downtown—with our attorney." Clearly uncomfortable, Martin Easley nodded, but his wife strode confidently to the door and opened it. "Good day, gentlemen."

Beecher would have tipped his hat if he wore one. "Thank you for your time."

Outside, he loosened his tie and unbuttoned the top of his shirt, and not because of the heat. "She's one beautiful woman."

Cash glanced back at the house. "Damn straight. Did you see how she took control of the conversation?"

"Yeah, and she knew more than she let on."

She sure as hell did. I should've pushed harder, made them talk. Should've. Both men got into the car.

"Bet she knows where the lieutenant is," Cash said.

"I bet she does too. If he's still alive." A sick feeling lodged in the pit of Beecher's belly. "Shit."

Chapter Forty-Four
A Rude Awakening

Diana rummaged through the closet and chose a chiffon print dress with ruffles bordering the low neckline. She'd never buy anything like that. Too fussy. After she put it on and primped in the mirror, she looked like another person. Wasn't that the point? She'd have to be another person to level the playing field. Her life and Lucier's counted on how she controlled what happened next. She stopped, shook her head, chuckling. What was she thinking? A camera leered down at her from inside a locked room. She wasn't at all in control.

If a ruffled dress played into their idea of who she needed to be, fine. She carefully applied her makeup and stood back one more time to take in the whole picture.

Here I am. Diana, Goddess of the Freaking Moon.

A knock on the door. Dinner, the voice said, and asked permission to enter. Diana said okay, and when the door slid open, a girl no more twelve or thirteen pushed a dinner cart holding plates with silver covers, then set the small table in the room with silver service and a bottle of expensive wine. A large man waited outside.

"The leader would like to see you after dinner, Ms. Racine," the girl said.

"Who might that be?"

"That's all I can say, but I was told to tell you there is nothing to fear."

Yeah, right. I'm locked in a room God knows where, Ernie's probably dead, or will be soon, and she says there's nothing to fear. Diana tried to erase the thought about Lucier from her mind, but it hung there like a recalcitrant child, unwilling to behave.

"You mean my food won't be laced with drugs?"

The girl frowned, obviously perplexed.

"You can tell whoever wants to see me that he can come in an hour's time."

She nodded and turned for the door without saying anything more, the perfect servant delivering a message from her master.

Leader. Is that what they called kidnappers these days? Diana referred to "the leader" as a man, and the girl made no correction. The women in Compton's circle seemed to be held in an exalted state, maybe even in control. She pictured Selene and the others as examples of how to act when *the leader* came. She pictured Sophia Reyes with her husband's hand tweaking her nipple while Diana watched. Was she in a bargaining position? She'd find out soon enough. If so, she'd do whatever it took to free Lucier. Then, one of those body shocks attacked her. The kind where her stomach somersaulted and her heart rate shot into the stratosphere. *Please, Ernie. Be alive.*

She willed away the bad thoughts and forced herself to eat. Whatever happened, she'd need strength. The drugs had zapped most of hers. Eating wasn't as much of a chore as she thought. Shrimp cocktail followed by prime rib, potatoes au gratin, and steamed green beans. Crème brulée for dessert. She devoured every morsel and felt better.

The knock on the door came in exactly one hour. "Who is it?" she asked.

"May I come in, Diana?"

The voice sounded vaguely familiar. It wasn't Compton's

rasp nor the cultured tenor of Phillip Crane. Diana gave her permission, playing the diva. When the key turned and the door opened, her jaw dropped at the sight of her visitor.

Her voice cracked in shock. "Edward."

"May I come in?" He stood outside, waiting for permission.

She managed a nod because words stuck in her throat. He stepped inside. "I don't understand. I thought—"

"I'm sorry I deceived you," he said. "I didn't think you'd understand."

She slumped into a chair, her mouth still open, and her hand pressed hard against her chest and rapidly beating heart. How could she have been so wrong? How could Edward Slater have fooled her so completely?

"I don't…understand," she stammered. "How could anyone understand this?"

"Give me a chance to explain," he said.

She shook her head slowly, rejecting in advance anything Slater said. "You explained once, and I believed you." She massaged her temples, trying to finesse away the vice-tightening sensation. *This isn't happening. I must be in the throes of another nightmare?*

"Lies. All lies," she mumbled. She faced him. "You had me going, Edward. What could you say now I'd believe? You drugged me, imprisoned me in a room somewhere on the planet, the object of a bizarre ritual to the devil, and I'm supposed to understand?"

"It's not like that."

"I suppose the cancer story was a lie, too, and that you have all the makings of a sex god to impregnate these young girls."

"No," he said emphatically. "That part was true. Almost."

"What is the truth?" Diana asked, not shrinking from his apologetic gaze.

"The cancer part but not the castration."

Diana got up and walked to the window. She wanted to scream but instead drew back the drapes and stared out into the abyss. A dark night in a dark world. No lights, no moon. Maybe she was on another planet. Mars, perhaps. Or Venus. Or a sick combination of both.

"Jesus. What a fool I am."

"Yes, Jesus, who turned his back on me and cast me into hell."

A slow bubbling concoction of shame and anger percolated inside. Lucier had been right all along. She'd been hoodwinked by a sad story, by the intellectual brilliance of a madman. "Hell is what you made it, Edward."

"Let me ask you, Diana. Could you love a man like me? Could you look beyond the abortion between my legs? Could you?"

He waited. When she didn't respond, he said, "As I thought."

She spun around to say something trite about love being in the eye of the beholder, but the words got lost in the sight before her. Edward Slater stood naked from the waist down, his pants draped at his feet. She gasped and backed against the window.

"Shocking, isn't it?" he said.

Tears flooded in her eyes. She managed to stagger to the bed before passing out.

* * * * *

His words echoed in her head from a far off place, becoming louder now, understandable. She had to readjust to the time and place. When she did, she wanted to go back to the never-

never land from which she had awakened.

"Again," he said, "I'm sorry."

Diana heard his words and opened her eyes. Slater hovered over her.

"That was cruel," he said.

He held a glass of water to her lips. She steadied his hand and sipped. It was the first time he let her touch him. He needn't have worried about setting off a psychic connection. He passed nothing to her, not even a blink of a vision. Where Edward Slater was concerned, she had lost her abilities. In fact, what she saw in the light of reality was far worse than any image he could have instilled through his touch.

"What have you done with Ernie?" she asked.

"He's safe. For now."

She allowed herself a monumental sigh of relief. *He's alive.* God had heard her prayer. "What do you mean, for now? Where is he?"

"Being well taken care of. We bound him at first, but he's not now."

Her high tumbled as reality sank in. She had jeopardized the life of the man she loved by being who she was—Diana, Goddess of the Moon. "Let him go. I'll do whatever you want. I'll be your goddamn goddess."

"Now see? That's the kind of love I'm talking about. You'd do anything for him, even turn yourself into a love machine, wouldn't you?"

Diana stared into Slater's steel-gray eyes that once had radiated kindness and warmth but now projected a cold arrogance. "Yes," she said, never flinching from his gaze. "Even that. Just let him go. He doesn't know where we are. If I'm right, he couldn't find this place with all the resources of the police department and the FBI put together. Please,

Edward."

"I can't do that. He knows too much, knows who we all are. We're not quite ready to change locations, although we may soon have to."

"He'll never say anything as long as you have me. He'd never put my life in danger."

Slater put the glass of water on the bedside table, then brushed a curl from Diana's forehead. She steeled herself against shivering at his touch, but she failed miserably and cringed.

Smiling, he said, "Do I disgust you that much?"

"No," she lied, and bit back the threatening nausea. Maybe this was a game after all, she reasoned, and playing was her way out. "You *did* fascinate me, Edward. Right from the beginning, even before I knew what you went through. The richness of your mind, your philosophy. Then, when I learned more about you, you became more fascinating. How you fought your way back to the living. I bought your story." A tear escaped from the corner of her eye. She didn't know why.

"Yes, I knew we shared an intellectual bond, and I think you were physically attracted to me—before you knew."

"Intellectually, yes, but not physically, although I thought…think you're an attractive man. I won't lie to make you believe there was anything more. I'm in love with Ernie, and that will never change."

"Pity. You still fascinate me. From the first time we met. You're unlike anyone, Diana. Beautiful, intelligent, compassionate. Of course, I realize when you learned about me, you felt sympathy, as did those few who knew. But I could make you ecstatically happy. I know how to do things that pleasure a woman in ways she can't imagine."

He gently caressed her cheek, leaving a burning trail from

his touch.

She took a deep breath and forced herself still. A cringe at that moment could ruin everything. "Let Ernie go first."

A momentary frown crossed Slater's face, then he smiled. "I haven't told you how very beautiful you look tonight." He ran a finger along her neckline. "Feminine. Ruffles suit you. You dress too simply, almost mannishly, with your jeans and man-tailored shirts. This is definitely more attractive."

"If you want me, release Ernie. I'll do anything you want—after I know he's safe."

Slater got up. His tone changed. "You're not in a bargaining position."

She couldn't let Lucier's life slip away. "I don't love you, Edward, but I can learn. We have things in common. Like you said, an intellectual bond. We can develop our relationship into something more."

"Don't patronize me, Diana," Slater snapped. "I'm not a stupid man."

"Then you know I'm not patronizing you. If you don't let him go, you'll need to drug me, because I'll never do anything willingly. That would spoil what we could have."

"Our drugs will make you beg to do whatever we want just to get your next fix, and they won't affect the fetus. You'll forget all about your cop lover."

His words instilled in Diana a fear she'd never known. Her insides quaked at the thought, because she believed him.

He sat next to her on the bed. "You'll want to love me, Diana." He brushed his finger back and forth inside her bottom lip. When she jerked her head away, he said, "You'll need to."

His gaze dropped from her eyes to her chest, and started to unbutton the top button of her dress. She got up. "Sit,

Diana, and don't move unless I tell you to."

She stood defiant.

"Sit," he commanded in a stern tone she hadn't heard before.

This wasn't the time to start trouble, so she sat.

He unbuttoned the top of her dress and eyed the oversized bra. "I see we miscalculated." He slipped the straps off her shoulders, and the bra fell, exposing her small breasts. He touched the tip of her nipple. "Like a china doll, so tiny."

Diana thought back to the night in the cabin and what that psychopath had done to her. *Put yourself in another place, Diana. Go to your fantasy tropical paradise, with the sun soaking into your salty skin.*

"No, dammit! Not this time." She pulled up her dress and slid off the bed. "Hook me on drugs. Do anything you want, but you'll never own me. Not until you release Ernie. Let him go, and I'll be yours."

Slater looked as if he'd been slapped, and Diana saw the conflicted, tortured being whose vulnerability made her believe him in the first place. But the man was also a monster—a twisted Jekyll and Hyde.

"You'll be who we want you to be," he said, his voice as calm and reasonable as if he were talking to a child. "Who *I* want you to be, because I'm the one who wanted you here. Phillip too, but for different reasons." Slater stood, his eyes steady on her. "You'll reproduce, willingly or not. In addition, you'll provide eggs to be planted in surrogates. Your psychic abilities will pass to your offspring. Not to all of them, of course, but surely to some." He pinched her chin. "And you will be mine."

Slater's cold determination almost stopped Diana's heart. She harnessed her voice from some place deep inside her and quivered when she spoke. "It doesn't work that way. I didn't inherit my gift from anyone. I'm a freak of nature. The percentage of passing on any ability I have is infinitesimal."

"Percentages change with volume." Slater smirked and left the room.

Diana shook as he locked the door behind him. Hurrying to the bathroom, she emptied her stomach of the wonderful dinner she enjoyed only an hour before.

Chapter Forty-Five
The Disciple

Maia watched Seth sleep. He passed out almost immediately. She didn't know what kind of pills Anat gave her, but if she ever needed something to sleep, she wanted those. She'd put two in Seth's coffee, just like Anat said, and hoped they'd keep him out for hours. Still, Maia couldn't take any chances. After she removed his key ring, she fastened both his wrists to the bed with the pair of handcuffs he kept in the room. That'd teach Seth to practice kinky sex. The titillating thought caused a brief distraction.

Stop! She couldn't let the memory of their lovemaking keep her from the plan. Focusing, she cut off three pieces of masking tape, also supplied by Anat, and fastened them across Seth's mouth. She fumbled to find the master key that would open most of the doors in the compound. Before she tried them, she ran back and kissed Seth's cheek.

"Sorry, love," she whispered.

Half a dozen keys hung on Seth's chain. The key on the fourth try turned the lock. She marked the key with a small piece of tape so she wouldn't have to hunt for it again. She glanced back at the sleeping figure, resisting the urge to undo what she'd already done. The plan must go forward, for her children. For all the children, and for the two people who shouldn't be here whose lives were in jeopardy. She cracked the door and listened. It was after midnight. Low light illuminated the quiet hallway.

Anat's suite was clear across the vast compound. One thing in Maia's favor: no one expected any mischief from her. She scanned the corridors, checking for cameras. None in this guest wing. Visitors wouldn't approve of someone watching their every move, especially those special men, and women too, Silas or Phillip lured into their fold with promises of sex and wealth in exchange for their superior genetic material. Maia marveled at how many were willing. Did they agree before they knew they were selling their souls? In the end, did it matter to them? She cringed at the thought while she hustled down the hall and out the back door.

After waiting for her eyes to adjust to the dark, she went over Anat's directions. The compound resembled a small town, cross-hatched with narrow paved streets. The road she'd take avoided them, in favor of a path at the edge of the forest. Lights went out at midnight, leaving the area black as coal. Only leaders and guards had the authority to breach curfew. Maia saw no one.

Anat gave her specific directions to Cal's building, situated on the border of the inner compound. Maia wasn't sure she could follow them in the dark. They'd constructed new buildings since her last visit which challenged her sense of direction.

Go to the end of your building, turn left onto the path, and go until you can't go any farther.

She'd never heard such silence. Was she being watched? Were there hidden cameras?

When you get to the end, a narrow road branches to the right. Take it.

There. She almost missed it in the dark.

Go for about three quarters of a mile.

Maia made her way carefully along the dirt path. She tripped on a fallen branch, swore, and kicked it out of the way.

You'll be behind three buildings at the end of the road. Cal's is the farthest.

Things had changed. As the group multiplied and the complex grew, the younger children lived in dormitories, like they would at sleep-away camp, always with an older member who acted as leader. Cal lived separately on the outskirts of the compound. He had free rein during the day but was locked in at night. What did they think he'd do? She found the master key, turned the latch, and slipped inside.

Up the stairs. End of the hall. On the right.

Maia had failed to ask if Cal expected her. Was he even awake? She opened the door just enough to slip through. Classical music played softly in the background. She moved into the apartment. Cal sat in bed reading, oblivious that someone had entered his domain. It gave Maia a chance to look around. His residence was much like her sister's: a two-room suite with a large balcony. Crammed bookcases lined the walls; a computer sat on the desk.

When he saw her, Cal hopped from the bed, wearing nothing but cotton drawstring pants. "There are no microphones," he said, "so no need to tiptoe." Though still thin, sinewy muscle replaced the softness she remembered, and he was more handsome than ever. He sauntered toward her and wrapped her in his arms, whispering in her ear.

"I hoped you were coming." Moving back, he said, "You heard about Diana Racine and the cop?"

"Yes."

"Bad enough they're kidnapping babies; this may wind up being murder. They can't let either of them go."

"How do you know everything, Cal?"

"I come and go as I please," he said, "except at night. The group isn't threatened by me, so no one has his guard up." He focused on her. "They think I'm a wimp. They think I'm a lot of things I'm not, and that's exactly the way I want it. Plus, I don't see any sense in resisting unless it's a means to an end." He moved back to the bedroom. "I need to get dressed. If I'd known for sure you were coming, I'd have been ready, but I honestly doubted Anat could talk you into this."

"I wasn't sure myself." She followed him. "If you can go wherever you want, why do you live out here all alone?"

"Being away from everyone else has its advantages."

Cal changed in front of her without inhibition. She guessed he retained some of the group's teachings. The body is a temple to be worshiped, and one should never feel embarrassment. Maia always thought the temple bit corny, but the philosophy had been drummed into her too.

He pulled on a pair of faded jeans and shrugged into a T-shirt. "This place is huge and growing until recently. I'm not sure why things are at a standstill, but I've got an idea. Not that it matters now. We need to get out of here, and the only way is by plane. One thing I do know—we're in the middle of fucking nowhere." He grabbed the keys from Maia. "Come on." He locked his door from the outside and checked the halls. "You came in the service entrance, didn't you?"

Maia nodded.

"Good girl. Now all we have to do is get to Anat without being seen."

"I thought everyone was asleep by twelve."

"The big guys can do whatever they want." Cal took Maia's hand. "Follow me. I know where they're keeping the Racine woman and have a pretty good idea where the cop is."

"You've been paying attention."

"Hasn't done any good until tonight," he said. "Stay close." He stopped short. "Are you sure Seth will be knocked out for a couple of hours?"

"More like till morning, and is he ever going to be pissed."

"Tough shit." He gazed at Maia apologetically. "Sorry. I forgot you and Seth were more than egg and sperm. He's better than most."

Maia wondered what Cal meant, but she didn't want to ask right now. She felt guilty enough. This man taking charge, showing no fear, was not who Anat described. More was going on than what they confided in her. Was she being used in some way? Too late to ask questions.

Cal led her down the stairs, stopping to check every time they came to an intersection. "I thought no one else was in the building."

"They use these buildings for mating. If something's going on, I always—shh." He pushed Maia back against the wall. "Someone is checking the perimeter," he whispered. "He usually makes his rounds earlier. Damn, why is he late tonight of all nights?"

Mating. Sounded like the birds and bees or animals in season. The group was expanding. Last time she saw more women from outside the family. Maia felt sick. They had upped *production*. Cal uttered an obscenity.

He held her back until the coast was clear, then they crept silently down the hall to a back exit. Cal opened it. They kept to the side of the building. Now that they were outside the building, Maia didn't have a clue where she was. She'd be lost without Cal.

"Anat's building is near the river," he said.

"I know. Her balcony hangs high over it. A sheer drop."

"Her only escape is to jump over and kill

herself—something she'd never do now that she has Chloe."

Maia struggled to keep up. "That's a coward's way out, not Anat's. She's too strong."

Cal turned. "She certainly is. One amazing woman." He latched onto her hand. "Come on. We've got more than a mile to go, and there's a new moon. Dark as pitch."

They hugged the backside of the building and headed toward the woods. As they were about to clear the paved area and veer onto the path, Cal pulled her down behind a line of shrubbery. He pointed ahead.

Two men came out of the last building. One second earlier and Maia and Cal would have been standing right in front of them. She'd never seen the big guy before, but she recognized Edward Slater. "What's he doing here?" she whispered.

Cal's face paled noticeably, even in the dim light. His body went rigid, and his upper lip curled in distaste. "Didn't you know? His so-called mission is the conduit to recruit the surrogates. He also convinced everyone to bring Diana Racine here. He and Phillip. Slater is Phillip's grandfather's prime disciple."

Maia needed a minute to digest what Cal said. "Disciple? But Phillip's grandfather has to be long dead."

"He was very old when Slater met him. I doubt he'd approve of what Slater's become."

"What do you mean?"

"Later," Cal said.

Maia always thought of Slater as an opportunist, sucking up to the rich guys for money to run his mission, but a major disciple? Cal's reaction upon seeing him told her there was more to Slater than her impression of him.

"I'll be damned," she said under her breath, then realized she probably already was. "Who's the other guy?"

"He's Ridley Deems's replacement. A couple more do the dirty work. They've stopped kidnapping babies for the time being in favor of taking care of anyone who gets in the way, like the New Orleans cop."

"How do you know so much?"

"I told you. I've created a persona they believe. I'm innocuous. I don't matter." He forced a tight smile, his eyes on Slater's back, waiting until he disappeared. "Of course, if we succeed tonight, they might change their opinion." He winked. "Come on, Maia. Let's go."

Chapter Forty-Six
Chameleon

The last thing Lucier remembered was Slater's sidekick, a huge creature he dubbed Mountain Man, injecting him with something. Everything went black until he woke last evening, stiff and groggy. He'd been moved into a rustic room with no windows and a lock to challenge Houdini on the only door. The place smelled musty and unused. The small bathroom contained a toilet, sink, a bar of soap and a towel. There was a cot bolted to the floor, a table, and one chair. No sheets or pillow. Better than a prisoner holding cell but not by much. This must be where they ostracized those undisciplined members who bucked the rules, he thought.

He'd been served dinner, and in the morning breakfast. A very good sandwich followed a few hours later. At least he was no longer trussed like a Thanksgiving turkey, and it didn't appear as if they were going to starve him to death.

He weighed his escape options the minute his head cleared. Nothing in the room worked as a weapon except the chair, except the only person to enter so far was a young girl who brought his three meals. He refused to put her in danger unless he had no other choice. Mountain Man accompanied her, but he stood outside the door, well out of reach of any attempt to take him down. They'd thought of everything.

This morning, he stretched, did a dozen pushups and a couple of deep knee bends to get his legs back, breathing heavily when he finished. He sure as hell wasn't in peak physical condition, and Slater's man looked like a pro wrestler who could put him down without working up a sweat. Lucier figured his life expectancy may span a few more days, but that's all. He was too much of a threat to keep alive, and they couldn't let him go.

He asked Mountain Man about Diana, and the man assured Lucier in monosyllables that she was fine. The answer didn't assuage the terror of remembering his last image of her, bound and unconscious.

Think, Ernie. He needed to find a way out and fast. One possibility kept cropping up, but he doubted this guy would fall for it. Maybe he was all brawn and no brain. With nothing to lose, Lucier made up his mind to try after dinner. Otherwise, he was a dead man.

To give himself an extra advantage, after the midday meal he launched into a serious set of push-ups and stretches. *Gotta get back in shape.*

* * * * *

Maia put her faith in Cal as they raced through the woods toward Anat's building. She heard the rapids, felt a fine mist in the air that turned her shirt into a soggy rag pasted to her skin. Cal thrust out his arm to slow her down when their destination emerged from the eerie shadow of trees.

Cal pointed skyward to the small black box high on a pole topped by a solar-generated light. "There's a camera aimed on the front door."

"How do we get inside?"

"A door in back. Stay here for a minute while I make sure the area's clear."

"But—"

Cal disappeared. What were they doing? Even with Anat

free, her plan depended on Seth, and Seth would surely fight what they needed him to do. Escaping from the compound, surrounded by mountains, woods, and rough-rapid waters would be impossible without him. No one walked out of there.

Cal stuck his head around the side of the building and crooked his finger for her to come. She followed his path to a narrow service door.

"We gotta make this fast," he whispered. He slipped the master key into the lock. It didn't work.

"Damn. They've even separated her by keys."

"I thought you visited."

"I do, but I have to get clearance. Anat and I eat together, spend some time, then I leave." Cal shrugged. "They're scared of her. Think she's plotting something, which of course she is."

The thought that her father and Phillip were afraid of Anat made her smile. They'd come this far and were in too deep. No stopping now.

Cal proceeded to try one key after the other until he found one that worked. They entered and climbed the four flights to Anat's aerie. When Cal opened the door, Anat ran to him and flung her arms around him. They kissed.

"Okay," Maia said, looking at Anat and Cal. "Now I'm totally confused. I thought—"

"I couldn't tell you," Anat said. "I wanted to, but I didn't know if I could trust you."

"Explanations later," Cal said. "We've got to get out of here. Give me the sling, Anat. I'll carry Chloe."

Anat picked up the sleeping child, and Cal arranged the sling on his chest. The baby didn't wake. They hustled out the door. Maia now believed Chloe was indeed Cal's daughter, but she didn't ask. Too many questions begged answers, and she hoped to live long enough to get them.

"Where's Diana Racine?" Maia asked as they hurried down the stairs to the back door.

When they got outside, Cal locked the door behind them. "She's in the visitor's quarters, receiving the royal treatment. Phillip uses the suite when he's tempting someone he regards deserving of our great order. The suite is newer and even more plush than his."

"Where's the cop?"

"In one of the out-cabins. They're secluded and soundproof." He held everyone back. "Wait. Let me look around."

"Are they the cluster of buildings on the other side, in the woods?" Maia asked Anat.

"Yes. Cal and I have both been guests there," Anat said. "Lovely place."

"Why?" Maia asked.

Cal returned and put his hand on Maia's shoulder. "Later, when we have more time."

"Bottom line is their conversion didn't work," Anat said." They gave up on the both of us."

"Later, ladies. Time is important, and we don't have much. The cabin is far. Are you up to making the trip, Anat?"

She nodded.

"What about me?"

"Anat and I have had this plan for a while, but we needed Seth, and you were the only one who could persuade him to go along with us."

"I haven't persuaded him, Cal. I drugged him. What makes you think he'll do what you want because I ask him?"

"I'm an optimist. I can't think otherwise. The kidnapping of the babies and the two outsiders make stopping this debacle necessary. Even to Seth. It also puts a kink in our plans because now we have more people to worry about."

Cal's gaze lingered on Anat. Such love passed between them that Maia felt like an intruder. He cuddled the baby close and rubbed his cheek on the sleeping child's head.

Turning his attention to Maia, he said, "You have the best chance of getting Diana Racine out of the suite."

"Me? How? They'll recognize me."

"Exactly the point. You're Silas Compton's daughter. No one will question whether you're supposed to be there, and unless they know you're being contained, they'll think you're doing your father's work. If Anat or I are seen, a red flag with sirens will go off."

"It's the middle of the night. Why would I want to see her?"

"Because your father is having a meeting to offer up Diana, Goddess of the Moon. Make up some bullshit about the stars being in the right place in conjunction with the new moon. They'll believe you. No one in that role is conditioned to question."

"Is my…father still here?" She almost choked on the word father, considering the picture forming of him. A picture she'd chosen to ignore for too long.

"I don't know," Cal said, "I haven't been privy to any information today. I know my father isn't here, nor are Anastasia and her sisters."

"Do you know why?"

"I have an idea."

Who was feeding Cal his information? "What if you're wrong?"

He held her gaze. "Then we're fucked. We haven't much time. If we can't convince Seth to join us when he wakes up, we're fucked anyway. We're past the point of no return. Go to the Racine woman, Maia. Get her out of the building. Anat and I will go to the cabins and release the cop. We'll meet in the middle, behind the school, unless something happens to one of us. If it does, we can't be any worse off than before we started, can we?"

Maia clasped the back of her neck and massaged. "Tell me what to do, then point me in the right direction."

Chapter Forty-Seven
A Pie in the Eye

During the six years between the death of his family and meeting Diana, Lucier either ate out or dined on a variety of supermarket frozen dinners. Occasionally, he feasted on leftovers at his friend's hotel. The food in this place vied with the best of New Orleans's famous kitchens. His hosts obviously believed the cultivation of a genetically mastered race depended as much on good nutrition as it did on DNA.

The pickup of his empty Styrofoam dishes from his meals occurred about an hour and a half after the young girl delivered his food, always with Mountain Man waiting outside the door. Two different girls had performed the chore, or maybe pleasure, of serving him. Anna, respectful and compliant, eagerly served him in the manner Lucier assumed she'd been taught. The other never gave her name, was quiet and sullen, seldom making eye contact. He hoped Anna showed up this evening. She'd be more apt to follow instructions. If he got that far.

He finished his dinner, a meaty white fish bathed in a butter/wine/garlic sauce, two vegetables, coffee, and dessert. The dessert was the important factor in his escape, and he worried that there wouldn't be one. He'd have made do with something else on the dinner plate if he needed to, but the lemon meringue pie with a graham cracker crust couldn't have been more perfect. The success of his plan rested on timing. It was a long shot, he knew, he had nothing to lose.

He heard the muffled words of the bodyguard and the girl's acquiescence as they approached. Lucier lowered himself to the floor, tucked his hand under his chest, and held his breath for as long as he could to cast a purplish hue to his coffee-colored skin. When the door opened, he saw Anna through the slit of one eye and groaned one word—heart.

The girl rushed to Lucier, calling Mountain Man to come inside. "He's having a heart attack. Mountain Man started to pull out his cell phone, but the she said in frantic desperation, "Hurry. He needs CPR. Turn him over and do it. You know how, don't you?"

"Yeah, but—"

"Do it," she ordered. "He can't die."

The big man slipped the phone back into his pocket and leaned over Lucier who took a deep breath and swung his fist full of lemon meringue directly in the man's eyes and nose.

Caught off guard, Mountain Man groped at the thick glop clouding his vision and clogging his breathing passage. His effort to wipe it away pushed the viscous substance further into his eyes. He inhaled some of the mixture and launched into a choking cough. Lucier sprang up, grabbed hold of the man's testicles, and yanked with all his might. Much better than a kick that sometimes failed to hit the mark.

"Sorry to resort to the old yank-the-balls cliché, man," Lucier said, "but it's either your nuts or mine." The guard released a horrifying wail and bounced around with one hand clutching his crotch, the other unsuccessfully wiping the goo from his eyes. Lucier decided to put him out of his misery. He picked up the wooden chair and smashed it over Mountain Man's head. The chair was solid, didn't even splinter. The goliath collapsed to the floor like a two hundred-fifty-pound boulder and lay as still.

The girl started screaming loud enough to alert anyone within hearing distance. He took a giant step toward her and clasped his hand over her mouth, muffling her cries. "I'm not going to hurt you if you stop screaming," he said calmly in her ear. "If you don't, you'll force me to put you to sleep too."

Panic flashed in the girl's eyes, round as marbles, her angelic face a mask of fear. Lucier assumed she was aware of what happened to anyone who didn't behave. He also assumed the kids here were taught to honor their elders. Even though he wasn't one of them, he hoped she'd respond to his demands as she would to any adult.

"I need your help," he said in his most soothing voice. "Will you scream if I remove my hand from your mouth?" She shook her head, and he uncovered her mouth. She whimpered but didn't cry out. He knew how scared she was and felt guilty. Lives depended on what he did now. "Stay here and don't move."

She nodded and he shut the door. He frisked Mountain Man and confiscated his gun and a switchblade strapped to his ankle. Next he took his keys and cell phone. The gun was a Glock. He checked the load—full—and tucked it into his waistband. He also relieved the big man of a prized find. Handcuffs. Lucier guessed they were for him if he gave any trouble. Who knew? Around here the cuffs might have a dual purpose.

Lucier hurried back to Anna, huddled where he'd left her. "They have a woman here they're going to harm. Diana Racine. Do you know her?"

Anna nodded and shrugged away from Lucier, but he kept a firm grasp on her arm. "They won't harm her," she said tentatively. "She wanted to come here. We worship her."

"People brought her here against her will." Lucier backed away to show he wouldn't hurt her but stayed close. "Do you think it's right to make someone do things against her will?"

Anna sniffled. "Sometimes you have to until they learn the right way. But I don't believe you. They wouldn't do that to her."

"Give me the benefit of the doubt, for now."

A moan from the unconscious man caused Lucier to check his life signs. He'd hit the brute hard enough to cause permanent damage. A finger to the big man's neck revealed a strong, steady pulse. He couldn't worry about it.

"Why do you think this man has a gun?"

Anna shrugged, but she wrinkled her brow. Thinking now, Lucier hoped. "What if your leaders tell you the wrong things? What then?"

The girl looked confused. "We're not supposed to question."

"They were going to kill me," he said, holding up the gun as evidence. "Then they'd say they sent me home, but they would have been lying."

"They'd...never lie. Lying is—it's a sin."

Lucier shook his head in exasperation. This place had been built on lies. A flashback memory surfaced of a lecture Lucier gave to his older son after catching him in a lie. It's a sin to lie, he'd told him. Lucier shook off the remembrance as he'd done so many times, snippets of another life popping up when he least expected them.

A snort from his unconscious captive snapped him back to the present. His groans indicated it wouldn't be long before he was awake and seriously pissed. The man had at least sixty pounds on Lucier and wasn't the type to fight fair. A smile curled his lips when he thought how he put down the hulk.

Not fair either.

Though the man was dead weight, Lucier dragged him to the cot, praying he didn't rouse. He hoisted his torso onto the mattress first, then his legs. His heart pounded from the residue of drugs still in his system, but he couldn't take time to catch his breath. He didn't want Mountain Man to wake before he had secured him.

He threaded one of Mountain Man's arms through the narrow space between two vertical slats in the headboard of the bed, pulled the other arm over the top rail, and cuffed the two wrists together. He used the knife to cut off the unconscious man's shirt and tear it into strips. He tied his ankles tightly to opposite bedposts and stuffed a wad of shirt into his mouth. With little leeway to move, one wrong turn and he'd break his wrist. When his captive woke, Lucier harbored no doubt he'd be wild with anger.

He turned to the girl, huddled into herself, terrified. "Where are we?" She didn't answer. "Where?" he demanded.

"I don't know if I should tell you. You're going to hurt people."

Lucier knelt down until he was level with her. He crooked his index finger under her chin and lifted her head until she raised an unsteady gaze to meet his. "I promise I won't hurt anyone who doesn't want to hurt Miss Racine or me. We were taken against our will. Kidnapped." A thought occurred. He needed to broach it delicately. "How old are you, Anna?"

"Fourteen."

"Have you been with boys?"

Cheeks flushing, she turned away and spoke softly. "Not yet."

"Is that what you want? To be with boys and make babies?"

"No," she answered quickly, then seemed ashamed of her response. "But that's what we're supposed to do."

More memories emerged, and Lucier spoke as the father he once was. "I had a little girl very much like you. She's dead now, but she's always in my thoughts. She would have wanted to go to college to become a doctor or a lawyer or even pursue a career in law enforcement like her dad. What she wouldn't want is what you will be forced to do if the people in control here aren't stopped." Anna sniffled, and Lucier asked one more question. "Do you spend time with your mother, Anna? Talk to her about these things?"

"I see my birth mother sometimes. Not enough, though. All the kids have lots of mothers. Fathers too. That's the way here."

"Would you like to spend more time with your mother?" he asked, wondering who Anna's mother was. Wondering what the population totaled in this pretend haven.

Anna nodded.

Mountain Man moaned louder now, distracting Lucier, but the sound came from deep in his throat. Best he could do with a gag in his mouth. Lucier wished he had some of the drug they gave him, because this guy looked like he could pull the cot from the floor bolts and walk through the door with it attached.

"I need your help. People will die without it."

Anna thought for a long time. "Are you sure you won't hurt anyone?"

A groan came from the cot. The big man's eyes sprang open, and he tried to get up. He realized he was tied to the bed and writhed and twisted, peppering his efforts with grunts and growls. Lucier was sure he wrenched his arm when he squealed in pain. The captive spit out his gag.

"When I get loose," he screamed, "I'm gonna kill you. Your girlfriend too. I don't care what anyone tells me. You're a fucking dead man, Lucier."

Anna flinched. Fear once more sparked her blue eyes. Lucier approached the restrained man and socked him squarely in the jaw. He looked dazed but still conscious. Lucier hit him again, and this time he fell back into dreamland. Lucier rubbed his throbbing knuckles, then wadded up a bigger chunk of fabric and forced it into the man's mouth, glad he didn't have to worry about losing his fingers in the clamp of teeth. Facing Anna, he asked again, "Now will you help me?"

With her frightened gaze on the tethered man, she said, "Yes."

Chapter Forty-Eight
The Truth Will Set You Free

Eggs floated in the air like little puffs of clouds. A magic wand kissed each one, cracking the shells, and infant Dianas pranced out, smiling and kicking, having the time of their baby lives. They crawled into her ears, talking, whispering sweet words, calling her Mama. Then their voices turned angry, urgent. Wake up. Wake up.

Diana sprang up from her bed, body soaked. Sweat dripped down her back and chest, yet the room was cool. Confused, she shook off her sleep and tried to focus. Dim light bathed the room. She stared at the picture on the wall until her head stopped spinning.

Voices still sounded in her ears. Was this a dream within a dream? No. People were talking outside her door. She couldn't make out what they said, but one voice was definitely a woman. They seemed to be arguing. Diana tiptoed to the door, and put her ear close.

"Why would I have the key to her room if my father hadn't sent me?" the woman said. "You know who my father is, don't you?"

"Yes, Miss Maia, I do, but no one informed me you were coming, especially at this late hour. I was told not to let anyone inside her room except your father, Mr. Crane, or Brother Osiris."

Diana covered her mouth, smothering a gasp. Maia. What was she doing here?

"Okay then, go ahead, call my father," Maia said confidently. "He's organizing the meeting and won't be happy to be disturbed. You know what he's like when he's mad. He'll probably chew you out, but do what you must."

After a long silence, the male voice said, "Well, okay. I guess it'll be all right."

Diana heard the jingle of keys, and the door opened.

Maia turned back to the guard outside. "We won't be long. She's expected at the meeting before the stars are in alignment. This is a private offering."

Diana moved back into the room. She started to say something, but Maia shook her head as a warning to play along.

"Okay, Miss Psychic, get dressed. Daddy wants you to perform tonight." She stared down the guard, who had inched into the room. "She can't dress with you in the room." Maia waved him out and closed the door. She turned to Diana and whispered. "No questions. Hurry up and dress. We have to get out of here."

Diana didn't have to be told twice. She yanked off the flimsy nightgown and searched through the closet. Oh for a pair of slacks. She found a silky blouse and a short stretchy knit skirt that allowed for movement.

"Hurry," Maia prompted.

"I'm done." she said. "What's go—"

"Shh. Not now." Maia slid the key into the door lock and pulled it to. Silas Compton and Edward Slater stood waiting. Compton, wrapped in a terrycloth robe, looked disheveled and sleepy, unlike Slater, wide awake and fully dressed.

"Where do you think you two are going?" Compton said, crossing his arms over his chest. "Maia, Maia. Did you really believe you could get away with this with us a stone's throw from this room?"

Slater pointed to the little red light in the vent and shook his head.

Diana glanced at Maia and jerked her head toward the camera with a shrug. "I forgot."

"The guard wasn't fooled," Slater said. "Our people are well taught. There are no surprises, even when the daughter of one of the directors tries to pull a fast one."

"I'm disappointed in you, Maia. Selene warned me, but I wouldn't listen. How could I imagine my own flesh and blood would betray me? Not once but twice."

Maia squared her shoulders and threw out her chin. "It's you who've betrayed me, Father, by making us all accomplices in your crimes. Federal crimes."

"You fail to comprehend the ultimate objective, my dear. The creation of a new world. One of beauty and sensuality and brilliance. The special babies will be nurtured in a paradise of intellectual stimulation. So what if a few people make sacrifices in the process? There's always collateral damage in the quest for a better life. The returns more than make up for the losses."

"Parents whose babies were stolen from them don't agree."

"They'll have others," Compton said. "If they knew the loving care and exaltation their offspring will enjoy, I'm sure they'd offer their babies to us without hesitation."

Maia clasped her hand over her heart and struggled for breath. "You're insane."

"I'm sorry you feel that way, but I won't let anything stop what we've started." He brushed her off. "We've wasted enough time and energy with traitors. Phillip is right. Time to rid the compound of all those who refuse to embrace our ideals. I'm afraid that includes two of my daughters. We will offer you to God's adversary, our supreme leader, as a measure of our devotion."

Maia stuttered in disbelief. "So…so you'll eliminate Anat and me and anyone else who hinders the propagation of your Utopia? Tell me, did you kill my mother, too, when she didn't go along?"

Compton straightened and settled his gaze on his daughter. "A necessary progression. Your mother didn't understand. She was lost to me after the death of your brother. So sad."

Maia's knees buckled, and she fell back against the wall in despair. Covering her mouth didn't muffle the unearthly wail that rose from her soul.

Diana moved to comfort her. Compton and his group of Satan worshipers were worse than she imagined. Now, with cold calculation, they were about to become murderers. A vision of Lucier smiling, his topaz eyes watching her, flashed in her mind, and the thought that she'd put his life in danger left her lightheaded. She looked up at Slater. "Edward, how…how can you let this happen?"

A small shrug. "Life is a series of tradeoffs, Diana. I traded off, for love not evil. You'll see. You'll be safe here, cherished. Just do what we ask of you and you'll live a charmed life."

Diana wanted to argue the point, but for once she decided to keep her mouth shut.

Inside her scream would not be silenced.

Ernie, where are you.

Chapter Forty-Nine
Breaking the Weak Link

Captain Jack Craven followed his gut, and he didn't like the warning sign churning there like a bad case of indigestion. Another day and no word from either Lucier or Diana Racine. So far, the police had kept their disappearances quiet, but that wouldn't last. Someone was bound to talk. If Jake Griffin got hold of the story, the implications would be disastrous.

No one accused men like Phillip Crane and Silas Compton of heading a satanic cult without irrefutable proof, and they didn't have it. One incriminating word and Compton's attorneys would come down on the district like an out-of-control meteor. Owning a house where satanic rituals were practiced didn't make Compton the devil.

Beecher's visit to the Easley home yesterday produced a big fat zero, other than to pinpoint the boss in the family. Martin Easley was a weak link, and Craven wanted to talk to him without his wife supplying the answers. He phoned Easley's office personally to make the request, but the secretary said he hadn't come in this morning. Then Craven called his home. The lack of response sent an even more ominous signal since Beecher mentioned they employed a housekeeper. Craven decided to follow up. In ten minutes, he and Beecher pulled into Easley's circular driveway."

"No cars," Craven said.

Beecher pointed to the back. "There's a three-car garage

behind the house."

The house appeared deserted, curtains pulled closed. They climbed the few steps to the gallery and rang the bell. When no one answered, Beecher lifted the fancy doorknocker and rapped. Nothing. He shrugged.

Tension in the air stretched tight. A spiral of fear slithered down Craven's back. He walked to the bay windows that flanked the right side of the door. A small crack in the drapes allowed for a peek inside. He waved Beecher over to take a look.

"Shit," Beecher said.

"Call for backup, an ambulance, and a crime scene unit," Craven ordered. He pulled out his weapon. "Probable cause." Then he shot the lock off the door.

* * * * *

Craven watched as Charlie Cothran, the coroner of Orleans Parish, bent over the body of Martin Easley and examined the knife stuck in his chest. "He's still in rigor. Best I can guess is death occurred sometime early this morning," Cothran said. "Can't pinpoint the exact time 'cause the air conditioner's off. Place is like an oven."

"Yeah, I know," Craven said. "Smelled death the minute I walked through the door. Still taste it on my tongue." He saw Ralph Stallings duck under the yellow crime scene tape that encircled the Easley home. The agent flashed his ID to the cop on guard and lumbered up the stairs to the front door. He donned booties and gloves and entered the house.

"Take over, Detective Beecher," Craven said.

Stallings nodded to Beecher. "Damn heat," he said, looking around. "Jesus, you got a mess here."

"Another body in the kitchen. The housekeeper." Craven said. He nodded toward Easley's body. "My weak link."

"Guess someone else thought so too."

"Long as they contained their little cult, Easley went along. But kidnapping babies and a cop involved set off his panic button. He harbored a pathological fear of the police."

"Yup. Read his file. No wonder."

Craven motioned Stallings into the kitchen. Blood covered the floor and spattered the cupboards. He'd already seen the slaughter, but his stomach lurched again. "Bigger mess here."

Stallings made a hissing sound at the sight of the woman lying with a gaping slice across her throat. "Jesus. "You never get used to carnage like this. Poor woman worked for the wrong people."

"Maybe she was a threat because she knew too much." Craven poked through the papers on the kitchen desk. "We're not going to find anything incriminating here, but we'll sift through them anyway."

After a visual sweep of the room, Stallings asked, "Where's the Missus?"

"Good question. One of the neighbors said she left with luggage early this morning. Neighbor didn't think much of it. The Easleys were always going somewhere, she said." Craven ran a hand across the back of his neck. "Wish I knew where."

"May be able to help you out." Stallings wrinkled his nose. "Let's get out of this room. I just had lunch." They walked outside into what seemed like frigid air after the house's sweltering interior. They leaned against Craven's car. "My investigators untangled a large tract of land from a land trust about five hundred miles from here in Oklahoma. It's remote, not too far from a national park. Might be what we're looking for." Stallings loosened his tie and unbuttoned the top of his shirt. "Crane's father bought the property way back when, and his lawyers shifted ownership from one shell company to another. Phillip Crane's geniuses did the same."

"Reckoned it was something like that."

"I guarantee when you find Mrs. Easley, she'll deny knowing anything about these murders."

"If we find her. Either Anastasia Easley killed her husband, or she called someone else in to do it, then she calmly packed her bags and left."

Stallings nodded in agreement. "I've already contacted our office in Oklahoma City. They're sending a chopper to scope out the area."

"I hope it's what we're looking for. After this scene I'm more worried about Ernie and the Racine woman. These people crossed the line too many times. There's no turning back. Crane and Compton tie up loose ends, and Ernie and Racine are loose ends." Craven related Cash's theory about the kidnapped babies. "Ernie was working on the idea, but frankly, it sounded too weird yesterday. Doesn't sound weird now."

"A genetically mastered race, huh?" Stallings said. "Somewhere in Oklahoma? I agree with you. Sounds far-fetched. Even if you're right, they have corporations, employees, houses. Christ, their families are in Louisiana."

"They wouldn't be giving up anything. Both the Crane and Compton corporations are intertwined and run by family members. They've probably funneled funds into emergency accounts all over the place, as well as property. If they felt it was time to pull out, they've protected their assets." Craven pushed himself off the car and paced a few steps. "From what Ernie said, Compton is an arrogant megalomaniac. He thinks we couldn't find our own dicks with both hands, let alone their private Hades."

"Maybe he's right," Stallings said. "The Oklahoma City

boys might not find a thing. And even we find them, owning property isn't a federal offense as long as they pay their taxes."

Fire roared in Craven's gut. "But kidnapping and murder are."

Chapter Fifty
Welcome to Paradise

Lucier waited a long minute for his eyes to adjust to the dark. He took some more time to scan the perimeter. Satisfied they were safe, he hopped inside the golf cart Mountain Man used to travel around the compound. Anna slid in beside him, issuing directions. He didn't move. Turning to the girl, he asked, "Are you with me, Anna?"

The young girl paused before she answered. "I came here when I was very young, so I don't remember much of the outside world. When new people came—not *our* people but surrogates and guards—they mentioned things. My friends and I talked about what we heard. We weren't supposed to, but we did. We're not allowed TV, and computers are loaded with studies the leaders choose, no Internet. Speak out and you disappear into these cabins or you're put in isolation, like Anat and Master Cal. We accepted the rules, but now…" she steadied her childlike blue eyes on him, "I guess it's time for me to be brave."

He let out a breath. Anna appeared to be processing whether to reject everything she'd been taught. Exactly how much did she know? How deep was the group's dogma implanted in this fourteen-year-old innocent's brain? She could lead him right to Slater or Compton and he wouldn't know the difference. With nothing and everything to lose, he had no choice but to trust her. "Okay. Who else is in these cabins?"

"You're the only one. They said you were going through indoctrination."

Lucier snorted. "Yeah, if you call indoctrination being tied to a chair and shot full of drugs for two days." The heavy weight of the Glock pressed against the small of his back gave him a measure of comfort. But one gun didn't mean much in a place where the only escape was a plane trip out.

"Where are they keeping Ms. Racine?" The girl hesitated. "It's a matter of life and death, Anna. Please."

Still wary, she glanced back at the cabin. "In...in the visitor's quarters. I served her."

"Now tell me, is Mr. Compton here? Mr. Crane? What about Mr. Slater?"

"You mean Brother Osiris?"

Lucier almost laughed. He wondered if Anna's mythology classes told the story of the mythical Osiris. Somehow he doubted it. "Yes."

"I think so. They'll want to hear how badly you've been treated."

Oh, for sure. Had this child already been taught to worship a dark god? Lucier doubted they were given a choice. He thought back to other compounds, other messianic cult leaders who led their flocks to follow, even to their deaths.

"I'm sure they will too, sweetheart. Now, how do we get to the visitors' quarters without exposing ourselves?"

She stared into the dark night. Was she having second thoughts? He was telling her to hide from people she'd trusted all her young life and help him, an outsider, who wanted to stop everything she'd ever known. He needed this girl to get him to Diana and figure out the next move. *Come on, Stallings. Keep searching those tangled deeds and trusts. Find this place.*

"Do you trust me, Anna?"

She hesitated. "I don't want anyone hurt."

"Has anyone been hurt?"

She didn't answer for an excruciatingly long time. Every minute meant more danger for Diana.

"Miss Maia is locked up, too."

Had he heard right? "Maia? Here?"

"She's always been my friend, and now I can't even talk to her. She's in a guest suite."

"If Maia is here, she's in danger too, Anna," Lucier said. "You must trust me."

Tears fell from the young girl's eyes. He understood her confusion. He'd made his case. Either she bought his story or she didn't.

"You wouldn't lie to me, would you? About Miss Maia, I mean."

He met her gaze. "I'm telling you the truth."

She nodded, let out a long breath. "I can get you to the building. After that, I can't guarantee no one will see us. I'm expected to return to my group with the man you left tied to the bed. Someone might be out looking for us already."

"Guess we'll have to take our chances."

"Okay."

Anna's directions led them on a dirt trail through the woods, skirting the main area of the compound. The drive went on forever. How big was this place? Where was it? He doubted most people there knew; otherwise, how could Compton keep the compound secret? Eventually someone would talk. A spike of reality caused a shiver. Talk to whom?

"Where are we? What state?" he asked.

"Paradise," she answered. "We've always been told we're in Paradise."

Chapter Fifty-One
Last Try, Do or Die

Compton and Slater left the two women in the suite, assuring them they'd return after their meeting to discuss the new problem. Diana lifted the whimpering Maia to her feet to direct her to one of the cushioned chairs. At her touch, a vision filled her head.

Maia with children clutching at her.

Fear as thick as morning fog.

What did that mean?

"Diana?"

Diana felt a tug on her arm.

"Diana?"

Maia's voice broke through her haze. "Wh…what?"

"Are you all right?"

Was she? "Yes, yes. I'm fine." Diana had experienced telepathic moments hundreds, no thousands, of times in her life, but she needed to put this one out of her mind. *Not now. Concentrate on getting out of here.* The red light twinkled in the vent. "Are there hidden microphones?"

"Only video unless they've changed the equipment."

Diana hoped she was right. "Who's in charge, Maia?"

Maia took her time. "Phillip Crane pulls the strings, but he lets my father think he's the boss. He's a wise old man from a long line of wise old men. Nothing goes on without his approval. Then there's Cybele and her devious daughters.

Now, because I screwed up, no one will ever know about this place and what they're doing."

"Don't be too sure. Ernie was working with the FBI to find the compound. They will."

"You heard my father. It'll be too late for me and for Anat and Cal. And for your policeman," she said apologetically. "They can't let him go."

Hearing the truth was much worse than thinking it. "I know. How will your father explain your disappearance?"

"I thought you were the psychic."

Diana managed a weak smile. "I thought so too, but Edward Slater fooled me completely. Good thing I retired."

"Edward surprised me too. As for my disappearance..." Maia drew a deep breath and let it out in a long, hissing stream. Her gaze connected with Diana's. "Oh, I'll go on an extended vacation, I guess. Maybe I'll be hypothetically kidnapped by terrorists while troubleshooting Compton business in the Middle East. I'd be the perfect target, wouldn't I? Daughter of a rich American held for ransom. Only they'll never find me. Silas could arrange that, in theory anyway. He'll be heartbroken for the world to see. He may even arrange for my body to be found. He'd enjoy the theater." Maia lifted her manicured fingers and massaged her temples. "I can't believe what he's done. He murdered my mother, Diana."

Diana sat on the arm of Maia's chair. "I'm so sorry."

"We didn't start out like this. Even though Dione and I hated Selene, we believed they were building a new world, where love and learning formed the basis for an advanced society. I thought of the Satan aspect more as a metaphor to lift the constrictions that religion burdened on the individual and free us of our inhibitions. Dione and I thought it was over the top, but we never believed we practiced a philosophy of evil.

"Not until the kidnappings.

"Then I saw what my father allowed Nona and Brigid to become. His own daughters. His and Selene's."

Diana got off the arm of the chair and crouched in front of Maia. "Those two girls are Silas's daughters? Your sisters?" Maia nodded, and Diana rose and paced the room. "Some psychic I am. I felt the evil, even saw it, but—" She couldn't go on. This was more perverse than a charred, skeletal hand prophesied. Silas Compton was a monster, and puppeteer Phillip Crane pulled the strings. To what ends would they go to advance their nightmarish ambitions? Diana had encountered the dark side many times in her life, but never to these unfathomable depths.

"Is there another compound? Somewhere they'd go if they had to abandon this place?"

"Not that I know. Why, do you think there is?"

"They knew when Ernie and I disappeared the feds would keep looking until they found us. So, yeah, there's another place, an escape route. One buried even deeper in red tape than this one."

Maia bit her bottom lip. She wiped away a tear. "Oh, my God. What have they done? What have I done?"

Diana wondered why Maia Compton never asked herself these questions before. She'd ignored all the signs. But this wasn't the time to add more guilt to her mounting list of regrets.

"Forget the self-incrimination for now." Maia sniffled and wiped her eyes. "How did you get free to come here?"

Maia told Diana what she, Anat, and Cal had done so far. "When Seth wakes, he'll be furious. How could we think he'd go against his father? He's been conditioned to obey. But—"

"But what?"

"Something he said—like no evil existed here until the kidnappings. I think he's wrestling with his conscience."

"We can only hope he's come to his senses. Not that it will do us any good tonight."

"What if they've found Anat and Cal and locked them in isolation?" Maia got up, walked to the window, and drew back the drapes. "It's so black outside. A big endless nowhere."

"Where are we?"

"Exactly? I don't know. Seth knows, but he would never say."

Didn't anyone ever question anything? Then she thought how she was raised to do what her father ordered. *Maybe we aren't so different after all.* "We've got to get out of here."

"I've given it my best shot. Besides, even if we could get out this window, it'd be on TV." Maia nodded at the vent.

"I tried disabling it, but—" She studied the vent. "Damn, why didn't I think of this before? I must have still been woozy from the drugs."

"What?"

"Listen up." She explained what she wanted Maia to do, then yanked the chenille lap blanket from the upholstered club chair. In the bathroom, she flattened it on the vanity and squirted toothpaste around the top edge until she emptied the tube. She carried it behind her back into the bedroom. Maia had moved the desk chair under the vent to the side. Diana got on the chair and pasted the blanket over the vent.

Please stick, Diana prayed, *at least long enough to do what we need to do.* Both gave thumbs up when the fabric held. They needed to work fast before it fell off.

Maia scurried behind the door with the chair in tow, and

Diana moved to the bedside table. Hopefully the guard wasn't glued to the screen. Diana lifted the lamp and crashed it to the floor. Maia drew a deep breath, raised the heavy chair over her head, and waited. She was taller with a better chance of succeeding. The key turned in the latch, and when the guard hurried inside to see what happened, Maia slammed the chair down on his head. He hit the floor like a felled tree. *Timber.*

Diana grabbed his keys and frisked him for a weapon and found one. This was the second time in her life she held a gun, and all within a few months. She tucked it into the waistband of her skirt.

"Okay, girlfriend," Diana said. "You're more familiar with this place than I am. Let's get the hell out of here before someone figures out what we've done."

Chapter Fifty-Two
Out of the Mouths of Babes

Lucier didn't play golf, so he marveled at the barely audible sound of the little electric vehicle. Another one sat at the end of the building. He saw no cars and guessed the carts provided the preferred mode of transportation around the compound. Anna pointed him in the direction of what she claimed was the guest house. He hoped she wasn't double-crossing him because he wouldn't know until it was too late.

"Slow down before the intersection," she said, "or they might spot you."

Her warning offered Lucier a measure of relief. If she was setting him up, she would have told him to barrel straight through.

"Where now?" he asked.

"I'll tell you, but you'd better tie me up or handcuff me, or else they'll know I helped you. This way, if you don't succeed, I can say you forced me with Steel's gun."

"Steel?"

"He's the guy you handcuffed to the bed. I don't know if it's his first name or his last."

"You knew I wouldn't hurt you if you refused to help me. So why did you?"

Anna thought for a long moment. "This place used to be a paradise, but things changed. Steel came, others too. They all look like the villains from comic books. Tonight, when Steel said he'd kill you and Miss Racine, that's not Paradise anymore." She pulled her legs into a yoga position and grew pensive. "But what really changed my mind were the new babies. They're not ours, which meant they belong to people outside the compound. That means they were stolen, and that's wrong. My friends and I—we're afraid now. That's why I'm helping."

She leapt from the cart and motioned Lucier to follow. When they got to the intersection, she pointed to a row of one-story buildings. "Those are the guest houses. Miss Racine is in the first one."

"You're sure?"

"I delivered food to her yesterday. I'm sure."

Lucier patted her head. "I don't know how to thank you."

"Don't. Just tie me to the steering wheel or something. Stuff my mouth so I can't yell, and make sure I can't get loose no matter what I do. You're not out of the woods yet. Even if you get her out, no one leaves here without a plane."

"I'll worry about if I get that far."

"You better be right. This place is all I've ever known. But I'm not ready to have kids. I'm still a kid myself."

Lucier wanted to smile, but he found nothing amusing about what she said.

She pointed to a copse of bushes. "Park over there. The cart will be harder to find, because when Steel doesn't return, they'll come looking."

"Damn, you're one smart kid."

"We're all smart here, and don't swear."

Now he did smile. He drove the cart into the brush, then took off his belt and wound it around her wrists and ankles and buckled it to the steering wheel so she couldn't move. He stuffed his handkerchief into her mouth. "Sorry, Anna, but you're right. I've gotta make this look good." She nodded. "You okay?" She nodded again. "I'll be back to get you if they don't get me first." He kissed her forehead and left.

Sticking to the perimeter of the wooded area, he dashed toward the back of the buildings. Voices filtered from around the front. Familiar voices. Lucier listened. He'd never forget Slater's, but the other one gave him pause until he realized it was Silas Compton's. He didn't recognize the third voice responding to Compton's orders.

"Don't release the two women for any reason. I don't care whether one of them goes into cardiac arrest. It'd be a ploy, and Diana Racine is the princess of ploys. My daughter is queen."

"Yes, sir," the third voice said.

Daughter. Had to be Maia, Lucier thought. She and Diana were locked up together. *That's a break. I think*. He waited a full ten minutes, until after the voices disappeared into the night. When he was about to start for the building, something pressed into his back, and a man's voice said, "Don't move."

Lucier raised his hands and sighed. *So close.*

He turned to face a handsome man, thin and wiry, holding a stick for a gun and carrying a baby in a sling. With him was one of the most beautiful women Lucier had ever seen, and he'd seen a lot of beautiful women lately.

"Are you the cop from New Orleans?" the man asked.

Lucier nodded.

"I'm Cal Easley. This is Anat Crane. We've come to get you out of here."

Chapter Fifty-Three
The Ticket to Ride

"Let's get as far away from here as we can," Diana said. "If we're going to be caught, I want to give them a run for their money."

"One thing in our favor. Silas won't wake Phillip in the middle of the night. He'll wait till morning. They've gone back to sleep." Maia grabbed Diana's arm, looked both ways outside the door, and hurried her out the building, heading for the woods.

"Diana."

She stopped in her tracks. *Ernie.* "I'd know that voice anywhere." She whirled around, saw Lucier with two other people, and ran into his arms with tears filling her eyes. Smothering him with kisses, she said, "God, I thought you were dead."

He held her close. "For a while, so did I. After Slater brought you into my prison, I was so worried. I—"

"Look," Cal said, interrupting. "I'm glad you two found each other and are both able to talk about it, but not here. Not now. We've got to move."

Maia and the woman Diana assumed was Anat Crane huddled in hushed conversation, obviously relieved to reconnect. Diana had no idea who the man carrying a baby in a sling was.

"Wait," Lucier said. "I left a young girl, Anna, tied up in

one of the golf carts. Someone's got to release her."

"Already did," Cal said. "She gave me a run-down of tonight's happenings. I told her to get back to her dormitory. The door will be locked, but if anyone asks about Steel, she's to say he's with you. She'll be okay. No one will suspect anything." He put his hand gently on Diana's back, leading her toward the cart. "I'm Cal Easley," he said.

Cal Easley's touch passed to Diana one of the oldest emotions known to man. Love. The love in his heart for the little girl he carried. The sensation was so intense it took Diana's breath away.

Unstrapping the baby's sling, Cal transferred her to Anat. "Come on." Both piled into their cart. "Do you fly a plane, Lieutenant?"

"No. Why, is there one in the compound?"

"A couple of them, plus a chopper."

"Do you?" Lucier asked Cal.

"No. Never mind." Cal said. "We'll need both carts. Follow us, be as quiet as possible."

"How did you know we were here?" Lucier asked.

"Little Anna." Cal started his cart. "It'll be dawn in a couple of hours. We have to be gone by then."

"What about Seth?" Maia asked. "What about my children?"

Cal turned back to face her. "We'll get your children. First Seth. He's our ticket out of here. Trust me, Maia." Then he took off.

Lucier turned to Maia in the back seat. "I don't know what his plan is, but it's better than mine."

Cal navigated the narrow paths as if he'd carved them out himself. Lucier followed. Tree branches crunched under the wheels as they tore through the dark. Diana heard the rush of water, smelled the damp earth. The air was cool, but she felt warm and sticky from the night's tension. Being free for the moment didn't instill a long-range sense of optimism. "For someone who's been under guard, Cal knows his way around."

"I've been snookered," Maia said. "Anat told me Cal's IQ is the highest of anyone here, but because he's gay, they won't use his sperm. No one pays him any mind, so he has free rein inside the compound."

Lucier laughed. "Gay my ass. He's as gay as I am. But I bet she's right about the IQ."

"And he's the baby's father," Diana said."

"I figured that out when I saw them together," Maia said. "I guess Anat didn't trust me enough to tell me the truth."

Lucier swerved out of the way from a hanging limb. "He's been putting on an act."

"Fooled me," Maia said, "until today."

"Those two have planned this escape for a while, and they would have succeeded except for a couple of minor details."

"Which are?"

"One, he can't fly a plane." Lucier tipped his head to the back seat. "But Seth can, can't he, Maia?"

"Yes, he flies."

Diana turned to Lucier. "What's the other thing, Ernie?"

"He needed help. Cal and Anat are very patient people. You're the key, Maia."

"Me?"

"How often do you come here? Every few months?"

"Usually."

"And I bet it was Anat who convinced you to drug Seth?" Diana asked.

Maia nodded.

"Where did she get the drugs?"

"She didn't really say who gave them to her exactly, but she saved them up."

"Bet innocuous Cal got them," Lucier said. "I assume there's a staff doctor who prescribed them to Cal to help assuage his inner demons."

"Yeah." Maia said as if she'd finally put it all together. "Poor, tortured, *gay* Cal." She laughed. "Brilliant."

"Maybe, but we're not out of here yet," Diana said. "Still, this might be our only chance."

"You got that right." Lucier slammed his foot on the accelerator to keep up with the cart leading the way through the black night in the dark forest.

Chapter Fifty-Four
Beat the Dawn

"What are you thinking?" Diana asked.

"I'm not thinking," Lucier said. "I'm hoping. Hoping the feds are close to finding this place. Even if we convince this Seth fellow to help us, we still need to get the plane off the ground. Getting Maia's kids first gives the bad guys more opportunity to catch us." He wondered if he should have verbalized his negative outlook.

Cal pulled behind one of the buildings at the end of the compound and waved them into the brush.

"That's where they put me this time," Maia said. "My regular apartment doesn't have security locks and cameras. This one does." She shrugged. "I've been deemed untrustworthy, I guess. Imagine."

"Big Brother's all over this place," Lucier said under his breath. "I gather Seth staying the night is a common occurrence?"

"Usually," Maia responded without embarrassment.

Lucier nodded. Clearly, the situation wasn't entirely against her will.

Cal jumped out of his cart and approached, keys in hand. Anat and the baby were already wending their way to the rear door.

"We're as safe here as anywhere," he said, "but not for long. If either Steel or the other guard gets free, people will be searching the compound. They'll find us eventually. Right now, the night's in our favor. All we have to do is convince Seth to fly us out of here before dawn." He followed Anat's path. "Just in case, be quiet."

"Seth is the only one who can get the children out of the dorm without raising suspicion," Maia said.

Lucier put his hand on Diana's back and guided her along the dark path. "I hope so."

Everyone bypassed the elevator and tiptoed up the stairs. Cal had already opened the door. Seth was groggy but awake, and from the narrowing of his eyes, not happy. Last in, Lucier closed the door.

Seth kept his stare riveted on Maia while she ripped the strips of tape off his mouth and undid the cuffs with the key from the key ring. Silent, he propped himself up on the bed and waited, his attitude a mixture of uncertainty and anger. Cal was the first to speak.

"You've got to help us, Seth."

Seth still didn't speak, even when Maia she sat next to him.

"We have to stop what's going on here," she said, "You're the only one who can do it."

"If I don't, what are you going to do, Maia, kill me? Spike my coffee again?"

"No," Lucier said moving closer, "but they'll kill me and probably arrange to kill Maia, if not technically, at least to the world."

"She knew the repercussions when she pulled the stunt with those two phony art thieves," Seth said. "Frankly, nothing would please me more than for Maia to be here on a permanent basis. At least that's the way I felt before tonight."

"My father said he'd get rid of all the troublemakers. That

means Anat and Cal too."

Seth shook his head. "He wouldn't."

"I'm afraid she's right," Diana said. "I heard him and Edward Slater discuss their plans, and Maia, Anat, and Cal weren't part of them. Don't forget what they plan for yours truly."

Maia raised her hand to his cheek. Seth shrugged it away and crossed his arms over his chest like a stubborn child.

"Someone in this compound is violating our child, Seth, maybe all the children. Is that all right with you?"

"Impossible." Seth said defensively. "I'd know."

"You're sure? Because I'm not." Tears rolled out of her eyes before hiccupping sobs shook her body. Anat moved to her and put an arm around her shoulder.

"Anyone with half a sense of reality knows that kidnapping babies from their birth parents is a crime," Lucier said. "By turning a blind eye, these people, you included, crossed the line. If murder is involved, you're an accessory."

Seth picked a residue of adhesive off his cheek, rolled it in his fingers, and flicked it into space. He expelled a ragged breath. "I didn't know about the babies until they were brought here. I objected." He focused on Lucier, then glanced at Maia. "I'm not a militant, nor am I a hero. Neither is my nature."

"Here's your chance to change," Cal said. "You might find doing so will save the lives of the people in this room, not to mention your children. I'll even venture to add all the children in this compound, because their treatment defies everything that's moral."

Maia reached out her hand again, but Seth refused to look at her. "Please, Seth. Help me get the children—all the children—away from here. They need help. I can't stop you if you want to return." She spoke in a whisper. "You must know that, deep in your heart. For once, don't be the loyal soldier. The war is over."

* * * * *

Steel got the wad of cotton out of his mouth, but no one would hear if he screamed bloody murder. That was the whole point of situating the cabins away from the main compound and soundproofing them—doubling the silence.

The son of a bitch cop had tied him up good. He was exhausted from trying to extricate himself. Every time he moved, one of his wrists twisted and stressed his forearm to the point of snapping. With his ankles tied to opposite sides, he couldn't use them to raise himself. The lemon meringue had crusted on his face, its glop still clouding his vision, and the cloying smell was turning his stomach.

The strips of cloth holding his feet were his best bet. He shimmied down as far as possible to get some movement in his legs and, scraping his heels against the posts, worked off his shoes. Now, if he could just stretch the cloth enough to slide his foot through the binding. He pointed the toes of his right foot and pulled and pushed.

"Damn," he howled. Fucking cramp. Spasms curled his toes, sending excruciating pain into the arch. When he tried to straighten it, a knot tightened in his calf and worked its way up his leg into his thigh. It felt like a vice clamped around his quadriceps. He lifted his middle up to stretch, but the contractions shot stabs of pain into his hip, and his arm wrenched from the maneuver.

He needed to walk out the cramp, but how in hell could he tied to the goddamn bed? *Relax, Steel. Let your body unwind.* Easier said than done when his whole body ached with every move. *Deep breaths.*

The pain diminished in small twitches, but he tried again without pointing his toes. That's what set off the cramp in the first place. This time, he pulled both feet toward the middle. The cloth stretched but not enough for either foot to slip through; however, the post on the right side moved.

Again, Steel.

He did and the post loosened some more. Again. And again, until it broke away from the bottom of the railing. He slid the tie down and freed his foot. He turned sideways, careful not to twist his shoulder, and pushed his free leg against the other post until it, too, came apart. He collapsed and took deep, calming breaths.

Big fucking deal, he thought. What now? How in hell would he get his wrists free? He could break the top rail, but he might break both arms in the process. He shimmied up straighter and turned slightly onto his side. Grabbing the top rail with one of his hands, he pulled himself up so his shoulder was level with the rail. Then he rammed into it, hoping one of the posts detached, but all he did was wrench his right forearm. He stopped to catch his breath before he tried again.

Thrusting harder, the rail loosened. He exerted more pressure and finally pulled it from the side post. He slid the cuffs to freedom. Using a liberated slat as a lever, he pried open one cuff; the other hung from his sore, swollen wrist.

He comforted himself by thinking how his hands would feel around the cop's neck. How he'd take his damn sweet time watching the fucker take his last breath.

Chapter Fifty-Five
Silent Confession

Lucier hadn't seen many people since he arrived, but he bet he was the only person of color in the whole place. So much reminded him of Nazi Germany that he shuddered when he thought of the eerie comparison.

He went with Seth to get the children while Cal stayed with the women. Lucier trusted Seth Crane about as far as he could throw him, which prompted his hand to curl around the gun's handle in his pocket.

Seth eyed the bulge. "You don't need a gun. I won't give you any trouble."

We'll see. "Who's watching the children?"

"A group leader. He'll be sleeping. There's never reason for anyone to be on alert. This isn't the kind of place where people are held at gunpoint."

"But it's the kind of place where people are put in cabins to go through indoctrination, huh? Everything's fine and dandy as long as no one questions the rules."

"Rarely happens."

"What about Anat?"

Lucier caught Seth's sidelong glance. "Anat is smart and manipulative. She planted the seed that someone was abusing Phillip to get Maia to do what she wanted, which is to get out of here. I'd know if something happened."

"Maybe. Or maybe the idea was so remote you never gave

it a thought."

"My father wouldn't let a perversion of that kind go on in his utopia."

"What do you call kidnapping babies if not a perversion?"

Seth didn't answer. Was internal angst causing a chink in this man's armor?

"Don't tell me there hasn't been any inbreeding here, because I won't believe you. With all the group's sons and daughters, sisters and brothers, nieces and nephews, they couldn't possibly keep at least cousins apart."

Again Seth didn't respond.

They arrived at a large building Lucier assumed—no *hoped*—was the dormitory. The space carved out of the forest for the dark cedar wood structure camouflaged it from an aerial view. Same with Maia's building. The compound hid in plain sight. He doubted they could hide a plane runway, though.

The design of the building alleviated Lucier's tension that Seth was taking him directly to either Crane or Compton. Neither man would reside in this simple no-frills building.

"Wait here," Seth said. "The kids will be sleepy, possibly cranky. If I'm lucky, they'll be quiet. I don't want to explain what I'm doing if anyone wakes up, and I sure don't want to explain you."

Okay, so he's maybe playing it straight. Still, Lucier felt like he stood on the fifty-yard line at the Super Bowl game, with all eyes on him. In another couple of hours, dawn would light the sky, but right then the area was as dark as pitch. No lights anywhere to give away their position from above. Crane and Compton money had created an entire town—no, a world—including their own water supply, construction, and power source. How did they accomplish this faux utopia without anyone exposing them? Money. It was all about money.

Seth carried out the youngest child with the other two trotting alongside. He signaled Lucier to take the driver's seat and hopped in. The older boy got in back, curled into a ball, and went to sleep. The little girl sat on her daddy's lap and cuddled her father and younger brother. A bomb wouldn't wake the little boy.

"Drive," Seth said. "Go back to Maia's apartment the way we came. As long as I'm here, you'll be safe."

Lucier turned the cart around. "What happens next?"

"I'll fly you out of here, but it won't be easy."

"You know I'll find this place and bring back the FBI, don't you?"

Seth didn't say anything for a long moment. "It really was a noble idea in the beginning," he mused, "but something went wrong. What do they say? Power corrupts; absolute power corrupts absolutely." He drew a breath.

"You went along," Lucier said.

Looking straight ahead, Seth Crane was a master of silence, but oh how his silence spoke volumes. His daughter squirmed in his arms, and he planted a kiss in the midst of her blonde curls.

"My father is a formidable man, Lieutenant, and my mother is in thrall to all he offers. It's not a complicated structure. My siblings and I were taught to love and to pleasure. We were instructed to read the great books of the world, to learn philosophy and metaphysics. Those higher planes of learning were the gods we worshiped."

Lucier wondered whether love and pleasuring went on within the household, but he didn't ask. He didn't want to know. "When did Satan enter into it?"

"Satan was presented no differently than other gods in other religions." Seth pointed. "Turn here."

Lucier pulled up to the back door and stopped.

"How can I explain something I grew up with and believed in? Were we all brainwashed? Were you brainwashed in the religion you grew up with? Somehow I doubt you see it that way, any more than I did. I still believe in much of what I've been taught—love, beauty, intellectual pursuit." He shrugged. "Hedonistic? Probably, but no one discards the teachings of a lifetime easily."

Unless his whole family is wiped out in one horrific moment.

"Like I said, the noble experiment went terribly wrong." Seth handed the young boy to Lucier, then leaned over his seat to wake Phillip. The boy got up without question and followed the two men into the house and to Maia's door. She took Leo from Lucier, kissed his cheek, and laid him on the bed; Seth did the same with Iris.

Maia went to Phillip. He pulled back, and she leaned down and put her hands on his shoulders. "Would you like to leave here, son?" she asked. Tears filled his eyes and he nodded.

Seth crouched by Maia's side. "Phillip, I know you're sleepy, but I'm going to ask you a question, and it's important you answer truthfully. You don't have to name names, but I'd like you to say yes or no. Okay?"

Phillip nodded. He rubbed his eyes and yawned.

Lucier noticed the boy hadn't spoken one word since Seth brought him out of the dormitory. Phillip did seem reserved for a boy his age, and Lucier began to understand Maia's concern.

Seth fingered through Phillip's hair and gently held the back of his head. "Has anyone here touched you or done anything to you in an inappropriate way?"

The boy's chin quivered. He stood with his arms rigid at his sides, avoiding eye contact with Seth. He neither moved nor looked for solace to either parent when he started to cry. In fact, he backed away from his father, who reached out for him.

Seth swallowed hard, and his jaw tightened in concert with a fiercely pulsing vein in his temple. He pulled the distressed child to him and wrapped him in his arms. Maia sat in semi-shock with the back of her hand across her mouth.

"Let's get to the plane," Seth said. "I'll get to the bottom of this when I return."

"You're coming back?" Maia asked. "Now that you know, how could you?"

"Like you, Maia, I'm a little late coming to the party. There are other kids here. I need to find out who's doing what and why. What's more important, who knows, and why they've let it continue."

"Don't forget the stolen babies," Diana said.

Seth met her gaze. "I haven't."

"I'm coming back with you," Lucier said. "With the authorities."

Seth fixed his eyes on Lucier and nodded.

Lucier checked his watch. Four a.m. They'd never get to the plane before the sky turned light. "Anyone at the airstrip?" he asked Seth.

"I doubt it. Two pilots are on call, and one or the other will make the round-trip when summoned. There's always a small plane here and a helo in case of emergency. My father and I are the only people who fly. He rarely does any more." He waved his hand at Lucier. "Follow me."

Seth drove one of the carts with Maia and their children. Phillip still sniffled, but he clung to his mother like a little boy terrified to let go. Lucier and Diana hopped in the back of the other cart. Cal drove with Anat and her baby in front. If one didn't know the situation, they looked like three couples with their kids out for a nighttime drive around the golf course.

How many more planes were at the disposal of Crane Corporation and Compton International? Was there a contingency plan to evacuate everyone if the need arose, and if so, where would they go? He only hoped Diana, the children, and those at risk were out of there before he found out.

Chapter Fifty-Six
Escape

Steel grunted along holding the arm he wrenched in his persistent effort to loosen the back of the headboard. His shoulder was killing him, the foot he used as a battering ram to break the door lock didn't feel much better, and his wrist might be broken. He put the pain aside, driven by so much rage for the damn cop. With no idea where the son of a bitch had gone, he decided to wake Slater for the verbal lashing he'd get for letting his prisoner subdue him—with a lemon meringue pie, for chrissakes. The more he thought about it, the madder he got.

The villas were empty unless one or the other boss men showed up. Slater came less often and usually alone, but he stayed longer—three or four days. Steel wasn't exactly sure of Slater's position. He wasn't a Crane in name or by marriage, but he acted like it. Steel didn't like the man's attitude, as if everyone in the room had just crawled up to vertical from all fours except him. Most of the women at the compound would do anything for him, though Steel couldn't understand why. It was as if the man had some kind of magnetic hold on them. As a guard, Steel's job description fell short of thinking. He did what he was told, and he'd screwed up royally.

* * * * *

Lucier held Diana's hand in the back seat of the golf cart while Cal followed Seth onto a bumpy path shrouded with an overhang of trees. "Are there any accessible phones anywhere, Cal?"

"All the links to the outside are coded. That's the one thing I haven't been able to crack."

"What about in the airstrip? There has to be communication equipment."

"Same," Cal said. "Locked and inaccessible. Believe me, whenever I had the chance, I tried."

Damn. These people had thought of everything. With an endless source of money, they'd constructed buildings that blended into their surroundings, hiding it from the world.

Seven or eight minutes later, they came to an airfield carved out of the mountains. A large camouflage-painted hangar sat at one end of a runway lined with recessed lights that rivaled any Lucier had seen. A helicopter sat to the right on a helipad with a removable cover, and a turbo prop took up one space inside the two-plane hangar. Lucier knew little about planes, though he'd flown both in a similar plane and a chopper to survey hurricane damage. This one seated maybe a dozen people.

Seth drove the cart to the right of the hangar and jumped out. He waved everyone to follow. "There's always more than enough fuel to get us back to New Orleans, but we'd better hurry. They'll know the kids are gone first. They'll check for the rest of us."

Cal parked beside Seth's cart. Diana helped Maia with the children, and Lucier followed Seth into the hangar with the others close behind. Seth rolled a stair truck to the entry door of the plane. "I need to get the key to open the door, and we'll be out of here within ten minutes. He separated one key from his ring. In the far corner of the hanger, he slipped the key into a locked cabinet and opened the door. He searched frantically inside.

"Shit," Seth said. "The key's always here."

"Is this what you're looking for?"

Seth swung around. "Edward."

Slater eased from behind the plane, holding the door key in the air. Steel stood beside him, glaring at Lucier with a triumphant sneer. Dried meringue stuck to the side of Steel's face, and handcuffs hung from one swollen, bruised wrist. In the other hand he clutched a gun, pointed at Lucier.

"Gimme my gun," Steel said. "Slow and easy. Fingertips."

Lucier pulled the gun from his waistband with his thumb and index finger. He thought briefly of getting off a shot, but he'd be dead before he got the chance, and he didn't want to risk anyone else getting hurt from a stray bullet.

"Put it on the ground and slide it to me," Steel said.

Lucier did what Steel said. He wouldn't need much of an excuse to shoot. *Bide your time, Ernie. Mountain Man won't do anything without an order, and right now, the boss is too busy to give directions.*

"You, Seth?" Slater said. "I'm disappointed."

Seth glanced at Lucier with an almost imperceptible shrug. "Let me fly these people out of here, Edward. You know what will happen to them if they remain. Do you really want to be responsible for the deaths of innocent people?"

Slater snorted. "Since when have you grown a conscience?"

"This isn't how it was supposed to be. We give life not take it."

"You still don't understand, do you, lover boy? This is bigger than the loss of a few innocent people, as you call them. We're creating an alternate universe, and nothing you do can stop us."

Soft whimpering broke the tension in the hangar. Seth turned to the sound. So did everyone else. Phillip cowered at Maia's side, clutching the hem of her shorts. He shook violently as he stared at Slater. Pee ran down his leg forming a puddle under his shoes.

Seth rotated slowly from his son to Slater. A creased deepened between his brows, and his mouth hung open for a long minute as realization struck. "You?"

Slater's face reddened. "I didn't hurt him. I was teaching him—"

Seth didn't wait for an explanation. He lunged for Slater's throat with the speed of a striking cobra. "You perverted—"

Steel shifted his vengeful focus from Lucier to the commotion for a split second, but that's all the time Lucier needed. He barreled in low, head-butting Steel's midsection with an upward thrust. Steel grunted and lost his footing, but righted himself and held on to the gun.

"Not again, *boy*," Steel sneered. "Not again."

Lucier had heard the demeaning word before, sloughed it off as meaningless because it was. The thought of letting down the people who counted on him bothered him more. The fate of the kids in the compound. The starry-eyed women too damaged to know they were being used. Maia, Anat, and their children. And Diana, whose determination never to give in would seal her destiny if he couldn't save her.

He marshaled all his strength against an adversary with nothing to lose and whose humiliation fueled his anger. Now victory depended on which man wanted to win more.

Lucier knew the big man hurt. He favored his arm, and his wrist looked like an eggplant. Lucier wanted to make him hurt more. Lucier grabbed hold of the handcuff and yanked it so hard, Steel wailed in pain. Lucier locked onto Steel's gun hand, pushing it to point at the hangar's ceiling. More twisting and squeezing. Harder and tighter.

In spite of his obvious pain, Steel fought with the determination of a feral animal and maneuvered the gun barrel toward Lucier.

I can't let him win.

A mythical strength, the kind that empowers those faced with do-or-die situations, surged into Lucier's body. He forced the gun from Steel's grip at the same time he twisted the cuff high on his back. The unmistakable snap of bone caused Steel to discharge an unearthly shriek. Lucier landed a forceful strike to Steel's knee, and Mountain Man hit the ground, writhing in pain. Lucier stomped down on Steel's wrist, then immediately scooped up the nearest gun. The big man's previous wail sounded like a whimper in comparison to what he was letting go now. Lucier socked him under the jaw with the butt of the gun to silence him, then hustled to retrieve the other gun, sticking it back into his waistband.

He'd been so involved in his own battle, he hadn't noticed the quiet inside the hangar. Seth Crane knelt in front of Slater, his hands encircling Slater's neck, squeezing and jerking the limp body in a fitful rage.

Lucier, breathing heavily, staggered to Crane and put a hand on his shoulder. Crane went still. He turned to Lucier as if he'd come out of a trance. Slater's eyes stared lifelessly, but Lucier put his finger to the side of his throat anyway. He couldn't find a pulse. "He's dead, Seth."

Crane fell back on his haunches. "I've never harmed a soul in my life. Never even cussed at anyone. Now I've murdered a man." He raised his tear-filled eyes to Lucier. "I kept thinking about what he must have done to my son, and I couldn't stop squeezing."

Lucier helped him up. He wanted to say killing Slater was self-defense, but it wasn't. Temporary insanity seemed a better justification. Lucier thought if Slater had molested one of his children, he would have reacted the same way, without a thread of guilt. "Come on. Let's find the others and get out of here. We'll bring the authorities back. They can take over."

He took Crane's arm, and they walked out of the hangar into the breaking dawn to a sight that changed everything. For the worse. Two men stood like military sentries pointing guns at them; another gunman held Diana and the rest at bay.

"Looks like we missed all the fun," Phillip Crane said. "Better late than never."

Silas Compton stood with a twisted smile distorting his lips. "We underestimated you, Ernie."

"Not for the first time, *Silas*."

Chapter Fifty-Seven
The Long-Awaited Reading

Diana stared down the barrel of the gun, wondering if she and Lucier would survive—if any of them would survive. One guard relieved Lucier of both guns.

"Shut up, Silas. *You* underestimated him, not me." Crane stepped forward and glared at Compton, the disdain in his voice palpable. "If you'd followed my instructions, the lieutenant would be dead now instead of Edward—the only person other than a true Crane who understood our mission. Now he's dead, murdered"—he glared at Seth with eyes as cold and icy as an Arctic wind—"by my son." He strode to stand before Seth. "My grandfather chose Brother Osiris to help me create what you almost destroyed. Obviously, he was more of a Crane than you."

Diana felt a wave of empathy for Seth. In the space of a few hours, his entire world had turned upside down. He'd realized his child, maybe more than one, had been violated, and now his own father declared him unworthy of the Crane name. Would Seth cave in the face of his father's accusations? How deep was his indoctrination?

Seth's cheeks turned scarlet. "Did your grandfather teach him to molest my children, Father? Molest others too, I presume. Or didn't you know about that?"

"Edward wouldn't do that," Crane said. "He loved those children."

"He sure as hell did," Maia said, "but not the way you mean." She held Phillip, his trembling arms wrapped around her, shorts showing the result of his fear. The other two children clung to her side. "No wonder this child is so withdrawn. Your grandfather's hand-picked messiah was a twisted pervert."

Slater's reluctance to touch Diana now made sense. He'd lost not only his God as a result of his calamity, he'd lost his soul. She wondered if the young Edward, the one who answered to a higher calling, had ever participated in a tortured dialogue with his darker self. The question would forever remain unanswered.

"How many others need help like my son?" Maia asked. She pulled her older son closer. "You can't stop us from leaving here, Phillip." She turned to Silas. "Tell him, Father."

"Silas tells me nothing," Crane snapped. "He'll do what I say."

Compton's eyes narrowed for a brief moment. Diana thought he was going to stand up for himself, but he lowered his head in obvious humiliation. Only two people held sway over Silas Compton—Phillip Crane and Selene.

"I'm in charge," Crane said, "and I'm afraid we can stop you from leaving. Truth is—we're the ones leaving. You, my dear Maia, will remain here with your friends, except for Diana, of course. She'll accompany us to our new location. My wife and daughters have already departed. You see, this runway can handle a plane big enough for everyone in this compound. It will arrive late tonight, and we'll have cleared out by midday tomorrow. When and if the authorities find this place, all they'll find is a burned out parcel of land in the middle of nowhere, because that's all that will be left."

Crane made a slow visual rotation of the property, a frown

creasing his forehead. "Pity, really. We weren't ready to move on quite yet, but I'm afraid your father gave us no choice, Cal. Martin's pathological fear that he would realize the same fate as his own father played right into the hands of the police. He verged on breaking. My daughter felt compelled to stop him."

Cal took a step backward. "Anastasia murdered my father?"

Phillip pursed his lips. "Umm, murder is a strong word. I prefer to describe her action as protecting the group. I knew about Martin when I recruited him, but he was a brilliant man and would produce brilliant children, like you and your siblings, only with Crane genes. I needed him." He sighed. "Who thought things would get so out of hand?"

"You don't subscribe to the devil, Phillip," Cal said. "You are the devil."

With an arched brow, Phillip said, "I do what needs to be done."

"Yet you did everything to involve the police," Lucier said. "Notes, druggings. Why?"

"Martin sent the notes. He wanted to stop this before it went further. He thought if he scared Diana away, the cops would stay away too. Had I known at the time, but..." He cocked his head toward Silas. "*He* wasn't as upset at Martin as I was. I should have paid more attention to a man whose ego made him think he could do anything and get away with it, like putting drugs in Diana's drink. If I'm being honest, his reprehensible behavior is what drew me to him in the first place. How could I ignore a man who blackmailed his own father-in-law into trading votes in the Senate for a government contract?"

"Blackmailed him?" Maia said. "How? Gault Fannon was a wonderful, kind man. What could you possibly have used against him?"

"Wonderful? Kind? Maybe," Silas said. "But your grandfather suffered from a similar perversion as poor Edward. He couldn't help himself. He hid it well, but I found out. The threat of exposure left him a broken man. In addition to the tragedy of your brother's death, learning about her father sent your mother over the edge." He shrugged helplessly. "With a little help."

Maia leaned against Seth. "A little help? You killed my mother, and you knew Edward was abusing the children? Your grandchildren? " Her knees gave way, and Seth reached his arm around her waist to keep her upright. "My precious babies?" She hugged Phillip closer. "You're evil, Father. Evil. Oh, God."

Seth took Phillip from her and whispered something in her ear. She calmed.

Diana sensed it had to do with upsetting the children, for Maia nodded and stood erect.

A little late to worry about your children, isn't it, Seth?

She hoped they were too young to understand what one grandfather had done and that the other planned to incinerate their parents like so much garbage.

"Sacrilege. Don't mention God in my presence, Maia," Phillip said.

"You'd do this to your own family?" Seth asked his father.

Cal stepped forward. "Oh, yes. Nothing stands in the way of the mighty Cranes. Anat has always been a thorn in his side. No tears will be shed over her demise. You stood a chance before today, Seth. The good soldier, only following orders, but you lost favor when you couldn't father more children. Now, unforgivably, you've screwed up by finally seeing the light. You're no good to them anymore." During his speech,

Cal took another step forward. No one noticed Lucier doing the same.

Diana needed to help. She had one thing in her favor. Phillip Crane wanted her alive. She stepped closer to Compton, the man who'd drugged her and placed her at Satan's altar. She'd improvise as she went along.

"If you don't care about me, Father," Maia said, "what about your grandchildren?"

"The children will come with us. They'll be safe, but I can't trust you any longer. And Anat—" He snorted.

"Anat what?" Anat said. "You're disappointed? I'm delighted."

Silas brushed her off with a flick of his wrist.

Diana moved closer to him. One of the thugs stepped up to her and jabbed his gun in her ribs. Lucier lurched toward her, but a second man waved him back with his weapon. Unfazed, Diana pushed the gun aside and reached for Compton's hand. He tried to pull away, but she wouldn't let go.

"What's the matter, Silas? You always wanted a reading, and I've never given you one, have I? Now is the perfect time, because after today, I probably won't be clearheaded enough to use the gift that makes me so valuable to your future generations."

"Get away from him, Diana," Phillip said.

Compton put up his hand. "No, she's right. Without Edward, who wanted her for himself, we don't need her lucid. We only need her fertile."

"You never learn, Silas. Go ahead, get your jollies."

The guards kept their guns steady, but the idea of her reading drew their focus. She went into full performance mode. Only Crane showed wariness, but eventually he, too, seemed drawn in.

I hope you know what I'm doing, Ernie, because it's now or never. She took Compton's hand. A moment of apprehension struck when she looked down. Nothing. No black skeleton, no nausea. She was in total control, onstage once again.

"I don't usually do this standing up with guns pointed at me." *Get that, Ernie? The guns are pointed at me.* "But I feel your vibes, Silas." *Definitely a load of bull.* She felt nothing but fear. "Just relax." Her soothing voice belied the tremors inside. The same voice she used to engage her subjects, including the serial killer intent on beating her at her own game. "Forget where you are. Forget what you're doing." She covered both his hands in hers and closed her eyes as she'd done thousands of times before.

She drew out the moment. Everyone was silent, fully engrossed. Compton didn't move. "I see a peaceful place with—"

She heard a scuffle.

A gunshot.

A groan.

Kids screaming.

Without turning around, she kneed a distracted Compton in the groin as hard as she could. Another groan. This one from Compton. His face contorted into a mask of pain. He drew a deep raspy breath and howled, clutching himself. She kicked him again, smashing his hand too. He dropped to the ground, and she stomped on his knee, relishing the crunch of bones.

Yes!

Compton curled on his side, writhing in agony, oblivious to the goings-on around him. She kicked him one more time for good measure.

A quick check showed Lucier trading punches with his guard, ducking a left hook and coming back with a right cross. He swung a low kick into his opponent's leg, throwing him off balance and sending him to the tarmac. The gun flew from his hand and skidded into the heavy brush surrounding the hangar. The guy hopped to his feet, limping and stunned, but still swinging.

Diana glanced at Compton—still out of commission, then at Cal, who held his own with a panting, overweight rival past his prime, and Seth, whose left arm hung useless at his side, blood covering shirt, gripped his adversary's gun with his good hand and turned the muzzle away. Anat, Maia, and the children were nowhere to be seen.

Diana skirted the melee to search for the gun in the brush. *Damn. Where did it go?* She kicked her way around the heavy growth. On her hands and knees, she plowed through the thicket. Sharp needles of dried brush pricked her skin, but she kept crawling, searching.

Checking back to gauge her time, she saw Seth head-butt the brute's nose. Blood splattered everywhere. He dropped his gun and clutched his nose with both hands. Seth crumpled to his knees, his face drained of color, and keeled over. Diana gave up her search, dodged Cal's scuffle, and dove for the gun near Seth before Broken Nose nabbed it first. Breathless, she lifted the weapon and shot twice in the air.

Cal's fat man lost focus at the sound of the gunshots, and Cal scooped the gun from his hand, wiping his sleeve across his forehead to keep the sweat from clouding his vision.

Lucier put his man down with a hard right to the jaw. He moved slowly toward Diana, who stood holding the gun in a death grip with a trembling hand. "You can let go now, my love," he said. "You've done enough." He kissed her head.

"More than enough."

She wanted to release the weapon, but she couldn't. Her fingers were locked onto the handle.

Lucier pried it from her hand. "Everything's okay, sweetheart. We're in control."

Diana responded to Lucier's calming voice and took stock of the scene. Sobbing noises came from around the side of the hangar, and Diana hustled to the sound, fearful someone was hurt. Maia and Anat huddled together with their wailing children.

Poor things, Diana thought. Fighting and gunshots had terrified them. "It's all over. Everything will be okay."

They all crept forward to survey the damage. Maia gasped. "Seth's hurt. Help him." She ran inside the hangar.

"You okay?" Cal asked Anat. When she nodded, he jogged after Maia.

Diana scanned the area. Phillip Crane was nowhere to be seen. The all-powerful Crane let others do the dirty work. Where had he gone?

Lucier motioned Crane's three flunkies together and leveled the gun at them.

A mechanized roar came from the hangar. "Crane's escaping," Diana yelled over the din.

Helpless to stop him, Lucier handed the gun to Diana and pointed to the three prisoners. "Shoot them if they move."

"My pleasure," she said.

Lucier helped Cal drag Seth out of the way. Everyone else moved back from the engine's thrust as the plane taxied onto the tarmac.

Just then, overhead, lights appeared in the early morning sky, and a brilliant spotlight illuminated the gathering on the tarmac. Lucier rushed out from the hangar and took the gun from Diana's hand. He pointed skyward. Shielding her eyes from the glare, she made out two dark ovals in the sky. Elation spread through her like wildfire, and she saw the three letters that would burn an image in her brain forever: FBI.

The earsplitting noise of the turboprop drowned out the whirring sound coming from above. The helicopters circled, hovered for a minute, then set down on the runway, blocking the path of the plane's escape. Diana couldn't see inside the plane, but the engines shut down. Crane didn't emerge.

Lucier grabbed her hand and squeezed it so hard her fingers went numb for a second. "You okay?"

She nestled next to him. "Never better."

Four men got out of each helicopter, guns drawn. They split. A few jogged to the hangar, one examining Slater. The rest tended to the group, except for the lead agent who headed their way. "You Lucier?"

Lucier nodded. "Boy, are we glad to see you."

The agent scanned the area, checking the men either down with injuries or being held at gunpoint. "Looks like you handled yourselves pretty well." He shook Lucier's hand. "Mike Cafferty. Stallings said if you were still alive to tell you he sends his regards."

"I wasn't sure I would be."

"Who's the guy in the plane?" the agent asked.

"Phillip Crane."

"The industrialist?"

"One and the same. The man coming to on the ground over there is Silas Compton. You have two of the richest guys in the country to load up, Cafferty. Big damn bust."

"I'm gonna love this."

"Mind if I yank Crane out of the cockpit?" Lucier asked.

"You think he has a weapon?"

"He didn't before he got in the plane, but I'm not sure if he had one stashed inside. Being Phillip Crane, he probably still thinks he's going to get away with this. That ain't gonna happen, not when all the facts come out. Your collar, Cafferty, but I'd like to cuff the slippery bastard myself."

"As long as I tag along." He must have noticed Lucier's frown. "Just to keep things kosher. Jurisdiction and all that."

Chapter Fifty-Eight
Amid the Confusion

Diana was exhausted, having slept little. She and Lucier filled in the disbelieving agents on Crane's plans for a new order. Federal agencies, child protection professionals, doctors, and counselors conducted interviews with both the staff and members of the group. Priests offered to conduct exorcisms to rid the evil spirits from Satan's damned. Their overtures were politely rejected.

The compound buzzed with planes landing and taking off. Fortunately, there were enough rooms to accommodate everyone trying to make sense out of a story that defied imagination. With few precedents, the state agencies proceeded one step at a time. Cafferty was right. Lucier had no jurisdiction in Oklahoma. He and Diana were star witnesses only.

"What happens now?" she asked Cafferty.

"All the psychologists and counselors agree that the children should remain here while they're being interrogated. Uprooting them from their parents or from the adults acting as their parents, before they understand what's happening would be more detrimental. Besides, it's easier to keep everyone together here. Doctors are taking DNA swabs from everyone in the complex."

"And the kidnapped babies?" Lucier asked.

"Two young women who said their names were Nona and

Brigid and claim to be daughters of Silas and Selene Compton, identified them. Our people are notifying the birth parents as we speak."

"What will happen to those girls?" Diana asked. "They've been so compromised."

Cafferty shook his head. "They'll need psychological counseling and deprogramming. They'll face criminal charges as well. There's a lot to iron out."

"You feel sorry for them, don't you?" Lucier asked her. He turned to Cafferty. "Diana feels sorry for everyone. She even felt sorry for a guy who wanted to kill her."

Yes, she felt sorry for the girls, but not for Compton and Crane. They were evil and should get the maximum sentence the law allows "It's not the same thing. Those girls have been brainwashed. They never knew what they were doing was wrong."

"Sorry, Ms. Racine, but they knew kidnapping babies from their birth parents was a crime."

Diana shrugged. "Well, yes. Still…"

"What about Anat Crane and Cal Easley?" Lucier asked.

"They're helping identify who belongs to whom, especially Easley. They've been trapped here a long time. Hope they can make it in the real world."

"They will because they kept their worlds real, even here." Lucier flipped through the papers of the human inventory. "There's a little girl named Anna. If it weren't for her, we wouldn't be having this conversation, and I think she fed information to Cal Easley."

"I'll look into her personally."

"Good. I'd hate to see anything happen to her."

Diana and Lucier got up to leave. A plane waited to take them back to New Orleans. Lucier turned. "Oh, one more thing. Seth Crane and Maia Compton. They helped us. What's going to happen to them?"

"They're gone." Cafferty said.

Lucier stopped. "Gone? Gone where?"

"Good question. The doctor fixed up his arm. The Compton woman and her children were with him. Then, during the night, they all disappeared."

Diana's mouth hung open. "Huh? But how?"

"They flew out of here."

"Planes blocked the runway," Lucier said.

"That's right. Crane took the helo."

"And you don't know where they went?"

"Not yet. They have to land somewhere. We'll get them."

Diana stole a quick glance at Lucier. *With an aircraft that can land just about anywhere? Don't bet on it.*

Chapter Fifty-Nine
Introspection

That evening, when Diana opened the door to her house, she and Lucier were met with that closed-up, musty smell, mixed with a hint of vanilla from the candles she loved. This was her home, and she loved the feeling of security. Tears filled her eyes. "Good to be home."

Lucier kicked the door closed and took her in his arms. "I wasn't sure we'd see either of our houses again."

"You're my hero, Lieutenant."

He kissed her lightly on the lips. "I didn't feel much like a hero when my face fell into the salmon. Quite the contrary. I should never have trusted those people. Knew it in the depths of my soul. Yet I let down my guard, disbelieving they'd do what they did."

"We were duped. No doubt about it."

"I talked to Captain Craven while you slept on the plane. He thought we were duped too. Said he missed me, but he's going to dock my pay."

Diana searched his face. "He's kidding, right? I mean you almost single-handedly broke up a kidnapping ring."

"I'm not sure. I hope so."

"I'll put on a pot of coffee, then I need to call my parents. I need a shot of caffeine to deal with them."

Diana spent half an hour alternating between answering questions from her mother and father. The FBI advised her and Lucier not to talk publicly about the case to avoid tainting the jury pool when the group went to trial, so she carefully avoided anything her publicity-hound father could "accidentally" release to a reporter.

"Cafferty called while you were on the phone," Lucier said when she hung up. "They tracked down the Crane Corporation pilot who flew Anastasia Easley to Canada to meet up with her mother and three sisters. All five are awaiting extradition back to the States, but there's a tricky situation with Anastasia Easley."

"What's that?"

"Canada won't extradite anyone facing a murder charge unless the death penalty is off the table, so she'll probably spend the rest of her life in prison."

"I can live with that."

"The men were denied bail in spite of protests from some of the highest-priced lawyers in the country."

"I hope they all rot in hell," Diana said. "They should be familiar with the place."

* * * * *

Diana and Lucier gave no interviews, but nothing stopped the media speculation. Diana opened the morning paper. "Will you look at this? Jake Griffin is having a field day. There are a dozen messages from him on the machine, but this time I'm not talking. That hasn't stopped him from reporting the story, from Ridley Deems to Brother Osiris and the Sunrise Mission, to the Cranes and Comptons as Satan worshippers. Jake's done his homework. He points out the irony of the mythology—Seth did kill Osiris in the end."

"There are too many victims in this story," Lucier said. "The full magnitude of human devastation won't be known for a long, long time. Years maybe."

"Speaking of Seth," Diana said.

"Still no sign of him, Maia Compton, and their children. I wonder if they'll ever turn up."

"If I had to guess, I'd say—"

"What?"

She studied him, knowing that part of Lucier didn't want them found. Even though Seth Crane was guilty of many things, Lucier, too, would have killed Edward Slater if he'd molested his child. "I honestly don't know."

Lucier held her gaze, smiling knowingly, and a moment passed between them before she returned to the newspaper.

"The story of a genetically engineered Utopia seems to have sparked hundreds of ethical debates. That ought to get the wingnuts spouting off on TV. Remind me not to watch any news channels for a while."

Diana pointed to a paragraph in the story. "Look at the litany of charges they're leveling at the group. Kidnapping, child endangerment, sexual abuse, *murder*. What a mess. This is one time Crane and Compton's money and influence can't help them."

Lucier poured both a second cup of coffee. "Don't be too sure. I spoke to Ralph Stallings this morning. He said Crane has been stoically silent, but Compton's lawyers are in discussions to plea bargain him. Even from a hospital bed, that son of a bitch says he'll tell them where the other compound is, off-shore accounts, and he'll roll on all of them, including his wife—for consideration."

"You mean he'd flip on the black widow?"

"That's what he said. You never liked her, did you?"

"No, and I was right. But I really screwed up with Slater." Lucier kept silent. She wondered what he was thinking. He was off limits to her psychically. She wouldn't read him, didn't want to. Hopefully, he couldn't read her right now either.

Yes, she'd been wrong about Edward Slater. He'd stimulated her intellectually in the beginning, stirred her curiosity, and his inner conflict touched her in a way she wasn't sure she understood to this day. Yet she had missed his essence—the twisted evil that corrupted him and drove him to unspeakable sins. Her feelings toward him never approached the physical. Those belonged to Lucier and always would.

She leaned over the table and kissed Lucier on the lips.

"What was that for?" he asked.

"Because I love you," she said. "No other reason."

He kissed her back. "That's a good enough reason for me."

ABOUT THE AUTHOR

Polly Iyer was born in a coastal city north of Boston. After studying at Massachusetts College of Art and Design, she lived in Italy, Atlanta, and now resides in the beautiful Piedmont region of South Carolina in an empty nest house with her husband and family pets. Writing novels turned into her passion after careers in fashion, art, and business. Now she spends her time being quite the hermit in comfortable clothes she wouldn't be caught dead wearing on the outside while she devises ways for life to be complicated for her characters. Better them than her.

Learn more about Polly and her books at
www.PollyIyer.com
The following is an excerpt from *InSight*.

InSight

Chapter One
The Helen Keller Alliance

Every morning, Abby ran her fingers over the cluster of raised dots on the sign outside her office door.

Dr. Abigael Gallant, Psychologist.

Above, serif letters spelled the same thing. She opened the door. "Morning, Cleo."

"Morning, Abby. Got everything ready for you."

"You always do." She sniffed. "Morning, Ellie."

"How do you always know I'm here?"

"I know." The too-sweet scent of her intern's perfume wafting in the air almost drowned out the rich aroma of coffee bubbling into the pot. Abby went into her office, unhooked Daisy's halter and gave her guide dog a neck rub. Then she and Daisy settled at her desk.

Cleo brought her a cup of coffee. "Thanks. What would I do without you?"

"You'd do it all by yourself like you did before you hired

me."

"But you make it so much easier."

"First appointment at nine," Cleo said. "New patient. Luke McCallister. Cop. Sergeant Dykstra said he has issues. It's all in the report." Abby flipped the crystal on her watch to finger the time.

"Okay, I've read the report, but I'll go over the information to refresh my memory." Cleo left and Abby got to work, reading the Braille printout of Hub City detective Luke McCallister's file. He'd lost his hearing in the line of duty, and *issues* was putting it mildly.

Half an hour later, Ellie knocked on the door. She came close to Abby's desk and whispered. "McCallister's here, and he's a hunk."

"Thanks for letting me know. Ask him if he'd mind waiting while I take a quick shower, change my clothes, and refresh my lipstick."

"Funny."

"Show him in. Oh, and, Ellie, stop panting. You sound like a teenage boy in heat."

Abby didn't hear McCallister's footsteps because he started speaking long before he reached the patient's chair.

"Well," he said, "put the two of us together and we have one Helen Keller."

She breathed in the scent of sandalwood, and her highly-tuned antennae picked up on the nervous quiver in his words, even though the detective tried to conceal it with sarcasm.

She followed McCallister's voice and faced in his direction. "Have a seat, Detective. I assume you read lips."

The leather seat cushion whooshed as he sat. "Read 'em, been known to kiss a few."

Arrogant SOB. This is going to be a long hour. She moved to the chair opposite McCallister, offering her best nice-to-meet-you smile. "We'll stay with the reading for now." She wanted to say she never kissed on a first consultation, but the ethically questionable response would probably give this patient the wrong idea. "Do you have any hearing at all?"

"None at normal decibels. I would hear enough of a siren to know one is wailing, feel the vibration from a loud noise, but that's about it."

Because she specialized in counseling the disabled, she knew a good lip-reader took in the whole face. She enunciated her words. "I'm pretty good at following sounds, but you'll need to tell me if I'm not facing you correctly. Ask me to repeat anything you don't understand, okay?"

"Fine, thanks. My speech reading instructor said I was her quickest study, but I still understand only about forty percent. I fudge the rest. Sometimes I tune out, or if a person talks fast or turns away, I'm lost. It's frustrating as hell. But if I can't keep up or miss something, I'll ask you to repeat."

"Forty percent is better than good."

"It still means I miss sixty percent."

"We'll work this out, and I can always write down anything you don't understand. Now, your sergeant said you weren't happy about counseling."

He shifted in his seat. "I'm fighting hard to stay in the department. If I didn't agree to see the shrink my bosses recommended, they'd have reason to can me."

An honest response. "So, will this be a battle of wills or a forced collaboration? I say 'forced' because I'm used to working with people who want what I have to offer."

Silence. Did he misinterpret her words or was he debating another smart-ass answer? She'd treated macho types before. Many relegated therapy to the weak-minded and struggled to adjust when faced with a life-altering disability. She waved her hand in the air. "Hel-lo. You haven't slipped out on me yet, have you?"

"I thought you people could hear better. You didn't hear me leave, did you?"

"*We people* hear better than you, but I'm not Superwoman. I suppose if you wanted to escape, you could sneak out and I wouldn't know."

"Ah, but then you'd report me, and I'd be out on my ass."

Abby stifled a smile. "Your choice."

"What does your voice sound like?"

She wondered if a little humor might help to connect. "Deep and husky. Bacall talking to Bogie."

He discharged a throaty laugh. "I remember that. Something about teaching him how to whistle. Put your lips together and…*blow*, wasn't it?"

The heat rose on Abby's face from the sexual implication of McCallister's tone. This man took pleasure in penetrating her professional façade. "Something to that effect, yes."

"Okay, you win. I give up."

"This isn't a win-lose game, Detective. You leave, you lose." She raised a small recorder. "If you agree, I'll record this session. It's the way I take notes. You see, we both have to make adjustments." He didn't argue. "I could ask you questions, but I'd rather you tell me how you felt after you learned you were deaf. How you still feel."

More shifting, a tongue click, a deep breath, a long exhalation. She waited.

"I was blindsided, totally unprepared." He hesitated. "Sorry, bad allusion."

"It's a perfect allusion. I know exactly how that feels, maybe better than you."

After a moment of silence, he said, "Yeah, I guess you do."

"Let's get one thing out of the way. I'm not big on political correctness. I don't tippy-toe around the facts or use words like visually impaired or audibly challenged. I'm blind, you're deaf. Continue."

"I didn't get all that, but enough. You're blind, I'm deaf. No tippy-toeing."

Silently chastising herself, she said, "Sorry. I'll speak slower."

"Don't worry about it. I got the gist of what you said. Now, where was I? Right, how I felt." He paused for a long moment. "I thought when I recovered I could go back to my old job. Instead, the brass assigned me to the damn computer—AFIS, tracking searches, stuff like that."

"AFIS?"

"Automated Fingerprint Identification System. I'm a street cop, Dr. Gallant. I don't do well sitting behind a desk."

"You're a liability on the street. You have to know that. You wouldn't want me on the road driving a car, would you?"

"That's different."

"Is it? Lives are at stake in both situations."

McCallister went into another prolonged silence as if he were thinking of the perfect response. Usually a patient's long pause preceded a significant confession. *Just tell the truth, McCallister.*

"You know, this is a mistake," he said. "I'm not comfortable opening up to a stranger."

She heard him rise.

"In fact, I'm not comfortable opening up to anyone."

She didn't want to lose him. How could she make him see that his job, maybe his future, depended on at least giving the first session his best shot? "What you say won't leave this room. I offer my professional opinion after we complete our sessions. If you can't continue, I'll send the report, and you can deal with your superiors." He didn't walk to the door. Then she heard the cushion whoosh again as he sat.

"I got enough of what you said to know I'm screwed either way, aren't I?"

"Like I said, your choice." She waited a good three minutes. After a deep sigh he started.

"At first, I didn't believe the doctors. I thought one morning I'd wake up to the sounds around me, but that didn't happen. Between the silence and tinnitus buzzing in my ears I thought I'd go out of my mind. I couldn't read anyone, couldn't respond, because I didn't know who said what. I tried to swallow my anger because I hate whiners, but it gnawed in my gut until I thought I'd explode."

Good. That's a start. "Your file says you're divorced. Did the injury have anything to do with your divorce?"

"I'm here about my job, Doctor, not my marriage." His tone took on a hard edge. "After I lost my hearing, I wasn't the same man my wife married. She deserved better. I'm not proud of it."

Now we're getting somewhere. "Do you think you're less of a man because you're deaf?"

This time she sensed his silent isolation. The quiet, always louder to her than to most, echoed off the walls.

After a while, he spoke. "Yes. I do."

"And does my blindness make me any less a woman?"

Before he could answer, Daisy got up from behind the desk, stretched, and sauntered to the water bowl. She slurped for half a minute, then burrowed her drooling head into her mistress's lap, greedy for affection. Abby scratched Daisy's ears, rubbed her neck, and settled her down.

"Is she how you get around?"

"She's my eyes, yes."

"You need to look at me. You looked toward the dog and I couldn't see what you said."

She was really screwing up with this patient. She faced in his direction, pictured him focused on her lips. "Yes, Daisy's my eyes."

"Good, thanks."

"A question, Detective McCallister. Have you considered a cochlear implant?"

"A gun shot off near my ear during the takedown of a meth lab. Most of the auditory nerve fibers were destroyed, making the effectiveness of an implant questionable. I'm still seeing specialists."

"I wouldn't give up. Improvements are being made every day."

"When I learned about this session, I researched you. Your résumé's impressive."

She ignored the personal reference. Some patients used the ploy to shift focus. "Quite a résumé yourself, especially your anti-drug work with kids in the projects."

"Don't tell me the dog reads too."

Abby smiled at the image. "She's pretty amazing, but no. I have a screen reader program on my computer that audibly reads what's on the screen, then I print it on a Braille embosser. It's the blind equivalent of texting." *Back to you, Detective.*

"It's weird to carry a phone I can't hear, but texting keeps me connected."

"Because technology has opened new worlds for the disabled, and a deaf patient who can't speak can text me, and my phone converts the text to speech. This was unheard of years back. I can hardly keep up with the advances."

"I'm big on email, too." McCallister hesitated. "This is a new world for me, and if I'm being honest, I'm not sure I'm up to it."

McCallister's revealing admission took Abby by surprise. She expected an hour's tug of war, but by session's end, he'd allowed some barriers to tumble. She fingered her watch. One more probing question. "What's been your darkest thought, Detective?"

He paused, but not for long.

"Eating my gun."

* * * * *

Ellie breezed through the door as soon as McCallister left. "Well, what did you think?"

Abby's fingertips skimmed the Braille printout of her next patient. She lifted her head in Ellie's direction. "About what?"

"You know, about Mr. Gorgeous."

"He's a patient, Ellie, off limits except for therapy. Besides, I have only your word he's good looking, not that it makes a difference."

"I didn't say good looking. He's better than that. Wait a minute." She called to the outer office, "Cleo, come here. Tell Abby what Detective McCallister looks like."

Abby wanted to stop this discussion, but Cleo's rolling chair moved back, and she entered the office. "Hunky. Six feet plus, cerulean eyes, and a body Calvin Klein would photograph in his tiniest bikini briefs."

"You must have X-ray vision to get that picture," Abby said. "And cerulean? Good thing you weren't paying attention. Dare I ask if he had any birthmarks?" She shuffled some papers to determine their order. "Anyway, I couldn't care less. He's a patient. It wouldn't matter if he were a Greek god or Quasimodo; I wouldn't know the difference. Stop trying to fix me up. You both know strict rules apply between therapist and patient."

Ellie leaned in close. "You need a man in your life, Abby, and this guy is all man."

A wave of sadness hit Abby as she thought back to the man who'd changed her life so irrevocably. "I've had a man in my life. One was enough, thank you." She could almost sense the exchange of raised eyebrows and shrugs. "Now, can we get our minds off men's butts and get back to business?"

"You still didn't tell me what you thought of him."

The last hour had generated a few silences, and now Abby contributed one more. She found Luke McCallister interesting, no question. The description of his looks meant nothing. No longer influenced by appearances, she found the tone of a voice and the inflections of a person's words revealed more than any visual. The cop showed a better grasp of his problems than most, but knowing them solved only part of the dilemma. She needed to convince him he still had value, even if in a different capacity than before he lost his hearing.

"I thought of him only as a patient," Abby said, answering Ellie's question. "Anything else would be inappropriate."

But Detective McCallister isn't quite ready to face the facts of his life, and I don't want to be anywhere near him when the volcano erupts.

ACKNOWLEDGEMENTS

To my good friend and critique partner, Ellis Vidler, for her constant support, encouragement, and generosity. She's forgotten more about writing than I'll ever know in my lifetime. To author Maggie Toussaint, whose critiques made this a much better book. To my family who cheered me on, and to my friends who rooted for my success, my heartfelt appreciation. I hope I haven't let you down.

Thank you all.

Made in the USA
San Bernardino, CA
15 April 2014